SURFACE
-and-
SHADOW

ISBN: 978-1-942428-98-5
First Edition
Printed and bound in the USA

Cover and interior design by Kelsey Rice

PRAISE FOR *SURFACE AND SHADOW*

"*Surface and Shadow* is an evocative portrayal of life in 1972 small-town North Carolina. Multiple challenges face newcomer Lydia Colton. How does she unravel the mysterious death of an heir to the town's major industry while safeguarding her husband's fledgling physician career? How does she navigate the bounds of sexism, racism, and classism tying her hands? How does she find a path to give her life meaning beyond her roles as wife and mother? This is fiction at its best—memorable and absorbing."

– JACQUELINE GUIDRY, AUTHOR OF *THE YEAR THE COLORED SISTERS CAME TO TOWN*

"While *Surface and Shadow* offers the compelling tensions of a mystery story, its deeper probing involves the unknowns of the central character, Lydia Colton. As she delves into the lives of others connected with the circumstances of a strange death from a half century before, Lydia comes to realize that she is also confronting the secrets of her own identity. The answer to one mystery is inseparable from an illumination of the second. What started as a concern about a long ago death becomes the source of lives renewed, for Lydia and for others. The resolution satisfies the reader as much as it does Lydia."

– WALTER CUMMINS, EDITOR EMERITUS OF *THE LITERARY REVIEW*

"Whitney gracefully captures the rhythm of life in a small southern town, creates complex characters who live and breathe, and explores large themes that affect us all. The story, beautifully told in an elegant but approachable style, unfolds at an energetic pace that will keep you reading from start to finish."

– MARK WILLEN, AUTHOR OF *HAWKE'S POINT*

"A first-rate mystery in the hands of an accomplished storyteller."
  – PHILIP CIOFFARI, AUTHOR OF *DARK ROAD, DEAD END;*
    JESUSVILLE; AND *CATHOLIC BOYS*

"Sally Whitney's literary style delivers a character driven novel set in Tanner, North Carolina, a small town with a southern sense of place where unspoken rules guard the family secrets of a prominent family. Lydia Colton, a young married woman, feels like an invisible outsider in Tanner until she initiates changes in her life and in the lives of others. She discovers ways to strengthen the fragile thread of humanity that runs through all of us when she searches to uncover details surrounding the death of a member of this prominent family. Vivid descriptions embrace the 1970s years with remarkable accuracy in this well-crafted narrative that crosses boundaries implanted in the old southern ways."
  – JUDITH BADER JONES, AUTHOR OF *THE LANGUAGE*
    OF SMALL ROOMS, MOON FLOWERS ON THE FENCE,
    AND *DELTA PEARLS*

SURFACE

-and-

SHADOW

SALLY WHITNEY

Pen-L Publishing
Fayetteville, Arkansas
Pen-L.com

For Greg

1

She slid the library card across the desk face down so the restless people waiting behind her wouldn't see that the name on the front, typed in boldface, was Dr. Jeffrey A. Colton. Creased in every direction and smudged with wallet dust, the paper card had the same lived-in, timeworn look as the library's scarred floors and shelves of frayed books, but the card had looked that way since the day she got it.

"It's not for my husband," she'd said when she first saw it. "It's for me. My name's Lydia Colton."

The librarian—a gentle woman with curly, gray-streaked hair and puffy cheeks—had cocked her head in surprise. "Honey, we always issue our cards in the husband's name. If the books don't come back, wives can be real hard to track down. Men are easier to find in the phone books and all, you know."

"I'd like to have one in my name," Lydia said as she crushed the card and handed it back.

"I can't do that, dear. We have rules, you know." The librarian ran her fingers across the card in long, smoothing strokes.

"Then I'd like to see the head librarian, somebody who can break the rules—you know."

"I'm the head librarian. I'm the only librarian, but I can't break the rules."

"Who made the rules?"

"The town council, I guess. You could write them a letter." The librarian smiled sweetly. "I wouldn't worry about it, dear. You can use this card anytime you want to."

Lydia snatched the crumpled card from the librarian's hand. "Thank you very much." She stuffed the card into her purse and left. She wrote to the town council, but they never wrote back. So she used the card anytime she wanted to, which was often, but now, a year later, she still put it face down.

In return for the card, the librarian took her book, stamped "April 21, 1972" on the sheet glued to the inside cover, right below "Property of Tanner Public Library, Tanner, North Carolina," and let her sign the check-out slip. In the canvas stroller next to Lydia, her four-month-old son, Malcolm, waved his tiny feet. Stroking his leg, Lydia wedged the book between his pudgy arm and the side of the stroller before hurrying out of the building to her aging Camaro. She'd stayed too long, and now she had to rush home.

Two hours earlier, she'd bolted from the townhouse where she lived. Right in the middle of paying bills, her stomach muscles had tightened and a haze seemed to drop before her eyes. It wasn't the first time the feeling had seized her. For several months it had crept up on her when she least expected it. She could be changing the baby or washing the dishes or even talking to her mother on the telephone when she would suddenly feel alone in a world pressing against her like Jell-O. Usually, she could manage it and do what she needed to do, but today she couldn't. She had to get out of there. She grabbed the baby and fled to the library, where she could bury herself in other people's thoughts and avoid her own.

Now it was way past time to start dinner, and the laundry was lying wet in the washing machine, but the feeling was gone. She savored its absence, fearing the feeling would return and praying that it wouldn't. Lord, something in her life had to change.

Back at home, she threw the laundry into the dryer and tossed green beans into a pot of water with a slab of fatback before settling into the easy chair to nurse the baby. When Dr. Jeffrey A. Colton (he of the library card) arrived, dinner was cooking, Malcolm was in his playpen, and Lydia was in the basement of the three-story townhouse folding clean bed sheets. She called up to Jeff that dinner was late. Soon he came down the stairs, a bottle of Budweiser in his hand. Leaving the beer on the washing machine, he pulled his golf bag from the corner and began to clean the clubs in the utility sink.

"What'd you do today?" he asked while his eyes still focused on the clubs.

"I went to the library."

Jeff looked up from the three-iron he'd plunged into the sink full of soapy water.

"Why?"

"To get out of the house," Lydia said. Then, softly, "I had one of those feelings I get." She knew the spells made no sense to him. When she'd tried to describe them back before they moved to Tanner, he told her she was working too hard. She had her job as a lab technician, and she had their apartment to look after. He thought she needed to find a girl to do the cleaning, but they couldn't afford to hire help. And that wasn't the problem, anyway. If it were, the feelings would have gone away when they moved to Tanner and she had no outside job, but they didn't.

"I wish you'd join some club," Jeff said as he rinsed the three-iron and dried it. "Something like the hospital auxiliary. That'd get you out of the house."

"I get out of the house." Lydia matched sheet corners to-gether. "I go to the library, and I think I'm going to go more." She didn't want to get into another discussion about the spells. "I met some interesting people there today."

Jeff raised an eyebrow. "Who?" He dunked a new club and washed it with a cloth.

"Nancy Galloway and Stella Waters." Lydia paused, waiting for Jeff to react. She knew the name "Galloway" would get his attention.

"Jesus, Lydia." Jeff's lips curled into a scowl. "What were you doing with Nancy Galloway? You know she's Henry Gal-loway's granddaughter, don't you? And who's Stella Waters?"

Lydia frowned. Everybody knew who the Galloways were. They owned the cotton mill in town. "Of course I know who Nancy is. And Stella's the woman who looks after her. You've seen her. She's an elderly black woman."

"What possessed you to talk to them? Did they approach you?"

"No. They were sitting by themselves, behind some of the stacks, over in a corner by the windows. Kind of pitiful, really. So I went over and introduced myself." Lydia tossed the folded sheet into the laundry basket, trying to sound nonchalant.

Jeff stared at her while the golf club in his hand dripped water in an ever-increasing circle on the concrete floor. "What did you talk about?"

"Books, mostly. We were in a library. Nancy told me what she was reading." Lydia reached for a pillowcase. "I liked her. I liked them both."

"And you didn't think Nancy's odd? She's retarded, you know." Jeff jerked a towel from the sink's edge. "That's why you don't see her out much. They don't let her go meandering around town by herself." He dried the golf club, shoved it back into the bag, and grabbed another one, pausing briefly to take a swallow from the beer sitting on the washing machine.

Lydia didn't like his tone. "She's not terribly retarded. You act like she's some kind of dummy. She talks a little slow, but she makes sense. She pointed out there was a new coleus plant on the window sill, which a lot of people wouldn't have noticed. I think she's delightful." Lydia folded the pillow case and laid it in the basket with the other linens. "And so is Stella, the woman she was with. Stella told me she raised four of her own kids and took care of two generations of Galloway children. Can you imagine? I liked talking to them. And Nancy wants me to meet her again sometime."

Jeff beat the nine-iron he was holding against the palm of his hand. His eyebrows converged behind the wayward hair hanging across his forehead. He kept his hair just long enough to be stylish, but monthly haircuts made sure it never got shaggy.

"I wouldn't do that if I were you," he said. "The Galloways don't like for Nancy to spend a lot of time with other folks. I knew that even when I was a kid. She's one of the most guarded people in the state."

"Why?" Lydia stopped folding the sheet in her hands. "That sounds cruel."

"I always heard they thought people were mean to her. And maybe they were when she was little. You know how kids can be. So the Galloways think they're protecting her."

"That's stupid. She's not a child anymore. She's probably as old as I am. And adults wouldn't be mean to her." Lydia was sure no one would mistreat a mentally retarded woman, even though she herself had felt less than welcome at times since she moved to Tanner. Among the groups Jeff had introduced her to, the women were cordial but seemed to have enough friends already. She had found her only friend in town on her own at the A&P. Maybe that's what the Galloways feared for Nancy. Not real meanness, just lack of interest.

"It doesn't matter what you think." Jeff swished the nine-iron through the water. "That's the way things are, and you have to respect them."

"Well, I think it's odd. In fact, I think the Galloway family is kind of odd."

"You might be odd too, if you had all their money."

Lydia stared at the sheet in her hands. "I doubt it."

"I'm just warning you that Nancy's family's not going to like you hanging around her. And I don't get why you want to. Or that colored woman, either. Why would you want to talk to her?"

Lydia thought for a moment. "I don't know. She interests me. Maybe because she's black. I've never known any black people. Not really. She's different. And Nancy's different. I would think you'd like me hobnobbing with one of the richest people in town."

"Not that rich person. Pick out somebody else." He turned his back, shoving the club into the bag.

Lydia snapped the towel she was holding. "I don't need you to tell me who my friends should be, thank you very much."

"I'm only trying to help." Jeff jerked the towel out of Lydia's hand. "And don't say 'thank you very much' to me like that. I know what you really mean."

"What do I mean?"

"'Go to hell' or something worse." He tried to pop Lydia with the towel, but she made a quick dodge. His lips approximated a smile, but his gray eyes glinted like steel.

Lydia held out her hand. "Give me the towel," she said, staying a few inches beyond his reach.

He tossed her the towel. "Seriously, Lydia," he said. "Keep away from Nancy Galloway. I'm warning you, her family won't like it."

"Her family won't like it, or *you* won't like it?" Sometimes Lydia couldn't tell where the unwritten rules came from.

"I'm only trying to look out for you. And believe me, I know what I'm talking about."

Lydia picked up the laundry basket and carried it upstairs. At the landing, she glanced back into the basement as Jeff plunged another club into the sink.

Two days later, Lydia put Malcolm into the Camaro and drove to the library. The more she thought about Nancy Galloway being kept away from other people, the madder she got. And the more she thought about Jeff telling her what to do, the more doubly mad she got. In the two years they'd been married, he'd somehow come to think his opinion mattered more than hers.

She set her jaw and breathed in the sweet spring air pouring through the open windows. Sunshine filled the car, raising a sprinkling of sweat on her neck beneath her thick hair. She'd inherited the hair from her paternal grandmother, a sizable woman who relatives said came from Cherokee ancestors, although there was no proof of Native Americans in the family tree. Lydia didn't get her grandmother's height, but she had inherited her raven hair, her high cheek bones, and her bronze complexion, which blazed like a blood orange when Lydia was angry.

To reach the library, she drove through the oldest section of Tanner, the neighborhoods closest to the river. Coming from the surrounding hills, the river flowed through the heart of Tanner on its way to South Carolina and, eventually, the Atlantic Ocean. Together, the river and hills gave the town a quiet beauty. At the western end of town, the river dropped sharply, and early in the town's development, the founding fathers reinforced the drop to create a scenic waterfall. Years later, when the town council decided Tanner needed a public library, they chose land next to the waterfall as the site.

The library was a homely building, as if it knew it couldn't outshine the natural beauty around it. Its one-story, red-brick exterior was distinguished only by a row of tall, gray windows and a narrow, dark door. The gentle librarian tried to brighten its appearance with pots of coleus in all the windows, but it still looked like somebody's drab sister.

Inside the library, Lydia found Nancy and Stella situated comfortably in two worn chairs next to windows overlooking the waterfall, the same place they had been before. They were easy to spot since Stella was the only black person in the library, and the few white folks who were there gathered on the opposite side of the room, like they were afraid of catching something. Gently pushing Malcolm's stroller back and forth, Lydia watched her new acquaintances for a while before approaching. In the stillness, her heart beat faster, and her fingers tingled. She hadn't been totally forthcoming with Jeff about her reasons for wanting to know Nancy.

In the months she'd been in Tanner, she'd marveled at the awe with which many of the townspeople regarded the Galloway family. Their attitude made her think of the Galloways as small-town royalty—a phenomenon she hadn't seen before and which she found a little disturbing. Because Stella and Nancy were part of the phenomenon, maybe getting to know them would help her understand it.

Nancy bent forward over a book with drawings of the solar system on its cover, her fine, red hair held out of her eyes with a flowered head band. The hair's texture allowed the breeze from the open windows to lift the ends, all except one bedraggled piece that Nancy curled and uncurled around her stubby finger.

Her pale skin seemed almost translucent in the incoming light. With an expression of concentration on her face, she could have been any twenty-something woman absorbed in a good book. The children's book she was holding was the only thing out of place.

Stella held the *Tanner Observer* folded between her thin hands. Her feet, which looked a little swollen in her dark hose and Oxfords, were propped on a short, wooden stool, and she occasionally dabbed at the corners of her mouth with a snow-white handkerchief she kept tucked in her pocket. Her wrinkled face and scarecrow-like limbs were a little disconcerting, but her eyes were soft. From time to time, she looked up from her reading and smiled at Nancy. At one of those times, she noticed Lydia, who pushed the stroller toward them.

"Hey," Lydia said softly. "Good to see y'all again."

Nancy's round face lit up. "Look, Stella," she said. "It's the lady with the baby." Stella nodded but said nothing. "Can I see the baby?" Nancy asked. Lydia pulled the blanket away from the sleeping infant's face. Nancy frowned when she saw him. "He's got a big nose," she said. Stella gave Nancy a scolding look, but Lydia smiled.

"You're right," she said. "But he'll grow into it." She covered him again with the blanket. "I came here to find him some books."

Nancy jumped out of her chair, letting her book fall to the floor. "I'll help you find some books. I know all about books for babies. I can show you the ones I liked when I was little." Her green eyes flashed.

"She might not want no help," Stella murmured in Nancy's direction.

"I could use some help, but we have to be quiet so we don't wake up Malcolm." Lydia pointed at the sleeping baby.

"Leave him here. I can watch him," Stella said, leaning toward the stroller.

After moving the baby next to Stella's chair, Lydia followed Nancy into the children's section, where they could talk more freely. The young woman knew exactly where the preschool and picture books were shelved. With their bright colors, the thin books had a kaleidoscope effect on that side of the room. "This one's good," Nancy said as she handed Lydia a copy of *Goodnight Moon*.

"How come you know so much about books?" Lydia asked.

"I like to read," Nancy said, pulling another book from the shelf. "We have a room full of books at home." She paused. "I can't read most of them. My mama reads them to me sometimes, but I like to read by myself. So Stella and I come here. There're lots of books here I can read." She looked at the book in her hand, then shoved it back between the others on the shelf.

Lydia mulled over this new information about the Galloways. She pictured Nancy's mother reading to her, although she'd never met Mrs. Galloway. She'd never met any of the family except Nancy. Nancy's father, she knew, had died in a car accident several years earlier, but other than that, they seemed to live a charmed existence. In addition to Nancy, her mother, and her grandfather, the family included Nancy's brother. Everybody knew they lived in a grand old house on the family farm a few miles outside of Tanner. The farm was named Foxrow, and Lydia wasn't sure which came first—the farm or the mill. The mill manufactured cotton fabrics sold under the Foxrow brand. Usually it was referred to simply as "the mill," so if anybody mentioned Foxrow, they meant the farm. "Does Stella live out at Foxrow?" Lydia asked.

"Of course," Nancy said. "Stella's like Mary Poppins. She lives with us and takes me places and shows me things."

"I ain't no Mary Poppins." Stella's harsh whisper startled the women. She stood behind them with the sleeping baby in his stroller beside her.

"Yes, you are," Nancy insisted. "Except Mary Poppins didn't have any family or a home of her own. Stella has us and a home at Foxrow." She nodded at Lydia.

"I got my own family too," Stella said. "And I'm mighty proud of my children. Ever one of 'em graduated from high school, and my son Sam just got a certificate for twenty years working at the mill."

"But you're still in our family," Nancy insisted. Then she turned to Lydia, handing her two more books. "Who's in your family?" she asked.

"Malcolm," Lydia said, pointing at the baby, "and my husband, Jeff."

"Does your husband work at the mill?" Nancy asked.

"No, he's a doctor."

Nancy nodded. "Doctors make good husbands," she said.

The innocent certainty in her new friend's voice reminded Lydia of voices she had heard growing up. Her childhood girlfriends thought doctors were ideal husbands. She looked at Nancy. "Good husbands make good husbands," she said.

Stella covered a chuckle with her hand, but Nancy turned her attention back to the books. Malcolm began to fidget in his sleep. He was going to wake up soon. With a sigh, Lydia reached for the stroller. "We have to go now," she said. "Thanks for your help."

When she finished checking out her books at the librarian's desk, she saw Nancy and Stella headed for the door, so she followed them out into the balmy day. Stella opened the door of an old Lincoln Continental Town Car.

"That's a nice car," Lydia said.

Stella smiled. "Nancy's grandfather give it to me."

Lydia ran her hand along the car's long, luxurious fender. Apparently, the king could be benevolent.

"We'll be back on Wednesday," Nancy said. "Can you come too?"

"Sure," Lydia said. The thought of seeing them again was exciting—and a little scary.

In the weeks that followed, the three women met at the library on Mondays, Wednesdays, and Fridays. Stella and Nancy welcomed Lydia so eagerly she wondered if anybody else had ever tried to befriend them. Some days they sat quietly and read side by side. Other days they talked until the chubby librarian told them to be quiet. Stella's favorite subject, besides her children, was religion.

"Some folks thought President Kennedy oughta not be president on account of he was a Catholic, but I never held with that," she told Lydia. "Jesus is the savior for anybody who believes in him, no matter what church they goes to."

"What if they don't go to church?" Nancy asked.

"Then we needs to get 'em to church," Stella said. "Just like that rowdy group of young'uns hanging round the store on my road. I told Pastor Jackson we needed to go down there and fetch those boys to Sunday school, but he said the church elders wouldn't never go along with that, and I oughta quit worrying about it." She shook her head. "Like I didn't know what I was talking about."

If the conversation didn't interest her, Stella sometimes dozed behind her newspaper or stared out the windows at the river, as if she had moved into a different dimension with its own sights and sounds.

Nancy loved to talk, and her favorite subject was her family, which was exactly what Lydia had hoped for. Even though Lydia's mother would have said gawking at rich people was beneath her, Lydia couldn't help wanting to know more about this family. In addition to her curiosity about their hold on the town, she was interested in their lifestyle. Her family never had a full-time cook or a nanny. And they certainly didn't drive Lincoln Continentals. So when Nancy talked about the Galloways, Lydia paid close attention.

"My granddaddy runs the mill," Nancy said one afternoon in mid-May when she, Stella, and Lydia had walked outside the library to sit in the white Adirondack chairs gracing the banks of the waterfall. Helicopter seeds falling from the maple trees along the river were making the twisting trip through the slowly flowing water over the fall to be crushed on the rocks below. "A lot of people work there, but it's my granddaddy's mill," Nancy said. "He got it from his daddy a long time ago."

"What made your great-grandfather decide to build a mill?" Lydia asked.

Nancy looked a little befuddled. She brushed a strand of hair from her eyes and looked away to follow the flight of a cardinal from one tree to another. When she looked back at Lydia, she was smiling.

"He built it so people could have cloth to make clothes. Then they wouldn't have to be naked." She giggled and stretched her arms over her head.

Lydia laughed. "And did he build Foxrow too?" she asked, meaning the farm and farmhouse.

Nancy nodded. "I think so."

"He must have had a big family to need so much room," Lydia said. "Did he have a bunch of kids?"

Nancy was suddenly pensive. "No," she said. "Just two. And one of them died."

Lydia was taken aback and wondered what old wound she'd accidentally opened. She'd been careful not to mention Nancy's father, but she didn't know about this other death.

Stella slid her chair closer to Nancy's and put her arm around the younger woman. "It's all right, baby," she said. "It happened a long time ago." Then she turned to Lydia. "Since her daddy passed, she get a little nervous talking about dead folks, but she all right."

"What happened, Stella?" Lydia asked. "Can you tell me?"

The old woman's heavy eyelids opened wide. "Don't know for sure," she said. She pressed Nancy's head against her skinny bosom, as if her thin flesh could prevent Nancy from hearing what she had to say. "It was right after the war. The first one. Nancy's granddaddy, Mr. Henry, and his twin, Mr. Howard, had both gone to fight for America, but Mr. Howard come home early. Didn't anybody know for sure why. He just come home. Then one night after it was all over and Mr. Henry had done come home, sometime in the summer of 1919, both of 'em was in the horse barn out to Foxrow. Some say they had some nasty girls in there with 'em, but nobody ever saw 'em. Then, sometime in the middle of the night, Mr. Henry come weaving up the driveway, drunk as a skunk. My cousin Christine told me all about it. She was living there and cooking for the Galloways then, and she was coming in from a late date herself and saw him." Stella stroked Nancy's hair and kissed the side of her head.

"Christine told me Mr. Henry like to fell down the front steps trying to get to the door. When he did get the door open, he tangled his feet up in the rug, fell flat on his face, and laid there. She ran for the back door, so's nobody would know she was out so late. For all she knew, he laid there till morning. When she heard the next day that they found Mr. Howard face down in the straw down to the barn, she figured he was passed out cold too. Well, he was cold, all right—dead cold." Stella's eyes glowed like polished onyx. "He was dead and drunk. Seems he got hold of some rotten moonshine. That's the devil's brew. It can eat your insides out, and it did him."

Lydia knew the danger of homemade liquor. It could blind you or kill you and would probably do both.

"Why would they drink that stuff?" she asked. "It's not like they couldn't afford regular whiskey."

"Some folks likes it better than store-bought whiskey," Stella said. "They says it's got a bigger kick. And in those days you couldn't buy nothing hard anywheres around here. The preachers had this town drier'n a creek in a drought. It was like they was getting ready for the next year, when you couldn't buy no legal whiskey at all." She shook her head slowly.

"Okay. I get it. But if Howard was drinking poison moonshine, why wasn't Henry?" Lydia leaned forward in the deep chair.

"Lord, honey, folks been asking that question for more'n fifty years." Stella let go of Nancy, allowing her to sit up straight in her chair. Her cheek had the imprint of the small, round button on the pocket of Stella's dress. "You don't have to listen if you don't wanna," Stella said to her.

"I know the story," Nancy said. She stared at the tumbling waterfall.

Stella went on. "According to Christine, Mr. Henry said he had his own pint jar of hooch, and Mr. Howard had his, and they never switched jars. Course, most folks find that hard to believe. Once you gets to drinking, you don't hardly know what jar you're drinking out of. But the police did find two near-empty jars in the barn. And sure enough, one had the poison, and the other one didn't." Stella nodded for emphasis. "The police spent a spell of time out to Foxrow, talking to everybody, even Christine, and she told me they near about tore that barn apart, but they couldn't find nothing to prove it was anything but an accident. And that's what they said it was. And they buried Mr. Howard down near the river. Ten years later they buried his daddy next to him and his mama not long after that."

Stella leaned closer to Lydia, and when she spoke again, her voice was barely audible. "But there's lots of folks who said it then and says it now, that it weren't no accident. People says those twins been drinking moonshine since they was old enough to get theirselves to the right places to get it. And they knew who to buy from and who not to buy from. And wasn't no way they could have been fooled into buying poison." Stella sucked in a raspy breath. "They says Mr. Henry give Mr. Howard that poison on purpose. They says Mr. Howard come home from the war early so's he could get himself set up as the one to run the mill. When Mr. Henry figured that out, he got mad, and he wanted the mill, so he bought that poison and give it to his brother. That's what folks says." Stella pulled the handkerchief from her pocket and wiped her mouth and eyes, both of which had become quite damp in telling the story.

"But the police never could prove that?" Lydia asked.

"No, ma'am," Stella said. "Or they didn't try. Some says old Mr. Galloway made sure they didn't try." She folded her arms across her chest and pursed her lips. Nancy tugged on her sleeve and pointed at three robins perched along the low branch of a maple tree. Stella nodded, patting Nancy's hand.

Lydia pictured Howard, dead on the barn floor. The image made her shudder. She had her own troubles, but at least she wasn't dead. "And nobody ever talks about this?" she asked.

"Not anymore," Stella said. "I suppose lots has forgotten."

Lydia wondered how anybody, especially the dead man's brother, could forget. "I'd sure like to know what happened," she said.

"It don't matter no more. It's best to leave it alone."

Lydia wanted to ask Stella if *she* thought it was more than an accident, but she felt uncomfortable asking the old woman such a personal question about her boss. Plus, Stella's eyes had lost their gleam, a sure sign she was done telling the story. Lydia waited quietly to see if Stella would continue, but she didn't. The rumor itched in Lydia's brain, like a scab that needed to be pulled off.

2

After hearing Stella's story about Howard and Henry, Lydia went to the library more often. She made sure she was there when Stella and Nancy were there, but she went on other days too. Those were her research days, when she combed through back issues of the *Tanner Observer*. If she held Malcolm on her lap facing the microfiche reader, the moving sheets of microfilm and the different images created by the light kept him entertained. He would've loved to grab the long strands of hair that usually hung about her face. Knowing he'd be in grabbing range for an hour or more, she'd tied her hair into a low ponytail with a purple scarf that was close to the color of her knit slacks. Most women in Tanner wore dresses to the library, but holding a baby on your lap when you're wearing a skirt that falls two inches above your knees can get sticky and revealing. So on research days, Lydia sneaked into the library basement wearing slacks.

With the microfiche, she was looking for anything that would help her know more about Henry Galloway, and since the newspaper wasn't indexed anywhere, it was pretty much a case of scanning all the issues. So she and Malcolm sat in the corner of the basement, hidden between stacks of reference books, and ran the reader until both they and it were too hot to continue.

Not much was written in the *Observer* about Henry or the mill during the 1950s. Aside from announcements of promotions, news about a building being added to the physical plant, and coverage of the annual Fourth of July picnic sponsored by the company, the names Galloway and Foxrow were hardly mentioned. In 1961, Foxrow Mills refurbished the YMCA facility it built for the people of Tanner in 1927, and a photograph of Henry and his son, Wallace, standing between the columns of the building's neoclassical façade, filled nearly half of the *Observer's* front page. Then, in 1965, another front-page article reported Wallace's untimely death.

According to the article, he had been driving home from a duck-hunting trip on the North Carolina coast. He was about five miles outside of Tanner on a two-lane road as the afternoon faded, and a deer darted in front of his car, causing him to swerve and crash headfirst into a bridge abutment. He was dead when the police and ambulance arrived. There were three photographs with that article: a large one of Wallace, a middle-sized one showing the crowds waiting outside the Tanner Episcopal Church to attend his funeral, and a small one of Wallace's wife and two children leaving the church.

Hugging Malcolm close to her, Lydia marveled that a family so blessed with all the material things could suffer so much sadness. Henry lost his brother and his son. She rolled the big sheets of microfilm forward and found nothing else about the Galloways until a photograph of Henry came up in September 1970, only two years ago. He was standing in a line with some of Tanner's town councilmen behind the mayor, who was putting a golf ball into the cup on the eighteenth green of the golf course. "Course Opens Nine New Holes," the headline announced.

Staring at a smiling Henry in the grainy photograph, Lydia wondered what he was really like. It was hard to believe such a pleasant-looking man was capable of murder. She needed to read the newspaper's accounts of Howard's death, but she wasn't going to do it there. The library's newspaper files went back only as far as 1947, the year the library was built.

Lydia's only choice was to visit the *Tanner Observer* offices on Main Street. In the months since she moved to town, she had never met Robert Kelly, the *Observer's* editor, but she felt like she knew him. He made his opinions, prejudices, and preferences quite clear in his editorials, and Lydia agreed with almost none of them. As far as she knew, she had never seen the man, so she had to have him pointed out to her when she arrived for their appointment at the dusty brick building, squeezed between the A&P and Penney's. The front door was hard to see with its narrow opening and dull-beige color, but you couldn't miss the picture window with gold-leaf letters, tall as a barrel, spelling out "*Tanner Observer*, Founded 1901."

The *Observer* offices were small. The reception area could accommodate a maximum of two people—or, in Lydia's case, one person and one baby stroller—and was surrounded by open doors leading to three closets with desks in them. An open set of double, swinging doors revealed a larger room with presses, paper cutters, typesetters, and other machines Lydia didn't recognize, all of which contributed to a deafening clacking noise.

Lydia stood in the reception area a few minutes, trying to decide which door was likely Robert's since none had a name printed on it. A harried young woman in a straight skirt, simple blouse, and six-inch heels came through the double doors, mercifully closing them behind her and softening the clacking to a low roar.

"Where can I find Robert Kelly?" Lydia asked. The woman pointed at the center door and hurried through the door next to it. Robert was sitting at his desk, smoking an unfiltered cigarette and using a fat red pencil to obliterate a neatly typed piece of copy. He looked up when Lydia knocked on the door jamb.

He was older than she expected. His gray hair was thin on top, but he appeared to be trying to compensate for that deficit with a set of thick muttonchops. He growled some sort of greeting and stared at her with clear-blue eyes, waiting.

"Hey," she said hesitantly. "I'm Lydia Colton."

The editor looked her up and down and nodded. "So you're Jeff Colton's wife. He did all right for himself. Kind of surprised me when he moved back to town, especially after his folks left. How long y'all been here now?"

"Nearly a year." *Although it seems like a whole lot longer,* she thought.

Robert sucked on his cigarette. "What can I do for you?"

When Lydia explained she wanted to read about Howard Galloway's death, he said, "Sweetheart, you're welcome to look as long as your little heart desires, but there ain't anything shocking—or even interesting—in those old stories. The Galloways had an even firmer grip on the *Observer* back then than they do now, and God knows, it's bad enough now." Lydia said she'd like to decide for herself about the articles, so he yelled, "Shirley!" The woman in the straight skirt appeared again. She led Lydia and Malcolm through the press room—where the screaming machines caused Malcolm to scream too—to a freight elevator, which took them to the dark and damp bowels of the building.

Shirley flipped on two overhead rows of flickering, pinkish fluorescent lights in a room to the right of the elevator, revealing floor-to-ceiling shelves stuffed with newspapers and books of clippings. "The morgue," she said solemnly and left.

The room was eerily silent after the thunder of the press room and chilly compared with the warm spring day and stuffy offices. Lydia tucked the blanket from the stroller around Malcolm, whose screams had resolved into whimpers, as she searched for the right stack of papers. From what Stella had said, she knew Howard died in the summer of 1919. She just wasn't sure exactly when. She took a guess and started with the papers in July. No luck there or with the first week in August.

As she moved on to the next week, Malcolm started crying again, and she realized he must be hungry. *Thank God for portable food supplies*, she thought as she pulled up her shirt and offered the baby her breast, which he latched onto eagerly. She was also grateful there were no prying eyes to telegraph their disapproval of what to her was a natural act, although most people seemed to think it needed to be done hidden away somewhere. Cradling Malcolm in her left arm, she squatted and then sat on the cold concrete floor next to the newspapers. With her right hand, she pulled the next one from the pile and hit pay dirt.

According to an article low on the front page, Howard's father, Arthur, found his son's body at the barn about three o'clock that morning. He had gotten out of bed to use the bathroom and heard a banging in the front hall. Suspecting a burglar, he took a rifle from the gun case and slowly crept down the stairs. Henry was lying just inside the front door. His feet prevented the door from closing, while a breeze occasionally banged the screen door against the jamb. Arthur tossed the rifle onto a table and tried to revive his son. After shaking him and rubbing his face with a wet washcloth, Arthur was able to get Henry to his feet, although he was unstable at best. "The drunkest I've ever seen him," the paper quoted Arthur as saying.

Arthur helped Henry stumble to his bedroom and dropped him onto his bed. Figuring that, if one son was that drunk, he'd better check on the other, Arthur walked through the bathroom the twins shared to Howard's room and found the four-poster bed empty. "I roused Henry again and demanded to know where his brother was," Arthur told the newspaper. "He mumbled something about the horse barn, so I went there immediately."

Howard was lying in one of the empty stalls, the paper said. He was fully clothed, but his shirt was stained with vomit. Arthur shook him like he had Henry, but there was no response. When he couldn't find a pulse, Arthur ran back to the house and telephoned the family doctor. It took the doctor nearly half an hour to get out to Foxrow, and he pronounced Howard dead at four twenty-five a.m. Together, the doctor and Arthur carried the body up to Howard's bedroom. Arthur woke up his wife, who, after sobbing at her son's bedside for nearly an hour, removed the dirty clothes, washed the body, and dressed him in clean pajamas.

At nine o'clock that morning, Arthur called the undertaker, who immediately called the chief of police. "Don't many twenty-four-year-old men die suddenly of natural causes—particularly rich ones," the undertaker told the *Observer*. The police chief said he would assume natural causes until he found otherwise. He planned to interview family members and search the barn.

Lydia folded that newspaper and moved on to the next one, which was published a week later. The first article had been on the front page, but the second one was on page seven, just above the obituaries. Lydia shifted Malcolm to her right breast and crouched over to read the newspaper lying on the floor. The article reported the Tanner Chief of Police had determined that Howard Galloway died from drinking illegal whisky. In their search of the barn where the body was discovered, police officers found two pint Mason jars, one with about two ounces and one with nearly five ounces of corn liquor in it. The department shipped the contents of both jars to the state bureau of investigation in Raleigh, which reported that the liquor in both jars contained grain alcohol, but the contents of one jar also had traces of lye, lead, and methanol. The bureau further stated that there were more than enough toxins in that fluid to kill a person.

Based on the report, the chief announced that he was closing his investigation because Howard's death was obviously an accident. "It's a crying shame," he said, "to have something like that happen to an upstanding young man. Let's hope all the young men in Tanner take this as a lesson and stay away from homemade spirits."

Lydia lifted Malcolm, who had fallen asleep, and rested his head against her shoulder. After tilting the back of the stroller to a reclining position, she laid the baby gently on his stomach. He fidgeted slightly but continued sleeping. Back with the newspapers, she searched the next five editions of the *Observer* for more information about Howard's death but could find nothing, not even an obituary. It seemed strange that no one at least tried to find out where the bad moonshine came from, or it never got into the newspaper if someone did. You would think a family would want to find out everything they could about a son's death.

Lydia kept reading, expecting she would find something about further investigation, but there was nothing. Howard's name wasn't mentioned again, but Henry's name came up in a few articles published several years after his brother's death. Apparently, workers at the mill had gone on strike to oppose something called the "stretch-out," which required them to work longer for no increase in pay. At that time, the mill provided houses to many of its employees, and according to the *Observer*, young Henry led the forces who physically evicted strikers from their mill-owned homes.

"We have to keep the mill safe for men who want to support their families," he was quoted as saying. "We don't have room for troublemakers at the mill or in Tanner." One of the articles featured a photograph of Henry carrying two chairs out of a worker's home.

Suddenly, Lydia heard the freight elevator creak open. Robert emerged from the dingy box, cigarette in hand, and Lydia noticed he was wearing both suspenders and a belt. "You been down here a long time," he said. "Digging up any dirt?"

"Just a bunch of things I don't understand," she said. "Like why nobody questioned where the whiskey that killed Howard came from. Or how he got hold of it. Police today would go after whoever sold him—or gave him—poison." She glanced at Malcolm to make sure the conversation hadn't disturbed him. His face was as peaceful as when she laid him down. "It doesn't make any sense to me. They should've gone after whoever he got the poison from."

"I can't tell you much about that," Robert said. "I wasn't here then. You oughta talk to Burt Evans. If I'm not mistaken, he was in practice with Calvin Cathey, and Calvin was the doctor who pronounced Howard dead."

Lydia's interest kicked into high gear. Burt Evans was the reason she was in Tanner. He was the doctor who brought Jeff to town to take over his practice when he retired. She would definitely talk to him.

"Even though you weren't here, don't you think it's odd the police don't seem to have been concerned about where Howard got the poison?" Lydia couldn't wrap her head around such incompetence.

"Listen, if old Mr. Galloway didn't want the police to look into where the liquor came from, they didn't look into it. I told you, he had his thumb on the newspaper. Believe me, he pressed just as hard on the police. You aren't familiar with small-town politics, are you?"

"Apparently not. It just seems so odd that somebody who's used to buying moonshine could make a mistake like that. And that nobody thought it was odd then."

"Well, dearie, that's my best guess as to what happened. Like I said, talk to Burt Evans. Now, I can tell you a little bit about *that*." Robert pointed with his foot at the photo of Henry carrying chairs.

"Henry Galloway hates the union more than most folks hate the devil. When I started at the *Observer* in 1934, five or six years after that happened"—he pointed at the photo again—"cotton mills in North Carolina were just fixing to join in an uprising that cost a lot of workers their lives and a lot more their jobs. They said it started with a wildcat strike in Alabama and then spread across the South. Folks at the Tanner mill walked out in September that year, yelling about too little wages for too much work. Arthur Galloway pretty much said the hell with the strikers—fired 'em and evicted 'em and said good riddance—and then started hiring other poor slobs from out in the country to replace 'em.

"Henry talked his father into putting armed guards at the mill gates to get rid of any strikers who tried to keep the replacements from going to work. As a result, several people got shot, and one got killed. Henry said they got what they deserved. In fact, he wrote an editorial that pretty much said that in the paper. Let's see here." Robert walked along the shelves for several yards, checking the dates on the newspapers. "Thirty-two, thirty-three. It should be right here." He pulled a stack of papers from a shelf and leafed through them. After a few minutes, he folded a page back and handed it to Lydia. "Read this," he said.

The editorial was titled "Bound by Duty." In it, Henry argued that the mill owners had a responsibility to workers who weren't on strike and to all of Tanner to keep the mill running and free of harassment for "decent, hard-working men who appreciate having a job in these hard times." He said he was "sorry that some were injured or lost their lives in a battle that could so easily have been avoided, but it was a choice they made—not only to walk out on their responsibilities but also to try to keep others from maintaining Tanner's stability through the stability of the mill." He said in the final paragraph, "Tanner's citizens can rest assured that the scoundrels who caused this turmoil, which resulted in injury and death, will not go unpunished. I promise to add the names of the leaders of this revolt to the others across the South who are now barred from getting jobs anywhere in this part of the United States."

"Barred from working anywhere?" Lydia asked. The punishment seemed unusually harsh. She wasn't familiar with the politics of labor, but she wondered if it was even legal to discriminate in hiring like that.

"Yep. That's what they did," Robert said. "And since it was the Depression and there weren't that many jobs anyway, a lot of those families had nowhere to live and didn't know where their next meal was coming from. They parceled their kids out to friends and relatives and did what they could for themselves."

"Were there a lot like that?" Lydia knew about the bread lines and hobo towns of the Depression and couldn't believe that someone would deliberately force a person into those situations.

"Not here. Just the strike organizers were blacklisted. Most of the others came back to work after a few weeks, and the Galloways took 'em back. Even gave some of 'em their houses back. But you can be sure the whole thing put the fear of God into 'em about unions. There ain't been a threat of a union or a strike in Tanner since then." Robert dropped his cigarette on the floor and crushed it out with his shoe.

"What do you think about Henry Galloway?" Lydia asked. "You've known him a long time."

Robert leaned against the shelves and looked up, as if he were talking to the ceiling. "He's a businessman—a damn smart businessman. Production and sales at the mill have increased almost every year since he took over."

"But what's he like personally?"

"Can't say. My relationship with him's purely professional. Almost like with a boss. If he tells our publisher he doesn't like what I'm doing, I figure I'm gone. Nobody ever told me that, but that's part of my business sense. Knowing which way the wind blows." He looked down at Lydia and smiled.

"You sound like you don't like him."

"I didn't say that. You can't live in Tanner and not appreciate what he and his father have done for this town. The schools, the churches, the merchants—everybody's benefited from the Galloways' generosity. We wouldn't have a YMCA or a municipal swimming pool if it weren't for them."

"Does he have a lot of friends?"

"I don't know. He and I, we don't travel in the same social circles. The only time I ever see him is at the Fourth of July picnic. The whole family always turns out for that. You can talk to him there yourself, if you want to." Robert pulled another Camel from a pack in his shirt pocket and lit it. "He's always real friendly at the picnic."

I guess I'll just do that, Lydia thought. "So nobody talks at all about Howard's death anymore. The family just sort of swept it under the rug and went on," she said.

"Why're you so interested in this?" Robert asked. "It was a long time ago, and the police chief said it was an accident, and that's all it was."

"I'm amazed at how it was handled. Or mishandled, I should say."

Robert took a long drag off his cigarette. "You better be finishing up now," he said. "It's getting late. We're fixing to close the office pretty soon."

The last thing Lydia wanted to do was leave. Nothing this interesting was waiting for her at home. "I'll be done in a little while," she said. "Just give me a few minutes to put all these papers back on the shelves."

"Shirley can do that," Robert said. "Come on. I'll walk you out." He waited for Lydia to make sure Malcolm was covered snugly, then walked behind her to the elevator.

The groaning and wheezing of the elevator ropes and the increasing clacking of the presses as they neared the main floor woke up the baby. By the time they entered the press room, he was wailing like someone had pinched him. Lydia pushed the stroller quickly between the machines and into the tiny reception area, where she waved and smiled at Robert over the wails, and then she hurried out into the late afternoon heat.

Robert waited until Lydia was halfway down the block before he returned to his office. The copy he had been editing was strewn across his desk, with the last page pinned damply under a glass of sweet tea and melted ice. He dropped into his swivel chair and pushed the papers and glass aside with one hand while he reached into a drawer with the other and pulled out a thin telephone directory. In a few minutes he had Jeff's receptionist on the phone.

"If he's with a patient, I can hold," Robert said. He didn't have to hold long. Soon Jeff's voice came over the line. "This is Robert Kelly down at the *Observer*," Robert said. "I just wanted to let you know that your wife was here this afternoon."

"What for?" Jeff sounded tired and a little annoyed.

"Well, that's why I'm calling. She was looking for old articles about Henry Galloway and his family." Jeff was quiet. "I don't think I have to tell you," Robert went on, "that the

Galloways don't like people messing in their business. I told your wife that, and I hope I scared her off, but I thought you oughta know. You sure as hell don't want Henry Galloway mad at you. I heard about a fellow once who got his house loan called in at the bank because he riled Henry. I just thought you oughta know."

3

Out on the street, cars and trucks grumbled past Lydia, belching exhaust fumes into the already hazy air. She glanced at her watch: four twenty. It was shift change at the mill, the only time Tanner had traffic problems. She darted along the cracked sidewalk, hoping the movement would lull Malcolm out of his tears. The Camaro was parked in the lot where the Tanner Presbyterian Church had been. At one time all the major churches—Methodist, Presbyterian, and Baptist— had been downtown, but as the residential areas expanded north and east, the churches went too, leaving gaping holes where their splendid old buildings had been demolished until parking lots and gas stations sprang up to fill them. The result was a much uglier, but more practical, commercial area.

Lydia was lifting Malcolm, still crying, out of his stroller when she decided she didn't want to fight the endless stream of vehicles, most of which had their windows down with Conway Twitty or Tammy Wynette blaring from the radio, and she didn't want to go home. So she grasped the baby against her shoulder, spoke to him softly to try to calm him down, wrestled the stroller into the trunk of the car, and walked past the line of auto supply stores, feed and seed stores, dime stores, and drug stores to visit her friend Suzanne, who lived in an apartment above the Tanner hardware store.

Suzanne had been kind to Lydia since the day they met at the A&P, when both were newly pregnant and miserably sick with colds. It had been another warm day, and Lydia had felt like her head was a steam engine about to blow. She was trying to figure out which cold medicine to buy when she noticed Suzanne staring at the list of ingredients on a box of Contac. As if she felt Lydia's gaze, Suzanne looked up and asked, "Do you know if this stuff makes you nauseated? I'm pregnant, and I can't keep a thing down, but I also can't breathe. I need help, bad."

"Me too," Lydia said and wiped her nose gingerly with a crumpled Kleenex. "I'm in the same fix."

Suzanne handed Lydia another tissue. "My condolences, then. Especially since the hottest part of the summer is yet to come. At least you're not showing yet, so maybe you won't be too miserable. That's what I'm counting on. If I can just stop vomiting and blowing my nose." Lydia laughed, which brought on a coughing fit. Suzanne whacked her on the back, and when Lydia was more under control, Suzanne said, "My apartment's not far from here. Why don't you come on home with me, and we'll have a steaming cup of herbal tea. Sounds boring as hell, but it shouldn't make us vomit, and maybe it'll help us breathe."

After that, they got together every week or so. Lydia liked Suzanne's irreverent comments and brash wit. She appeared worldly, although she grew up in Tanner and left North Carolina only for vacations. Having quit college after her first year, she told Lydia she learned most of what she knew from watching television, particularly *Jeopardy!* and *General Hospital.* She was taller than most women, with a buxom figure that really showed off the peasant blouses she liked to wear. She was convinced she didn't have to worry about her husband straying as long as her boobs didn't start to sag. Her daughter, Lily, was five years old when she and Lydia met. Lydia was glad to know someone who had been through pregnancy and childbirth before, although Suzanne's observations were not always comforting.

"Ask for all the drugs you can get," was her primary advice.

In the afternoon, Suzanne worked part-time for Everclean, a vacuum cleaner company that sold its products through home demonstrations. Her job was to telephone prospective customers and persuade them to let a sales team give a demonstration in their home, preferably that evening. She earned a small salary, but most of her income came from the percentage she received if she set up an appointment that resulted in a sale.

"Talking to those folks gets kind of repetitious," she told Lydia, "so if they don't sound very interested and I need a little excitement, I tell them I'm talking to them buck naked and see what their reaction is. You'd be surprised how many—men and women—ask me if I want them to take their clothes off too."

The afternoon of Lydia's visit to the *Observer*, Suzanne answered her knock on the door with a quick "Come on in. I'm on the phone." Malcolm had calmed down, so Lydia slipped quietly into the apartment and settled both of them on the couch with the tie-dyed slip cover. She was eager to hear Suzanne's conversation in hopes that it might be one of the "naked" calls, because she wasn't sure Suzanne ever actually said that. She could tell from Suzanne's side of the conversation that it was an Everclean call, but it seemed to be going well, so Suzanne would have to stay with her pitch. Disappointed, Lydia reached around Malcolm to the coffee table and picked up a copy of *Time* with George McGovern's picture on the cover.

Inside the magazine, a ranking of Democratic presidential candidates put McGovern in the lead, which didn't surprise Lydia, but she was surprised to see that Shirley Chisholm was still in the race. No woman had ever run for president before, and certainly not a black woman. Lydia wondered why a woman would want to be president. Shirley Chisholm didn't have any children, so they wouldn't be a problem for her like they would for most women, but what about her husband? Would he be the "first gentleman"? Not that there was anything wrong with having a first gentleman, but it just seemed odd.

"Well, great," Suzanne said, signaling to Lydia that the call was almost over. "Someone from our team will be at your house at eight o'clock tonight. And be sure and have your husband there. He'll wanna see what a fine machine the Everclean is. Good-bye now." She hung up the phone. "My Lord, that is a sale if I ever set one up. Woman's dumb as a stick, but by God, her house is gonna be cleaner than her neighbor's. Lily, sweetie, that is money in the bank for us." She grabbed her daughter, who was lying on the floor watching television with the sound off, and tickled her between her ribs, causing the child to squirm and giggle. "So, Lydia. What are you and Malcolm up to today?"

"More than usual. We just paid a visit to the *Tanner Observer* and had a little chat with Mr. Robert Kelly himself." Lydia picked a rattle up off the floor and handed it to Malcolm, who was beginning to fidget.

"I hope that old coot didn't make any stupid proclamations while you were there. For somebody in charge of a weekly newspaper in a town with only a few thousand people, he sure has a high opinion of himself." Suzanne kissed Lily on her cheek and moved to a Kennedy Rocker, where she nearly always sat when she slowed down for a few minutes. "Did you read that dumb editorial he wrote about Memorial Day? About how it doesn't mean anything anymore, how it's just another day off from work since Congress made it into a three-day weekend? Guess he thinks he's smarter than Congress. I, for one, am glad it's a three-day weekend because it gives me three whole days when Frank is home to give me some help with these kids."

She glanced at Lily to make sure she wasn't listening. Suzanne's husband, Frank Jessop, was a first-line supervisor at the mill who often had to work on Saturday, but unless production was way behind schedule, the mill seldom ran on holiday weekends.

"But I know that's not why you went," she continued. "Did Sir Kelly have anything to say about Howard and Henry?" Lydia had told Suzanne Stella's story about Howard's death, and Suzanne said she had heard the rumor before.

"Not much. I just read the newspaper accounts."

"What is it with you and that old story?" Suzanne asked. "That's such old news, it's rotting."

"It's not just that," Lydia said. "It's the whole family, even Stella. They fascinate me. They're different from the rest of us."

"No joke," Suzanne said.

"Not just because they're rich." Lydia sighed. "There's something haunting about them. And besides, Nancy and Stella like me."

Suzanne shrugged. "Don't you have enough to think about without getting your ass snagged in this?"

Lydia ran her fingers through Malcolm's silky hair. "Nothing as intriguing as this." She paused. "And I need something like that in my life. I feel like something's missing."

"Maybe you oughta get a job."

"Jeff doesn't want me to work. He made that quite clear when I got pregnant. And, besides, I want to stay home with Malcolm. It's the right thing to do. I don't think that's the problem, anyway. I've been without a job before and never felt like this. It's like I've lost something, but I don't know what it is. I've even had dreams about losing things."

"Fear of loss is our most primal fear. They say a baby's first fear is fear of abandonment. Fear that he'll lose his parents or whoever takes care of him. Maybe the feeling and the dreams aren't about what you've lost, but what you're afraid of losing. Are you afraid of losing something?"

"No. I feel empty, like whatever it is, it's gone already. And you know those spells I get."

"Did you ever see a doctor about those?" Suzanne frowned.

"I tried to explain them to Dr. Greene when I went for my last checkup. He said it was just hormones. But I felt like this before I got pregnant. In fact, I thought having a baby would cure it, but it's been five months since Malcolm was born, and I still feel this way."

"What's Jeff say?"

"That it's all in my head."

"Men are so dense." Suzanne rocked with a deliberate sway that underscored her point.

"You know, I thought Jeff was totally tuned in to me back when we were dating, a real man of the '60s. Sympathy, love, harmony—all that shit. He listened to what I said, or at least he pretended to, and a lot of the time he actually agreed with me. I thought getting married would bring us even closer, but it's been sort of the opposite. It's like he lives in a different world. I know he feels pressured to be as good as Dr. Evans, and he thinks the whole town's watching him, but that's not his entire life. I really thought being married to Jeff would be different." Lydia sighed again, thinking back to the handsome med student she had fallen in love with. His hair was a little longer then, and the extra pounds he carried gave him a real presence. She had wanted to be with him all the time.

"Life changes when the real world comes crashing down on you," Suzanne said. "Frank gets preoccupied with work too, but

I snap him back by going off and leaving him with the kids for a few hours."

Lydia laughed. "Jeff would have to fit that in between work and golf, but I could try."

"What's he think about you and the Galloways?" Suzanne asked. She gathered up some Cheerios on the table next to her and slipped them into her pocket.

"He told me to stay away from Nancy. He said the Galloways don't want other people bothering her. Did you know that?"

"Yeah, I've heard it. I always thought it wasn't the Galloways so much as people just didn't wanna be around her. She's retarded—and kind of weird. So are you gonna stay away?"

"I don't know. Probably not." Lydia remembered Jeff's face the last time the subject of Nancy came up. For the first weeks after she told him about Nancy and Stella, she kept their library meetings a secret, figuring he would care less as time went by. But a few days ago, one of his patients mentioned to him that she saw Lydia talking with Nancy at the library. When Jeff confronted Lydia, she said she was bound to run into Nancy occasionally since there was only one library in Tanner and they both liked to go there. Jeff's glower showed that wasn't the answer he wanted, and he spent the rest of the evening in a sulk.

"What's he gonna do when he finds out you're poking around in Howard's death?" Suzanne asked.

"I'm not going to tell him—at least not for a while. I want him to get used to the idea of Nancy and me first. There's no way me being friends with that girl is going to stir up any trouble. Jeff's just thinking like the little boy he was when he lived here before. He needs to grow up. And when I think he's ready, I'll tell him what I'm doing about Howard." Lydia had never kept anything from Jeff before, and it made her stomach churn to do it now.

A lonesome cry from the bedroom sent Suzanne to check on the newest member of her family, Frank Junior. She came back carrying the baby, who squirmed in delight when he saw Malcolm. After spreading a blanket on the floor and retrieving a few toys from behind the TV, she laid her son on the blanket and motioned for Lydia to do the same. "All right, little bruisers. Here's y'all's chance to mess with each other." Then she pulled a cigarette from a pack of Newports on the coffee table and lit it. "Maybe it won't matter whether you tell Jeff what you're doing or not because you're not gonna find anything."

"But there're so many missing pieces. What do you know about moonshine? I looked up methanol in the encyclopedia at the library, and what I read implied that it has a funny smell. Wouldn't Howard have smelled it or tasted it, even, if there was enough in that booze to kill him?"

Suzanne exhaled a long stream of smoke. "My uncle claimed to know some bootleggers back when I was a little girl. He told my daddy the rule was to always smell moonshine before you drink it, and even if it doesn't smell funny, put some in a spoon and set it on fire. If it burns any color but blue, don't drink it. It's got lead or methanol or some other chemical in it."

"So see. Howard should have known."

"But maybe that's not true all the time. My uncle didn't always know what he was talking about. And maybe Henry got him so drunk on the safe stuff first that he could slip him the bad stuff without his knowing it."

Lydia pondered this idea for a few seconds. "You still have to admit, it doesn't sound like an accident, and there are a lot of loose ends. And a lot of possibilities that nobody mentioned at the time. Something else occurred to me last night. What if somebody had a bone to pick with the Galloways and deliberately gave the boys that poison moonshine? Do you reckon the Galloways had any real enemies back then?"

"Sure they did. They still do. You can't run a mill and a town without picking up some enemies along the way."

"Like who?"

"Damned if I know. Especially way back then." Suzanne puffed on her cigarette. "But smell or no smell, enemy or no enemy, I'll tell you this. If you really wanna know about the Galloways, you need to finagle yourself an invitation out to Foxrow. They're all there, including the old man. I'll bet, when you meet them for real, you won't care anymore. Maybe it's just Nancy you're really interested in, although, for the life of me, I can't see why."

"She's kind of sad, in a way," Lydia said. "Cooped up like a—what's that saying?—like a bird in a gilded cage. Sometimes she almost breaks my heart. And I don't know why nobody else can see it. But you're on to something about going out to Foxrow."

Jeff didn't get home that night until nearly seven o'clock. "Appointments ran late," he said as he pulled off his necktie and went to the kitchen for a beer. Lydia had finished nursing Malcolm and was getting ready to give him a bath, but Jeff told her to wait. He wanted to talk to her.

"What were you doing at the *Observer*, looking up information about Henry Galloway?" he asked in a stern voice as he perched on the edge of his easy chair with his beer. "Kelly told me you were there."

Lydia pondered what he said in amazement. It had been only a few hours since she left the *Observer*. And Jeff already knew. She groped for an answer that would satisfy him.

Sally Whitney

"It's Nancy. I'm worried about her," she said. "I know you told me to stay away from her, but she's so cut off from the world. And I don't understand why they do that to her. I thought if I knew more about her family and some of its history, I might understand. She needs a friend." Lydia's stomach flittered. She should tell him the whole truth, but he wasn't ready to hear it yet.

"Well, it doesn't have to be you. She'd probably rather be around somebody more like her, anyway." Jeff's mouth tightened. The small port-wine birthmark in front of his left ear grew darker. It was the face Lydia had come to know as his business face, the one he put on when she said something he didn't agree with.

"What do you mean? Somebody who's retarded, like her? For crying out loud, Jeff, she can be friends with normal people too. But I don't think they ever let her go anywhere to meet anybody." It was true the only friend Nancy talked about was Stella.

Jeff sat back in the chair and crossed his arms. "You know what? This may be a lesson you have to learn for yourself. If you keep hanging around Nancy and looking for newspaper articles about her family, one of them's going to tell you off. It's just a matter of time. And when it happens, you're going to be so humiliated, so mortified, you'll wish you'd listened to me. Why don't you save yourself and me the embarrassment?"

Lydia thought about that for a few seconds. Could everything she was doing end up making her feel even worse about herself? Maybe she'd be better off just acting like Mrs. Jeffrey Colton and never doing anything more daring than suggesting a new color for the smocks the hospital auxiliary ladies wore. Jeff would like that, and she wanted to please him. Maybe that's what she agreed to when she married him. No. That couldn't be true. Nobody told her that.

"I'll be careful," she said. "And I'll try not to embarrass you."

The next time Lydia met Nancy and Stella at the library, she had devised a plan she was sure would get her invited to the farm. Nancy loved to talk about anything she owned—books, souvenirs, jewelry—and she especially liked it when Lydia showed interest in her things. As soon as Stella was deep into the current issue of *Reader's Digest*, Lydia asked Nancy to tell her about her room at Foxrow.

"It's green," Nancy said eagerly. "And there's wallpaper with green grapes on it. I picked it out." She pushed up the sleeves of her oversized shirt, showing freckles on her rounded arms.

"What about the furniture?" Lydia asked.

"It's white. With silver trim painted on it." Nancy closed the book she'd been reading and began to gesture as she talked. "I have white curtains too. They have little balls hanging around the edges. There're pictures on the walls. There's a picture of Mama and me when I was a baby and a picture of a horse eating grass in a big field. I've always wanted a horse. Mama won't let me have one. She's afraid I'll get hurt. I love the horse in the picture. You should see it sometime." Nancy's eyes brightened, and she smiled with excitement. "Come see it, Lydia," she said. "Come to my house. I'll show you my room and all my pictures." She clapped her hands, letting her book drop into her lap.

Stella looked up from her *Reader's Digest*. Lydia hoped none of the other people in the library heard the noise, but she figured they were all across the room on the other side of the shelves, as usual.

"Hush, sugar," Stella said. "You supposed to be quiet in a library. What's all the fuss about, anyhow?"

"Lydia's going to come to my house and see my room," Nancy exclaimed. "She's going to see my bed and the picture of my horse and—"

Stella patted her knee and made a "sh" sound. Saliva glistened in the corners of the old woman's mouth, and her eyes were soft with kindness. "You oughta see what your mama thinks about it before you goes inviting folks to come to your house," she said. Nancy's face crumpled in disappointment. "But just this once, I'll tell her I said it's all right for this one to come on out."

She nodded at Lydia with a stern look that seemed to say, if Lydia did anything to hurt Nancy, she'd have Stella to answer to.

And so the visit was arranged for a Saturday afternoon. Jeff was playing golf, so Lydia hired a babysitter for Malcolm and drove to the farm. She didn't tell Jeff where she was going, even though he had implied she could go ahead and get herself in trouble if she wanted to. She figured he didn't really mean that. He hoped the sarcasm would shame her into giving up. She felt bad about lying by omission, as her mother called it, but it was for the best. Jeff had been in a bad mood ever since he talked to Robert Kelly.

Memorial Day had passed a week earlier, and every lush tree and vibrant wildflower along the way announced summer had arrived. Lydia turned the Camaro from the highway onto the red dirt road that cut across the fields and forests of Foxrow. For as far as she could see, the land spread out like an oil painting, rich with colors and textures and life. Branching off from the main road were side roads she assumed led to different parts of the farm. A horse barn, visible down one of the roads next to a small corral, sent a shiver through her. It was probably where Howard died. Another road rolled past fields of half-grown corn, and a third led into a dense thicket that may have been an orchard. Lydia was tempted to go exploring, but she was afraid she'd get lost in the maze of roads, and she didn't want to be late to see Nancy.

She stayed on the main road, and suddenly, there it was, rising up behind a cluster of century-old oaks. The two-story farmhouse loomed larger than she expected, gleaming white in the afternoon sun. A broad porch stretched across the entire front and down one side of the house. The yard appeared close to an acre by itself, covered with thick grass, separated into sections by boxwood bushes the size of boulders. In the side yard, a flower garden was bursting with crimson daylilies and lavender hyacinths, and beyond that, patches of river shone between the oaks and pine trees lining the edge of the fields.

Lydia parked her car on the gravel driveway that looped in front of the house. Slowly, she climbed the wooden steps leading to the porch. White wicker sofas and chairs with paisley cushions stood guard at various spots on both sides of the heavy double front door. All of the windows were flanked by deep-blue wooden shutters, with hinges that suggested they actually closed and latched. Lydia took a deep breath and twisted the vintage buzzer.

Almost immediately, the door was opened by an attractive, middle-aged woman, whose deep-red hair had a richness of color not found in most women past their thirties. "I'm Caroline Galloway," she said. "Please come in."

After waiting for her visitor to enter, she extended her hand. She was taller than Lydia, with a substantial but proportionate figure, which gave her a commanding presence. Her skin was as pale as her daughter's, but her eyes were darker, somewhere between hazel and light brown. Her firm handshake surprised Lydia and reminded her she was in the presence of power.

Inside the double front door, a mammoth center hall ran the length of the house and held a wide, heart pine staircase, winding up to the second floor. Caroline gestured for Lydia to follow her through a door on the left to an equally cavernous living room.

Nancy sat at one end of a long, green velvet couch. With a gentle smile, she said, "Hi, Lydia," then fell silent. Caroline invited Lydia to sit on the couch near Nancy and arranged herself in a wing chair with crewel upholstery. Feeling the need to say something, Lydia started the conversation by remarking how beautiful Foxrow was and asking about its history.

"Foxrow's been home to four generations of the Galloway family," Caroline said. "My husband's grandfather, Arthur Galloway, bought the land and built the house shortly after he started the mill in 1890." With her, "house" sounded like "hoose," Lydia noticed, marking her as a transplant from Virginia.

Lydia nodded. "He sure was ambitious."

"Well, in addition to his interest in cotton processing, Arthur liked to think of himself as a gentleman farmer, who grew some of the cotton he used," Caroline said. "So he bought five hundred acres of river bottom land that was already a working farm, hired the hands to run it, built the house, and sat back on his porch to survey his holdings when he wasn't spending long hours at the mill. They say he named the place Foxrow because of the red foxes that shared the land, and then he gave the name to the mill, as well. In the beginning, when the mill just made cotton yarn, they took bales of cotton straight from the farm." She folded her hands and smiled. "Would you like a glass of ice tea?" When Lydia accepted the offer, Caroline asked Nancy to go to the kitchen and bring back tea for all of them.

"As I was driving up to the house, I saw corn growing, but no cotton," Lydia said in an effort to keep the conversation going after Nancy left.

Caroline shifted in her chair, which Lydia was beginning to think of as a throne. "My father-in-law is not as interested in farming as Arthur was, so he leased most of the land to tenant farmers, and they prefer to grow some corn and mostly tobacco," she said. "Henry doesn't care because the amount of cotton Foxrow produced was such a small percentage of what the mill needs that it doesn't affect purchasing one way or the other." Caroline tilted her head in a gesture of indifference.

Lydia thought about Henry Galloway and his fierce opposition to the union. He didn't seem to have the temperament of a farmer.

Nancy returned with a small tray holding three glasses of iced tea garnished with lemon. As she walked, she concentrated on balancing the glasses and passing them out. Caroline took a glass and sipped from it quietly while appearing to study Lydia's face.

"How long have you lived in Tanner?" she asked after a few minutes, letting Lydia know she was aware that her guest was not a native.

"A little over a year," Lydia said, "but my husband grew up here."

"And what do you think of our town?" Caroline asked, taking another sip of tea.

"I like it. The hills and river are beautiful."

"Yes, it really is a lovely place," Caroline said. "Arthur picked the right spot along the river to build his mill. We love it here, don't we, Nancy?"

"Yes, ma'am," Nancy said. She was strangely reticent, unlike her chattering at the library.

"I knew it was a great place to live the first time I came here," Caroline went on. "I'm originally from Richmond, but I came to visit a friend and met my husband, Wallace, and never wanted to leave." Her smile tightened, pulling her lips into a thin line. "And, of course, when I saw this house with its antique charm and family history, I knew there was no place I could be happier. Where are you from, Mrs. Colton?"

"Charlotte," Lydia said. "My parents still live there."

"How nice," Caroline said. "Has your family always lived there?"

"Yes. At least for several generations." Lydia replied. "My grandparents and my great-grandparents on both sides lived there." *I could qualify for Daughters of the Confederacy, if I wanted to*, she thought, but she didn't say it.

"What's your maiden name?"

"Lawrence," Lydia said.

Caroline frowned. "I don't know any Lawrences from Charlotte. What was your mother's name?"

"Harris. She's remotely related to the man who started Harris-Teeter grocery stores. Some distant cousin." *Grocery stores may not be as aristocratic as cotton mills, but they make lots of money.*

"Did you attend Queens College in Charlotte?" Caroline asked, pointedly ignoring the remark about the grocery stores.

"No, ma'am. I went to Elon College. I was a chemistry major."

"Chemistry?" Caroline smirked. "That's an unusual major for a woman. Why on earth did you choose that?"

"I didn't want to be a teacher or a nurse."

Caroline's eyes widened. "I imagine you wanted to be a wife and mother."

"Yes, ma'am," Lydia said. It was true, it had never occurred to her she would not be a wife and mother. It came after college, like college came after high school.

In the silence that followed, Nancy looked up from staring at her lap. "May we please go upstairs now?" she asked. "I want to show Lydia my room."

"I suppose so," Caroline said. As the two women rose from the couch, she said, "It was a pleasure to meet you, Mrs. Colton."

"I enjoyed meeting you too," Lydia said.

Nancy took Lydia's hand and pulled her toward the door.

They left the room and climbed the steps, each of which had a small dip in the center, worn by the rubbing of so many feet over so many years. At the top of the stairs, the heart pine flooring flowed into a center hall as large as the one below it. Five doors opened off the hall, two on each side and one at the back.

"Which room's yours?" Lydia asked.

"That one," Nancy said, pointing to the first door on the left. "That one's Granddaddy's," she said, pointing to the door across the hall from hers. "The one next to it is Tom's."

"And Tom's your brother," Lydia said.

"Right. My big brother. He works at the mill."

Lydia remembered reading about Tom in the *Observer* or hearing Jeff mention him. He was the heir apparent to the family dynasty. Supposedly, he was working his way up through the mill, keeping a low profile for the time being, except that everybody in town recognized his silver Corvette.

"The one next to mine is the guest room," Nancy continued. "The door at the back goes to the back staircase and to Stella's room over the kitchen. Mama's room is downstairs."

Lydia stared at the door to Henry's room, wondering if he was in there. While she was pondering what she would say to the old man if he appeared, Nancy dragged her into a room that was indeed a cloud of green and white. Nancy started the tour with the horse picture and was moving on to the photograph of her mother and her when Stella appeared at the door.

"I'm supposed to give y'all about thirty minutes and then fetch you back downstairs," she said, "but I reckon I can give y'all an extra five." She looked at the heavy watch with a rectangular face on her thin wrist. It was obviously a man's watch, and Lydia wondered if Henry or Wallace or maybe Tom had given it to her.

Stella stationed herself in a chair in the hall while Nancy continued to describe the furnishings in her room. She was very proud of her things and had a story to tell about most of them. When she had shown Lydia almost everything sitting on her chest of drawers or dressing table or hanging on the walls, she took an eight-by-ten photograph in a cardboard folder out of one of the drawers. The picture showed Nancy plus four other young women in fancy dresses and two young men in suits, standing in front of a water fountain in a garden.

"These are my friends from school," Nancy said. "This was the day we graduated."

"Congratulations. You're a great-looking group. What are your friends doing now?"

"I don't know. I haven't seen them since then."

"Why not?" Lydia asked.

"They live too far away for Mama or Stella to take me."

"Don't you miss them?" Lydia was amazed that nobody would make the effort to get the group together.

"No," Nancy said quickly. "I have Stella. She's my friend. And now I have you." She put her arms around Lydia, giving her an awkward hug.

As Lydia pulled away, she noticed an unusual runner on a small table in the corner. The long, narrow cloth was actually several pieces of material in various prints, sewn together in no apparent pattern. "What's this?" she asked.

Nancy blushed. "I made it," she said. "Tom brings me cloth from the mill. I cut it into shapes and sew them together."

"For heaven's sake," Lydia said, causing Nancy's blush to deepen. "It's beautiful. I didn't know you could sew." Lydia had not picked up a needle and thread since home economics class in ninth grade.

"Here. Let me show you." Nancy lifted the vase of flowers sitting on the runner.

Lydia admired the neat seams and straight edges. "Who taught you how to sew?" she asked.

"She did," Nancy said, pointing at Stella, who had stepped inside the door. "She takes me to Belk's to buy needles and thread. The stitches don't show if the thread's the same color as the material. I can use a thimble. Can you use a thimble?"

"I'm afraid not," Lydia said. "Maybe that's something you can teach me." As she spoke the words, she stifled the joy that threatened to creep across her face. She knew where her next invitation to Foxrow was coming from.

Stella cleared her throat. "We got to go now," she said. "Miss Caroline's gonna come looking for y'all pretty soon, and we all be in trouble."

Sadly, Nancy replaced the vase before she and Lydia followed Stella down the stairs. In the first floor hall, Lydia peered into the living room, expecting to see Caroline, but no one was there. Stella and Nancy told her good-bye, and she left through the double front door, hearing it click solidly shut behind her.

4

Nancy spent the rest of the weekend planning to have Lydia visit Foxrow again. She knew her mother wouldn't like it, but her mind was made up. It had been a long time since anyone had shown any desire to come see her, and she wasn't going to let this new friend slip away.

At Sunday dinner, Caroline said that, although Lydia seemed nice, she didn't share the same interests as Nancy and wouldn't make a good friend for her. Nancy, however, knew her mother was wrong. Lydia was interested in sewing, and she would show her how. After dinner, Nancy went out to the kitchen and told Stella her plan.

"Now, honey, a person usually waits till they's invited to their guest's house before they invites the same guest for another visit," Stella said. "Just be patient. If y'all meant to be friends, it'll happen."

But Nancy couldn't wait. She spent all day Monday going through runners and tablecloths she had made and deciding which ones she would show Lydia. She also checked her sewing basket and discovered she had only one thimble. She would need another if she and Lydia were going to sew at the same time. She had a lot to do to get ready for the visit, but first she had to ask her mother.

When Caroline returned home from bridge club, Nancy was sitting in the living room, stitching two swatches of material together and watching TV. "It's such a pretty day. Why aren't you sewing in the garden?" Caroline asked.

"'Cause I want to see you, Mama," Nancy said. She stuck her needle into the cloth and looked up at her mother as warm blood flooded her cheeks. Caroline sat down in the wing chair and folded her hands in her lap. She glanced at her watch, although she barely turned her head or her wrist, and returned her gaze quickly to Nancy, who was breathing deeply through her mouth. As neither one spoke, voices from the television covered the silence until Caroline walked across the room and turned it off. Before she returned to her seat, Nancy said, "I want Lydia to come see me again," the words whooshing out in a rush.

Caroline shook her head slowly. "We talked about this," she said, changing direction and walking toward Nancy instead of the chair. Standing in front of her daughter, she touched her cheek lightly. "She's not right for you. And you hardly know her." Nancy and Stella had not told Caroline how often they saw Lydia at the library. "We'll find you another friend."

"Like who?" Nancy cried. "Who? I don't know anybody else. You keep saying you'll find me a friend, and you never do. Just your friends. They don't like me." The flush on her face ran like prickly heat down her neck.

"They do like you," Caroline said, running her hand over Nancy's hair.

"They don't even know me. They won't talk to me." Nancy's green eyes grew watery.

"You don't spend much time with them, but never mind them. We'll find somebody else for you."

"No. I want Lydia. We're going to sew together in my room or maybe out in the garden." Nancy glared at her mother.

"I told you, we'll find somebody else," Caroline said, but before she could say any more, Henry Galloway strode into the room. He appeared cool and collected at the end of the hot day, despite his three-piece suit and tightly knotted necktie. With his thick mane of white hair, he reminded Nancy of Harry Reasoner, the man her mother watched on TV every night.

"Where the hell is the newspaper?" Henry said. "Did one of y'all bring it in here?" He stood barely inside the door and raised his voice, as if he were afraid they couldn't hear him on the other side of the large room. Nancy looked away from him when he spoke. The physical force of his words frightened her.

"I haven't seen the paper since you had it at breakfast this morning, Henry," Caroline said. "Why don't you ask Pansy?" Pansy was the Galloways' cook, who shared the servants' quarters above the kitchen with Stella. "Maybe she put it somewhere in the kitchen instead of the study."

"Damn woman knows where I like it," Henry said. "She's only been putting it there for the past ten years." He scowled and stared at various tables. Not finding the newspaper, he left the room, slamming the door behind him.

Nancy raised her head and saw her mother's bitter stare. To break the moment as much as get her attention, she reached for Caroline's hand. "Please, Mama," she said. "Please let Lydia come see me."

Caroline's face softened, but she didn't smile. When she turned to Nancy, her expression was one she would give to an injured kitten. "All right," she said. "Maybe one more time, but if she does anything that you think is bad or hurts your feelings at all, you tell me, you understand?"

"Yes, ma'am," Nancy said, a bubble of happiness swelling inside her chest.

⸺

The visit was set for the following Saturday afternoon. At Caroline's request, Nancy asked Lydia to come on Friday afternoon, when Caroline said they wouldn't have to worry about bothering Henry. Lydia said Saturday was the only day she could get a babysitter for Malcolm, and she was afraid he would spoil the visit if she brought him. Nancy thought she would die if she had to wait another day, but Stella told her it was good because it would give her another day to get ready. Together they planned the afternoon's sewing lesson and went to Belk on Thursday to get supplies.

The trip to Belk was something they had done many times before. Tanner had two other department stores—JCPenney and locally-owned Davis's—but Nancy liked Belk the best. Stella parked the Lincoln in the parking lot where the Presbyterian church had been. From there it was only two blocks to the store, which was about as far as Stella liked to walk at one time. She would have parked closer, but that required parallel parking. As she told Nancy, "The Lord didn't mean for no car this long to back into no piece of street that short."

Nancy could feel the heat of the sidewalk through the soles of her Capezios, and she was glad when they reached the cool interior of the store. The sweet aromas of the perfume counter and scented candle section were also a welcome change from the outdoor odors of warm asphalt and restaurant grease. Nancy stopped by the perfume testers and squirted herself with Tabu, as she always did. She liked the smell and the heart-shaped bottle it came in. Stella stood behind her while she went through the ritual with the tester, but never squirted any on herself.

The next step in their shopping expedition was to stroll past the jewelry cases with their winking glass rings and milky cultured pearl necklaces. Nancy gazed at the gleaming displays and fingered the gold and silver earrings hanging from racks on top of the cases. Saleswomen watched as she passed through the aisles, but rarely approached her. They knew she was only looking. She always followed the same path through her favorite areas before she and Stella descended the narrow stairs in the corner of the store to the basement level, where the yard goods and sewing notions were located.

Normally, Nancy took her time studying the various spools of thread, while Stella perused the table linens and dishtowels across the aisle. On that particular shopping expedition, however, they had a new mission: select a thimble for Lydia. Nancy went immediately to the rack of thread and began searching the counter on both sides. She walked around the corner of the counter, but still no thimbles. Bolts of cloth, needles, hemming tape, hooks and eyes, snaps, but no thimbles. What if she couldn't find a thimble for Lydia? Then she couldn't teach Lydia to sew, and Lydia might be mad at her. The thought of disappointing Lydia hurt like a sudden stomach ache. She turned to Stella, who immediately grabbed her hand.

"What's wrong, baby?" Stella asked. "Oh, now I remembers. You wants a thimble." Nancy nodded and touched a finger to her quivering lips. "Well, let's see here now."

Stella led her back around the counter and down the aisle till the notions ended. Still no thimbles. The only saleswoman in the area was refolding a disheveled pile of men's T-shirts one aisle over. She looked up at Nancy and Stella and went back to her task. Although Nancy recognized most of the people who worked at Belk, she didn't remember this one. The woman was younger than most of the employees and had a bland, washed-out face. Stella cleared her throat softly, causing the woman to look up again, but she quickly turned her back and walked toward the rear of the store.

"Well, that's a fine how-do-you-do," Stella whispered.

"What's the matter with her?" Nancy demanded. "Why won't she help us?"

"Don't you worry none. It ain't got nothing to with you," Stella murmured. "She just don't like the looks of me. Some folks never change." Stella gazed after the woman, her lips set in a thin line. "C'mon, baby," she said. "There's other places that sells thimbles." She pulled Nancy toward the stairs.

"Nancy, dear, can I help you?" a voice called loudly. Nancy stopped walking, causing Stella, whose hand she was still holding, to stop too. One of the regular saleswomen rushed up to them, the heels of her pointed-toe pumps clicking against the cement floor. "Can I help y'all find something?" she asked.

"That other girl wouldn't help us," Nancy said, even though Stella squeezed her hand hard. The saleswoman's forehead wrinkled. "Stella said it was because of her. That the girl didn't like the way she looks. That's mean. Stella looks fine. She's just old." Nancy studied her friend's familiar face. How could anyone not like Stella?

The saleswoman sighed. "I'm sorry if Gail was rude to y'all. She's new here. I'll talk to her about it."

"You better tell her she hurt Stella's feelings, and that's not nice." Nancy could feel Stella pulling on her hand, but she wanted to make her point.

"I'll be sure to tell her. Now what can I do for y'all?"

"I need a thimble," Nancy said. "My friend's coming to see me. I'm going to teach her how to sew." She tried to drop Stella's hand, but the older woman wouldn't let go.

"Well, isn't that nice," the saleswoman said. "Of course we have thimbles. They're right back here." She returned to the thread rack and opened a drawer in the counter. "We don't have enough space to display everything. We're so cramped here in the basement. What size did you need?"

Nancy had no idea what size Lydia's finger was. She turned a troubled face to Stella, who said, "Get one that fits her." She pointed at the saleswoman. "Her and Lydia about the same size."

The thimble purchase completed, Nancy and Stella left Belk by the side door at the top of the stairs and made their way along the sidewalk toward the parking lot. As they waited for the first traffic light to change so they could cross, Nancy said, "I don't like that girl who wouldn't wait on us."

"I told you not to worry none about that," Stella said. "You just think about tomorrow."

Nancy nodded. Some people weren't nice to everybody, but Lydia was. And Lydia was coming tomorrow.

While Nancy and Stella shopped for a thimble, Jeff Colton was checking on patients at Arthur Galloway Memorial Hospital. It was a small hospital, but well-appointed because of the endowment Arthur set up for it when it was built in 1925. For its first years, it was called Tanner Hospital, but as soon as Arthur died, the town council voted to change the name. It had been Galloway Memorial ever since.

Only four stories tall, the building rested peacefully atop a small hill in what had been the outskirts of town in the 1920s, although houses grew up around it in the ensuing years. People who lived in those houses said they lived on "hospital hill," and everybody knew immediately what they meant. Fortunately, the builders preserved ample land for the parking lots the 1950's car boom made necessary, so while the hospital had to give up its rolling green grounds, it remained isolated in a sea of asphalt. Its yellow brick mellowed with age, giving a creampuff appearance to its narrow façade and long side walls.

At one time or another, nearly everybody in Tanner had passed between the four white columns lining its front door. Like a lot of teenagers, Jeff had become familiar with its emergency room, so when he arrived back at Galloway Memorial, it seemed like home. Also, its halls were filled with people he knew, old friends and acquaintances, who were now doctors, nurses, and orderlies. One of them was Joanna Philips.

Jeff had run into Joanna his first day on the job. Dr. Evans had admitted two patients to the hospital just before Jeff took over the practice, so the young doctor had to catch up with them and their cases. The first one he went to see had a pinched nerve and was being treated with traction. In a bed surrounded with bars, weights, and straps, the man was reduced to a small, red face inside all the paraphernalia.

When Jeff had entered the room, a slender nurse with blonde hair twirled into a French twist was adjusting the weights at the head of the bed. Her crisp, white dress showed off her tiny waist and delicate arms. She seemed too dainty to handle such heavy equipment, but she lifted and pulled like it was all made of air. In a single fluid motion, she removed the largest cylinder and placed it in a box on the floor behind her. The patient moaned and grabbed the bars on the side of the bed.

"Just a minute, Mr. Cockerham," the nurse had murmured. "I'll have the weight right back on there and relieve the pressure. We have to step you down on the weights, or you won't get any better."

"Good morning, Mr. Cockerham," Jeff said.

The nurse looked up in surprise, another weight clasped in her hands. Without the bangs he remembered, her face had a different shape, but she was still beautiful. "Joanna," he said. "I didn't know you were here."

She smiled, crinkling her eyes like the teenager he had known, as she slipped the weight onto the line extending from the pulley. Mr. Cockerham sighed as the new weight moved his vertebrae away from the nerve in question.

"Dr. Colton, welcome to Galloway Memorial," Joanna said. She closed the box of weights and wrote a note on the patient's chart. Her awkward, left-handed grip of the pen was the same as it had been in high school when she wrote Jeff notes and went with him to the senior prom. "This is Dr. Colton, Mr. Cockerham," she said. "He's taking over for Dr. Evans."

Jeff moved closer to the bed. "How's the pain today?"

Mr. Cockerham winced. "Some better."

"It takes a while for the muscle to relax and the nerve to heal. You'll see a big difference tomorrow." Jeff felt the man's shoulders gently, then checked the weights behind him. "Looks like you're in good hands," he said. "I'll see you tomorrow." Joanna followed him out the door.

"Good Lord, when did you get to be a doctor?" she'd asked as they walked down the hall. "Last time I saw you, you were an obnoxious frat boy."

"Me? How about you? I thought you gave up the notion of nursing to be a stewardess."

"I got tired of traveling." She laughed. "This is more my speed." She couldn't have surprised him more if she had said she decided to become a rocket scientist. He had liked her in high school, but he thought she was frivolous, not serious enough for any kind of medical career.

Memories of that frivolous schoolgirl flashed across his mind when he happened to catch sight of Joanna on the day of

Nancy and Stella's visit to Belk. She was just inside one of the hospital rooms, bent over a patient's outstretched arm as she started a new IV.

"It'll be just a little pinch, and then you won't feel a thing," she said softly, and she was right. Jeff could see there was none of the vein gouging he observed so often with less competent nurses. If he could have seen that side of her when he knew her before, their relationship might have lasted longer.

As it was, she was far from his mind when he met Lydia. A third-year medical student, he was too busy to date, but a friend had insisted he go out with Lydia. "Get your head out of the books," the friend had said. "Have yourself some fun for a change."

"Okay. But just this once."

To Jeff's surprise, he had liked her. She was smart and interested in what he was studying, and the "once" turned into several dates, which extended into several years. Being with her made him happier than he had ever been. Since neither of them had much money, they spent their evenings in the Duke Gardens in warm weather and watching TV or listening to music (usually The Beatles or Creedence Clearwater Revival) when it was cold, but they always ended up in Jeff's bed, where she made him happiest of all.

He asked her to marry him in the middle of his residency, mostly because she threatened to move to Atlanta. "A lot of my friends went there after college, and they all love it," she said. "Maybe I could get a job in the Coca-Cola labs. They must need chemistry majors. I could come up with a new soft drink. Could be a lot of money in that."

Jeff wasn't sure if she really intended to move, but the idea of living apart from her pushed him over the edge. He didn't even care if she was trying to hurry him along. He loved her, and six months later, they were married.

They had rented a tiny apartment close to the hospital, and Lydia worked at a cosmetics factory near Raleigh. The life of a resident was hard, with long, grueling hours at the hospital, but they made their way through the rough spots and arrived, still together, at Jeff's decision to take over the old doctor's practice in Tanner.

"You'll love Tanner," Jeff had told Lydia on a stormy Sunday afternoon. A hurricane making its way up the North Carolina coast was sending torrents of rain inland, darkening the sky so that midafternoon looked like evening. "It's small enough to know most of the people in town, but large enough so that everybody doesn't know your business."

"I was hoping for some place like Atlanta or Richmond," Lydia said. She was sitting at their kitchen table, making out a grocery list.

"Give it a try," Jeff urged. He sat down next to her in the other chair at the table and took the pencil out of her hand. "I have a ton of student loans to pay back, and this is an up-and-going practice being dropped in my lap. How can I turn it down?"

Lydia looked up from the list. "Tell them no."

"Don't be so catty. I promise you'll like it." He twisted the pencil in his fingers, surprised and irritated at the resistance in her eyes. This was his big break. She should be thrilled for him, instead of digging in her heels. His success would be her success too.

"What am I going to do there? Do they make anything there, or are they all farmers?" Lydia turned away from Jeff and stared out the window at the rain. Her face was as dark and disturbed as the trees, their limbs windblown toward the west.

"There's a cotton mill that employs people from Tanner and way beyond. And there're a couple of small factories. I think one makes some kind of women's underwear, and another one makes electronic equipment. But you don't have to worry about that." Jeff leaned over and kissed her forehead. "You don't have to work anymore. Once my practice gets going, we can start a family."

Lydia's face brightened. She put her arms around his shoulders and pulled him closer to her, kissing him full on the lips. That was more the reaction he expected. But then she pulled away. "If this place is so wonderful, why did your family leave?"

Jeff had taken a quick breath. "My father got a new job. It had nothing to do with the town." At least he didn't think it had anything to do with the town. It was a good town.

It is a good town, he thought now as he watched Joanna care for her patient. She spoke softly to the sick old man about friends of his she had seen at the bank, and she could do that easily because she had known him and them most of her life. People in Tanner weren't perfect, but they were good people, with a core of respectability as strong and stubborn as the kudzu covering the roadside trees and bushes. More than anything, Jeff wanted that respectability for himself and Lydia and Malcolm.

Joanna checked her patient's IV one more time and squeezed his hand before she left. Jeff looked in on his patient in the next room before he headed to the nurses' station to say he was leaving for the day and they could reach him at his office. Joanna was in a huddle of nurses at the desk.

"Look here," a nurse said as she pushed a mail-order catalog into Joanna's hand. Jeff glanced over her shoulder at a picture of three female models, wearing white slacks and tunics. "They're the latest uniforms for us," the nurse said. "Aren't they cool?"

"They'll never let us wear them here," Joanna said as she handed the catalog back. She turned and caught Jeff standing behind her. "Sorry," she said. "I didn't see you there."

"Just checking out," Jeff said.

Joanna nodded. "How's Lydia?" she asked. "I hardly ever see her around town." She paused. "But I did see her at the library not too long ago." Joanna's carefully sculpted eyebrows rose slightly.

"She's fine." Jeff kept his tone nonchalant, but he immediately wondered if Joanna had seen his wife with Nancy Galloway. The phone call from Robert Kelly had shaken him, but Lydia hadn't mentioned the Galloways in weeks. "She stays pretty busy with the baby and doesn't get out a lot," he said. "Did you talk to her?"

A lopsided smile curled Joanna's lips. "Nope. She was talking to Nancy Galloway, so I left them alone. How does she know Nancy?"

Jeff's heart banged like a bass drum. "She doesn't know Nancy. Nancy must have said something to her."

"Well, tell Lydia I said hey."

Jeff nodded and watched her walk away. One of his patients, Robert Kelly, and now Joanna. Gossip about Lydia and Nancy must be spreading. He would have to put his foot down. Wives were supposed to do what their husbands wanted. The question was how to convince her of that.

5

Foxrow, on the day of Lydia's second visit, was even more genteel than she remembered. The porch floor sagged slightly, with a dip that suggested years of experience its fresh paint couldn't hide. A warm breeze stirred the oak leaves and rippled through the neatly trimmed boxwoods. It was hard to believe anything evil could have happened in such a refined environment, but that made the possibility even more intriguing. Lifetimes of propriety could mask a single wanton act. Lydia twisted the buzzer by the front door.

To her surprise, a black woman in a gingham bib apron opened the door. She was much younger than Stella and at least thirty pounds heavier, with a fluff of dark hair making a halo around her oval face in the latest "Afro" style. Her chestnut eyes sparkled as she looked Lydia up and down for a few seconds and then stepped away from the doorway.

"Come on in," she said. "Who you here to see?"

"Nancy," Lydia said, trying to figure out who the woman was.

As if she sensed Lydia's puzzlement, the woman said, "I'm Pansy, the Galloways' cook. Most times, I don't answer the door, but I was passing through when the buzzer rang, and I figured why not save somebody a trot. Trouble is, I don't know where Nancy is. Have a seat, and I'll see if I can find her." She gestured toward a wooden settee in the wide entry hall that swept through the center of the house.

Lydia sat and studied the room-like hall. On her first visit, Caroline had taken her through it so quickly, she hadn't noticed its interesting collection of furnishings. Against the wall across from her was a huge Victorian hall tree with a storage bench. A faded wool rug with a Native American design covered most of the wide-plank floor from the front door, past the staircase, and into the shadows beyond. Between the door to the living room and another door that Lydia hadn't seen before was a narrow table holding a large wooden box with a handle on one side. Lydia was about to venture over to examine the box when Pansy reappeared from the unidentified door followed by Nancy, who was nearly dancing with excitement.

"Here she is," Pansy said. "Found her out in the kitchen snitching cookies, like I didn't just feed her a lunch fit for a queen." She shook her head and went back through the door.

Nancy ran up to Lydia and grabbed her hand. "I got everything we need to sew," she said. "We're going to have so much fun." She pulled Lydia toward the grand staircase that wound up to the second floor.

Climbing the stairs, Lydia could hear every squeak and sigh of the old boards. The relative silence of the house made her uneasy.

"Where is everybody?" she asked.

"Everybody who?" Nancy replied.

"You know. Your mother. And your grandfather. The other people who live here."

"Well," Nancy said in a slightly exasperated voice as she began to count off the missing persons on her fingers. "Mama's playing tennis at the country club. Today she stayed for lunch. Tom went riding. Tom got a new horse, but I haven't seen it yet. He promised to take me down to the barn tomorrow. Granddaddy went to the mill. That's everybody."

Lydia nodded. She was pleased at having the house pretty much to herself and Nancy, at least for a while. Nancy hadn't mentioned Stella, but surely she got a day off occasionally. Lydia was surprised that Caroline had left the house, knowing she was coming, but she felt sure the woman would be back soon.

Nancy had dozens of multi-colored scraps of material spread out on her bed. The prized new thimble sat on her dressing table in an open velvet-lined ring box. The two women were hardly in the room before Nancy carefully picked up the box and, cradling it in her palm, presented it to Lydia.

"Put it on your middle finger," she said, and Lydia did as she was told. "Does it fit?" Nancy asked. "It looks like it fits." She nodded with glee as Lydia confirmed that yes, the thimble did fit.

Lydia couldn't remember ever seeing such joy on another person's face over such a simple little gesture. She knew from the ring box that the thimble was special to Nancy, and she really wanted Lydia to like it, but Nancy's happiness at seeing the thimble on Lydia's finger was surprisingly touching. Lydia squeezed the young woman's hand.

Nancy pulled her dressing table chair and her desk chair over to the bed so she could begin the sewing lesson. Lydia settled onto the desk chair and vowed to be an attentive student, even though her thoughts were elsewhere.

"Did anybody in your family ever sew?" Nancy asked as Lydia awkwardly moved her needle through the fabric.

A vision of her mother clutching an embroidery hoop came to Lydia's mind. "Not really," she said, "except my mother used to do some cross-stitching. She made me a pillow when I was a little girl. I think I still have it. I'll show it to you sometime." Nancy's face glowed with happy anticipation.

After thirty minutes and four pieces of material sewn together, Lydia began to worry that the upstairs would soon be invaded by other family members. Before she left that afternoon, she was determined to look around Henry Galloway's bedroom. She didn't expect to find anything that had to do with his brother's death, but the room could give her a better sense of the kind of man Henry was. About all she knew so far was that he was an aggressive businessman, who donated money to his town but was willing to throw employees out of their jobs and homes if they crossed him. She knew nothing about his relationship with his brother.

If she asked Nancy to show her the room, the young woman might do it, but Lydia didn't want that because she couldn't trust Nancy not to tell somebody. No, she had to do the exploring on her own, without Nancy realizing it, so it would have to be a quick look, a very quick look. Nancy had mentioned that her grandfather's room was across the hall from hers during Lydia's first visit, so at least she knew where she was going. She just had to figure out how.

When Nancy said she was going downstairs to ask Pansy if she and her friend could have the rest of the cookies, Lydia knew it was the best chance she was going to get. As the stairs began to creak, she closed the door to the bathroom that joined Nancy's room with the guest room, hoping that, if Nancy returned first, she would think Lydia was in the bathroom and not go looking for her. Then she crept across the hall and carefully turned the old porcelain doorknob. Fortunately, the door was not locked, and the hinges must have been recently oiled because they hardly made a sound as she pushed her way into the room. Across the threshold, she paused and listened for any sounds on the steps. If Nancy or Pansy or, God forbid, an early returning Henry or Caroline caught her in Henry's room, she'd be banned from Foxrow forever and probably from Tanner too. Jeff would never forgive her. She drew a deep breath and dared to look around the room.

The old man was certainly neat. His four-poster bed with the antique coverlet was precisely made up, not a wrinkle showing anywhere. The three ladder-back chairs gracing separate corners of the room were free of hastily tossed shirts or pajamas. Heavy draperies were cast to the sides of the windows, letting the afternoon light spill across the room. A roll-top desk in the fourth corner was open, revealing cubbyholes filled with orderly envelopes and index cards. A single stack of papers rested in front of the cubbyholes, held in place by a brass paperweight.

Lydia was torn between searching through the papers in the desk and the personal items arranged in a row on top of the bureau. She had to decide immediately. As a pair of shiny gold cufflinks on the dresser caught her eye, she moved in that direction. The cufflinks were the only items that looked as if they might have been left on the bureau as an afterthought. Staring up at her from their positions side by side were a small brass dish filled with pennies, a glass business card holder with five or six cards, a rectangular satinwood hair brush, a black Swiss army knife engraved with the initials HLG, and an alligator eyeglasses case.

Lydia flipped through the business cards, but didn't recognize any of the names or businesses. The glasses case was empty. Behind the row of personal items was a walnut shaving mirror with two drawers in the casement. Lydia eased open the drawer on the right. A retractable tape measure, an expired passport, and a silver cigarette lighter lay beside a stack of monogrammed—again HLG—white handkerchiefs. Lydia lifted the stack of handkerchiefs and felt something heavy in the pile. As she tilted her hand, a silver pocket watch landed on the dresser top with a thud. Unlike the cigarette lighter, it looked as if it had not seen a jar of silver polish in a long time. Lydia released the tarnished latch, and the cover flew up immediately.

The face had probably once been white, but had now yellowed, making the gray Roman numerals less distinct. The manufacturer's name had so faded into the yellow that it was illegible—some name starting with a W. A small second hand had its own dial in the lower portion of the face, but neither it nor the main hands were moving. Lydia closed the cover and stroked the cold, smooth case. It reminded her of a stone stolen from a mountain creek bed; even its ashen color was stone-like. Instinctively, she flipped the watch over. On the back of the case, nearly hidden by tarnish, was an engraving. Lydia rubbed the watch on her skirt to try to remove some of the oxidation. The color lightened a bit, but the engraving was still difficult to read.

Hoping more light would help, she carried the watch to the window and held it in the sunbeams. At last she could read the words on the watch: "To Howard From Father. Graduation May 1914." Lydia wondered if Henry had a matching watch and if the words referred to college or high school graduation. She tried to do the arithmetic in her head, remembering that the newspaper account said Howard was twenty-six when he died. That would make him about twenty in 1914. Probably college graduation. She wondered where he went to college and whether both twins graduated.

There were so many questions she wanted answered. She had to find someone in town who would tell her the truth about the Galloways. Burt Evans flashed across her mind. When she was at the newspaper office, Robert Kelly told her Dr. Evans knew the Galloways and the doctor they called the night Howard died. That was the person she needed to talk to. She rubbed the cover of the watch against her skirt to see if it had an engraving she missed at first, but nothing appeared. As she slipped the watch and handkerchief back into the drawer, she heard the front door open and close.

"Hey, Mama." Nancy's voice resounded up the stairwell.

"Hello, Nancy." Caroline's voice was softer, more restrained. "Where's your brother?"

"He went riding." The silence that followed Nancy's answer made Lydia freeze for fear of being heard, despite the fact she was all the way upstairs.

"Where's Pansy?" Caroline asked next. "Pansy!" she shouted. Then in a more composed voice, "Is Lydia here yet?"

"Yes, ma'am. She's in my room."

"Did you call me, Mrs. Galloway?" Pansy's voice entered the conversation.

"Yes, I did. Did Tom say anything to you before he left to go riding? Was there some reason he had to leave when he did? I told him specifically not to leave the house until I returned."

"No, ma'am. He didn't say nothing special. Just that he was going riding."

More silence. Lydia was afraid to move, but she knew Nancy was heading up the stairs and Caroline might be with her. If she could step on the oval rug at the foot of Henry's bed, her shoes would make less noise than they would against the pine floor, and the rug extended almost to the door. Holding the corner of the bureau for balance, she extended her leg and thrust herself over to the rug. Hardly a sound.

"All right, Pansy. That's all," Caroline said. Lydia scurried lightly across the rug and peered out of the door to see if Nancy had made the turn in the stairs. "I'll go up and speak to Lydia," Caroline continued. The stairs began to groan, and Lydia knew her time was up. She darted into the hall and saw Nancy coming around the stairs so she was directly facing her friend.

"Were you looking for me?" Nancy asked.

"Yeah. I wondered what was taking you so long," Lydia said, relieved to have an explanation for her presence in the hall thrown to her so easily.

"Mama's home. She's coming up to see you."

Caroline followed a few steps behind Nancy.

"Hello, Mrs. Galloway," Lydia said when the woman reached the second-floor hall.

"Hello, Mrs. Colton," Caroline said, her face all smiles around her piercing eyes. "I hope you're enjoying your visit. What have you and Nancy been doing?" Her appearance was regal, even in her white tennis dress. Lydia felt as common as she had the first time they met.

"We're sewing, Mama. I told you we would," Nancy said. "Come see." She took her mother's hand and led her into the bedroom. Lydia followed. Seeing the patched pieces lying on the bed, Lydia could easily tell which ones she had sewn and which ones Nancy had sewn. Nancy's were much better.

As Caroline studied her daughter's sewing efforts for a few seconds, a shadow of tenderness stole across her face. "You know, Nancy," she said, "Pansy should've fixed y'all something to drink with those cookies—some lemonade, maybe. Why don't you go back downstairs and ask her for some lemonade or ice tea or maybe a couple of Cokes? And don't hurry. I want to talk to Mrs. Colton alone for a little while."

Lydia sucked in a gulp of air. Could Caroline know she'd been in Henry's room? Her mind raced to find an explanation for being there. She could say she went in the bathroom and came out on the wrong side and got confused about which room was Nancy's, or she could say she thought she heard Nancy in Henry's room and went to look for her, or there must be something more believable she could say.

Nancy set the cookies on her dressing table and obediently left the room. Lydia thought Caroline might sit down, but instead, the older woman stood silently until Nancy's footsteps made it down the stairs. Then she gently closed the door and turned to face Lydia. Lydia met her gaze, but Caroline's eyes didn't flicker.

"I don't understand why Nancy thinks your friendship is so important," she said. "And frankly, I don't know why you want to be around her. Surely you recognize her limitations. She has the mind of a seven-year-old. You don't strike me as being slow or naïve, so you must enjoy the company of normal adults. If you feel sorry for Nancy, she doesn't need your sympathy."

Lydia started to protest, but Caroline continued talking.

"We've seen to it that she has everything she needs to lead a happy life. I know very little about you or the family you come from, and I certainly don't know what kind of person you are. Letting Nancy associate with you is a gamble for us, and we've never gambled on anything concerning Nancy in her life." She paused.

Lydia spoke up quickly. "You may not know anything about me, Mrs. Galloway, but I promise you I'll never do anything to hurt Nancy. I'm a good person, and I like Nancy. I think she's charming, and she needs some friends her own age."

"You think you like her, but you're just fascinated by her, like a quirky relative or a new pet," Caroline said. "That'll wear off soon. You'll get bored with her and move on to other amusements, and she'll be left alone, wondering what happened. It's better if she doesn't get too attached to you. I didn't want you to come today, but Nancy begged me so much, and I just can't deny her anything she truly wants. So I let you come." Caroline stared at Lydia

"Well, thank you very much." Lydia stared back. "And I will not leave Nancy and move on to someone else. I will never walk out on her unless you make me, and that'll hurt her for sure." Lydia drew a quick breath. She couldn't believe she said that.

Caroline's response was swift. "How dare you talk to me like that?" She took a step toward Lydia. "I know what's best for Nancy. So don't be surprised when her invitations stop coming. And I don't want you to see her outside of Foxrow. You understand, don't you?" Caroline smiled as if she were giving directions to a buried treasure or a birthday party.

Lydia wanted to slap her well-bred face. "I can't promise you I won't run into Nancy in town," she said.

"I'm sure you'll work it out," Caroline replied. She opened the bedroom door to signal the conversation was over. "Nancy should be here soon with the drinks. I'll just wait until she returns." She walked into the hall and pretended to examine the towels and blankets stacked in a cupboard next to the stairs.

Nancy returned with lemonade a minute later. She exchanged a few words with her mother, and then the sound of Caroline's steps grew fainter as she descended the stairs.

"Did you and Mama have a nice talk?" Nancy asked Lydia.

"Oh, yes," Lydia said.

At least the conversation let her know she would need every trick she could think of to stay friends with Nancy.

⁓

That same Saturday afternoon, Jeff Colton shot his best golf score of the season. The score pleased him, and it made his partner, the chief of emergency at Galloway Memorial, ecstatic.

"Thanks a million, Jeff," Steven exclaimed, waving the score card in the air. "Your eighty-one means we get to stay dry." To raise the stakes, Jeff's foursome had agreed that the losing team would sit in the dunking booth at the Fourth of July picnic.

The victory was especially sweet for Jeff because Charley, a childhood pal of his, had cajoled the group into the wager and ended up one of the losers. As the head of raw materials purchasing at the mill, Charley had gotten stuck with managing several of the amusements at the picnic. When he ran into trouble getting participants for the dunking booth, he pressured his golf buddies.

"See? Serves you right," Jeff told him as they walked from the eighteenth green to the clubhouse. "A duffer like you shouldn't try to put one over on pros like us. And I'm going to see to it that your ass stays in the water all day."

Charley shook his head. "Yeah, right. You think you can hit that bull's-eye? You couldn't hit it if it was ten feet tall. You're just trying to get even with me, anyway, for snaking your clothes when you were in the shower at the gym back in high school."

"Maybe so, but I'm going to love seeing you dunked."

The group dropped their golf bags on the pro shop porch and went inside.

"Four cold Buds," Charley called as they settled at one of the few tables in the small shop.

"Make it three," said Charley's partner. "I promised my wife I'd be home by four." He gulped water from the fountain as the others looked at him in disgust.

"I'm not going home till I have to," Charley mumbled. "Or at least not until it's time for the PGA on TV. That way I don't have to listen to Susan tell me everything the kids did while I was gone."

"Does your wife do that too?" Steven asked as he popped the top off his beer. "That's all Barbara talks about. The kids did this. The kids did that. After a while, I can't take it anymore."

"Kind of makes you want to find another woman to talk to, huh?" Charley said with a grin. Two of the guys grinned back; Jeff stared at his beer. They all knew Charley was having an affair with a waitress, but Jeff figured that was Charley's business, and he never asked him about it. There were some things a man should keep to himself. Still, everybody in town seemed to know about it except Charley's wife. Jeff felt sorry for her. A husband was supposed to take care of his wife, not humiliate her. That was what he was trying to do for Lydia—take care of her. If she could just figure that out.

His spirits rose on his way home. *This couldn't be a finer afternoon*, he thought as he drove his '65 Mustang through the farmland that separated the country club from Tanner. The June sky sparkled pure azure before it faded behind the late summer haze. Crisp-white wildflowers filled the ditches along the highway. The Mustang responded smoothly to his touch as he pushed it as fast as he dared through the curves, his fingers keeping time to The Rolling Stones' "Tumbling Dice" on the radio. He was happy about his golf score, happy about escaping the dunking booth, and looking forward to seeing Lydia and Malcolm.

He parked the Mustang on the street in front of his building, a rectangular red-brick structure with individual white doors leading to its four townhouse units. *Next apartment has to have off-street parking*, he vowed as he always did when he arrived home. Or maybe their next home would be a house. He was ready for a house of their own. Something new, with all the modern appliances. Lydia would like that. She'd never said anything about wanting a house, but that didn't mean she didn't want one.

Maybe the two of them should start looking at houses for sale in the area. They could follow Charley's advice and buy out near the golf course. Totally modern. Maybe all electric. A Gold Medallion Home—that's what he wanted. After church on Sunday, he could take Lydia and Malcolm on a ride out toward the country club and look at what houses were available. See what they cost. He pictured Lydia smiling with pleasure. Yeah, her own home, that's what she needed. Maybe they could buy one now.

This idea pleased Jeff. He walked through the front door, planning how he would tell Lydia about it. A teenager who lived down the street slouched on the couch reading *Redbook* while Malcolm slept in his playpen.

"Where's Lydia?" Jeff asked, more sharply than he intended.

"She went out to Foxrow." The girl dropped her magazine, sat up, then added, "But she'll be back any time now," as if she sensed his surprise and disappointment. Jeff paid her what she asked for and sent her home. After opening a Budweiser, he sat in his favorite chair and read *Golf Digest* while he waited for Lydia to come home.

If she was surprised to see him when she arrived, she didn't show it. She opened the door quietly, smiled at Jeff, and immediately saw the sleeping baby. "Hey," she said softly.

Jeff set the empty beer bottle on the floor next to his chair. "Why didn't you tell me you were going out this afternoon?"

"It happened at the last minute. I forgot." She pointed at Malcolm. "Keep your voice down."

She dropped her purse on a chair and scurried up the stairs. Jeff got up and followed her, nearly kicking over the beer bottle.

"What in God's name were you doing at Foxrow?" he called from the bottom of the stairs as she reached the top. When she didn't answer, he ran after her.

Lydia swept into the small master bedroom, squatted, and opened the bottom drawer of her bureau. Two bureaus, a dressing table, and a double bed with end tables left little walking space in the room. Since Jeff couldn't get past the bent form of his wife, he stopped just inside the door at the side of the bed.

"Why did you go out there?" he asked again.

"Nancy invited me." Lydia removed bright wool sweaters from the drawer and laid them on the floor without looking up.

Stay calm, Jeff told himself as he sucked in the room's warm air with its lingering odor of dusting powder and sleep. Since his conversation with Joanna on Thursday, he'd been waiting for the right moment to ask Lydia about the Galloways. Now it was thrown in his face. Reading old newspapers at the *Observer* office and being seen with Nancy were bad enough, but showing up at Foxrow meant Henry and the other Galloways knew what was going on. *Don't get angry until you find out what happened*, he thought, *but why the hell didn't she do what I told her to?* A window, raised about an inch, offered street noise but no breeze. Jeff leaned against the door jamb, his arms folded across his chest.

"I told you to leave Nancy alone," he said.

"No, you said it was a lesson I'd have to learn for myself." Lydia took some old post cards and photos from the drawer, leaving a large empty space.

"I didn't think you'd take that seriously. I thought you'd have enough sense to realize I was right. Why can't you leave that girl alone?"

Lydia sat back on the floor and leaned against the bed. "If I tell you, will you believe me?" Jeff nodded, amazed she would ask such a question. Lydia fiddled with her skirt, straightening it against her thighs. Finally she spoke. "She needs me. She's the loneliest person I've ever known. Her mother won't even take her to see the people she met in school. She doesn't do anything all day except read books and sew scraps of material together. I know that's not all she wants to do, but she doesn't have any choice. Those idiots are so afraid something will happen to her, they won't let her do anything."

Jeff rubbed the back of his head. "Lydia. It's nice of you to be concerned, but it's not your problem. They're going to do what they want to do, no matter what you think. Did somebody besides Nancy say you could come out there today?" Jeff was counting on the Galloways to back him up in telling Lydia to stay away.

Lydia turned her gaze from Jeff toward the window. "I talked to Nancy's mother. She said I could come." A satisfied smile crossed her lips as she glanced back at him.

"What about Henry Galloway?"

"I didn't see him."

"He's the one we have to worry about. Him and all the other people in town. I'm telling you, Lydia, it looks bad for you to be hanging around a retarded girl, particularly a Galloway. People will think you're dumb yourself, or else you're trying to score points with the Galloways, and neither one is good. I still think this is wrong."

"Well, I don't." Lydia stood up. "And answer me this. How come your opinion is always more important than mine?"

"It's not."

"You act like it is." She kicked the bottom drawer of the bureau shut and pulled open the next one up. "This time I want my opinion to count."

Jeff had no idea what she was talking about. In this situation, he knew better because he understood small-town dynamics better than she did. But she made it sound like it happened all the time. Suddenly he wasn't just angry at her for going out to Foxrow; he was mad because she was making him into someone he wasn't.

"You're blowing things out of proportion," he said. "This is just one time."

"What about when you joined the country club, even though I wanted to put that money into a college fund for Malcolm? And then those pea brains wouldn't put my name on the membership. Just yours." Lydia plowed through nightgowns and sweatshirts, not looking at Jeff.

"Malcolm wasn't even born yet." Jeff's voice grew louder, although he was trying to keep it under control. "And we need to belong to the country club to meet people. That's the way things are. Just like with the name on the membership. That's just the way things are, and there's nothing we can do about it. I don't see why it's such a big deal." He reached around Lydia and closed the drawer in front of her. Then he took hold of her shoulders and turned her to face him. "You can't change the world. You can't change Tanner, and you sure as hell can't change the Galloways. The sooner you get that through your head, the better off we'll all be." He shook her lightly to try to drive home his point.

She twisted loose from his grasp, jerked open the bureau drawer, and grabbed a frayed cross-stitched pillow. "I told Nancy I'd show her this pillow, and that's what I'm going to do."

Before Jeff could answer, she ran down the stairs as the baby started to cry. Jeff punched at the wall, just hard enough to bruise his knuckles but not enough to dent the wall.

6

Lydia was bursting to tell someone about the pocket watch in Henry's room, but she sure couldn't tell Jeff. After getting so riled up on Saturday, he hardly spoke to her the rest of the weekend. The silence gave her plenty of time to think about what she was doing.

She was disgusted with the fix Nancy was in, with everybody telling her what to do, and she wanted to help. She also needed Nancy to help her get into Foxrow to learn more about Howard. The idea of finding out whether Howard's death was really an accident excited her, and if she could do something for Nancy along the way, so much the better. But Jeff would never understand that, just like he didn't understand a lot of what was happening to her. Those spells of restlessness, for instance, which, by the way, she hadn't had since she met Nancy.

As soon as Jeff left for work on Monday, she called Suzanne to tell her about the watch.

"Holy shit," Suzanne exclaimed. "Girl, you are gonna get yourself strung up by the thumbs, but I wanna know every detail."

"It's amazing, isn't it?" Lydia replied. "I can't believe I went into Henry's room. My mother would die if she knew I did something like that. My pulse was throbbing the whole time. What do you think about the watch?"

"Maybe it's a souvenir from the victim. They say killers like Richard Speck sometimes save souvenirs."

"If this was murder, it was no thrill kill." Lydia was sure of that. "Supposedly, Henry wanted the mill all to himself, so there was motivation. It's not the kind of thing you'd keep a souvenir from, but maybe he kept it out of guilt."

The sound of cigarette smoke being exhaled came across the line before Suzanne spoke. "I don't think so. If you killed your brother, you wouldn't want something of his anywhere near you." She paused for a few seconds. "So what does Jeff think about the watch?"

"I didn't tell him. I haven't told him anything about me trying to find out what happened to Howard." Guilt rose like a cloud of acid in Lydia's stomach.

"But he knows you talked to Kelly down at the newspaper."

"Yeah, and Saturday he got home before I did, so the baby-sitter told him I was out at Foxrow."

Suzanne exhaled again. "What'd he say?"

"He got mad—again—and told me I couldn't change Nancy or Tanner. Lord knows what he'll do if he ever finds out what else I'm up to. I guess I'm a pitiful excuse for a person. Anybody who's willing to aggravate her husband like this has got to be a terrible wife and a pretty bad mother." Lydia's voice wavered. "Am I that awful? I don't mean to be, but I have to do this. I've got everything I ever wanted, but sometimes I just feel like I'm nobody. Like there's not one person, except maybe you, who really sees me—like I'm invisible. If I do this, though, I think it'll make me feel real. Have you ever felt like that?" An unexpected pressure seized the back of her throat, and tears flooded her eyes. "Have you ever felt like you had to do something like this?"

"Not anything like this," Suzanne said. "Not in this town, anyway. And I'm beginning to think there isn't anybody like you in this town. I just hope what you're doing is worth it in the end."

Lydia forced away the tears. "It will be. I'm sure of it. There's something out there that needs to be found." She was glad Suzanne didn't ask her what needed to be found. She wasn't sure exactly what it was, but it had to do with a family clinging so desperately to silence and secrecy that they couldn't or wouldn't investigate the death of one of them. And she was determined to be the one who found it.

All Suzanne said was, "I hope you find what you're looking for, and since your only clue so far seems to be that watch, you better find somebody who knows something about it. And no, you're not a bad person."

Lydia hoped Suzanne was right. "I'm going to start with Dr. Evans," she said. "He's the only really old person I know in Tanner. Plus, I heard he has a connection to the night Howard died."

"The man who brought Jeff to Tanner," Suzanne mused. "You just love tempting trouble, don't you? You know if you ask him questions about Howard Galloway, he's gonna tell Jeff."

Lydia nodded. "He might. Or maybe he won't. Of all the people in this town, he might be the one who has enough respect for me that he won't go running to Jeff. I don't know." A cold feeling of dread touched her. "For now, I'm taking things one step at a time."

Another warm day with no promise of rain greeted Lydia as she left home to visit Dr. Evans. June had so far been unusually warm and dry. The real dry spells tended to come during the dog days of August.

The old doctor sounded surprised when she called to ask if she could visit him, but being a gentleman, he invited her for lunch. To reach his house, she drove through downtown Tanner, which was quiet that morning. Traffic was light, and few people appeared on the sidewalks. Maybe the heat was keeping people indoors, but the stillness in the air felt to Lydia like the whole town was holding its breath. Could be it was just the buildup to the Fourth of July picnic, the biggest social event in Tanner.

Lydia read one of the colorful posters advertising the picnic while she waited for a traffic light to turn green. Designed by the New York agency that did the advertising for Foxrow retail fabrics, the posters were plastered all over town, as if there might be some poor soul within a thirty-mile radius of Tanner so cut off from reality that he or she didn't know the picnic was coming up. The posters promised good food (fried chicken with all the trimmings, hot dogs, hamburgers, watermelon, and homemade ice cream), good times (pony rides, carnival games, sack races, dancing after dark), and good prizes (free tickets to the movie theater, coupons for the grocery stores, cases of Cokes, and a grand prize of a brand-new 1972 Ford Thunderbird). At the last picnic, Lydia had been so nauseated the smell of chicken and cotton candy sent her running for the bathrooms, but this year, she was looking forward to it.

Burt Evans' home sat high on a hill above Emory Street, one of many that looked out over the houses on the other side of the street and, beyond that, the river. The oldest residential street in Tanner, Emory ran from the downtown commercial area out to the library on the western edge of town. Most of the houses on the street were white weatherboard, with a few red brick ones mixed in. They were all at least two stories tall, unlike Lydia's neighborhood, where the single-family homes tended to be bungalows or Cape Cods. Burt's house had a long sidewalk, leading to a tall stone porch. The steep driveway was two separate strips of concrete that passed under a tall portico next to another set of stone steps, leading to a smaller porch on the side of the house.

Lydia debated whether to attempt navigating the driveway and decided to park on Emory Street and walk the uphill climb to the front porch. Having rehearsed what she would say to him during the drive over, she repeated it to herself as she made her way up the sidewalk. She couldn't say how she actually found the watch, so she made up a story in which Nancy told her about it. Instead of saying she was trying to find out if Howard's death was an accident, she decided to say that she thought she could be a better friend to Nancy if she knew more about her family, but she didn't want to upset her new friend or her mother by asking questions.

Burt greeted her at the door wearing a light-blue linen suit, white shirt, and navy necktie. Jeff had said once he thought Dr. Evans was in his seventies, although he looked younger than that. The hair on top of his head reminded Lydia of strings on a violin, but it was still brown, and the denser growth around the lower part of his skull was gray only at the temples. His posture was slightly stooped, but stable. Today, she noticed his face was marked with pouches beneath his eyes, visible through a pair of heavy bifocals, but few wrinkles.

He led her into the living room, a comfortable area dominated by a huge stone fireplace at one end. Because it was summer, someone had filled the space between the andirons with an arrangement of Magnolia leaves, probably picked from the magnificent tree in the front yard. Lydia could imagine Dr. Evans picking the leaves, but not doing the arranging. Probably that had been done by his housekeeper, Lucille.

When Jeff first explained about the medical practice in Tanner, he told Lydia that Burt's wife died of leukemia in 1966. Since then, it had been just him and Lucille in the house, with her doing the cooking and cleaning and whatever else needed doing along those lines. She was apparently doing a good job: the living room was spotless, from the well-made draperies to the neatly upholstered Victorian furniture.

"Lunch'll be ready soon. Would you like a glass of ice tea?" Burt said as Lydia made herself comfortable on the tufted loveseat. She accepted the offer, and he went into the adjoining dining room and called for Lucille.

Soon the housekeeper appeared, carrying two tall glasses of tea garnished with lemon wedges and mint. She wore a pale-pink shirtwaist dress that contrasted sharply with her dark skin, and when she entered the room, Lydia smelled a light scent of lavender. She nodded to Lydia, smiled briefly at Dr. Evans, and disappeared as quietly as she had come.

"I'm tickled to spend some time with you," Burt said after a sip of tea. "I don't think I've really talked with you since you moved to Tanner. I hope our town is living up to your expectations."

"It's fine," Lydia said. *Jeff likes it a lot, and that's what matters, I guess,* she thought.

"Have you made some friends?" The old doctor's eyebrows rose in anticipation.

Lydia seized her chance. "As a matter of fact, I have. And one of my new friends is why I asked to see you today." Cautiously, she explained her mission the way she rehearsed it, as innocently as she could. "Weren't you the Galloways' family doctor after Dr. Cathey retired?" she asked to try to lead Burt into a discussion of the family.

"Nope. They were his patients when I started working with him, but after he retired, they started going to somebody else. I think Henry thought I was too wet behind the ears to take care of his family, although I'm not a whole lot younger than he is." The doctor smiled.

"But you must know something about the family history," Lydia pressed on. "I'm sure there're things that everybody knows except me because I'm new here. Like has Nancy always lived at Foxrow, or did her parents live somewhere else when she was little and her grandmother was alive?"

"She's always lived there," Burt said with a look of misgiving. "The only Galloway to move away from Foxrow was Alice, Nancy's aunt. She and Ralph Otis bought their own place as soon as they got married."

Gradually, Lydia walked the old doctor back through the years, listening attentively to anecdotes about life in Tanner that related to the Galloways only marginally as well as those that involved them more directly. Wallace had been the Galloway he knew best, and his old face sagged in sadness when he talked about his death. But he smiled when he told the story of how Wallace met Caroline.

Caroline was from Richmond, and while she was at Hollins College in Roanoke, she met a girl from Tanner, who invited her home for a visit. To entertain her, the girl invited over some friends, including Wallace. After drinking several cups of lemonade laced with vodka, Wallace managed to fall off the porch where the group was gathered. Embarrassed by the incident, he called Caroline the next day to apologize and ended up asking her to go the movies with him that night. They were married two years later.

"Some folks say she was after him all along," Dr. Evans said with a chuckle.

"What about Henry Galloway?" Lydia asked when he finished the story about Wallace. "Do you know him well?"

"He was close to Dr. Cathey, but, like I said, he never took to me too well."

"What about the night Howard died? Were you there with Dr. Cathey that night?"

"Hold on now. I'm not that old." The doctor reared up in mock indignation. "I was still in school when that happened. I didn't go into practice with Calvin until ten years later."

Lydia smiled to hide her disappointment. She had hoped Dr. Evans could fill in some details concerning that night, but she wasn't about to give up. "Did Dr. Cathey ever tell you anything about that night?" she asked. "Did he ever talk about it?"

Burt shifted his position on the Victorian chair where he was sitting. It occurred to Lydia that his wife surely picked out this living room furniture, and he had never changed it. The incongruity of the very masculine doctor with the dainty chair accentuated his obvious discomfort. A look of relief swept across his face when Lucille appeared at the dining room door and announced lunch was ready.

"After you," Dr. Evans said as he stood and followed Lydia to the table covered with a beige linen table cloth trimmed in lace and set with brown transferware china. Baked chicken, green beans, and sliced tomatoes were arranged nicely on the plates at the two settings. "Lucille sure knows how to make lunch look good, doesn't she?" the doctor said.

Lydia hated losing the momentum she had going in the living room, so she plunged back in. It wasn't exactly light lunch conversation, but she couldn't let whatever Dr. Evans knew get away from her. "Did Dr. Cathey tell you anything unusual about the night Howard died?" she asked.

Burt picked at his chicken and stirred his green beans a bit. "He didn't like to talk about it. He said it was one of the saddest nights of his life, a young man like that." He took a swallow of iced tea and tapped his fork on his plate. "There wasn't much more to tell, other than what was in the papers," he said slowly. "Howard was dead when Calvin got there. He'd obviously been drinking a lot. Calvin pronounced him dead, and that was about it for his part, except for trying to console Mr. Arthur and his wife." Burt put a bite of chicken in his mouth and chewed deliberately, as if he'd rather chew than talk.

But Lydia pressed him again. "Was there anything Dr. Cathey noticed about the barn that night or about Howard that wasn't in the paper?"

Dr. Evans continued to chew his chicken, as though the tender pieces were tough and dry. Behind the heavy glasses, his eyes narrowed. Finally, he swallowed. "It seems to me, Lydia, that you're awfully curious for somebody who just wants to be a friend to Nancy. What exactly are you up to?"

"I promise you, I started out with that intention," Lydia said. "I like Nancy, but I don't understand her life. She might as well be in a nunnery, the way they keep her cooped up out at Foxrow and away from anybody in Tanner. So I'm trying to understand why the family does some of the things it does, and when you start asking questions about the Galloways, you have to ask about Howard's death."

"Why?"

"Because it's like this big black cloud hanging over the family, or at least it seems that way to me. I can't understand why they didn't investigate it more than they did. It's like they just let him disappear."

"So you're doing your own investigation?"

"Sort of. But I really just want to understand the family."

The doctor ate a mouthful of green beans before he spoke again. "I don't know about you poking into the Galloways' business. You might turn up something that's better left unturned. Most likely, though, you won't find anything, and I believe your intentions are honest, so I'll tell you the one piece of information that never got into the newspaper because nobody thought it was important. But Calvin said he always wondered about it."

Burt got up from his seat and looked through the door leading to the kitchen. From where she was sitting, Lydia could see Lucille was no longer in the room. Nevertheless, Burt pulled the door almost shut.

"That night, when Dr. Cathey and Mr. Arthur got ready to carry Howard back to the house," he said after he sat back down, "Calvin looked around the stall where Howard was lying to see if there was a jacket or blanket or anything they could wrap him in. He said he saw an empty Mason jar sitting on top of the divider between the stalls and a jar that was partly full with what turned out to be the poison liquor on the floor not far from Howard. But he said he also saw a third jar that was at least half full, and maybe more, shoved against the back of the stall. Turned out the liquor in that jar was fine, but Calvin always wondered why there were three jars if just Howard and Henry were there. Seemed like there should've been two or four. And why was so little liquor gone out of that jar, and why was it shoved into the back of the stall? Apparently, nobody ever thought much about it because it wasn't poison, but Dr. Cathey said it always gave him pause because it didn't make much sense. Now, if you can figure out what the extra jar means, I hope you'll tell me." Dr. Evans put another bite of chicken into his mouth.

Lydia hadn't eaten much of her lunch during their conversation, so she dug into the beans while she thought about what the doctor had said. An extra jar of moonshine could mean a lot of things. Maybe that was all the boys could afford that night. Maybe Henry drank one whole jar and a little of that third one before he staggered home. If there had been a third person there, Henry would have told the police, although the idea of a third person reminded her of what Stella said about rumors of "nasty girls." But if that were true, they had mysteriously disappeared after Henry left. It wasn't likely they had their own car. The third jar also made Lydia wonder again about some enemy of the Galloways giving the boys the poison. Maybe another person slipped in with the jar of poison after Henry was too drunk to remember.

"Somebody told me that Henry and Howard bought a lot of moonshine, so they knew the safe bootleggers to buy from," Lydia said. "So it seems totally unlikely to me that they would have gotten hold of a bad jar by accident." She waited for Burt to comment, but he just shrugged and went on eating. "Did anybody hate the Galloways enough back then to bring that jar of poison out there to Howard or to sell it to the brothers in the first place?" Lydia asked.

Dr. Evans swallowed and rubbed his chin. "You mean hate them personally or because of the mill?"

"Either one. I'd guess the two were so tied up together you couldn't pull them apart. I know Henry and his father had some run-ins with the union later. Was anything like that going on then?"

"Not that I know of, but like I said, I wasn't here then. Still, that sounds pretty unlikely to me." He went back to concentrating on his chicken.

"How about another mill owner? Somebody who was competing with Foxrow Mills?"

Burt looked up from his chicken, exasperation beginning to show in his eyes. "Do you have any idea how many cotton mills there were in North Carolina then? Taking out one wouldn't help anybody much."

"It just nags at me that, from all I can tell, nobody tried to find out where that poison liquor came from. They must have all been a bunch of scaredy cats, or they plain didn't care. Or they were stupid." Lydia laid her fork on her plate and folded her arms.

"Don't get yourself all riled up now," Dr. Evans said gently. "Finish your lunch. You'll hurt Lucille's feelings if you don't." Lydia smiled and took a bite of tomato. In addition to wanting to be the one who found out what happened to Howard, she was beginning to realize how unfair it was to Howard that there were still questions about it after fifty years.

Before long, Lucille appeared and asked if they were ready for dessert. If she thought it odd that the door to the kitchen was closed, she didn't say so. Dessert was chess tarts with whipped cream that tasted like Lucille had whipped it herself. It was creamier and sweeter than any Lydia had ever bought at the grocery store.

As she ate, Dr. Evans asked her about Malcolm and Jeff and the medical practice. She answered his questions to be polite, thinking all the while that she had to get the conversation back to the Galloways because she wanted to ask about the watch. The doctor gave her the opportunity when he brought up the Fourth of July picnic.

"I didn't enjoy it much last year because I was pregnant," Lydia said, "but I'm looking forward to it this year. Everybody seems to have a big time. It's awfully nice of the Galloways to give it every year."

"It's nice," Burt said, "but it's pretty typical of mill towns. I'll bet there's a picnic just like it—probably even better ones—in dozens of towns in this state. Maybe we should go picnic hopping." He smiled for the first time since they began to eat.

"I still think it's nice of the Galloways." Lydia said. "They may be mysterious, but they seem awfully refined and generous and well-educated. Do you know if Howard and Henry went to college?"

Dr. Evans stopped smiling. "Back to your favorite subject, I see."

"Well, I do have one more question to ask you, and then I promise I won't bring them up again."

"Okay. We've come this far. Go ahead and ask. But let's go in the living room where the furniture's more comfortable." The old gentleman stood and helped Lydia slide her chair away from the table. As they left the dining room, Lucille came in silently behind them and began clearing the table, the lavender scent floating around her.

Settled again on the Victorian loveseat, Lydia posed the question she came to ask. "Nancy once told me about a silver pocket watch that apparently Arthur gave to Howard for a graduation gift. I wondered if it was high school or college graduation and if Arthur also gave a watch to Henry. I thought it might tell me something about the twins and their relationship with their father and maybe with each other."

"That's going way back before my time," Burt said. "I told you I didn't come to know Henry until ten years after Howard was dead, and I've never known him very well. You need more of an old-timer than me."

"Like who?"

Burt crossed his legs and laced his fingers on top of his belly. "Wilbur Meacham's the only one who comes to mind. He was a vice president down at the mill for decades, and I heard he grew up in Tanner. Chances are he's known Henry longer than anybody else around here."

"Where can I find him? Will he talk to me?"

Burt nodded, which caused the strands of hair across his skull to slide forward. "Oh, he'll be tickled to talk to you. And he's easy to find. He fell several months ago and broke his hip. I've been told the hip isn't healing the way it should, so the hospital moved him up to the fourth floor, where the long-term patients are. And because he's Wilbur Meacham, they'll let him stay as long as he wants to. They say he likes flirting with the nurses and the lady patients, so he may stay forever. You won't have any trouble getting him to talk."

———

A short while later, walking down the long sidewalk to Emory Street, Lydia was grateful that Dr. Evans had shared so much information with her. He was a kind man, which was one reason he had been an excellent doctor, and he cared about everyone, not just his patients. If he was willing to give her information to help in her mission, then what she was doing must be worthwhile, she was sure of it. She told Suzanne as much when she picked up Malcolm, whom Suzanne had been keeping during her lunch date.

"You can twist anything to mean what you want it to," Suzanne said, "but I'm sucked into this thing as much you are, so I'm not gonna tell you to stop now."

"Then you'll keep Malcolm while I go see Wilbur Meacham?"

"Of course," Suzanne said.

7

Nearly a week passed before Lydia went to see Wilbur Meacham. In the meantime, she met Nancy and Stella at the library twice. She decided to tell Stella what Caroline said about not seeing Nancy away from Foxrow because her gut feeling told her the old woman wouldn't support that idea.

"Nancy, she needs a friend like you," Stella said. "I'll make sure Miss Caroline don't know nothing about us here at the library."

Nancy was already talking about another visit to Foxrow, but Lydia decided to put her off for a while. She had another lead to follow, and she didn't want to wear out her welcome at Foxrow before she really needed it.

In planning her trip to see Wilbur, she took a chance and asked Jeff about the hospital's fourth floor. When he asked her why she was suddenly interested in the hospital, she said she heard a lady at church talking about an uncle who had been sent to the fourth floor, and she wondered what that meant.

"It's a hodgepodge," Jeff said. "Some of the patients actually need to be in the hospital for a few months because they have some chronic illness or failing organs or complications from surgery. Others don't need full-time doctors and could be taken care of at the nursing home, but maybe the nursing home doesn't have any empty beds at the moment, and they're waiting at the hospital until that happens. And some just don't want to go home, so they bribe or cajole the doctors in some way not to release them, and the insurance companies pick up the tab. It's a scam, but what can you do? You feel sorry for the old folks—and most of them are old—because some of them don't have anybody at home to look after them."

It was one of the longest conversations Jeff and Lydia had had since their argument about Foxrow. He hadn't brought up the subject of her visits with Nancy again, but he'd been very distant. They said what they had to say to get through the day and take care of Malcolm, and occasionally they had a conversation, but talking with Jeff was like talking with a refugee from *Invasion of the Body Snatchers*. He looked and sounded the same, but there was no feeling in what he said.

The one time they'd made love since the argument was a disaster. They couldn't seem to communicate on any level, and she felt like it was all her fault. Why couldn't she just do what he wanted? The question ate at her constantly, but every time she got ready to walk away from Nancy and Howard, a nagging little voice said, "Someday he'll realize you're right."

What Jeff didn't tell her about the hospital's fourth floor was that some of the patients had mental problems. The first thing she heard when she got off the elevator was a man's voice hollering curse words from a room down the hall. A passing nurse patted her shoulder saying, "Don't worry, honey. He doesn't know what he's saying. It must be time for his meds." Lydia shrugged and thanked her.

The hall was long and narrow, with the usual hospital paraphernalia lining the walls. One difference Lydia noticed that set the hall apart from the other hospital areas she had seen was the decorations on the doors. Several of the doors had wreaths or photos taped above the numbers. Wilbur Meacham's door had a photo of him on a motorcycle that must have been taken at least twenty years earlier.

When Lydia called Wilbur to ask if she could visit him, he said he had no idea who she was, but if she was under fifty and pretty, she could come. She assured him she was under fifty and said he would have to decide whether she was pretty, which he said he would be happy to do. His door was nearly closed, so Lydia knocked lightly.

"Is that you, Nurse Hazel?" a deep voice called out. "Come in here and give me some sugar."

"It's Lydia Colton, Mr. Meacham," Lydia replied. "Remember, I called you yesterday."

A nurse came up behind her and pushed the door open. "Go on in," she said. "He's decent. I was just in there."

Lydia took a few steps into the room and found herself facing men in two beds. The one on the left was propped up on pillows, wearing a crisp, blue pajama top above the covers and calmly reading the *Tanner Observer*. The one on the right, who she knew immediately must be Wilbur Meacham, was wearing a striped pajama top, fastened around the collar with a red bow tie. His round face and bald head made Lydia think of Dwight Eisenhower. The FM radio next to his bed was playing gospel music with an upbeat tempo.

"Come in, darlin'," he said. "Let me get a look at you."

As Lydia walked toward his bed, the other man looked out from behind his newspaper. He raised the bushy eyebrows behind his horn rims for an instant, then went back to his reading.

"Now don't you go making eyes at every pretty woman who comes to see me, Lester," Wilbur said. "You get your own women. Come 'round the bed, Miss Colton. There's a chair over here, and it's as far away from that old wolf as you can get."

Lydia sat down, as told, next to the bedside table and the radio. Since the music was louder there, she couldn't help looking in its direction.

"That's The Chuck Wagon Gang," Wilbur said. "Don't you just love them? That's some of the best four-part harmony you'll ever hear. And they're singing one of my favorites, to boot: 'Have a Little Talk With Jesus.'" He paused for a few seconds and then joined in on the chorus in a deep, rich baritone.

"Shut up, Wilbur," the man in the other bed said. "That young lady just got here. Don't run her off."

"Shut up, yourself," Wilbur said. "She might like gospel music." He turned to Lydia. "What do you think? Aren't they great?"

Actually, they stink, Lydia thought, having never listened to gospel music in her life. When she was growing up, the music in her house had been classical, except when she was alone in her bedroom with her record player and her rock-and-roll 45s.

"They're terrific, Mr. Meacham," she said. "I could listen to them all day."

"See there, Lester," Wilbur said. "So just mind your own damn business." Lester uttered an exasperated sigh and hid behind his paper again. "So, Miss Colton," Wilbur said, "why did you come see an old geezer like me?"

"Actually, it's Mrs. Colton, but you can call me Lydia."

"Who's the lucky guy?" Wilbur smiled as he turned the volume on the radio down slightly. The Chuck Wagon Gang had come to the end of "Have a Little Talk With Jesus." Lydia explained about Jeff and how they had come to Tanner and the role Dr. Evans played. "Oh, yeah," Wilbur said. "Young Doc Colton. I've heard of him. Even seen him around the hospital a time or two. Never knew he had such a pretty wife." Lydia smiled appreciatively. "So are you on some kind of goodwill mission for your husband? Be nice to the old guys on the fourth floor?"

"No, Mr. Meacham, I'm here totally of my own accord. Actually, Dr. Evans suggested I talk with you because he said you're probably the only person in town who could tell me about Tanner before the Depression. I like the town a lot, and I'm trying to learn more about its history." This explanation was completely unplanned and came to Lydia out of the blue.

"Before the Depression, huh? Let's see. I was thirty-nine when the stock market crashed, so I have a few memories before then." He laughed. "At least of the few things that happened when I wasn't drunk or trying to get that way. You might could say I had a flamboyant youth." He laughed again, a resonating laugh that echoed his deep voice. Lester sighed loudly again. "What exactly is it you want to know?" Wilbur asked.

The hospital loudspeaker began paging one of the doctors, giving Lydia a few seconds to pose her question in her mind. Wilbur scratched his neck beneath the bow tie and straightened the collar of his pajama top.

"To start with, Mr. Meacham," Lydia said when the blaring loudspeaker trailed off, "how large was Tanner around the turn of the century?"

"Now you're asking me to stretch way back. I was just a kid in 1900."

"Well, say a little later then. When you graduated from high school. How many folks were in your graduating class?"

Wilbur nodded and began ticking off his classmates on his fingers. "Esther, Mabel . . ." He went through the list and at the end said, "About twenty, give or take a few."

"Are any of them still living, besides you?"

"Not that I know of."

"What about Henry Galloway? Was he in your class?"

"Lord, no. Henry and Howard—that was his twin, you know—were four or five years behind me. I was already working at the mill when they started there."

"Do you know if Henry went to college?"

"Yep. He and Howard both went to the university at Chapel Hill."

"Did you go to college?"

"Nope. I worked my way up through the mill by my wits and my grits. Started off in the spinning room and made it all the way to the officers' club. Not bad, I'd say. Course, it didn't hurt that old Mr. Arthur—the twins' father, you know—liked me a lot. The twins liked me too. Henry and I used to double date. He had his eye on the youngest Loudermilk gal, and I was already dating her older sister. We spent a lot of time parked in Henry's Buick." Wilbur laughed his resonating laugh again, even heartier than before.

Hot damn, Lydia thought. "So you know Henry well, and you knew Howard too?"

"Sure, I know—knew—them both. Did I already tell you they were twins? Didn't look a thing alike, though. Henry was heavyset, with a full head of thick hair. Howard was tall and skinny, made me think of Ichabod Crane. Even his hair was skinny. But he was a fine man. Really sad what happened to him. You heard about that, didn't you?"

Lydia nodded. "Did Henry ever talk to you about his brother's death?"

"He never talked to anybody much about it. He was pretty torn up. Right after that, he quit dating the Loudermilk gal and started dating Elizabeth Calhoun. She was more his type—went to some girls' finishing school, I think—and after about a year they got married. He settled down pretty much after that. Don't know if it was Howard's death or marriage or maybe a little bit of both."

"That and his daddy was getting him ready to run the mill," Wilbur's roommate said smugly.

"I told you to butt out, Lester." Wilbur's voice had some edge to it, different from his tone only a few minutes earlier. "You don't even know Henry. You just wish you did." Lester turned a page of the newspaper with great commotion.

"So Henry's father had a lot of influence on him?" Lydia asked. "Was he like that with Howard too?"

"I guess so." Wilbur sucked in his thin lips. "One time, when Henry and me and the Loudermilk girls stopped by Foxrow to pick up something Henry wanted—I forget what it was—I heard Mr. Arthur yelling at Howard. Henry hustled us all out of the house so we wouldn't hear any more, but he told me later that Mr. Arthur was mad at Howard for something that happened down at the mill. He wanted Howard to show more gumption. Take charge, you know?"

"Did he yell at Henry too?"

"Not so much, I don't think. But Henry didn't vex him like Howard did. Around the mill, I got the feeling that Mr. Arthur favored Henry over Howard. He bragged on Henry a lot. But it was just a feeling. I don't know for sure. Maybe Henry gave him more reason to brag."

"How could he favor one son over the other?" Lydia's motherly instinct reared up inside her head.

Wilbur tugged at his bowtie. "Most likely, he didn't. I shouldn't have said that. Henry was just such a star. A real go-getter. And a real charmer with the ladies." He swallowed as the twinkle crept back into his eye.

"A charmer? How so?" Lydia didn't see Henry as a ladies' man.

"He was a lot of fun. Went to a lot of parties. Always had a pretty girl by his side. This was back before Howard died. Henry was the social one of the pair. Howard was quieter, more serious. Didn't go out much. Henry always said his brother was home reading, if anybody asked. Mr. Arthur gave the twins a Buick Roadster—the one I told you we double-dated in—

when they went off to college. Said it was transportation to and from school. I never saw Howard drive it, though. In fact, I rarely saw him in it. Henry pretty much had it all to himself."

An announcer came on the radio, saying The Chuck Wagon Gang hour had come to a close, and he was kicking off the next hour with Donna Fargo singing "The Happiest Girl in the Whole U.S.A." Wilbur turned off the radio in a hurry.

"I don't like these new singers, do you?" he asked.

"I haven't heard any of them," Lydia said.

"Haven't missed much." Wilbur smiled.

Lydia was afraid he was getting off track, so she spoke quickly to bring the conversation back where she wanted it. "Didn't Howard ever go out with the other kids? Who were his friends?"

Wilbur's expression suggested he was trying to recall something that he couldn't quite pull up. Lester peered around his newspaper and waited for an answer along with Lydia. Finally, Wilbur said, "I don't remember him hanging around with anybody in particular. The only times I remember seeing him in town, he was with Henry or by himself. After he came home from the war, I'd see him by himself, since Henry was still overseas." He paused. "Yep, I remember him at the drug store, buying hard candy. He always wore these plain, brown trousers and a white shirt. He was never much for fashion. Henry was the one who was up on all the latest styles."

"Do you know why he came home from the war, Mr. Meacham?" Lydia asked. "From what I understand, he wasn't wounded. Somebody told me he may have finagled a way to get home so he could set himself up to take over the mill. Do you know anything about that?"

Wilbur looked over at Lester, who had ducked behind his newspaper again.

"Come closer," he said to Lydia and gestured with his hand. Lydia leaned toward the old man until she could see the white whiskers springing from the folds in his neck and smell the Ben-Gay on his hip. "Nobody outside the family ever knew why he came home," he whispered. "It was all hush-hush around town, and you knew better than to ask anybody who might know. We were all supposed to act like boys came home from the war unharmed every day. Frankly, I never believed those takeover tales. Howard didn't seem to have it in him, but, you know, sometimes the quiet ones are the ones you have to watch out for the most." He ran his tongue over his dry lips.

"What I heard from some of the insiders at the mill was that Howard was sent home for medical reasons, maybe psychiatric. He was sensitive and pretty much a loner, like I said, so that could have been true. Maybe he froze on the battlefield." Wilbur cut his eyes over to the bed next to him, where Lester had put down the *Observer* and lay with his eyes closed, like he was asleep. Wilbur grunted with satisfaction and continued.

"All I know is, I barely saw him until Henry came home, and then the two of them started showing up in town again, and Mr. Arthur put them both to work at the mill in the dye house. I remember thinking that was one of the nastiest places in the whole mill and wondering why he put his sons there." He shook his head and scratched his neck again. When he spoke, he was no longer whispering. "Mostly, I was just glad he didn't put me out there."

Lydia leaned back in her chair and patted his hand. He was an interesting old fellow, who obviously had been around the Galloways a long time. But he also obviously had a flair for mischief, and she wondered how reliable he was as a source of information. He admitted he used to drink a lot, and he seemed to be the type of person who would tell you something just to get a rise out of you, but something about him also seemed sincere. Nobody would pretend to like gospel music.

"When you were double-dating with Henry," Lydia asked, "before he went to war, did he have a silver pocket watch? Maybe it was a gift from his dad when he graduated from college."

"Henry didn't have any kind of timepiece in those days," Wilbur said emphatically. "He was notorious for not knowing what time it was. And because the girls always had curfews, we'd have to ride downtown past the big clock at the bank on the corner several times a night to keep them happy. I used to tell the older Loudermilk gal that I got to kiss her every time we drove by the clock, so for propriety's sake, she quit asking so much, but Henry still went down there. It was all right with me." He winked at Lydia.

So no pocket watch for Henry. Or at least he didn't carry it. Then Lydia had an idea. "Did Henry graduate from the university?"

"Of course he did. Magna cum laude. Both brothers. There was a big write-up in the *Observer* about it. They were both smart as whips. UNC even asked Henry to be on their board of trustees a while back."

Things aren't adding up, Lydia thought. If Arthur gave Howard a watch, he most likely gave one to Henry, especially if he liked Henry better than Howard. But if he did, Henry didn't carry it. And she couldn't think of any kind of illness that would get Howard out of the army but wouldn't keep him from working at the mill. Lydia looked at Wilbur and tried to imagine him as a young man. Once upon a time, he and Henry and Howard had been young, with hopes, fears, desires, and frustrations, probably not that different from what she felt. Yet Wilbur and Henry made it out alive and Howard didn't. Now she wondered if Arthur had anything to do with that. A sadness filled Lydia.

"What's the matter, darlin'?" Wilbur asked. "You look like your cat just died."

"Maybe I'm a little tired. And you must be too, after all this talking. I think it's time for me to go."

"Don't rush off. I'm never too tired for a pretty lady." Wilbur's sagging eyelids rose to show more of his rheumy eyes.

"You wish you were never too tired," Lester said without ever opening his eyes.

"Shut up, Lester," Wilbur said.

"Thanks for talking with me, Mr. Meacham. It's been a real pleasure." Lydia stood and pushed her chair against the wall. She extended her hand to shake his, but he kissed it gently instead.

"Please come again," he said. "Nothing like a pretty face to brighten a day."

Jeff hadn't planned to go to the hospital that afternoon, but his last appointment cancelled. He wanted Steven to read an article in *Golf Digest* before their Saturday match, so he ran by home, grabbed the magazine, and hoped to catch the doctor before he left the emergency room for the day. As he drove the Mustang past the visitor parking lot, Lydia's Camaro pulled out onto the street. It could have been another blue Camaro, but he caught a glimpse of her long, dark hair before the car slipped out of sight. Puzzled, he grabbed the closest parking space and ran into the lobby.

"Was my wife just in here?" he asked the receptionist, a thin woman with a narrow, pinched nose.

The woman smiled faintly. "Sure was. You just missed her."

"Was she looking for me?"

"Said she was here to see Wilbur Meacham. Now, isn't that sweet? Visiting that old man." The woman's smile broadened, showing lipstick on her teeth.

Jeff thanked her and wandered through the halls toward the emergency room. There was only one reason Lydia would go see Wilbur Meacham—to dig up dirt about the Galloways. The same thing she did with Burt Evans. Dr. Evans had called Jeff a few days earlier to tell him about Lydia's visit.

"I don't think she means any harm," the doctor said, "but she asked me about the night Howard Galloway died. That's such an old story most people don't pay it any mind, but it's best to leave it that way. I told her what I know—which isn't a lot—but she needs to leave it alone."

Since the call, Jeff had tried to figure out a way to make her stop, but he'd come up dry. And now Wilbur Meacham. No telling what that man could think of to tell her. *Oh, God.* He might even tell her that old rumor about Henry killing Howard. Jeff stopped walking. What if she started asking people about that? Jeff's breath came in short bursts. He shoved the magazine he was carrying under his arm and ran to the nearest door. He had to talk to Lydia.

No one was home when Jeff reached the townhouse. Lydia must have stopped off somewhere, but he knew she wouldn't be much later. It was dinnertime. He left the front door open, leaned against the jamb, and waited. Finally, the Camaro pulled up next to the sidewalk. After gathering her purse, the diaper bag, and Malcolm, Lydia walked toward the door. Jeff pushed the screen door open and let her pass by. "I saw you leave the hospital," he said. "They told me you went to see Wilbur Meacham."

Lydia set the baby in the playpen and handed him a few toys. "He's a nice man," she said.

"And I know why you went." Jeff moved toward her as she turned away from the playpen. His breath quickened. "To ask him about Howard Galloway. And he probably told you the rumor about Henry."

A flash of surprise crossed Lydia's face. "No. He didn't tell me the rumor. I already knew it."

"But you asked him about it, didn't you?"

"No, but some people think—"

"I know what some people think. Some people who are really stupid. Let me tell you about that old Galloway rumor. My father warned me about that story when I was just a kid. He must have heard Charley and me talking about it because he ran into my room with his face red as a firecracker. I'll never forget it. I can tell you his exact words. He said, 'If you boys want your fathers to have a job, you better stop that kind of talk this minute.' Charley and I never mentioned it again, and you better not, either."

Lydia fingered the candlestick on the table next to the couch. Without looking at Jeff, she said, "Somebody ought to mention it. I don't know if Henry killed his brother. I don't know what happened to Howard. But it drives me crazy that they called it an accident and never even went after the guy who sold him the poison. Would they have done that if Henry had been the one who died?"

"What the hell are you talking about?"

Lydia looked up from the candlestick. "The family just let him die without making any fuss about it. Wilbur said Henry was the golden boy. They treated Howard like some redheaded stepchild. How can a family do that?"

This was not what Jeff expected. "Wait a minute," he said. "You've gone from talking about Howard to Henry being some kind of favorite son. And last week you said all you were interested in was Nancy. What's going on, Lydia?"

Sally Whitney

"I wanted to tell you about Howard." Tears dampened Lydia's eyes. "I wanted to tell you how important it is to me to find out if it really was an accident. But you were so damned mad at me already about seeing Nancy that I couldn't." She wiped her eyes with the back of her hand.

"How did pity for Nancy turn into a crusade for Howard?" Jeff really wanted to understand.

Lydia sighed. "It started out as an interesting story. Stella told me the rumor. And when I thought about it and maybe finding out if it were true, I didn't feel so insignificant anymore. You know, I haven't had one of those restless spells since I met Nancy."

Oh, God, the spells again. Jeff started to say something about them, but stopped himself. This was more serious than Lydia's spells. "Okay, but you can be interested in something without sticking your nose in it."

"It started as an interesting story, but the more I learned about it, the more I realized how unfair the whole thing was to Howard. Nobody seems to know where they got the poison. Nobody seems to know if some thug had a grudge against the Galloways and went after Howard. Nobody knows if his father had it in for him, or maybe what they say is true, and his brother had it in for him. The point is, nobody seems to know, and nobody tried to find out." Her eyes were dry now.

"That doesn't mean you have to find out."

"Why not me? I found out something awful in college and maybe saved some lives, even though it took me a long time to own up to what I knew."

"What did you do to save lives?" Jeff asked. The story was getting wilder the longer Lydia talked.

"I was a lab assistant for a chemistry professor," she said. "He had a grant for a research project, and while I was typing his notes, I realized he was reporting results for tests he hadn't even run. I was scared, but I finally confronted him. He denied it, and he fired me as his assistant, but I found out from the new assistant that he left the project. And it's a good thing too. He was supposed to be testing the toxic effects of insecticides used on soybeans. A lot of people ate those soybeans."

Jeff rubbed his forehead. Who was this woman? She'd never told him that story before. "That's different," he said. "You weren't risking your family's reputation and profession."

"It cost me my job," she said, "and it could have cost me more. Looking back on it, I realize that guy could have bad-mouthed me to the other professors or to the dean. He could have made up all kinds of lies about me. He probably could have jeopardized my job applications after college. I sure as hell couldn't use him as a reference. But you know what? Even knowing all that now, I'd do it again. It was worth the risk. And besides, I don't see how I'm risking our family's reputation and profession by finding out what happened to Howard. You don't even work at the mill."

Jeff fumed. She had no idea about small towns and the turmoil she was creating. "The Galloways run this town, Lydia. If you do something they don't like, they have ways to make you pay for it. And if you go up against them, you won't find anybody on your side because they all have to live here too, and they know how it works. You're the only one who doesn't."

"I'm not scared."

"You should be." Heat rose in his cheeks. "They could turn the whole town against me. I could lose my practice. Give it up, Lydia."

"I can't."

From the playpen, Malcolm began to howl. Lydia rushed over and picked him up. "What's the matter, sweetie?" she asked.

Her maddeningly calm voice grated against Jeff's nerves. She was so damned headstrong. "You have nothing to gain from this and everything to lose," he said. "What's it to you what happened to some man fifty years ago, anyway?"

Lydia settled onto the couch with Malcolm and offered him a breast. He began nursing hungrily. "It's a matter of truth," she said. "Maybe I'll learn the truth, and I won't tell anybody, but I'll know."

"Goddamn." Jeff clinched his fists. "I'm telling you, you can't do this. We'll have to leave town."

"Maybe it really was an accident. If I find that out, nobody'll be upset."

"Even if it was an accident, they won't want all that old business stirred up. Just stay away from this and from the Galloways. How many times have I told you that?"

The look on her face told him there was no point in trying to reason with her now. If they talked about it much longer, he would do or say something he'd regret. He stomped off to the kitchen, got a beer, and slouched in a chair at the kitchen table. What she needed was something else to think about. A distraction. He remembered Charley's enthusiasm about the houses out at the country club. If she wouldn't find another interest for herself, he would find one for her.

8

B right sunlight caused Jeff to squint as he looked out across the half acre of yard that separated the spacious patio he was standing on from the fifteenth hole of the golf course. A sparse line of pine trees marked the course's boundary, revealing two golfers moving in and out of sight as they carried their clubs up the fairway. Jeff could picture himself sitting on the patio with a beer after playing eighteen holes, watching golfers take their shots between the trees.

"So what do you think?" the realtor asked.

This was the third house they had looked at, and Jeff liked all three. All three backed up to the golf course. All three had screened-in porches and patios. All three had two-car garages so he'd never have to park on the street again. All three were all electric. Two houses were brand new, and the third one, where they were now, was only a few years old.

The catch, of course, would be getting Lydia to like them. The third one might appeal to her most. Its fireplace and wallpaper reminded Jeff of a dollhouse Lydia's father built for her when she was a child. *Maybe we can even set up the dollhouse in this house, if we can get the old man to part with it,* Jeff thought, remembering how proud Lydia's father was of his creation. He showed it to Jeff the day they met, soon after Christmas in 1967.

Lydia had invited Jeff to spend some time with her family in Charlotte, and although he thought she was rushing things, he had already told her he didn't have plans for that week, so he had to go. All he knew about her parents was that her mother was a homemaker and her father was an architect. When he arrived at their house, he was greeted by her mother, a small woman who flitted about like a hummingbird, her voice marked with a drawl that suggested her roots were south of North Carolina. She served Jeff eggnog that was heavy on the nutmeg and rum. Lydia's father did most of the talking. He was a rugged-looking fellow, but his pitch-black hair didn't go with the rest of his face. Jeff tried to figure out the mismatch and decided it was probably too much Clairol for Men. There should have been some gray there.

He immediately pointed out the dollhouse. As tall as the fireplace across from it, it sat in an elaborate cabinet with doors that could be locked, although at the time they were fully open. It had numerous rooms, each filled with furniture built to scale, a few holding finely dressed dolls. The interior walls were decorated with elaborate wallpaper, matched with luxurious draperies adorning the little windows. Jeff was impressed by the details, especially when he noticed an Irish Setter, each long, red hair frozen in place, resting next to the kitchen stove. He let out a long, low whistle. "This took a lot of work," he said.

"You bet it did. I designed it for Lydia with the best miniature artists I could find. It's a real show place."

Lydia's mother crept up behind the two men. "He even gave one of the artists a picture of Lydia so the mother doll looks like her." She held up the doll so Jeff could get a closer look. "See the long, dark hair? And the children dolls have dark hair too." Jeff couldn't see any resemblance between the doll and Lydia, but, hey, it was the thought that counted.

He thought about Lydia in the house he was standing in today and hoped she could see the resemblance to the dollhouse. "I think this might suit my wife and me fine. The location's great, and it's move-in ready. We wouldn't have to do a thing to it. Just move our stuff over here."

The realtor chuckled as he made a note in his folder. "So you got your eye on this one?"

"Actually, I like them all," Jeff said. "They've got everything we need, but I'm afraid that may be a problem." The realtor's broad smile sagged as his forehead wrinkled. "See, I want something that my wife can sink her hands into. Something she can decorate and mess with as much as possible." Jeff hoped he didn't sound like a lunatic. Most men wanted a finished deal. Who wanted to go through the hassle of picking out doorknobs and wallpaper with his wife?

"Your wife can redecorate this house to her heart's content," the realtor said quickly. "She can pick out wallpaper and paint and curtains and blinds. She can change all the hardware on the outlets and the light switches, if she wants to. And she can even pick out new knobs for the kitchen cabinets. There's plenty in any house you buy to keep her busy. Y'all will see."

Jeff tried to imagine Lydia getting excited about redecorating a house. He had almost no idea what that would involve, but surely she would think of all kinds of things that needed to be done. "I reckon you're right," he said.

The realtor resumed his professional smile. "If you want to see more houses, I've got others in town I can show you, but these are the only ones for sale on the golf course."

Jeff told him he would have to think it over, and of course, he would want to bring his wife out to see the houses. The realtor said he would get in touch with Jeff in about a week, but he warned him not to wait too long because houses on the golf course got snapped up. Jeff knew several new doctors—specialists mostly, urologists and gynecologists—had moved to town in the past year, so the realtor was probably right. He would have to work quickly.

Before leaving the area, Jeff drove back past all three houses. Because they were new, or relatively new, they were all in good shape, and they all cost about the same. The down payment would drain their savings account, but they needed to do it. It was time they had a house. The townhouse was already a little cramped since Malcolm was born, and Jeff wanted another child as soon as possible. He figured they would start trying again when Malcolm was nearly a year old. That would space the children about two years apart. *A good distance,* he thought. A few years after that, he wanted a third child, and that would really require more space. The houses he looked at had four bedrooms: a master bedroom, plus one for each of the children. Perfect for his plans. Having a house in Tanner would be good for his career. It showed he planned to be a permanent resident of the town and would give him room to entertain other up-and-comers.

But more important than all of that, they needed a house to get Lydia out of her infatuation with the Galloways. When Dr. Evans had called him about Lydia's visit, he told Jeff to keep her busy with other things. "She's acting obsessed," he'd said, "and people get obsessed when they're lonely or frustrated. I know that's not the case with Lydia, but something new in her life would be good."

The house was the something new that would distract her from the Galloways. After their most recent argument, Jeff was afraid she was changing into somebody else. She had always been opinionated and willful, but never so in-your-face. Not like she was lately. If she continued to defy him, would she up and walk out on their marriage someday soon? He had to bring the real Lydia back.

To get away by himself to look at houses that Sunday afternoon, he told Lydia he had notes to catch up on at the office, and he needed to stop by the hospital to see a couple of patients. He had been gone nearly two hours, but it wouldn't hurt to be gone a little longer. He really did have one patient he wanted to check on at the hospital—a sixteen-year-old girl with mononucleosis. He had hospitalized her because she had shown very little improvement after three weeks with the illness, and he wanted to run some tests on her liver and spleen. He also wanted to make sure she was getting the rest he prescribed.

He drove toward the hospital, but before he got there, he made a right turn that took him in a different direction toward another section of town. He wasn't sure why he made the turn; he just felt compelled to do it. He cruised down one of the streets that were developed right after World War II, with lots of small houses built for returning servicemen who took advantage of low-interest home loans provided by the GI Bill. At the end of that street, he took another right and then a left, and he was in the Tanner neighborhood he knew best—the one he had lived in when he was young.

When he and Lydia moved to Tanner, he drove her through the neighborhood and was a little embarrassed by the modest homes. They were all attractive and well kept, but they were smaller than he remembered. Most had been built in the early 1950s, about the time his family came to Tanner. Their house had been a new construction. He pulled up in front of it and parked the Mustang, taking the time to study it that he hadn't wanted to take with Lydia.

It hadn't changed much. There wasn't much to change. It was red brick with white trim and a one-car garage. The only visible difference from the original house was a change his family had made—a den addition attached to the left side. He remembered the day his father told him they were going to build a den.

"I don't think we need it, but your mother wants it," his father said. "Houses are a big deal to women. If it makes her happy, I'm happy." It was the first confidence he could remember his father sharing with him, and it made him feel very grown-up.

Today, two children were playing in the yard around a large maple tree. His father had planted that tree; it had sure grown in a hurry. He hoped the children were happy in the house. He had been. He hoped Lydia would be happy in the house he was going to buy for her. If his father was right about houses and women, this should do the trick—bring the real Lydia back.

Jeff pulled away from the curb and turned on the radio. Music suited his mood. A quick swing by the hospital and he'd be headed for home to tell Lydia about the houses he'd seen. The hospital visitors' parking lot was full, but Jeff swept past it to the doctors' lot, which had plenty of spaces. He rushed in through a back door, almost colliding with Joanna Phillips, who was on her way out, dressed in shorts and a sleeveless blouse.

"Watch it there, doc," she said. "There's a shortage of nurses, you know."

"Sorry. I didn't see you coming," Jeff said, but his attention suddenly fixed on her slender thighs and the creamy skin of her upper arms. "Is that the new weekend uniform? If so, I vote to make it required all week."

Joanna laughed and put her finger to her lips. "Shhh," she said. "Don't tell anybody you saw me like this. I just got off shift, and I'm on my way to a picnic down by the river. I didn't have time to go home and change, so I changed in the ladies' room. I didn't think I'd see anybody at this door."

Her eyes flashed with mischief, reminding Jeff of the effervescent high school girl who used to kiss him in the closet where the chemistry beakers were stored. Any boy in his class would have given his right arm to be him back then.

"Want to join us?" Joanna asked. "It's a few nurses and some guys who work at the mill. You're more than welcome." She was standing so close to him he could see the bobby pin indentations in her hair where her nurse's cap had been secured. He wanted to reach out and smooth the fluffy hair.

"No, thanks," he said, although every nerve in his body screamed *go*. "I've got to check on a patient. Maybe next time. Y'all have fun."

"Sure. See you tomorrow." Joanna waved and dashed out the door.

Jeff watched the shapely hips and buttocks move across the parking lot with an ache in his groin. His sex life with Lydia had been irregular, at best, since Malcolm was born and nearly nonexistent in the past several weeks. He had to do something about that soon. As Joanna climbed into her Corvair convertible, he got one last glimpse of calf and thigh. Sucking in a few deep breaths, he walked slowly toward the elevator.

His mononucleosis patient was glad to see him and appeared to be following doctor's orders. "Like I can do anything else in here but rest," she said. "They even limit my phone calls. I get to have exactly two a day, and they can't last more than fifteen minutes. That's barbaric. And visitors? Forget it. Nobody except my parents allowed in. Not that I want anybody to see me like this anyway." She huffed and looked down at her lap. The swelling in her glands had gone down.

"You're looking much better," Jeff said. "Maybe you can go home in a few days. You tell me when you think you look all right to go home." He glanced at her chart and spoke to her nurse at the nurses' station before he left. She was definitely improving.

Now he could go home to Lydia. He had photos and floor plans of the houses tucked into a big folder the realtor gave him. He just hoped she was home. He wasn't ready for another argument about her going out to Foxrow. She hadn't said anything about going out that afternoon, but that didn't mean she hadn't.

He was relieved to see her car parked in front of their building. He parked behind her and strolled into the townhouse, full of anticipation.

"Sure, I'll keep Frankie with Malcolm while you take Lily on the pony rides and anything else you want to do, if you'll watch Malcolm for an hour or so to give me time to talk to some people." Lydia's voice came from the dining room.

Oh, shit—company, Jeff thought, until he looked around the corner and saw she was talking on the telephone. She saw him come into the room and waved.

"Got to go, Suzanne. Jeff's home," she said and hung up the phone.

"Anything exciting going on?" Jeff asked.

"Just talking to Suzanne about the Fourth of July picnic. I'm going to really enjoy it this year." Lydia sounded more enthusiastic than she usually did about Tanner events. Jeff was encouraged and a little wary.

"What's so special about this year?" he asked.

"For one thing, I'm not pregnant. And they say the food is delicious." Lydia smiled. "And maybe I'll meet some new people. Are you going to be able to go?"

"Yeah, for at least part of it. I have to see patients at the hospital in the morning, and I'm on call all day, so I could be busy. But sure, I'll go for part of it. I wouldn't want you to have to go alone." He wanted to be sure she talked with the right people, especially the wives of the guys on the town council and the new doctors in town.

"You don't have to worry about me. I'll go with Suzanne and Frank, if you're busy. Frank'll want to hang out at the horseshoe pits with his buddies, so Suzanne will need some company," Lydia said a little too quickly. Jeff stared at her, trying to read her face. "And you can join us later," she added.

Jeff felt another argument coming on. He sensed she didn't really want him there, which made him suspicious. And hurt his feelings. Her obsession with the Galloways seemed to be so much more important to her than he was. He'd make damn sure he was at that picnic. "Okay," he said. "I'll get there as soon as I can."

Lydia nodded and went down the steps to the basement. In a few minutes, the door to the clothes dryer clicked open and slammed shut. Soon she would come up the stairs, carrying a basket full of laundry. Jeff shut the door to the basement so she would have to ask him to open it before she came back into the room.

Quickly, he took the photos and house plans out of the folder and spread them on the dining room table. He was arranging them in order of preference when Lydia yelled from the basement stairs. "Jeff, open the door. Why'd you close it?"

He straightened the papers and reached for the door. Lydia strode into the room with an overflowing laundry basket and a scowl. She started to say something to him but noticed the material on the table and peered at it over the basket. Then she set the basket on the edge of the table and picked up one of the photos. "Not a bad looking house," she said, "but I'm not crazy about the tan roof."

"What about the rest of it?" Jeff asked. "It has a brick fireplace and a great floor plan. Look." He handed Lydia the sheet with the floor plan.

She set the clothes basket on the floor and looked at the information about that house and then the other houses. "What is this, Jeff?" she asked. "Why is this stuff here?"

"We're moving!" he exclaimed. "It's time we got out of this tiny place. These houses are all for sale out at the country club. Aren't they great? They have four bedrooms and two baths and a two-car garage."

Lydia dropped the paper she was holding. "How could you make a decision like that without asking me? How could you even think that we're ready to buy a house without discussing it with me?" Her dark eyes flashed with familiar ire.

"Hold on a minute. Don't get your nose out of joint." Jeff raised his hands in a defensive gesture. "I haven't bought anything yet. I'm just looking. I want you to go look at them with me."

"We can't afford a house." Lydia's expression was firm.

"Yes, we can. I talked with Avery down at the bank, and we can get a loan to cover any of these."

"What about all those student loans you're always moaning about? That's all we need. One more loan to pay back. It's too soon, Jeff." She leaned down to pick up the laundry basket.

"No, it's not. Trust me." Jeff grabbed her elbow. "Just think about the houses. I saw them all today, and they're great. Especially this one." He thrust the photo of the older home toward her. "See, its roof's black. It's a little older than the others, but it's in good shape."

Lydia studied the picture for a few seconds, then threw it onto the table. "No houses, Jeff." She said. "I don't want a house."

Jeff couldn't believe what he was hearing. Her reaction didn't make any sense. They had talked back when they were dating about the house they would live in one day. She wanted a house then.

"Why don't you want a house?" he asked.

"It's just more of the same."

Now he was really confused. More of the same what? "At least give these houses a chance," he said. "Go see them with me. I promise you'll like them. Wait till you see the big yards for Malcolm to play in. Will you at least look at them with me?"

"Why should I?" Lydia said as she grabbed the basket.

"For us. For me. Do it for me and Malcolm, if nothing else."

Lydia set the basket on the table. "You know, you've been saying that a lot lately. Do it for me. Trust me. I've always wanted to please you, and God knows, I've tried, but I swear these days it seems like you're asking me to give up a lot of my- self to keep on pleasing you." She folded her arms as her stare hardened. "I came to Tanner because that's what you wanted. I've met the people you wanted me to meet. At least let me live where I want to live."

"Just wait till you see these houses. You'll want to live in them." Jeff scrambled for the right words. "Tell you what. We'll wait till after the picnic. Give you some time to think about it. Okay?"

Lydia turned from him and carried the clothes basket to- ward the stairs, her face stiff and unsmiling.

Jeff gathered the pictures and papers and shoved them back into the folder. He was wrong to try to tempt her with photos. She needed to see the real thing, and he would make sure she did.

9

Fourth of July fell on a Tuesday that year, so if they had enough vacation days, a lot of people took Monday off to have a four-day weekend. Frank Jessop said he pitied the new workers at the mill, who only got a week's vacation and had to take that the week the mill shut down in August. "It's a free country, and a man oughta be able to take his vacation whenever he wants to," Frank said.

As a supervisor and a mill employee for ten years, he got two weeks' vacation, and he mostly spread out the second week around the holidays. His plan for the Fourth of July was to go fishing on Monday because Suzanne insisted he go to the town picnic on Tuesday. Suzanne told Lydia that Frank would be happy to be their escort to the picnic if Jeff had to work, and she should meet them at their apartment at ten o'clock sharp. They couldn't all go in one car because there wasn't room to stow a second stroller.

Lydia was glad to take her own car because she didn't want to have to leave when the Jessops were ready to go if she didn't want to. Jeff went to the hospital that morning, like always.

Before he left, he promised to come to the picnic as soon as he could, and he kissed Lydia good-bye, something he hadn't done in weeks. Lydia was pleased, but she wondered about the change.

"What's with Daddy?" she asked Malcolm when Jeff was gone. She was dressing the baby in shorts and a T-shirt. The forecast called for temperatures in the high eighties, and she didn't want him to get heat rash. "I hope he's not mad at me any longer," she said to the smiling baby. "Or maybe he's just all caught up in his dream of being a homeowner."

She felt bad about the way she talked to him when he told her about the houses. It was mean to be so rude to him, but he had no right to assume what she wanted or didn't want. And she meant what she said about giving up another piece of herself. Still, she'd have to make it up to him. She sighed and stuffed more diapers into the diaper bag.

At ten o'clock, the two of them rang Suzanne's doorbell. After a last-minute search for Lily's sandals, which had found their way into the toy chest, the group was on its way.

By the time they arrived, at least half of Tanner was there. Lydia had never seen so many people milling around Municipal Park. Apparently, the possibility of winning a new Ford Thunderbird had drawn a bigger crowd than usual. The car was displayed near the center of the park on a specially constructed platform, high enough to be seen from almost every corner of the grounds. It was painted deep gold, with a black vinyl roof and black interior. Plastic red-and-blue flags flew on wires stretched from the platform out to the game and food booths.

Lines at the booths were already long, with children darting in and out, eating snow cones and playing with yo-yos, lariats, and other prizes. Mixed aromas of fried chicken, hamburgers, and cotton candy permeated the air, except close to the pony rides, where manure was the prominent odor. The most popular DJ from the Tanner radio station, WFOX, had set up near the dance pavilion and was playing rock music, interspersed with a few patriotic marches and anthems, over screeching loudspeakers hung on poles and in trees.

Frank herded his brood through the crowd straight to the Thunderbird, which he examined inside and out until Lily started whining and Suzanne complained there was a whole picnic yet to see. Lydia used the vantage point of the platform to survey the crowd for Henry Galloway. She'd never seen him in person, but she was sure she'd recognize him. No one in the multitude even resembled him, however, so she spent the next hour with the Jessops, strolling past all the games, stopping every so often to let Lily try her luck. By the time they reached the horseshoe pits, Frank claimed he promised to meet some friends there and disappeared into the group of men crowded around the fields.

"Don't lose too much money on those bets y'all are not supposed to make," Suzanne said before she moved on toward the area where the sack races were about to begin.

While Lily picked out a sack, Suzanne and Lydia found seats in the shade so they could offer apple juice to Frankie and Malcolm. Lydia continued watching for Henry, but the only people she recognized were acquaintances from church or merchants she did business with occasionally or Jeff's friends and their wives. Nobody she really wanted to talk to. Then she spotted Robert Kelly with a young photographer. After promising Suzanne she'd be back shortly, she pushed the stroller over and caught up with Robert at the dunking booth. The mayor of Tanner was the current victim and a popular one at that, judging from the number of people lined up to take a turn. Robert said a few words to the photographer before he backed away to let him start shooting.

"Counting on that one for the front page?" Lydia asked.

Robert stared at her for a few seconds before he smiled. "Well, if it ain't little miss snoop," he said. "Glad I haven't seen you in my newspaper's morgue lately. Have you found something else to keep you busy?"

"I stay busy enough," Lydia said.

"Good for you. Gotta watch out for wagging tongues. You know gossip travels faster'n spit, and you don't want the Galloways to think you're poking around in their business." He pulled a Camel from the pack in his shirt pocket and lit it.

"Do they know I came to your office?" Lydia wasn't sure where Kelly's loyalty lay.

"I sure didn't tell 'em, if that's what you're getting at. I believe in freedom of the press. Anybody's got a right to read anything they want to in a newspaper, whether it's new or old. My morgue's open to the public, no matter what they want to read. But others may not be so open-minded. So here's some free advice: read something else." He drew on the cigarette and exhaled loudly.

"Well, thank you very much," Lydia said. "I'll keep that in mind, if I ever come to your office again."

She started to say something about what she would read next time, but he raised his hand to signal her to be quiet. The photographer walked up behind her, his cheap cologne cutting through the various picnic odors.

"Did you get the mayor in the water?" Robert asked. The photographer, whose pimply skin suggested he wasn't far out of his teens, promised he had some good shots, including the mayor, dripping wet. "Then go look for some other council members. Try to catch 'em doing something stupid, like running around with a greasy watermelon. I'll check on you in a little while to see if you got anything good." Robert dismissed the photographer with his gaze and turned back to Lydia. "He's a summer intern, studying journalism down at Chapel Hill. Doesn't know one iota about what he's doing."

"You told me Henry Galloway would be at this picnic, but I haven't seen him. Is he here?" Lydia was beginning to worry that Jeff would show up soon. It was almost noon, and unless one of his patients had a serious problem, it couldn't take him that long to finish rounds at the hospital.

Robert shook his head. "You weren't listening while ago, were you? Well, don't worry. They'll all be here." He puffed on the cigarette again. "Tom'll put in an appearance and then disappear. The old man usually hangs around for a while and visits the game booths to give away prizes to kids who haven't won any. He makes damn sure everybody enjoys his picnic. And you better believe he'll be here when they draw the winning ticket for the car."

"When's that happen?"

"About three o'clock, probably. That's when the most people are usually here. Hey," he turned his head suddenly, "there's George Ashby." A beefy older man, sporting a plaid cap and yellow slacks, approached them. "Good to see you, you old coot," Robert said. "Too bad I need sunglasses to look at you."

"You just wish you looked this good," George said. "And who's this young lady?"

"Lydia. She's Jeff Colton's wife."

"Jeff Colton. Sure. He was a fine boy. I always knew he'd make something of himself, and here he is, a doctor. You're a lucky lady." George tipped his cap to Lydia and smiled.

"Nice to meet you," Lydia murmured.

"Sorry, but I gotta run," Robert said. "Can't leave that kid by himself for too long, if I wanna have anything decent to print." He crushed his cigarette into the grass and took off toward the water pistol area.

"Where are you and your lovely child headed next?" George asked Lydia. "I'd be happy to walk you there."

"That's a nice offer, but we're fine," Lydia said. "We're fixin' to catch up with some friends over at the races."

"Enjoy the picnic." George tipped his cap again and walked away.

Left alone, Lydia scanned the crowd for any of the Galloways. Surely, Nancy and Stella would be there, or maybe Nancy was coming with her mother. Maybe Stella would come with some of her friends. A group of black families was gathered around several picnic tables at the edge of the park. Lydia recognized Pansy among them, but she didn't see Stella.

Since the only part of the picnic she hadn't visited was the arts and crafts booths on the other side of the park, she began pushing Malcolm's stroller in that direction. Along the way, she passed back by the game booths and the activities field, where Suzanne was tying Lily's leg to the leg of another little girl so they could compete in the three-legged race. A stab of guilt hit Lydia as she remembered her promise to look after Frankie so Suzanne could spend time with Lily. He was fidgeting a bit in his stroller, but for the most part, he looked okay. She would get back to them.

Between songs at the dance pavilion, the DJ was babbling about the patriotic significance of the picnic and how everybody was making a statement just by being there. Lydia was taking a short cut between the pavilion and the edge of the activities field when she saw Dr. Evans, sitting in a folding chair in the door of the first-aid tent. With a straw hat perched jauntily over his thinning hair, he was a picture of casual grace. He saw her about the same time she saw him and waved merrily.

"Hey there," he called. "Is the picnic living up to your unpregnant expectations?"

"So far," she answered, "but I haven't tried any food."

"I highly recommend the barbequed chicken, the potato salad, and the homemade ice cream," Burt said, patting his stomach. "I just had them all for lunch." Lydia pushed Malcolm close to the doctor's chair. He leaned down and stroked the baby's cheek. "This one's worth a lot of ruined picnics," he said. "He's filling out nicely. I predict he'll be quite a handsome fellow." Malcolm twitched and tried to brush the doctor's hand away. "Looks like he's as feisty as his mother too."

Lydia couldn't help blushing. She really didn't care what most of the people in Tanner thought of her, but she did care about the old doctor. With his beloved position in town, his blessing was like the Good Housekeeping Seal of Approval. She hoped his jovial comments meant he didn't resent her for asking questions about the Galloways.

Jeff was annoyed with himself for staying so long at the hospital. He planned to make rounds and be at the picnic before eleven, but one of his elderly patients spiked a fever for no apparent reason. He waited around for results from the tests he ordered. By the time he found out it was a common infection, he had let some of the nurses, including Joanna, talk him into joining them to eat a piece of the red, white, and blue cake a patient's wife had brought, and he didn't think he should disappoint them. So it was well after noon when he finally got to the picnic.

My Lord, he thought as he took in the swarms of children running around their crowded elders, the tinny music bouncing among the loudspeakers, and the myriad smells of cooking food. He didn't remember the picnic being such a circus, but then it had been years since he had stayed very long. He didn't know how he was going to find Lydia in all this mess. He didn't even know what she was wearing.

He started his search at the pony ride and petting zoo, figuring she might have taken Malcolm to see the animals. Nothing there but a lot of smelly animals, excited kids, and agitated adults. As he passed the horseshoe pits, he got a glimpse of Dallas Freeman walking in his direction, so he turned abruptly and went toward the crowd at the food stands. Dallas was an old classmate of Jeff's, who in seventh grade organized the "Clobber Colton" club—a group of boys who had punched or pushed him every chance they got. The club didn't last long, but Jeff never forgot it, and he still didn't like Dallas Freeman.

He walked on past the arts and crafts booths filled with quilted potholders, needlepoint wall hangings, and watercolor landscapes, all by local artists, and was almost to the activities field when he saw Lydia at the first-aid tent talking to Dr. Evans. "She damn well better not be pressing him for more information about the Galloways," Jeff whispered as he hurried over to her.

"I made it," he called. "Sorry I'm so late." Lydia smiled, but didn't move. Burt waved as Malcolm reached his little hands up to his daddy. Jeff picked up the baby and jostled him on his hip. "Did I miss anything?" he asked.

"Nothing exciting, except maybe his honor getting dunked," Burt said. "He went down with a heck of a splash."

"I can live without seeing that," Jeff said, "but I sure hope Charley hasn't been in the booth yet. I promised him a good swim. How long are they going to keep you stranded here at first-aid?"

"Till my replacement comes, I guess. It's a good place for an old codger like me. While y'all young docs are out saving lives, I can cover the skinned knees and bee stings. Fortunately, I haven't had much business."

Since Lydia wasn't asking about the Galloways, Jeff was glad she was talking to Dr. Evans. He was a good man and a good friend to their family. But there were other people he wanted her to spend time with. "Care to join us for lunch, Dr. Evans?" he asked.

The doctor declined, reminding Lydia of his food recommendations. Lydia said she'd try them and walked with Jeff to the food booths. Jeff didn't think he could handle barbequed chicken. All he wanted was a couple of hot dogs and some ice cream. Something easy to eat while he visited with the townspeople. Lydia said she'd wait to eat until after she fed Malcolm. He was beginning to fuss, so she knew he was hungry and tired.

"You're not going to nurse him here, are you?" Jeff asked. He still hadn't gotten used to having her breast feed in public. She insisted it was perfectly acceptable if done with modesty, but it made him uncomfortable, even if none of her breast was showing.

"I'll go off by myself for just a little while," Lydia said. "It'll help him fall asleep. He needs a nap." Jeff groaned softly. "What else am I supposed to do? I didn't bring any formula, and he can't eat a hot dog."

Lydia took the baby from Jeff and went off toward a small grove of trees, away from the general hubbub. Jeff saw her point, but it still bothered him. A little old-fashioned decorum was nice. He didn't see any other women nursing babies at the picnic. Trying to remember what Dr. Evans recommended and whether Lydia really wanted it, he bought hot dogs for himself and then bought two more for Lydia. If that wasn't what she wanted, he could probably eat them too. He thought he remembered potato salad, so he bought some of that and two Cokes.

As he made his way toward the grove, he saw Lydia sitting on the ground, her back propped against a tree, with the baby cuddled in her arms. It was a beautifully serene picture—Lydia curved gently over the baby, her long, dark hair loose on her shoulders, the tall grass almost hiding her legs and feet. Jeff smiled as he sat down beside her and opened the bag of food.

"Hot dogs all right?" he asked.

"Sure," she said, extending her free hand. Jeff unwrapped a hot dog and put it into her palm. She took a big bite, causing mustard to squirt out and drip down both sides of her chin. "Damn," she said through a mouthful of food.

Jeff used a paper napkin to wipe the mustard away. Gently touching her lower lip, he remembered the first time he traced the outline of those lips with his finger and told her how beautiful they were. She had thought he was putting her on, but he meant it. He loved every feature on her face. Just as he had back then, he leaned closer and kissed her.

"Is that better?" he asked as he pulled away.

"Six hundred percent," she said with a smile.

When it came time for the potato salad, Lydia had switched Malcolm to her right breast. There was no way she was going to manage the fork with her left hand, so Jeff fed it to her, one small bite after another. The relaxation and peace in her eyes made him want to go on feeding her forever. By the time she finished eating, Malcolm was sound asleep in the crook of her arm.

"Thanks," she said softly. "I don't know what I'd do without you."

Jeff folded down the back of the stroller and helped Lydia nestle the baby under the canopy. What a great family he had.

"Let's go back to civilization," he said. He was afraid some people might leave before he and Lydia had a chance to talk with them.

Around two o'clock, Stella parked the Lincoln Town Car in the field designated for picnic parking. "Lord have mercy," she said to Nancy. "We gonna have to walk a mile before we even gets to the picnic." Stella had wanted to come in the morning when it was cooler and she could park closer to the festivities. She had also wanted to come with her son, Sam, and his family, but Caroline Galloway had been fighting a miserable summer cold for several days, and that morning she wasn't at all sure she was going to be able to take Nancy to the picnic.

"I really want to take her," Caroline said, and Stella knew she meant it. "Just give me a little time for the medicine to kick in. I know I'll feel better." But her watery eyes and swollen nose told Stella she most likely wasn't going anyplace that day, and Nancy had been looking forward to the picnic for weeks.

There was no use thinking Henry or Tom would take Nancy since they had their own responsibilities at the picnic. Well, Tom might, but his grandfather wouldn't like it. So that meant, if Caroline couldn't go, only Stella was left to take Nancy. They waited around and waited around for Caroline to feel better until finally, after lunch, Stella said they couldn't wait any longer, and Miss Caroline should go take a nap. Caroline protested feebly, but soon gave in.

Nancy was disappointed that her mother wasn't going, but Stella convinced her it was better than not getting to go at all. So there they were, tromping across the ruts of the field, Stella moving her hands from one car to the next to keep her balance, and Nancy squealing for Stella to hurry up. When they reached the picnic, Stella sat down on the first bench to catch her breath, although she told Nancy they needed to sit a while to plan what they would do first.

"I want a fudge royale ice cream cone, and I want to run in the races," Nancy said.

"We'll get you the ice cream," Stella said, "but you know I promised your granddaddy not to let you run in no races. You gets so overheated and all."

Or so Henry had said, but Stella suspected he was embarrassed by Nancy's attempts to do anything athletic. She was all left feet when it came to activities like that. And she was likely to be the only grown-up in the race since the women never participated, and the men only competed against each other in the grosser contests like pie eating and mud ball flinging. Stella breathed slowly while she waited for her heart to settle down. Most days she didn't feel her seventy-two years, but walking did take it out of her.

"Alrighty, sweetie. Let's us go see the sewing first," she said when she felt better. "I hear they got crocheted doilies and homemade skirts. You just might get a notion for something new to make. It'd do you good to try something new." She led Nancy toward the arts and crafts booths, cringing at the screaming guitar sounds coming out of the loudspeakers as they neared the dance pavilion.

On the other side of the pavilion, Nancy pulled Stella's arm and pointed, giddy with excitement. "Look," she cried. "Look over there. It's Lydia and baby Malcolm."

Stella squinted behind her trifocals to see where Nancy was pointing. Sure enough, there were Lydia and the baby and a man Stella figured was her husband. His knit shirt, creased trousers, and smart expression looked like they belonged to a doctor. It was the first time Stella had seen him. They did make a nice-looking couple. They were talking to another couple who were older, at least middle-aged or better.

"Come on," Nancy said, pulling harder on Stella's arm. "Let's say hey."

"They talking to other folks," Stella said as she grabbed Nancy's hand and held her still. "Let's us wait till they through talking. We don't wanna be rude." But Nancy pulled away from the old woman's grasp and ran to her friend. Stella followed as quickly as she could.

When they reached the group, the middle-aged man was saying, "There's no way North Carolina will ever ratify the equal rights amendment. Sam Ervin will see to that."

"Hey, Lydia," Nancy exclaimed, and the man fell silent.

Lydia introduced Nancy and Stella, and the two shook hands all around. Jeff was not as handsome as Stella had thought from a distance, but that was probably because his face was creased with disapproval. She knew they wouldn't want to be interrupted. If only she could've held Nancy back. At the moment, Nancy was asking to play with Malcolm, but Lydia told her not to wake him up.

The other couple excused themselves and walked away, causing Jeff's grimace to deepen. He took hold of Lydia's elbow and put his other hand on the stroller handle, as if they were about to walk away too, when the beeper on his belt sounded. With a disgusted sigh, he glanced at the beeper.

"Excuse me," he said. "I have to find a telephone." Then, to Lydia, "Stay right here. I need to talk to you in case I have to leave." Then he walked toward the park concession stand, the only permanent building on the grounds besides the dance pavilion.

"It's so good to see y'all," Lydia said after he left. "I was hoping you'd be here. Have y'all had any food or played any games?"

"No, ma'am. We just got here. Miss Caroline got a bad head cold, and we waited out to the house to see if she was gonna feel good enough to come to the picnic, but she never did," Stella said.

"I want to eat some ice cream and play some games," Nancy said. Her eyes sparkled as she kept turning her head to take in all the sights.

In a few minutes, Jeff returned. "I have to go back to the hospital," he said. "I think it'd be a good idea, Lydia, if y'all went on home. Malcolm's been out here long enough."

"I'll go in a little while," Lydia said. "I need to find Suzanne and tell her I'm leaving so she won't be looking for me." Jeff frowned at her. "It's okay," she said. "You go on. I'll only stay a little while longer." Reluctantly, Jeff left.

"Now, let's go get some ice cream," Lydia said to Nancy.

"Ain't y'all leaving?" Stella asked.

"In a little while," Lydia said. "I told him I'd leave in a little while."

The two scoops of fudge royale ice cream dripped down Nancy's cone and onto her arm like a brown-and-white volcano. By the time she finished eating, she was so sticky Lydia figured she might attract flies. Stella took one look at the mess and insisted they go to the restroom so Nancy could wash up. "And I needs to go, anyways," she said.

The restrooms at the park were old wooden enclosures, standing about six feet apart, clearly marked "Ladies" and "Men." Inside the ladies' building, two sinks faced two stalls across the narrow cement floor. One of the stalls was occupied, so Stella slipped into the other while Nancy washed her hands. Lydia stood in a corner, out of the way.

As Nancy was drying her hands on the pull-down cloth roll, a woman with dull-blonde hair and sunburned cheeks came inside, accompanied by a taller woman in a wrap-around skirt. Seeing that the stalls were full, they joined Lydia in the corner. A few seconds later, as Stella emerged from her stall, the newcomers turned to Lydia. When Lydia shook her head, they looked at each other.

"You go ahead, then," the sunburned woman said to her friend. "I'll wait."

"No, I can wait," the woman in the wrap-around skirt replied. "I don't have to go that bad."

"Me neither."

The sunburned woman turned her head and spoke in what was supposed to be a whisper but was impossible not to hear in the small room. "You know I don't like to use a commode right after one of them uses it."

Stella let go of the pull-down cloth and crossed her arms. Lydia searched for the right words to fire at the woman, but Nancy beat her to it. "Stella's very clean. She's probably cleaner than you are."

The two women stared at Nancy, as Lydia began to giggle. Leave it to Nancy to tell it like it is. Lydia flung her arm around Nancy's shoulders and walked her out of the restroom behind Stella. Nancy might have her shortcomings, but nobody had a more tender heart or greater loyalty.

Outside, in the bright sunlight, Lydia expected Stella to say something about the incident, but she didn't. She just kept walking toward the booths where the crowd was. Nancy shook off Lydia's grasp on her shoulders and hurried to catch up with Stella, who took her to the arts and crafts booth, where the quilts and pot holders were.

While Nancy perused the handsewn items, Lydia and Stella found a bench to rest on. If Stella wasn't going to bring up what happened in the restroom, Lydia wasn't going to, either. Instead, she tried to figure out a way to ask the old woman if Henry was at the picnic, without arousing her suspicions. She was getting anxious because she still hadn't seen him, and she really wanted to meet him.

"I'm sorry about Mrs. Galloway's cold," she said cautiously. "Is Mr. Galloway sick too?"

"No, he fine," Stella said, wiping perspiration from the folds in her face. "Him and Tom was fixing to leave the house soon after Nancy and me left. Let's see here." She stuffed her hand-kerchief into a pocket on her seersucker dress and held up her narrow wrist so she could see the oversized watch attached to it. "It's nearabout three o'clock. I expect they here already. We just ain't seen 'em yet."

Lydia studied the silver watch with its square, Arabic numerals and tiny second-hand face. She had noticed it before, but now its incompatibility with the wearer captivated her. "Where'd you get such an unusual watch?" she asked.

"Mercy, honey, I've had this watch longer'n you been on this earth. Mr. Henry give it to me less'n a week after I first come to Foxrow to take care of Mr. Wallace when he was just a little bitty baby, smaller'n yours. Mr. Henry said he wanted me to be out to Foxrow on time every morning because that was when I lived in town with my husband, Rufus, before I moved out to Foxrow after Rufus died. I told him the only clock I had didn't always keep good time, so he give me this watch. I took good care of it all these years, and it still keeps good time." She rubbed the watch with her skirt to clean the crystal. "Course, he give me umpteen other watches since then, but I like this one. I waited long enough to wear it."

"What do you mean, you waited long enough to wear it?" Lydia asked.

"Mr. Henry got this watch from his daddy when he graduated from school, but he mostly despised it. He wanted a pocket watch, like the one his daddy give Mr. Howard. My cousin Christine heard Mr. Arthur tell Miss Sarah—that was his wife—that he thought Mr. Henry would think this watch was fine, him being such a high stepper and fancy dresser and all. Wrist watches was all the rage back then. The latest thing, you know? And Mr. Arthur, he figured Mr. Howard was such a fuddy-duddy that a pocket watch would suit him. Well, maybe he was right about Mr. Howard, but, Lord, was he wrong about

Mr. Henry." Stella chuckled and shook her head. "Or maybe Mr. Henry just wanted the pocket watch because Mr. Howard had it." She laughed again. "Anyhow, I ended up with the wrist watch, but I was afraid to wear it out to Foxrow till after Mr. Arthur died, and that took close to fifteen years."

So that explained the pocket watch. At least, to some extent.

"Were the twins jealous of each other, do you know?" Lydia asked. If Henry was the favored son, why did he want what Howard had?

"Lord only knows. They was thick as thieves, Christine said, but they could scrap like cats and dogs."

Stella's last word was almost drowned out by a clash of cymbals and the blare of trumpets and trombones. Malcolm woke up screaming, and Nancy came running back from the booths. "It's a parade!" she cried.

The parade was actually the Tanner High School marching band, moving in formation about thirty feet from the bench where Stella and Lydia sat. In their orange-and-green wool uniforms, the band members were likely to pass out from heatstroke, but they looked great. They progressed through a strip of grass marked off for them with red-and-blue flags, playing "Stars and Stripes Forever" with more zeal than accuracy. Malcolm stopped crying when Lydia held him up where he could see the band. Nancy clapped her hands and wanted to walk along with the marchers, but Stella told her she could see them better if she stayed in one place.

The band members followed their path to the center of the park and went through several drills on the grass in front of the platform that held the prize car. They switched from "Stars and Stripes Forever" to "God Bless America," then stood at attention as Henry Galloway climbed the stairs to the platform, the picture of propriety in his suit and tie. The moment he stepped behind the microphone, the crowd fell silent, giving him their undivided attention. Using a portable amplifier with screechy feedback, he welcomed everybody to the picnic.

"Eat lots of food, and win lots of prizes," he said. "Y'all live in the greatest little town in North Carolina, so y'all deserve it." Picnickers clustered around the platform cheered and then immediately hushed, waiting for what Henry was going to say next. "In a few minutes," he continued, "we'll start drawing raffle tickets for the big prizes and then," he paused, "for the grand prize. A 1972 Ford Thunderbird."

Cheers rose again, as swarms of other picnickers moved from the booths and games toward the platform, crowding in with each other, elbow to elbow. As Lydia, Stella, and Nancy were swept along, Suzanne appeared beside them. Lily, a little sunburned and dusty, trailed behind her, and Frank, carrying Frank, Jr., was visible farther back in the crowd.

"I thought y'all might have left," Suzanne said. "It's so damn hot. We're gonna go as soon as they announce the winners." She looked with curiosity at Lydia's companions. Lydia went through the introductions, and when Nancy and Stella turned their attention back to Henry, Suzanne whispered, "Have you talked to the big guy yet?"

"I hadn't even seen him till just now," Lydia whispered back. "I'm going to corral him when he's finished."

A small boy, whom Henry called up out of the crowd, was drawing the first tickets for the movie passes. When those winners left the platform, Henry brought up a little girl to draw for the cases of Coke. Excitement built as a young woman drew tickets for the grocery coupons, since everybody knew the car would be given away next.

"How come she's dawdling so much?" asked Frank, who had caught up with Suzanne. "She's acting like those tickets weigh a ton."

Finally, the coupons were given away. Henry announced that since the Galloway family wasn't eligible to win the Thunderbird, and he thought it might seem rigged to let anybody who was eligible do the drawing, he was going to have his grandson, Tom, pull out the winning ticket. Tom climbed the stairs to the platform like an old man with arthritic knees, a look of duty on his face.

"Well, don't be so thrilled about it," Frank said. Suzanne told him to shut up.

Tom reached into the cardboard barrel and held up a ticket. Henry looked at the ticket, cleared his throat into the microphone, and called out, "Shirley Osborn." Shirley ran out of the crowd and bounded up the steps.

"Who the hell is that?" Frank said.

"She works at the newspaper office," Lydia said, causing Frank to stare at her with surprise. "I ran into her there once," she said quickly.

After giving the keys to the Thunderbird to Shirley, Henry opened the door for her to sit in the driver's seat. Then he motioned for her husband to join her in the car. Disappointed, the crowd began to move back toward other parts of the picnic or, in the case of many of them, toward the parking lot.

"See y'all later. We got to go," Suzanne said as she hurried off to join her family, who were already with the parking lot group.

Lydia turned to Stella and Nancy, who was asking for more ice cream. "I need to go see somebody now," she said, "but I'll catch up with y'all later." She would have liked for Nancy to introduce her to her grandfather, but after Caroline forbade her to see Nancy outside of Foxrow, she couldn't pop up with her at the picnic. She put Malcolm back into his stroller and pushed him as quickly as she could through the crowd. Henry was on the ground next to the platform, shaking hands with the men and hugging the older women. His white hair gleamed in the sun, accentuating his ruddy complexion. Everybody appeared happy to see him.

As Lydia approached him, he was talking to two men not much younger than he was. Patiently, she waited while the three chatted pleasantly until one moved away. She was about to step in when Henry turned to the other man and said, "He's an idiot. Get him off the school board at the next election."

Startled, Lydia almost missed her chance to get Henry's attention as someone greeted him from the other direction.

"Mr. Galloway," she called before he could move away. He looked at her with no sign of recognition. In fact, she could see his indecision about whether to acknowledge that he had heard her. She didn't give him a chance to ignore her. "Mr. Galloway," she said again, "there's a snake next to your foot." Now she had his attention. And the attention of the people closest to him, who gasped and backed quickly away.

Henry stood still, staring at her. "Which foot?" he asked in a booming voice.

Without diverting her eyes, she said, "Left." They looked down simultaneously. "Must have been the wind rippling the grass," Lydia said, "but it sure looked like a snake to me."

"I knew there wasn't a snake there," Henry said. "You would have moved your baby out of the way if you really saw a snake."

"I know better than to make sudden moves when I see a snake. I noticed you didn't move, either." The picnickers who had stepped away from Henry at the mention of a snake began to close in again.

Henry's eyes softened as his lips curled into a smile. "Thank you for the warning, anyway," he said. "And I'm glad nothing happened to this adorable child." He leaned over and patted the top of Malcolm's head. "I don't believe I've had the pleasure of making your acquaintance. I'm Henry Galloway." He extended his hand to Lydia, who shook it firmly. It was a thick hand, well-manicured, with no rings adorning it. Not exactly what Lydia expected. But Henry wasn't what she expected, either.

In photographs, he looked pompous, a fellow pleased with himself and sure of his authority. Today, he seemed more down-to-earth, maybe even a little vulnerable. His shirt collar was damp where it touched his neck, and the knot in his tie had loosened ever so slightly. Lydia couldn't tell for sure if the pleasure in his expression was genuine or rehearsed, but she felt drawn to it.

"I'm Lydia Colton," she said. "I've lived in Tanner a little over a year now. My family and I live on Singer Street. We moved here from Durham."

Henry waited, as if expecting her to say more. After an awkward silence, he said, "Durham. Interesting town. Tobacco factories and Duke University."

Lydia was about to say that Jeff graduated from Duke when Tanner's mayor, in fresh clothes after his stint in the dunking booth, stepped out of the crowd and spoke to Henry.

"Sorry to interrupt your conversation, Mr. Galloway," he said, "but Kelly wants some photographs of you with the winner of the car." Henry apologized to Lydia and returned to the platform.

Not much of a conversation to interrupt, Lydia thought. *Sure as hell not worth waiting all day for.* She toyed with the idea of trying to corner Henry again but decided it would be better to see him at Foxrow, where there wouldn't be so many distractions. Now that they had been introduced, it would be natural for her to talk with him, if she could just arrange to run into him at the house. Her mind was swirling with plans for another trip to Foxrow, when Tom Galloway touched her forearm.

"Don't get bummed out," he said. "Sometimes he can't help giving people the brush-off." His voice was light and playful, with none of his grandfather's seriousness. Having seen him only at a distance, Lydia was surprised at how young he appeared up close. His cheeks were smooth, with no suggestion of beard shadow, while his hair was the strawberry blond that usually turns dark on adults.

"I'm Tom Galloway," he said. "Nancy's told me a lot about you. She thinks you're pretty neat. Sorry I missed your visits to Foxrow." He was obviously flirting with her, and she couldn't decide whether to be offended or flattered. Mostly, she was curious. She didn't know how he fit into the Galloway puzzle. He seemed always to be in the background, a shadow in his own family.

"I really just see Nancy when I'm at Foxrow," Lydia said. "She's the one who invites me."

"I know," Tom said. "I'd like to talk with you about that sometime."

"Go ahead." Lydia braced herself for another admonishment about leaving Nancy alone.

"Not here. There're too many ears. I want to talk with you in private."

"Okay. I'll give you my phone number. God knows, I'm home most of the time."

"I'd rather do it in person."

Lydia wondered if he was serious about wanting to discuss her friendship with Nancy or if he just wanted to get her alone. She brushed aside the latter thought as ridiculous, letting her curiosity take over.

"Can you meet me at a friend's house Thursday night?" she asked. She didn't want his Corvette parked in front of her townhouse, and she couldn't meet him in public. Thursday was Frank Jessop's bowling night, Jeff had Kiwanis Club, and

Suzanne would want to know every word Tom had to say, anyway. She gave him Suzanne's address and suggested he park in the old Presbyterian Church parking lot, rather than on the street.

As he disappeared back into the crowd, Lydia began pushing Malcolm's stroller toward the parking lot. It hadn't been such a bad picnic after all.

10

"Girl, you are gonna get us both tarred and feathered!" Suzanne screamed when Lydia told her about the plans for Thursday night. "You and me, meeting Tom Galloway on the sly. This is better than anything I ever made up to tell those dumb Everclean folks."

She was so excited about having Tom Galloway in her apartment that she told the Everclean manager she was too sick to make phone calls on Wednesday and Thursday so she could spend both days cleaning. When Frank asked what had gotten into her, she kissed him and said her libido was peaking too early in the week and she wanted to save it for the weekend, so she was diffusing energy through house cleaning. He said he would be happy to forgo bowling Thursday night and stay home to oblige her, but she assured him she had great plans for Saturday that were worth waiting for.

Lydia congratulated her when she arrived because the apartment had never looked better. Not a single abandoned toy underfoot or an unnoticed dollop of oatmeal anywhere. Even the old tie-dyed couch looked like it had been recently shampooed. The usual odor of Play-Doh and magic markers had been replaced with a spicy clove scent. Suzanne was wearing a conservative v-neck blouse with a cotton skirt, "because this is business," she said. The women put the children to bed, as planned, with Malcolm on a pallet on the floor in the bedroom.

The doorbell rang at eight. Lydia opened the door to find Tom standing in the hallway in shorts and an Izod golf shirt. He thanked Suzanne for allowing him to visit and accepted the Coke she offered him. After a few minutes of chitchat about the picnic, he turned the conversation to his sister. "Whatever happens, Lydia, don't let my mother run you off." His cobalt-blue eyes were stern.

Lydia blinked. This man was a mystery. "Don't worry. I'm not in the habit of letting anybody tell me what to do," she said.

"That's for sure," Suzanne added.

"Yeah, but you don't know my mother. She can be a real bitch," Tom said, "and if she has Grandpa on her side, the two of them are like the Berlin Wall. If they had their way, they'd keep Nancy away from everybody."

He knows, Lydia thought. *Somebody in that family knows what they're doing to her.* "Why do they treat her like that? What are they afraid of?"

Tom cleared his throat. "Well," he said, "it hasn't been easy for Nancy. Kids at Tanner Elementary either made fun of her or ignored her, and she couldn't keep up, anyway, so they sent her to a special school in Charlotte. That was okay, except the kids there lived in Charlotte or someplace out in the boonies, so it was hard to get her together with them outside of school. When she was a teenager, Mom tried to hook up her up with a church group, but that didn't work out either.

"I guess the crowning blow came at one of Mom's garden club meetings. Some new lady, who didn't know Nancy, was

SURFACE *and* SHADOW

giving the program, and she called on Nancy to tell the group what her latest gardening project was. Nancy said weeding, which was an appropriate answer, but some of the ladies snickered. Nancy burst into tears, and Mom had to take her home. I think one reason Mom's wary of you is that you're new." Lydia frowned at him, but he frowned right back. "Don't look at me like that. In a town where most folks have been here since they were born, you're new."

"What about your grandfather?"

"I don't know about him. Probably, Nancy embarrasses him. He's never said so, but it's the only thing I can figure out. He mostly ignores her. Maybe he just can't be bothered." Tom paused. "Anyway, Nancy likes you, and I don't want them to scare you off."

"They won't." Lydia wondered what Nancy's relationship was with this brother. She'd never seen the two of them together. "I'm bound and determined to go on being friends with her, so if you can do anything to help me with that, I'd appreciate it."

Tom nodded, but before he could speak, a gurgle followed by a swoosh of running water sounded from the kitchen. "What the hell?" Suzanne exclaimed as she rushed out of the living room. Tom and Lydia followed her but stopped at the edge of the linoleum, where soapy water was spreading from under the dishwasher in a fan-like pattern.

"Get some towels from the bathroom," Suzanne called. "Oh, my God. I thought this would be on the dry cycle by now." When Tom and Lydia returned with the bath towels, Suzanne had thrown two dishtowels into the creeping water, temporarily slowing its flow.

"What happened?" Lydia asked.

"Damn dishwasher's falling apart," Suzanne cried, running her fingers through her hair and waving her elbows next to her

145

head. "I've told the landlord a hundred times it needs work, but does he pay any attention to me? No! He's too cheap to pay a repairman and too busy hunting raccoons to work on it himself." She grabbed a towel from Lydia and threw it on top of the dishtowels.

Tom knelt next to the water and started making a dam with the towels he was carrying. "Where's your cutoff valve?" he asked.

"Under the sink," Suzanne replied, eyeing him with caution.

Tom squished across the wet floor and reached into the cabinet beneath the sink. In a few seconds, the swooshing sound stopped. "Get me a screwdriver and a flashlight. I'll see if I can figure out what's wrong," he said. The women exchanged surprised looks before Suzanne dashed toward the bedroom.

"What I started to tell you," Tom said as he pushed towels into the remaining water with his foot, "is that maybe I can bring my mother around when it comes to you and Nancy. She'll probably ignore me, but I can try." He looked up from the water.

"Stella's big on you too, you know. She thinks you're the best thing to happen to Nancy in a long time. She's seen Nancy shoved aside too many times, but she says something about you is cool. She's right, isn't she?" His expression darkened, temporarily hiding the light he seemed to exude.

"I really like Nancy," Lydia said. "She's smarter in some ways than people give her credit for. And she needs me. I'll be around as long as I can, but sometimes, though, I wonder what's going to happen to her."

Suzanne barged back into the room, lugging a heavy metal tool box. "Here's all Frank's stuff," she said. "Take what you need."

Tom helped himself to a couple of screwdrivers and quickly removed the skirt of the dishwasher. After wiping up more water, he lay down on the floor and shined a flashlight beam under the appliance. "What do you mean, you wonder what's going to happen to Nancy?" he asked while peering at the jungle of hoses and dust balls the beam revealed.

"Well, Stella's an old woman," Lydia said. "She can't look after her much longer. What happens then? Will your mother or your grandfather hire somebody else to be her caretaker? And what about after they're dead? Then she's your responsibility. How will you take care of her?" Lydia hadn't meant to blurt out so much. She hadn't even realized she was thinking along those lines.

Tom sat up abruptly. "Hey, wait a minute," he said. "This conversation's getting out of control." His voice was harsh, and he set the flashlight down on its face. Suzanne backed away, as if startled by his tone.

"I'm not looking at Nancy's life for the next forty years," Tom declared. "I just think she's happier since she met you, and I don't want her to lose that. That's it. No hitches, no commitments, no save-the-world attitudes." His boyish airiness had disappeared. "Just keep coming to see her. That's all I'm saying." He lay down again on his stomach with the light pointed under the dishwasher.

Lydia had to recover his confidence. "You can count on that," she said. "Wild horses couldn't keep me away from Foxrow."

"Yeah," Suzanne said. "It's like she's obsessed with the place."

Lydia glared at her friend, who backed away farther.

"Obsessed?" Some of the calm returned to Tom's voice as he reached under the dishwasher and felt along its underside. "What's there to be obsessed about at Foxrow?"

"The house's been in your family a long time," Lydia said casually. "And the history of the house is part of the history of Tanner."

"Do y'all have a screwdriver with a stubby handle?" Tom interjected.

Suzanne seized a handful of tools and shoved them at Tom, but none seemed to be what he wanted, so she rifled around in the bottom of the box and came up with a screwdriver no bigger than the palm of her hand.

"Lydia's real interested in history and things that happened a long time ago," she said, as if trying to make up for her earlier slip. "She spends a lot of time in the library, reading about the past."

"Yeah, I heard about those trips to the library," Tom said as he took the screwdriver and thrust it neatly under the dishwasher. "Nancy says you meet Stella and her there."

Lydia was taken aback by his knowledge of the group's secret meetings. Suzanne's eyes showed surprise too. Neither one said anything as Tom attempted to manipulate the screwdriver under the appliance. Finally, he withdrew his hand and sat up. He was quiet for a few seconds, as if considering his next remark. When he spoke, his eyes were calm, but controlling. "I also heard you made a trip to visit Wilbur Meacham in the hospital and that you were asking questions about my grandfather."

Lydia flinched. "How did you hear about that?"

"I'm tight with one of the nurses. Was that trip because of your interest in the history of Tanner? Or are you just nosy?" The playful light was back in his eyes.

Lydia sensed that he might be an ally. He didn't seem upset about her conversation with Wilbur. "A little of both, actually," she said. "The history of your grandfather is the history of Tanner, don't you think?"

"I guess so, but there are other people who're Tanner's history too."

Lydia took the plunge. "Yeah, I know. Like your grandfather's brother."

Suzanne grinned. This was turning out to be better than she expected.

Tom's reply was quick. "What do you know about him?"

"That he died very young. And there were questions about his death."

"No questions. It was an accident," Tom said in an even voice. He stood and put the screwdrivers back into the tool box. "Your dishwasher's fixed," he said to Suzanne.

"I just heard there were some odd circumstances," Lydia said.

"Like what?" Tom's voice hardened again.

Lydia realized she'd better back off. "I don't know. Never mind. It's not important." He might be looking out for his sister, but he was no different from anybody else when it came to this subject.

Tom said nothing, creating an awkward silence that Suzanne jumped in to fill. "Thanks for fixing the dishwasher. What was wrong with it?"

"Just a loose hose clamp." Tom never took his eyes off Lydia.

The intensity of his gaze made Lydia's insides squirm, forcing her to say something. "Thanks for helping me with Nancy," she blurted out. "I'll be back out at Foxrow as soon as she invites me."

"I'll see what I can do to make sure that happens," Tom said with no emotion. He reached under the sink and turned the water back on. "Tell your husband about the clamp," he said to Suzanne. "He may want to watch it, in case it works loose again."

"How come you know so much about dishwashers?" Suzanne asked. "Excuse me for saying so, but you don't seem like the type to mess around with machinery."

Tom smiled at her assumption. "That's because you don't know me," he said.

"So what exactly do you do at the mill?" Suzanne asked.

"Nothing to do with machinery right now. I'm in the main office. That's where all the orders come in, and I have to see that they're filled. Grandpa thinks it's a good place for me to learn about customer relations." He laughed.

Suzanne offered him another Coke or a cup of coffee—or a beer, if he wanted it, a sure sign she found him acceptable—but he declined everything and headed home instead.

"So what do you think?" she asked Lydia when he was gone. "I think he's cute as pie."

"I'm not sure I trust him," Lydia said. "I'd like to think he honestly believes they're smothering Nancy, but he may be up to something with that. He seems sort of sneaky, and he clammed up real quick when I mentioned Howard. He was also flirting with me at the picnic. Maybe he's just a jerk."

"Don't be so catty. If he flirted with me, I'd flirt back, especially if I thought I couldn't trust him." Suzanne winked at Lydia as she pulled a Newport from the pack on the coffee table and lit it. "As for Howard, why'd you bring that up, anyway?"

"Because Tom could help me, if he wanted to. But obviously, he doesn't. He's just like all the rest." Lydia dropped into Frank's La-Z-Boy recliner.

Suzanne settled in the rocking chair. "So how are things between you and Jeff? Any better?"

"Maybe some. I told you he threw a fit when he figured out I was asking people about Howard's death. Then he didn't speak to me for nearly a week. Now he's got this wild idea that we should buy a house. Why on earth he thinks that, I don't know, but at least he's speaking to me again. In fact, he's being pretty nice. It's like old times. The problem is, I don't want a house."

"You don't want a house?" Suzanne almost choked on her cigarette smoke. "Why the hell not? I'd give anything to get out of this dump and into a house."

"Because it's just going to be more of what I already have. If I thought a house would make me feel better, I'd be all for it, but it won't."

"So what would make you feel better?"

"I don't know."

"Have you ever thought about taking Malcolm and moving back to Charlotte?"

"You mean leave Jeff?"

Suzanne nodded.

"That's an awfully big step. A scary step. And I'm not sure it's the answer. The problem's more with me than Jeff. Something's missing with me. Sometimes I feel as thin as smoke. I need something to give me some substance. Maybe finding out what happened to Howard Galloway would do it." For the first time, Lydia realized how much she believed what she was saying.

Suzanne let out a long breath. "Not if old man Galloway runs y'all out of town, like Jeff thinks he will." She raised her eyebrows and cocked her head toward Lydia.

"You know," Lydia said slowly, "that's a risk I might be willing to take. There're lots of other towns, and they all need doctors."

Suzanne shook her head. "You are something else. But I like you. I just wish I knew what it is you want so badly." She put her cigarette into the ashtray beside the rocking chair. "You make me think of those women's libbers. They're an unhappy bunch, and I can't figure out why. I love being a woman. I love having Frank take care of me. And you're better off than I am. Your husband's a doctor, for crying out loud."

"I'm not a women's libber," Lydia said. "I don't want to burn my bra, and I don't think men are chauvinist pigs. And I sure as hell don't want to run for president. I just want something that I don't have now."

"And what might that be?" Suzanne asked, pausing after every word.

Lydia tried to come up with an answer, but she didn't have a name for the longing she felt or for what would make it go away. There had been a time when she would have agreed with Suzanne, when she wanted a husband to take care of her, but not anymore. Somebody taking care of you could be a real pain in the ass. She wondered if Nancy ever felt like that. Maybe she would ask her sometime.

"As soon as I know for sure," she said to Suzanne, "you'll be one of the first people I'll tell."

11

Two years, four years, six years? Tom Galloway couldn't remember how long it had been since an interesting woman lived in Tanner. When he was in prep school, all girls were interesting. While he was in college, a few of his friends' younger sisters blossomed so nicely that he was intrigued by the contrast with the kids he had known.

By the time he graduated from college and came back to Tanner to live full time, they had all scattered, but a new crop of teachers had been attracted to the town's good schools and were ripe for dating. He made his way through them and the new ones who came the next year until that grew old, and he couldn't help being drawn to the wives of several of his colleagues at the mill. Henry put a stop to that when he found out about it, causing Tom to turn his sights to larger cities surrounding Tanner. And that's where he had stayed on the weekends, except for a brief encounter with a lady lawyer who, for some reason she never told him, worked in a local law practice for several months before moving on to Raleigh. She, he decided, was the last interesting woman in Tanner, but she hardly stayed long enough to count.

And now there was Lydia Colton.

He couldn't believe she had lived in town for over a year without his noticing her. Particularly somebody with her energy and nerve. Nobody had tried to be friends with Nancy since she was a child, and nobody ever asked questions about his grandfather's brother. She was a spitfire, all right. He wondered if she knew anything about Howard's death that he didn't know. If she did, he wanted to know it too. He especially wanted to know if there was any evidence that his grandfather was involved. He would have asked her at Suzanne's, but she'd be more likely to tell him what she knew when she was more comfortable with him, and he didn't like having Suzanne there. He would prefer to be with Lydia alone. He had the perfect setup for that—get her back out to Foxrow to visit Nancy.

He started planting that seed in Nancy's mind the next day by telling her how much he enjoyed meeting Lydia at the picnic. Nancy was elated that her big brother liked her new friend, although Stella remarked, "You just remember, Tom Galloway, that she's Nancy's friend, not yours."

"I know that," he said quickly. "I just wanted y'all to know I'm on your side about her, even though Mom's not much of a fan."

"All right, but you best leave her alone," Stella replied. "She don't need you to scare her off when Miss Caroline already giving her a fit."

With Tom's encouragement, Nancy invited Lydia to Foxrow on a Saturday in the middle of July. Caroline was scheduled to be at the Outer Banks with friends for the week. When Nancy asked her permission for the visit, she flat-out refused, but Tom sweet-talked her for three days to change her mind. It took some doing, but he finally convinced her that he and Stella would be home during Lydia's visit. If Nancy had any problems, surely the two of them could handle them.

As the warm, clear morning on the day of the visit turned to afternoon, dark clouds began to gather over the river and spread across the farm. Nancy fretted that Lydia might not come if a storm arose, but Stella said, "That woman ain't scared of no rain. Not by a long shot, child."

As it turned out, Lydia parked the Camaro in the driveway and darted up the walkway and stairs just as the first fat raindrops fell, playing isolated notes on the porch's tin roof.

"Hustle on in here quick now," Stella called from the open front door, "before you gets yourself drenched."

Tom watched her arrival from an upstairs window. He liked the quickness of her movements, the way she lowered her head and ran from the car, rather than bother with an umbrella. No put-on, southern-lady airs about her. When he heard the front door close, he walked to the head of the stairs to listen to the conversation going on below.

"I wanted us to sew in the garden today," Nancy said. "Now with this old rain, we can't." The whine in her voice told him her face was all puckered up.

"I'd just as soon sew in your room," Lydia said. "Or we could sit on the front porch and watch the rain. I bet it's beautiful coming across that field in front of your house."

"No sitting on the porch," Stella said. "Could come up a lightning streak. Why don't y'all do something other'n sew today? Y'all could go in the study, since Mr. Henry ain't here. He ain't getting back from his business trip till evening. You got some nice books in there you could show Lydia. Since we ain't at the library and don't have to be quiet, you could read a little for her. You know how you loves to read out loud."

The sound of footsteps going down the hall meant Nancy liked the idea and was leading Lydia to the study at the back of the house. Tom was glad they weren't going out to the garden. He wanted to get Nancy out of the way so he could have some time with Lydia alone, and that was easier to do if they were in the house. Since his plan involved the television, if he had to drag them in from the garden, it could be hard.

Originally, he had planned to have Pansy offer the women refreshments in the living room about the time that one of the networks showed reruns of *Dennis the Menace*, which Nancy loved, but he couldn't believe his luck. On that particular Saturday afternoon, the PBS station was showing an old Walt Disney movie that Nancy had never seen. It could keep her spellbound for over an hour.

At two o'clock, he put the plan into action. Pansy went into the study and told Nancy and Lydia that she had served popcorn and Cokes for them in the living room. Tom turned on the TV and went to the kitchen to wait.

"You up to no good," said Stella as she rocked in a chair by the kitchen window, watching the rain and crocheting. "You don't never hang around the kitchen on Saturday afternoon. Ain't you gonna go see one of your city gals?"

"For your information, I don't have a date tonight." Tom smiled his most charming smile. "And if I want to sit in my own kitchen and feed my face, I can." He reached for the small bowl of popcorn Pansy had left for him. Stella snorted her disapproval while she stared at the rain.

At two twenty, Tom went into the living room and found both women watching the movie. "Sorry to bother y'all," he said, "but I need to borrow Lydia for a few minutes." He motioned to Lydia to follow him to the door.

"Okay," Nancy said, hardly taking her eyes off the TV screen.

Once in the hall, he told Lydia to come with him to the study.

"So what can I do for you?" Lydia asked as she sat down in one of the study's leather club chairs. She looked as much at home in luxury leather as she had in Frank Jessop's La-Z-Boy recliner.

"Tell me what you know about my grandfather and his brother's death." Tom kept his voice flat and calm. He didn't want to scare her, just get her to talk.

"I don't know much," Lydia began.

Shit, Tom thought. She was dodging the question. "But you must know something, after all your snooping."

"Why do you want to know?" Her voice was as calm as Tom's.

"Because you're not going to leave it alone, and somebody needs to look out for the family's interests. Somebody who won't explode at the suggestion of any Galloway sins."

Lydia nodded. "And what do I get out of letting you in on anything I know?"

"You get to keep coming to see Nancy. And I might be able to help you."

The only sign that Lydia was at all disturbed by his proposal was the methodical swinging of her right leg, which was crossed over her left. Her eyes were cool and her face, composed.

"All right," she said finally, "but here's what I want. I want access to any family records about Howard. I want letters, photos, school records, army discharge papers—anything that will tell me who he was. And I want the same information about Henry. I want to know exactly what their relationship was." Her cool eyes came alive with a heat Tom found exhilarating and frightening at the same time.

"It's a deal," he said. "But first I want to hear what you've learned."

Lydia told him about the newspaper account of Howard's death and the reports of Henry's passionate stand against the union, most of which Tom had already heard from his father.

"Grandpa's got a temper, all right, and I know he had a wild streak when he was young," he said. "I also know he was so plastered the night of the accident that he couldn't remember anything that happened, except that he and Howard were down at the barn drinking. It had something to do with a wager about which one could drink the most moonshine without passing out."

"I'll bet you didn't know this," Lydia said and told him about the third jar of liquor Dr. Cathey had seen in the barn. That was definitely news to Tom. He hadn't heard the story about the two watches, either, although it didn't surprise him. Refusing to wear the wrist watch sounded like something his grandfather would do. The third jar, however, didn't make much sense.

"Why do you reckon they had that third jar?" he asked.

"Seems like maybe there was somebody else there," Lydia said, "but I don't know who it would have been."

"It doesn't sound to me like you've turned up much that's new," Tom said in an effort to keep Lydia from having the upper hand in their relationship. "If I take you record hunting, you have to promise to clue me in on anything you learn from now on." The fire in Lydia's eyes still burned, but she nodded her agreement. "Come on, then," he said. "Let's start in Howard's old room, which just happens to now be mine."

"What about Nancy?" Lydia asked. "She must miss me by now."

"I'd say we have about thirty minutes before she flips out because you haven't come back. She knows you're gone, but she probably doesn't realize how long it's been. Come on, we have to hurry."

He reached for her hand and was surprised that she didn't pull away but followed him up the hall stairs. Fortunately, neither Stella nor Pansy had come out of the kitchen, so nobody was around to see the furtive couple or hear the old stairs creak. Upstairs, Tom and Lydia passed Henry's room on the right and Nancy's on the left and ducked into Tom's room next to Henry's. "Here it is," he said. "I'll show you the part that's practically unchanged."

"Hasn't anybody ever lived here except you and Howard?" Lydia asked.

"Nope. It's been sort of like musical bedrooms at Foxrow over the years, but nobody wanted this one, for obvious reasons. When I was about five, my parents put me in here so I could share the adjoining bathroom with Grandpa and leave the one across the hall free for guests. Nobody had been in this room much at all until then. Maybe enough time had passed that they figured any ghosts or living dead that might have been here had disappeared. It always looked to me like they just shoved all Howard's stuff in one of the closets to make room for me and my stuff, and that suited me fine. So here we are," he said as he threw open the closet door.

The smell of old cardboard and leather hit Lydia's nostrils as soon as the door was open. The closet was shallow, probably added after the house was built, and filled with boxes, a few suitcases, and clothes hanging on a rusty metal rod that ran the length of the small space. Everything was dusty, especially the clothes. When Lydia touched the sleeve of a pinstriped suit, she shuddered as the dust fell on her hand.

"Why didn't anybody get rid of these things?" she asked. "Didn't you want the space for your stuff?"

"Guess they forgot about them," Tom said. "And my stuff fits okay in the other closet. But that may be lucky for you." He lifted a large box off one of the stacks and set it on the floor. "This is the only one I've actually looked in. It's pretty boring stuff, but you can check it out." He tore off a few strips of package sealing tape that were obviously newer than the box and pulled back the flaps.

Inside the box were rectangular sheets of paper, arranged neatly in four piles. Lydia turned one of the sheets so she could read the writing. "Woodberry Forest School, Woodberry Forest, Virginia," was printed neatly at the top of the page. Below it were lines and squares, filled in with an elaborate script written in faded ink. "It's a report card," she said. "Looks like it was Howard's in ninth grade."

"You said you wanted school records," Tom said, lifting one of the papers and glancing over it. "Hmmm. This one is Henry's at about the same time. What's Henry's report card doing in a box of Howard's things?" He dug deeper into the same pile. "These are all Henry's. Ninth grade, tenth grade, eleventh grade."

Lydia looked at the papers below the one she had seen first. "These are all Howard's. Same grades. If these are prep school report cards, then what are these?" She grabbed a paper from another pile. "University of North Carolina. I should have known. But why did they save all these?" She read through some of the Woodberry Forest papers quickly. "What kind of grades did Henry make?"

"Mostly As and Bs, looks like. How about Howard?"

"Mostly As and Bs. Here's an odd one. Some of the As are circled in what was probably red ink, although it's pretty much pink now. Do you see anything like that in Henry's papers?"

Tom shuffled through his stack of papers. "Yeah, there're a couple like that," he said. "What's the date of the one you have?"

"May 25, 1909. The spring Henry finished tenth grade."

"This one's Howard's on the same date, and it has circles."

They put the two report cards side by side and discovered that if Henry had a circled A in a course, Howard made a B in the same course and vice versa. "It's like they were comparing grades," Tom said, "and marking the one who did better in the course. See, if they both made an A, the grades aren't circled."

"Good Lord, they were competitive," Lydia said. "I wonder if they put that on themselves or if Arthur pushed them into it."

"My grandfather's probably the only one who knows the answer to that, and I've never heard him talk about it. I've never heard him talk about Howard at all."

"What else is in here?" Lydia reached for another box, this one tied with dilapidated cotton string. When Tom pulled on the string, it tore like a paper ribbon. The opened box flaps revealed metal objects in various shapes.

"This is heavy," Lydia said as she lifted one of the objects. Out of the box, the cup and handles were unmistakable.

"It's a trophy," the two said almost simultaneously. The other objects were also trophies—some the traditional loving cup and others more like shields or plaques.

"They're all for tennis," Tom said after reading the inscriptions. "Some are Grandpa's and some are Howard's. That makes sense. Grandpa played tennis all the time until he got too old, and he still plays doubles sometimes."

"I bet they were as competitive in sports as they were in school," Lydia said. "Wait a minute." She set aside one of the plaques and picked up a silver plate about the size of a dinner plate. "This one's different." Holding it up to the light to make the tarnished engraving more legible, she read, "For outstanding achievement in the field of philosophy, Howard Lee Galloway." She shook her head. "Philosophy? This must be some sort of academic award." She handed it to Tom.

Tom looked it over. "Interesting that it's in philosophy. Grandpa studied economics and engineering. I know because he's told me a million times. You'd think Howard probably studied the same things."

"Let's see." Lydia flipped back through the college report cards. "Yeah. Henry took a lot of engineering courses. And some in economics." She pulled out another stack of cards. "Howard has the same courses, at least for his junior and senior years. But look here. His freshman year, he took two philosophy courses, and two more his sophomore year. But none after that. If he was so good at it, wonder what happened."

Tom took the cards from her. "If Arthur was anything like Henry is now, he told Howard what he was going to study, and you can bet it wasn't philosophy. Not practical enough for a businessman."

Lydia felt a sadness settle in her gut. She could see the young Howard, being pushed into a field he didn't care anything about.

"He should have stood up for himself," she said. "I had to do that when I was in college. My parents wanted me to take education courses, but there was no way I was going to be a teacher. My father said I'd need a teaching certificate to get a job, but I didn't care. I was going to be a scientist—at least until I got married."

"I'm guessing Arthur really didn't give him a choice." Tom tossed the report cards back into the box.

"Have you ever heard anything about Arthur liking Henry better than he did Howard?"

Tom shook his head. "Where did you hear that?"

"Somebody mentioned it. But they weren't sure. I thought maybe this was why. If Howard wanted to do something different." The sadness Lydia felt for Howard was working itself up into anger. Maybe he was pushed around all his life.

"I don't know," Tom said. "I told you, nobody talks about Howard around here."

Lydia turned her wrist over so she could see her watch. "It's after three o'clock. I've got to get back to Nancy. She's bound to miss me by now. How about you go through these boxes and tell me if you find anything? You've got constant access and plenty of time."

Tom smiled his slow, charming smile. "But it's so much more fun with you," he said.

Lydia knew she ought to say something catty to put him in his place after a remark like that with a sultry look in his eyes, but she needed his help. She could handle him, if she had to. So she gave him a disgusted sneer and said, "Just go through the boxes. Please." Then she left.

As she descended the stairs, the sound of the TV drifted from the living room. She slipped back through the door and took her seat next to Nancy, who turned to her with no sign of surprise.

"You haven't drunk your Coke," Nancy said and pointed to the full bottle on the table next to Lydia.

"I was too preoccupied," Lydia said and took a long swallow of the drink.

After the movie, Nancy told Lydia to wait in the living room while she ran up to her room. She seemed suddenly excited. When she returned, she was carrying a small package, wrapped in polka-dotted paper with a red ribbon. "It's for you," she exclaimed, thrusting the package toward Lydia.

"It's not my birthday," Lydia said.

"I know, but I made it for you anyway." Nancy's face was bright with anticipation.

Lydia took the package, which felt soft and pliable, and ripped off the ribbon and paper. Inside was a piece of cloth about twelve inches wide and three feet long. Most of it was made of Nancy's usual colorful scraps, sewn together with dainty, short stitches. In the center, however, was a circle of white cloth, probably cut from a bed sheet or pillowcase. On the white material, Nancy had used tiny stitches to draw outlines of two women holding hands. One woman had black hair, like Lydia; the other's hair was red, like Nancy's. Lydia recognized the significance of the piece immediately. A rush of tenderness swept through her. "Nobody's ever sewn a picture of me before," she said.

Nancy seized her in a crushing hug. "I love you, Lydia," she said. "You're my best friend."

"I love you too," Lydia said as she returned the hug. When she pulled away from Nancy, she studied the woman's innocent face. How could she have taken advantage of this trusting soul, particularly when Nancy was trying so hard to be a good friend? Lydia swore she would make it up to her as soon as she found out what really happened to Howard.

"I'll give this beautiful drawing a place of honor on my dining room table," she said, "and every time I look at it, I'll think of you."

Nancy beamed her gratitude as she shyly touched her work. She was obviously so proud of it. Just then Stella slipped into the living room to see if they needed anything.

"Lordy, ain't that pretty?" she said when she saw Nancy's handiwork. "You sure do have a gift with a needle." Nancy beamed even more. "Well, y'all have fun. Just remember, Mr. Henry gets home about five." And then she was gone.

Lydia knew the mention of Henry was a hint that she should probably leave by then. She would love to stay and try to get a few minutes alone with him, but this was not the time.

The rain had let up when she left the old house, allowing random rays of sunlight to break through the clouds. The sparkle of moisture on the bushes and flowers reminded her how dazzled she had been by the yard and garden on her first trip to

Foxrow. Today, the boxwoods seemed even bigger, while the hyacinths and daylilies had given way to flaming gladioli and piercing-blue hydrangea. Breathing in the fresh post-rain air, Lydia felt a tingle of satisfaction. Foxrow was alive with an energy that would push its secret to the surface.

On her drive home, the sun came out in full, causing puffs of steam to rise from the road. She was enjoying watching the little clouds disappear into the air when she had a disturbing thought. The rain might have lasted long enough to force Jeff off the golf course. It had come down pretty hard for a while, but she had been too busy to notice when it stopped. She did not want Jeff waiting for her at home.

At the Fourth of July picnic, he had seemed almost his old self, and she hoped he was going to stay that way. The old Jeff was affectionate, attentive, not so damn controlling. When had he started pushing her into the background? It had happened so gradually, she couldn't remember. Was it right after they got married? A year later? Maybe it had always been there, but she didn't notice. Maybe it wasn't just him. Maybe it was this town making her feel like such a second-class citizen. If that was the case, then it was only fair that the town would also provide her salvation with the mystery about Howard Galloway. If only Jeff could accept that.

To her relief, the Mustang wasn't parked on their street. She hurried across the yard, pausing only to wave at one of the neighbors as the woman pulled weeds out of her tiny rose garden. With only two scrawny plants on her small patch of dirt, Lydia admired her neighbor's fortitude.

"Mighty pretty, Miss Bessie," she called before she darted inside.

After paying the babysitter and sending her home, Lydia hid Nancy's needlework in her bureau drawer. She was casually reading a magazine while Malcolm played with his toys when Jeff arrived.

"Shot a seventy-nine," he announced as he came through the door. "Next thing you know, I'll be on the pro tour." He grinned. "What do you say I take a quick shower, and let's all ride out to look at houses? I drove by them as I was leaving and they said, 'Y'all come back, now.'" He made motioning movements with his hands. "'Y'all come back, and bring the family.'"

Lydia looked down at her magazine. "Not this afternoon. I really don't feel like it." She was tired after the trip to Foxrow.

"But you said you'd look at them after the picnic. It's been over a week since the picnic. They're going to be sold soon." The pleasantness in his face turned to pleading. "Please."

Lydia didn't know if she felt guilty about sneaking off to Foxrow again or repentant because she enjoyed the way Tom Galloway flirted with her or if she just didn't want another argument, but whatever the reason, she gave in. While Jeff called the realtor, she packed up the baby, the stroller, and the diapers, and off they went.

She had to admit, the houses had some good features. The rooms were larger than the ones in their townhouse, and the yards were level and grassy. Swing sets and tricycles dotted the neighborhood, so Malcolm would have other children to play with. But the walls were plasterboard, the doors were hollow, and the ceilings were low. The whole atmosphere seemed phony. Lydia couldn't explain that to Jeff, so instead she said, "They're nice houses, I guess, but they don't have any character."

"Y'all can give them character." The realtor jumped in on that.

"Sure we can," Jeff said. "We can decorate any way you want to. We'll do wallpaper, carpet, paint. Maybe someday, we can add a room. Or," his eyes grew wide, "maybe even a swimming pool."

"Why would we want a pool when we can walk to the country club?"

Jeff looked so hurt that Lydia immediately regretted her comment and especially her tone.

"Because maybe you don't want to walk to the country club," he said. "If we were going to buy one of these houses, which one do you like best?"

"I don't know. Maybe this one," Lydia said, feeling trapped. They were standing in the family room of the house that was five years old. It had a wide brick fireplace and a door leading out to a screened porch. The open door allowed a warm breeze to come inside. Balls, puzzles, and building blocks were pushed into a corner. It could be a happy room for somebody, just not for her.

"I thought you'd like this one," Jeff said. "The fireplace and wallpaper remind me of the dollhouse your dad built. But if you think this room's too dark, we could strip the wallpaper."

"No, the wallpaper's fine," Lydia said. *It's the whole damn idea I can't stand.*

"See, there are things you like about this house," Jeff said, smiling again.

"Not really." *Pay attention, Jeff.*

"Tell you what," Jeff said to the realtor. "Let us go home and talk this over. It may just take some getting used to."

Lydia looked around the family room again and out into the backyard. Maybe she could be happy here. Maybe she and Jeff could be more tolerant of each other if they had more space to spread out so they weren't on top of each other all the time. Since Malcolm had taken over the spare bedroom, there was nowhere in the townhouse to get away by herself. She tried to imagine herself happy in this new house, but even with all the rooms, she felt boxed in. The desperation that sent her flying from the house the day she met Nancy and Stella stirred in her stomach.

"I'm not ready for this," she said. "Let's go home."

Jeff said a few parting words to the realtor and walked her toward the car.

12

Lydia might think she wasn't ready for a house, but Jeff was certain they were. It just might take a little while to convince her. She hadn't wanted to move to Tanner, but he convinced her it was the right thing to do. When they were dating, she had wanted to go on a cruise to the Bahamas, but he told her she couldn't afford it. Granted, he couldn't always change her mind. He couldn't talk her out of breast feeding in public, and he couldn't talk her out of her fixation on the Galloways. But otherwise, his track record was pretty good. He would get her to come around about the house.

Feeling reassured kept him cheerful the rest of the weekend, and he was smiling when he got to the hospital on Monday. Against his better judgment, he had promised to stop by a birthday party for one of the nurses. He planned to duck in and out as quickly as possible. The affair was nearly over when he arrived, but he stayed long enough to choke down some birthday cake that tasted like cotton. Joanna caught his eye as she was cutting a slice of cake for herself.

"Want another piece?" she asked him.

"No," he said. "I've had my limit on sugary mush for today. We're lucky we don't have any dentists on staff."

"Party food's no fun if it's good for you," Joanna said. "Besides, those of us who worked all weekend need that sugar rush to keep going." She smiled at him with blue eyes that didn't appear weary or sleep deprived at all. It was amazing how that perky-teenager look could dart in and out of her face so quickly. His heart beat faster.

"I need to get going," he said.

"You look happier today," Joanna said, "happier than you have in a while. I've been worried about you. Something's bugging you. If you want to talk about it, I'll listen." Such intimacy coming from Joanna astonished Jeff, and he wasn't sure how to respond. "Don't get all worked up," she said quickly. "I know you're married. I'm speaking strictly as a friend. You've always been too serious, but lately you look like somebody stole your car."

"I'm fine, Joanna," he said. "Really, I am." As he turned to walk away, the loudspeaker paged him to go to the fourth floor. "Room four eleven?" he said. "I don't have anybody up there." Joanna shrugged and told him again she'd be happy to talk if he wanted.

Hazel Edwards was waiting for him outside room four eleven. A heavy-set, middle-aged nurse, she was a mainstay at the hospital, who had worked in nearly every unit and was loved and feared by doctors and patients alike.

"I knew you'd wonder what in the Sam Hill was going on, so I wanted to give you a quick rundown," she said, but Jeff had already recognized the name and photograph on the door.

"Wilbur Meacham?" he said. "He's not my patient."

"He asked for you," Hazel said. "Dr. Johnson is his regular doctor, but he had a heart attack day before yesterday."

"Is he okay?" Jeff had known Dr. Johnson for years.

"He'll be fine, but they sent him to Charlotte Presbyterian to be on the safe side. Wilbur may be worse off. His fever's way up, and his chest sounds like double pneumonia." She handed his chart to Jeff. "The old guy was cracking jokes yesterday, and today he can barely sit up. I told him he needed to get his butt out of that bed and go home weeks ago, but I think he's afraid of being alone."

Jeff didn't know much about Wilbur Meacham except who he was and that he used to be a bigwig at the mill. Stories that floated around the hospital when Wilbur arrived with his broken hip involved a wife who died of cancer years earlier and ungrateful offspring, who disappeared to the far corners of the earth and never came home to see their dad. *What makes a child do that to a parent?* Jeff wondered. He vowed that he would do everything he could to make sure Malcolm and his future brothers and sisters didn't turn on their parents.

After scanning the many pages of Wilbur's chart, he went into his room. The man lying in the bed was not what he expected. Comments he had heard around the hospital painted Wilbur as a live wire—a refreshing break in the ongoing procession of melancholy sick people—but this man did not look capable of even smiling. His puffy cheeks and hairless head were shiny with perspiration and so pale that blue veins stood out, crossing each other like a road map.

"Hello, Mr. Meacham," Jeff said, and to his surprise, Wilbur did smile.

"Hello, Doc," Wilbur said. "You're not gonna have a heart attack on me now, are you? I don't need any more doctors dropping before I do."

"I'm fine," Jeff said. "What's going on with you?" He helped the old man sit up and pushed his stethoscope against the papery skin beneath the damp pajama top. Hazel's diagnosis was right. He could hear moisture in both lungs, with a heavy dose of bronchitis. He checked Wilbur's eyes, ears, and throat for signs of infection, but they appeared clear. His heart beat was faint but steady.

In the middle of a cough, Wilbur put his hand to his chest, as if he were in pain. "I figured Nurse Hazel wasn't giving me enough attention, so I scared up a way to get more," he said. "Lester over there's not much company."

He peered around Jeff to glare at his roommate, but Lester didn't reply. He looked worried.

"I'm going to give you a chance to charm some new nurses," Jeff said, patting Wilbur lightly on the shoulder. "I want you to have some blood tests and a chest x-ray, and then I'm moving you down to the second floor," he leaned in and whispered loudly, "where the prettiest nurses are." He helped Wilbur lie back down and made some notes on his chart. "I'm going to take good care of you, Mr. Meacham, but I'm curious. Why'd you ask for me?"

Wilbur's eyes brightened slightly behind their watery glaze. He coughed again and spit some phlegm into a plastic cup on the table beside him.

"It's that little wife of yours. She's one feisty gal. I figured, if you have half as much gumption as she does, you'll do all right by me." He made a sound that started out as a chuckle but turned into another cough. Jeff looked quickly down at the chart to hide his fear about what else Wilbur might be thinking.

"Yep," Wilbur said when the cough had passed. "That lady's full of spit and vinegar, with a mind of her own. I could tell because I know women." He paused, as if he was expecting a retort, but both Jeff and Lester were silent.

"Yeah, I know women," he went on, "and I could tell she's up to something. She's got an unnatural curiosity about the Galloway family. She acted like she was interested in Tanner, but I could tell. It's the Galloways she's hankering after. And that's okay. They're a fine, upstanding family. And I should know." He closed his eyes and wiped his forehead with the corner of the bed sheet.

"But, you know, there's an emptiness about them that I never could quite put my finger on. Like a hole where some feeling should be, but it's not. Especially Henry." He sighed without opening his eyes. "Maybe your wife can figure it out, find out what's missing. Might be the best thing that ever happened to them or this town."

His breathing seemed shallower, and Jeff, who had been totally caught up in Wilbur's observations, jerked his focus back to Wilbur as a patient. "I'm going to leave now," he said, "to find Hazel and have her start you on an antibiotic and oxygen immediately. I'll order the x-ray and the blood tests, and when I see you tomorrow, you'll be in your new room downstairs."

Wilbur opened his eyes and nodded before closing them again, but he didn't speak. Apparently, their short conversation had taken a great deal of effort for Wilbur, and Jeff worried about his having enough strength to fight this new illness. As his doctor, Jeff would have to review all the information about his hip, any therapy he was receiving, and the condition of his overall health. He didn't want Wilbur Meacham to check out under his watch. He patted Wilbur's shoulder again and waved good-bye to Lester.

After handing his orders over to Hazel, he walked out to the staff patio, which was amazingly vacant on such a pretty day. He had felt so good about his plan to distract Lydia with the house, but Wilbur's comments worried him. The old guy seemed to think some good could come out of her probing. For the life of him, Jeff couldn't see what that could be, and the last thing he needed was for Lydia to get any encouragement, particularly from somebody with Wilbur Meacham's status. That might blow up the situation—and his marriage—to where no house was ever going to fix them.

⁓

Tom Galloway hoped Lydia appreciated the time he was spending in that musty closet. If anybody else had told him to go through boxes, he would have told them what they could do with those boxes, but she was such a doll. So that Monday he opened a few boxes, and a few more on Tuesday. He dutifully kept after it until he had been through nearly every one, but he didn't have much to show for his effort.

He had hoped to come up with some really telling piece of evidence, but no such luck. He'd found a few more boxes of trophies, some UNC yearbooks, a wooden globe, several novels, including *Of Human Bondage* and *The Scarlet Pimpernel*, lots of old shoes and pants and shirts, a broken phonograph, and some silver cufflinks, but nothing that gave any clues to Howard's death or to his relationship with his brother.

Late one sultry afternoon, he was sitting in the closet on a wooden chair he had moved in there to save his back from bending over so much when he came to the last box. The heat in the closet was intense, even though the window air conditioner in his bedroom was running as hard as it could. The cold air it was pushing out just couldn't penetrate the dusty confines of the closet. Tom had shed the shirt he wore to work and peeled off his undershirt to wipe the sweat out of his eyes.

This is it, he thought. *Last chance to find something real in here.* He was ripping open the tired old box when he heard the floorboards in his room sigh.

"Who's there?" he called out.

"Just me." Stella poked her head around the closet door and stared at the half-naked man. "What you doing in here?" she asked as she quickly surveyed the opened boxes. "Lord, Tom, ain't nobody looked at this stuff in twenty years, not since your daddy boxed it up and put it in here. Why you tearing it all out now?" Her wrinkled face squeezed into a frown.

"Because it's about time," he said. "It's been taking up space in my room for years, and I want to know what it is." He hoped she bought that, but he had a feeling she wouldn't.

"If it's been here all that time, how come you just now got up an interest?" Her black eyes held no room for waffling. "Could be it's got something to do with Miss Lydia Colton?" She put her spidery hands on her hips and leaned forward.

"No. Why would it have anything to do with Lydia?" Tom rose and took a step toward Stella, hoping to back her out of the closet, but she didn't move.

"Don't think I didn't see you two run up here last time she was visiting Nancy. I knew you was up to no good that day, and I was right, wasn't I? If she wasn't a decent married woman, I'd know what you up to, but this has got me bamboozled." She was so close to Tom that he was looking straight down into her face and could smell her lilac talcum powder. In a gentle but firm gesture, he put his hand on her waist and pushed past her into the bedroom. "Don't you run away from me, Tom Galloway. I wants an answer." She turned on her heel and followed him across the floor.

"You'll have to excuse me, Stella," Tom said. "It's almost time for dinner, and I need to get cleaned up after being in that dirty closet." He unbuckled his belt, as if he were about to remove his pants.

"Don't you excuse nobody," Stella said. "You know well as I do dinner in this house ain't for another hour. Now sit yourself down on that bed and tell me what's going on." She pointed at his bed, where he had tossed his shirt and tie.

Resigned, he did what she said, but he wasn't sure how much he could tell her. Steely in her resolve, she could be a strong ally or a strong adversary, and he was always better off in family matters if she was on his side. The older Galloways respected her and valued her opinions—as much as their sense of propriety would let them value the opinions of a black servant. And maybe she knew something about Howard or Henry that would shed some light on the mystery. He decided to take the chance.

"It has to do with Grandpa's brother's death," he said and told her about Lydia's quest to find out what really happened in the barn so many years ago. "What do you know about it, Stella?" he asked. "Anything that everybody else doesn't know?"

"Lord have mercy, I'm the one that told Lydia about what folks suspect in the first place. And I don't know no more than I told her. And that's just what Christine told me." She sat down in his desk chair, tucking the skirt of her cotton house dress neatly beneath her. "And how come a nice girl like Lydia wanna stir up that old story?"

The air conditioner continued to grind, as if it were in a constant battle with the old house, whose cracks and crevices graciously invited the summer evening inside. Seeing the open boxes and facing his aging friend, Tom felt Howard's presence in the room as he had never felt it before.

"I don't know, Stella," he said. "But she's burning up with it, and she's lit a spark in me that makes me want to find out too, for Howard's sake."

"Tommy, Tommy. You ain't never done nothing for nobody else that didn't help you somehow. If you got a hand in this, then there's something in it for you someplace. You got your eye on that married woman, don't you?" Stella pulled a handkerchief out of her pocket and dabbed at her cheeks.

Stung by her criticism, Tom said nothing. Sure, he was interested in Lydia Colton. That's what he rationalized was pushing him into this search, but there was more, something he was just beginning to recognize. He couldn't talk about that, not even to Stella, so he took the easy way out.

"Yeah, Stella," he said, trying to look apologetic about his feelings. "I do like her. She's a good-looking woman." He shrugged. "But I learned my lesson, so I won't take it too far. And this is one way I can get her to spend time with me. Don't rat on me." He smiled his charming smile at the old woman.

"You got any idea what a snakes' nest you stirring up?" Stella asked, her dark eyes flashing. "You ain't learned no lesson at all. Not about women and not about your family. Didn't your daddy tell you when you was a little boy that your granddaddy's brother's death was an accident, and you wasn't supposed to think nothing else? It's one thing for somebody outside the family to go poking, but it's another thing entirely for you."

She dabbed at her face and the corners of her mouth. Her left foot, still covered in dark hose and shoved in a heavy Oxford shoe, despite the heat, tapped loudly on the hardwood floor.

Tom had had enough of her accusations. She'd been with his family a long time, but that didn't entitle her to talk to him this way. He was a grown man now, not a child under her care.

"I know what I'm doing, Stella, and it'll be all right," he said. She continued to stare at him and tap her foot. "You really need to go now," he said. "I do have to get ready for dinner."

Stella stood slowly, never taking her eyes off him. "You too smart for this," she said. She tucked her handkerchief back into her pocket and crossed her arms. "This ain't just about no woman. There's something else going on here. Gimme some time and I'll figure it out."

She made her way to the door and then looked back, chewing on her thin lower lip. Nodding her head thoughtfully, she went on down the hall. Her footsteps reached the stairway and then faded away.

Tom was sweating more now than he had been in the closet. He opened the bottom drawer of his dresser and took out the bottle of Johnny Walker Black he kept there. He poured a few ounces into the bathroom glass and downed them quickly. Then he poured a few more. Clutching the glass, he sat on the bed again and stretched his long legs across the quilted bedspread. Yeah, she might figure it out, but not before he figured it out himself. Turning to face the closet with the open boxes, he raised his glass.

"You see, Howard," he said softly, then paused to take a swallow of scotch, "I have a secret. But I'll tell you what it is because I don't think you'll tell." He took another swallow of scotch. "I hate Tanner, and I hate that mill even more."

He lowered his head with the despair of his confession. He wasn't sure when this hatred started. Probably when he first realized there was so much more to the world than this tiny little town. But it was a hatred that grew with summer jobs in the un-air-conditioned weave room, where the temperature topped a hundred degrees every day, and with long nights with nothing to do but go to the movies or watch TV, and with college beer joints, where friends talked of going north to find their first jobs. And it ripened when he received a job offer from General Electric, but his grandfather told him, "You already have a job. You'll have to turn that one down."

And for what? A cotton factory in the boondocks of North Carolina. Maybe, he remembered thinking, just maybe, if he got a good job with a company in the Fortune 500, his grandfather would let him go. But it was wishful thinking. Henry faced him on that fateful day, when he told him about the offer from GE, and made it clear that he had an obligation to the family business.

"Why?" Tom had asked. "Why am I trapped here? I didn't ask to do this. I don't want to do this. I am not a goddamn lint head."

Henry ignored the slur, but held his ground. "Maybe if your father had lived, you could have a few years to see the world, if that's what you want. But now the future of Foxrow Mills depends solely on you."

So Tom devised a different plan, a plan that took shape slowly over his first years working full time at the mill. If they wanted him to take over the Foxrow empire, then he damn well would, and the sooner, the better. Because when he did take over, he would sell it—every last smelly cotton bale and clacking loom. Everything except the farm, which he would keep so Nancy and his mother would have a place to live. And if that hurt anybody's feelings, or if it had a devastating impact on Tanner, well, so be it.

He couldn't be responsible for everybody. And he wasn't misleading them, either. He wasn't playing the role of the town's golden boy. Hadn't done that for years. The truth was, he avoided most people in Tanner as much as he could now— spent every weekend and as much of his other free time as possible away from the place—at least he had until he met Lydia. But that was all part of the plan. He didn't want any close ties in Tanner because, when the axe fell, they were all going to hate him, and it would be easier all around if they didn't know him very well.

He was biding his time now and trying to practice patience. It was going to be years before his grandfather died and he inherited the business. The old man could still walk for hours around the farm and give his opinion on every decision made at the mill.

But then Lydia Colton fell into Tom's life, with all her beauty and energy, and in addition to her sex appeal, he sensed that her plotting and probing could work to his advantage. He just wasn't quite sure how. Staring at the scotch in his glass, he ran his finger around the rim.

"Tell me, Howard, did you really want this fucking mill so bad that you got out of the army to come get it? And did that cost you your life?"

He took a deep swallow and tried to imagine his granduncle as a man about his age. There weren't any photos of Howard after his senior year in college, so the only face Tom could call up was the face of a twenty-year-old, a youthful face, with round eyes and hair parted down the middle.

"If it cost you your life, then we have something in common because it's sure as hell costing me mine." Tom drank some more scotch and almost choked on it as he blurted out, "And all because of the same person."

And then it came to him. Why it was important that he find out what really happened to Howard. If Henry did kill his twin brother, then all his preaching about family responsibility and family honor wouldn't amount to a hill of beans. There would be no responsibility or honor in the Galloway family, and no one could make demands on a fourth-generation heir who just wanted to get away from it all.

"Howard, my man," Tom said, raising his glass once again. "Maybe you and I can both get some justice out of this. Yours has been a long time coming, and mine can't get here fast enough, but I think I'm about to speed it up." With a smile, he drained his glass.

If he was lucky, the closet's last box held the key.

13

For Lydia, the days after her visit to Foxrow crept by like ants—one after the other, and every one the same. "I really need to get back out to Foxrow and see what else is in Howard's old room," she told Suzanne on the phone one unending afternoon. "I keep meeting Nancy and Stella at the library, but Nancy never mentions having me back out to the farm. I'm afraid Tom may have screwed things up."

"I thought you decided he was okay after all," Suzanne said.

"Yeah, but he makes me jittery. He obviously likes me, but he seems awfully eager to know about his grandfather's brother too. He could be a big help to me, I'm sure, but I get the feeling he may be using me. I don't want trusting him to end up biting me in the butt."

"That could happen, I reckon, but I bet he's not your problem." Suzanne exhaled cigarette smoke. "Mrs. Galloway wasn't too crazy about your visits, was she?"

"No. She doesn't want me anywhere near Nancy." Lydia remembered Caroline's promise to end the invitations to Foxrow. Maybe she had made good on it.

But a week later, Nancy came through.

It was another hot morning at the library as Stella, Nancy, and Lydia met for their usual get-together. Summer was sliding into August with an intensity that suggested the dog days might be particularly miserable that year. Malcolm had been fussy for a couple of days, causing Lydia to suspect teething, and she almost kept him home, but she was grateful she didn't. Nancy explained she had wanted to have Lydia back out for a visit, but her mother had been very busy.

"She working on Mr. Nixon's reelection campaign," Stella elaborated, "though Lord knows why."

"Come next Saturday, and we'll sew some more," Nancy said. "Maybe it'll be pretty, so we can go out in the garden."

Lydia wondered if Tom knew about this visit and would be there to help her do some exploring. If not, she was back to her own devices, but that hadn't stopped her before.

Sure enough, the weather was clear on Saturday and plenty warm. Nancy met Lydia at the door, with Caroline close behind. "We can go outside," Nancy exclaimed, nearly dancing with excitement. Caroline agreed that was a good plan.

"But remember to stay in the garden," she said. She had greeted Lydia politely, with maybe a little less irritation. "I'll come check on y'all in a little while," she said.

Nancy had all the sewing supplies ready for transport in a wicker picnic basket, which she lifted from a table in the entry hall before she led Lydia out the door and down the wide porch steps. The garden was in full bloom with blues, purples, and reds flashing across the green stems, and the warm aroma of fresh air and plants circulated everywhere. Lydia understood why Nancy liked it here so much. It was a world unto itself. When they sat down on the blanket Nancy pulled out of the basket, only the looming second story of the house, the tops of the oak trees, and the sky suggested the existence of any world beyond their flower walls. They were alone with only the sound of bees.

Nancy had saved Lydia's handiwork from the earlier visit and gave it to her now, along with her thimble and thread and new fabric to add to her work. For herself, she pulled out a new arrangement of ginghams, different from the one Lydia had seen at their last sewing lesson, making her wonder how much time Nancy spent with her needlework. They sewed along in companionable silence for a while and then talked about a movie Nancy had seen on TV. Lydia was starting to ask her about a book on elephants she had been reading at the library, when a loud "achoo" interrupted them.

"Damn flowers. They gang up on my allergies." Tom was suddenly standing above them, wiping his nose with a hand-kerchief.

"Hey, Tom," Nancy called out. "Want to sew with us?"

Tom squatted near the two women, but didn't sit. The sun caught his hair, making it glow like burnished gold. "Not now, sweetie," he said. "I just came to see how you ladies are doing." He glanced at his watch.

"We're doing just fine," Lydia said. "Nancy's being very patient with old bumble-fingers me. Maybe someday my stitches will be as neat as hers."

Nancy beamed with pleasure at the compliment and pushed her needlework toward Tom for his inspection. He was offering more praise for her sewing when the roar of a car engine and the scratch of tires on gravel sounded from the driveway. Nancy dropped her work in Tom's hands and stood up.

"It's a blue car," she said. Tom began folding the fabric as the car door slammed. "It's Mrs. Pettigrew." Nancy turned to Tom. "What's she doing here?"

"Visiting Mother, I guess," Tom said. He seemed totally uninterested in the visitor's arrival. Lydia was about to ask who

Mrs. Pettigrew was when Tom said, "You know, it's hot as blazes out here. Why don't y'all come inside for a while? You can sew in Nancy's room, or you can help me with a treasure hunt in my room."

Nancy's face fell at the suggestion of going inside, but she perked up immediately when he mentioned a treasure hunt. "A treasure hunt, yes!" she said, clapping her hands.

She began to gather the sewing supplies and put them back into the picnic basket. Lydia folded her small piece of work as she wondered what Tom was up to. She was glad to get a chance to go back to Howard's old room, but taking Nancy along was a risk. Maybe Tom had a plan for distracting her once they got upstairs. When the three of them finished folding the blanket, Tom threw it over his arm and started toward the rear of the house.

"Where're you going?" Nancy asked.

"I thought we'd go in the back door," Tom said. "Maybe we can swipe some cookies in the kitchen." Nancy smiled at the mention of cookies, and she and Lydia fell into step behind her brother.

The wooden door to the kitchen was open, allowing what little breeze there was to come through the screen door, which banged with a warm resonance as they passed through. Pansy was peeling Russet potatoes as she sat at the large farm table the family used for breakfast and sometimes lunch. She greeted the threesome without missing a beat in her peeling.

"Can we raid the cookie jar?" Tom asked cheerfully.

"Help yourselves," Pansy said and went on peeling.

They were happily munching oatmeal raisin cookies when a voice came from a corner near the fireplace at the far end of the kitchen. "What happened to y'all's sewing party out in the garden?"

Lydia was startled by the sound since she hadn't noticed that there was anyone else in the room. She turned and saw Stella sitting in a rocking chair, fanning herself with a magazine. A deep crease crossed the old woman's forehead, giving her a sterner look than usual. Nancy began to say something, but Tom cut her off. "They decided it's too hot outside, so they're coming in for a while," he said.

"*They* decided?" Stella asked.

"Yes, ma'am," Lydia said quickly, as Tom turned away from Stella to face Nancy and put his finger to his lips in a "sh" gesture. "We thought we'd be more comfortable up in Nancy's room."

"Well, long as it was y'all's idea," Stella said with a sharp gaze at Tom. Then, smiling at Nancy, "I'll come up later and see if y'all needs anything."

Tom, Lydia, and Nancy hurried up the narrow back stairs. When they reached the center hall, Nancy darted toward the bathroom. As soon as she was out of earshot, Lydia turned on Tom. "Have you lost your mind? Telling Nancy we're going on a treasure hunt and parading the three of us right past Stella."

"Hey, parading us past Stella was a hell of a lot better than walking by the living room where my mother is, don't you think?" Tom's eyes sparkled with mischief.

"And what about your mother? We can't count on that woman to keep her occupied forever." *Not after the bitch promised to come check on me*, Lydia thought.

"With *that* woman, we can," Tom said. "You don't think she came all the way out here by chance, do you? I ran into her at the drug store last night, and while I was trying to avoid her, it dawned on me that she could be a big help. I read in the *Observer* that she's in charge of the Woman's Club bazaar this year, so I told her Mother would be home this afternoon, and it would be a good time to hit her up for help with the bazaar.

Mrs. Pettigrew won't leave until Mom agrees to do something, and Mom will never agree because she'd rather just give money, so they'll be busy for a while."

Lydia shook her head with astonishment. *You conniving weasel*, she thought. *I can't wait to hear your next answer.* "And how are you going to explain to Nancy what we're doing?"

"It's gotten too complicated to keep what we're doing from my mother and your husband and Nancy, so I've decided to let Nancy in on it. If we tell her it's a secret, I don't think she'll give us away."

Lydia wasn't sure that was the case, but she didn't have much choice. Tom had plunged into her mission up to his armpits and seemed to relish every twist and turn. She still questioned why he was so interested, but that just ramped up her curiosity about the whole Galloway family. Before she could tell Tom he might be making a mistake about his sister, Nancy came out of her room, calling, "Let's start the treasure hunt."

"You're on," Tom said, motioning for the two women to come into his room. "I finished going through the boxes and didn't find anything," he said to Lydia, "so I guess the next thing to do is check out the furniture that belonged to Howard. I don't have much hope there, but we might as well try." Then he turned to Nancy. "It's like this," he said. "If you can find anything that has Grandpa's name on it—Henry, remember?—or that has his brother Howard's name on it, you win the prize. Okay?" Nancy nodded without smiling, appearing to take the hunt quite seriously.

"The only pieces of furniture that I know were Howard's," Tom went on, "are the desk and the chest of drawers. You take the chest, Nancy. Just push my clothes out of the way and look for any scraps of paper caught in between where the sides of the drawers meet the bottoms or maybe . . ." He stopped in mid-sentence and looked at the closet. "No, wait a minute. There's one more box you can go through." He went into the closet and dragged a half-opened box through the door. "You and Lydia can go through this together, while I work on the desk." He opened the slant top of the old piece of furniture to reveal a double row of small drawers under cubbyholes stuffed with papers.

Nancy seized the box and began tearing off the remaining shreds of string, while Lydia wondered why this particular box was left alone, especially when Tom said he had been through all of them. After sitting down on the floor next to Nancy, she opened the box's flaps. More stacks of paper. She picked up one and saw it was an old newspaper clipping glued to a piece of construction paper with a ragged edge, like it had been ripped out of a scrapbook. The clipping was an article about the sixth game of the 1918 World Series, which Boston won to take the series. *Sports fans, typical guys, big deal,* Lydia thought and tossed the paper aside. The next sheet was an article about the fifth game of the same series. Nancy was starring at similar clippings.

"What's a World Series?" she asked.

"Something baseball players dreamed up to make more money," Tom said.

"Don't worry about it," Lydia said. "There's not likely to be anything about your granddaddy or his brother in anything about baseball."

The two women went back to sorting through the papers and suddenly came to the last ones. Beneath them were stacks of phonograph records.

"Look at this," Lydia exclaimed, holding up one of the records with a "Victor" label. "Al Jolson. Enrico Caruso. Howard must have liked the latest music."

"Who are those people?" Nancy asked, her face showing tinges of exasperation.

"Just some old singers," Lydia said. "Nobody you would've ever heard of."

Nancy glanced at a few of the records, then tossed them on the floor beside her. "This treasure hunt is boring," she said. "I don't see granddaddy's name anyplace. I want to sew." She stood up and wiped her hands on her Bermuda shorts. "Let's go to my room, Lydia."

"Tell you what," Lydia said as Tom looked up from the desk, obviously annoyed. "Why don't you bring your sewing in here and do it on Tom's bed while I keep on hunting? If I find something, I'll share the prize with you."

"What's the prize?" Nancy asked with renewed interest.

"The prize is a trip to Lake Norman to go swimming," Tom said. Lydia stared at him in disbelief. She couldn't go to Lake Norman with the two of them.

Nancy was thrilled with the idea. "You keep hunting," she said to Lydia. "I'd rather go with you, anyway." Then she left to get her sewing.

"You are a damn lunatic," Lydia said, glaring at Tom. "I can't go running off to Lake Norman with you all."

"We'll worry about that when we find something," Tom said. His eyes glowed with the thrill of the hunt, and Lydia was surprised to feel a tingle shake her shoulders.

She was attracted to him, no doubt, but it was different from a sexual attraction. Instead of touching his body, she wanted to touch inside him. Beneath his cocky, flirtatious exterior, she sensed anger and dark determination. He was way too eager for this.

"Anything in the desk?" she asked.

"Nothing that's not mine. But I did find a couple of old bank statements I thought I'd lost." He shoved some papers into a cubby hole and opened the drawer below it.

Nancy came back into the room with the picnic basket and spread the pieces of material and spools of thread on the bed. After arranging her latest work on her lap, she lifted the needle from the corner where she had stuck it when they left the garden. With quiet concentration and an expression of contentment, she made careful, even stitches in an arrangement of ginghams that began to take on the appearance of a pattern. Watching her, Lydia was again impressed with her dedication to her work and her skill, and suddenly she had an idea that was so exciting she couldn't believe she hadn't thought of it before.

"Nancy," she said, "have you ever thought about sewing for somebody besides yourself?"

"Who would I sew for?" Nancy asked.

"I don't know, but there's bound to be somebody who needs a person who can sew like you do." Lydia envisioned embroidery and monogramming and running stitches around the edges of tablecloths. Nancy could learn to do that.

"Hold on a minute," Tom said. "Let's not get carried away here. Why would Nancy want to do work for other people?"

"To show off what she can do. To get out and meet people. Just for a change. She could even make a little money." Lydia was irked that he didn't see the genius of the idea.

"She doesn't need any money. Believe me, she's well taken care of."

"She may not need money, but let me tell you, in this world, earning money is the way we measure what a person contributes or how good they are at something. It's our only yardstick for value."

"She doesn't care about that."

"You might be surprised."

Nancy looked from Tom to Lydia. "It'd be fun to see if other people liked my sewing."

"I thought so," Lydia said. "Then you need to find some-place to do it besides your room and the garden."

"Don't push her." Tom frowned. "She's happy doing what she's doing, aren't you, Nancy?" Nancy nodded, but Lydia had a feeling the young woman liked the idea better than she let on. Nancy did that sometimes—mulled over something she had heard and then suddenly, days or weeks later, brought it up again with her own reactions. "I give up on this desk," Tom said as he slammed the last drawer shut. "Are you done with that box?"

"Yeah, nothing here." Lydia piled the pages of newspaper clippings back on top of the records. Instead of standing up and lifting the box, she crawled on her knees, pushing the box ahead of her on the heart-pine floor. Once she had it inside the closet, she sat down on the floor again and leaned against a stack of boxes shoved to the back wall. Her neck and shoulders were tired from bending over the sewing and then the papers in the box, so she leaned her head back on top of one of the boxes.

The light in the closet was dim. There was no overhead fix-ture, so the only illumination came in through the door and didn't quite reach the corners. Yet, with her head tilted back, Lydia thought she saw a bulge on the underside of a shelf that ran the width of the closet just above the hanging bar. It would have been impossible to see if clothes had been hanging in front of it, but in their searching, she and Tom had pushed all the hanging clothes to the other side of the closet.

Lydia scrambled to her feet and stretched to reach over the boxes piled between her and the questionable spot on the shelf. With her arm fully extended, her fingers grazed the bulge. It was rough and spongy. She tried to get her whole hand against it, but couldn't, so she grabbed the box pressing against her stomach and pushed it out into the bedroom.

"What's going on?" Tom looked up from the papers he was gathering into a pile on the desk. Nancy stopped sewing and watched Lydia turn back into the closet.

"I may have found something." Lydia set another box on the bedroom floor. Tom dropped his papers and came up behind her in the closet. "See," she said. "There's something under that shelf." Tom got in front of her in the space where the boxes had been and ran his hand along the mass protruding below the shelf.

"It's heavy paper," he said. "Seems like it's stuck to the shelf."

"Don't tear it." Lydia craned to see around his elbow.

"Give me some room. I think I can get it loose." He tugged at the package for a few seconds, then lowered his hands. "Damn. Feels like it's tacked or nailed to the shelf. I need something to pry it loose. Nancy, hand me your scissors, will you?"

Nancy, who was giggling at Tom's use of a curse word, put down her sewing, brought him the scissors, and stood behind Lydia to watch what he was doing. Using both hands to feel his way in the dim light, Tom worked to force one of the scissors blades under whatever was holding the paper in place. With a quick jerk, he knocked the piece of metal to the floor. Lydia leaned over and scooped it up.

"Looks like an old tack," she said.

"Yeah. Well, there's a bunch more." In a few minutes, two more clattered on the floor. Tom lowered his hands to wipe sweat from his forehead. "How about y'all back off and give me some air?" Lydia and Nancy backed up about two steps each.

A fourth tack hit the floor a few seconds before Stella walked into the bedroom. Thin arms crossed at her waist, she strode across the room to stare at the closet shelf with the others. "What in heaven's name y'all doing?" she asked. "Y'all said you was gonna sew in Nancy's room."

Nancy immediately looked at the floor, but Tom never flinched. "I was stacking these boxes back in the closet and found something weird, so I asked them to come help me get it loose. I think I've almost got it." He popped another tack onto the floor.

Stella's steely gaze swept across the fabric and spools on the bed, but she didn't say anything. She also didn't move. Tom pried out two more tacks, and a large brown envelope fell into his hands. Except for the holes the tacks made and some gray-ish grime and dust, the envelope was in good shape. There were no tears, and the flap was glued shut. Tom turned it over a couple of times, revealing no writing on either side.

"If I was you, I'd put that right back wheres I found it," Stella said.

"Why?" Tom said. "It's my room, so technically I have a right to anything in it."

"You knows why," Stella said.

"What is it?' Nancy asked.

Lydia was dying to open the envelope, but she wasn't about to get between Tom and Stella.

"Let's check it out," Tom said, avoiding Stella's stormy eyes. He slid the blade of the scissors under the flap, slicing the envelope open. Then he reached in and pulled out a few sheets of thin, brown paper. A military seal appeared at the top of the first page with the words "Army of the United States" inscribed in a half circle above it.

"It's Howard's army discharge papers," Tom said with awe in his voice.

"What do they say?" Lydia was on the verge of jerking the papers out of his hand.

"They don't say nothing you needs to know," Stella said with a penetrating frown.

"Let me see," Nancy cried.

Tom turned away from the women and scanned the papers. "It's a medical discharge," he said.

Then Wilbur was right, Lydia thought.

"It says," Tom went on, "that he was released from duty because of mental infirmities." Tom's mouth twisted into a frown. "What infirmities?"

"I told you it wasn't nothing you needs to know," Stella said. "And it sure ain't nothing for your little sister to know." Nancy was standing quietly, waiting for Tom to explain what he had just said.

"Now, it's high time Nancy and Lydia went back to Nancy's room." Stella took Nancy's hand and led her toward the door. Lydia gathered the sewing supplies from the bed, gave Tom a resigned smile, and followed them into the hall. "It ain't nothing for you to worry about," Stella was saying. "Just some old papers that don't mean nothing."

"What about Lake Norman?" Nancy asked.

"We ain't talking about Lake Norman," Stella said.

Stella and Nancy had disappeared into Nancy's room, leaving Lydia trailing behind, when the door to Henry's room flew open, and Henry stepped into the hall. Clutching the picnic basket, various swatches of material, and spools of thread, Lydia grasped for the right thing to say. Henry's face showed no sign of recognition, but then he smiled.

"Mrs. Colton from Durham," he said. "The snake seer." He was wearing slacks and a short-sleeve shirt, casual clothes that didn't suit Lydia's image of him. "What are you doing in my upstairs hall?"

"Visiting Nancy," Lydia replied. "We've become friends this summer." Henry's frown suggested this information didn't fit in with his ideas about the women. "I'm glad to see you again," Lydia said hurriedly. "I wanted to talk with you more at the picnic. One thing I wanted to explain is that I'm not actually from Durham. My husband went to school there, so we lived there a few years."

Henry's silver eyebrows rose, whether in interest or disdain, Lydia wasn't sure. "So your husband's a Duke graduate," he said. "I'm a Carolina man myself."

"Yes, I know. I've read about your involvement with the university. You're a very active alum." Lydia's face grew warm as she stumbled over the words, making small talk while she tried to think of a way to get him to talk about himself and maybe reveal something she didn't know. One of the spools fell out of her hand and rolled along the floor. "Aren't you on the board of trustees?"

Henry picked up the spool, which had rolled against his foot. "Not any longer. I retired from that a few years ago."

Nancy's voice grew louder inside her room. In a few minutes, she would come looking for Lydia, which meant Lydia had to act fast if she was going to learn anything new from Henry. The only thing she could think of to do was mention Howard and see how he reacted.

"Didn't I also read that your family set up a scholarship at UNC in your brother Howard's name after he died?" She had read no such thing, but she thought it sounded plausible.

Henry's ruddy complexion darkened. "We established a scholarship, but it's named for my father." He twisted the spool in his hand. "And why exactly are you visiting my granddaughter, Mrs. Colton?"

"She's teaching me to sew." Lydia held up the material and basket as evidence. *Think, you idiot*, she said to herself. *Get him to say something about Howard.*

"Then you will need this," Henry said, handing her the spool. "Good afternoon."

He turned away from her and started down the steps, where he met Caroline coming up. They nodded to each other and passed on. The corners of Caroline's lips sagged toward her chin, driving the grooves on either side of her mouth deeper into her skin.

"Where's Nancy?" she asked. "I thought you two were going to stay in the garden."

"She's in her room with Stella. We came in to cool off a little. I've got the sewing supplies." Once again, Lydia held up the material, spools, and basket.

Caroline hurried into Nancy's room, calling to her daughter in softer tones, while Lydia followed. Nancy and Stella stood at the window, holding back the ball fringe curtains. Neither turned to acknowledge Caroline or Lydia, so Caroline slid her arm around her daughter's waist. "I think it's time for Lydia to go home," she said.

Nancy jerked her head around to stare at her mother. "Why?"

"Because she's been here long enough. It's late."

"Lydia's never here long enough. I wish she lived here."

Nancy slid out of Caroline's grasp and moved closer to Lydia. Stella turned from the window with a look of shock on her face. Lydia was surprised too, to hear Nancy speak so sharply to her mother. Ever since Nancy gave her the table runner, Lydia had known how much the young woman cared about her, but she didn't expect her to confront her mother like this. Lydia wondered if she'd ever had any other friends who were as devoted as Nancy.

"I'm sorry, but Lydia needs to leave." Caroline's voice grew stern around the edges.

"But she hasn't seen the cardinal yet."

"There'll be other cardinals for her to see. I'll walk you to the door, Lydia."

Lydia put the sewing supplies on the bed. "We'll see each other again soon," she said and waved to Nancy before descending the stairs with Caroline. She vowed once more to make it up to Nancy for using her to get close to Henry. She also vowed that the next time she saw Henry, she would be more prepared.

⁂

The cardinal flitted from branch to branch in the old maple tree, his scarlet body disappearing behind the leaves and re-appearing like a drop of blood. A second cardinal joined him from time to time before flying off to other trees, but the first bird seemed to like that particular maple. With her nose nearly touching the window, Nancy hoped more birds, different birds, would join him. Cardinals were her favorite, but she also liked goldfinches and even the little brown wrens.

"Come on," she said. "Come to the big tree."

"It's too hot for them birds to fly around much," Stella said. "They smarter than that. They stays in the shade or near the water."

"But they might come. I love it when they come close to my window. I feel like I can reach out and touch them." Nancy imagined the softness of their feathers, slick and smooth as the satin ribbons she sometimes wore in her hair.

"You don't wanna touch no birds. They got lice. Just look at 'em, and think about how beautiful they is."

"I would touch one if I could. I want to know what they feel like." The cardinal took a final sweep from one side of the tree to the other before he flew off toward the river. Nancy watched the tree patiently for several minutes, then dropped the curtain. "They're gone. What can we do now?"

Stella dropped her curtain as well and retrieved a handkerchief from the pocket of her dress to wipe her nose and mouth. "I needs to go see how Pansy's coming with dinner. She likes to watch them ballgames on TV, and sometimes she gets behind.

But I reckon I got a few minutes to do something with you. Want to sew some more or play a game?"

Nancy shook her head and sat down on the bed. Her mind was awash with the strange turns the afternoon had taken—from Tom's inviting her to play a game with him, even if the game was boring, to Lydia's saying she could sew for other people, to finding something hidden in Tom's closet, although she didn't understand what it was.

"What's the matter, sugar?" Stella asked. "You not fretting about them old papers, are you?"

Nancy shook her head again. She didn't care about some dirty old papers. She ran her fingers across her new patchwork runner, which Lydia had left on the bed. It was pretty, probably the best one she had ever done. Maybe somebody would like to have it.

"Do you think I'm a good sewer, Stella?"

"Course you is. I been telling you that a long time. Look at them tiny, even stitches." Stella pointed at the perfect seam between a green gingham and a red one. "Can't just anybody do that. Takes years of practice and fistfuls of talent handed down from the Lord." She patted Nancy's cheek.

"Would somebody ever want something I sewed?" Nancy had never before thought she could do anything that another person might want. Usually when she was around people outside her family, they talked to her for a few minutes and then ignored her. But Lydia wasn't in her family, and Lydia said other people would like the way she sewed.

"What somebody you talking about?" Stella smiled gently.

"Somebody besides you and Mama and Tom. Somebody who doesn't live at Foxrow."

Stella leaned back against the bedpost, lacing her fingers except for the two pointers, which she pressed together and rubbed against her chin.

"What put this notion in your head about sewing for other folks?"

"Lydia did. She said other people would like the way I sew. She said they might want me to sew something for them."

"Uh huh." Stella closed her eyes and spoke so softly Nancy wondered if the old woman was still speaking to her. "I knew that girl was gonna cause a ruckus the day I met her." She went on rubbing her chin with her pointer fingers and said nothing more until Nancy tapped her on the leg. Then she opened her eyes and smiled. "Well, I expect there's folks out there that would like your sewing, and I bet Lydia's gonna find out who. You just gotta be ready when the time comes, if you wanna do it. And that's all any of us can do. Watch and wait and be ready 'cause you never knows when you'll be called."

Nancy wasn't sure what Stella meant by "be ready," but she would try her best to do whatever she needed to do. She just hoped it didn't take too long.

Tom had been standing barely inside his door when Henry spoke to Lydia in the hall. He wanted to tell her he would try to find out more about the discharge papers, but when he heard his grandfather's voice, he stopped where he was. He couldn't let Henry see Lydia and him together. He regretted his decision to hang back as soon as he heard Lydia mention Howard. The mere fact that she referred to the dead brother, which nobody in Tanner ever did in Henry's presence, would alert him that something was going on. So Tom wasn't surprised when Henry said at dinner that he'd like his grandson to walk with him down to the horse barn after the meal.

"I haven't seen that new filly of yours in a few weeks. I want to be sure you're taking care of my investment," he said, but

Tom knew there was more to it than that. When Pansy came to clear the dessert plates, he said he needed to use the bathroom before he left with Henry. What he really needed was time to prepare for the onslaught.

The evening air was still sweltering as the two men set out on the dirt road leading to the barn. Tom offered to drive them down, but Henry said exercise after dinner was good for digestion, so they walked through the dust while the sun threw their elongated shadows before them. Only the good-night laments of the mourning doves interrupted the silence until they reached the barn's shadowy confines, where horses munched on their evening feed. Henry threw the light switch and proceeded directly to the buckskin quarter horse Tom purchased earlier in the summer. She had finished her feed and looked eagerly at the approaching humans. Henry ran his hand along her muscled back.

"Seems in good shape," he said, "but I don't think anybody's groomed her today." He lifted two curry combs from the storage cabinet beside the stall and tossed one to Tom. "Give me a hand," he said. Tom started combing at the top of the horse's neck on her left side; Henry did the same on the right. When they reached her withers, Henry asked, "What do you know about Lydia Colton, that woman who was visiting Nancy this afternoon?"

"Not much," Tom replied, keeping his eyes focused on the horse.

"Bullshit." Henry raised his head behind the horse's mane. "I saw her coming out of your room this afternoon. She's decent looking, so I'm sure you've been sniffing around. But I'm more interested in why she asked me about Howard. Tell me what you know." His voice was low and firm, with a tone he used most often in business meetings.

"I know her husband's a doctor. See, I do know she's married. And Nancy's seemed a lot happier since she's been around." Tom moved his comb in a circular motion along the horse's ribcage.

"If you've been carrying on with her, we'll deal with that later. What I want to know now is why she's asking questions about us." The frown lines in Henry's forehead pushed down against his eyebrows as he fixed his grandson with a glower that Tom had seen cause seasoned board members to wither. "I know she's talking about us with people in town. I want you to tell me what she's up to."

Tom tightened his grip on the curry comb and turned away from his grandfather's gaze. The old man thought he could control everything. There was nothing Tom would have liked more than to wipe that confidence off his face. He stopped combing. "Why don't you ask her yourself, if you're so damned concerned about what she's doing?"

"You can bet your ass I will. But it might make it easier for her if you tell me." Henry moved his comb down to the horse's belly. "Tell me, because I'm going to find out anyway."

That's the fucking truth, Tom thought. What Henry wanted, Henry got. But maybe Tom could make it seem less threatening so his grandfather would leave Lydia alone. "She's just curious, that's all. Somebody told her about Howard, and she's intrigued. Don't make a big deal out of it. She'll get tired of it and quit."

The horse's skin rippled. She was enjoying the combing. Henry traded his comb for a stiff-bristled brush. "Like hell she will. You don't believe that any more than I do. What's she trying to prove?" He flicked the brush against the horse's neck.

"She's not trying to prove anything. Like I said, she's just curious."

"Well, I won't have it." Henry flicked harder at the horse's flesh. "I won't have anybody prying into our family's business. And I mean that."

Tom walked around the horse to the cabinet and took out a brush. "Why do you care, if there's nothing for her to find?" he asked as he passed Henry. The old man's eyes flashed and he paused, holding the brush in the air. For a second, Tom thought his grandfather was going to hit him. It wouldn't be the first time the old man pounded a guy who sassed him.

A few years earlier, a low-life from up the river broke into the house at Foxrow late one night and ran smack into Henry, who'd gotten up to use the bathroom. When Henry grabbed his collar, the guy called him a moneygrubbing asshole, so Henry threw a punch that broke his nose. Tom remembered blood spewing down the man's face. This time, Henry drew a deep breath and lowered the brush to the horse's shoulder instead.

"Is there anything for her to find?" Tom asked when he was safely back on the other side of the horse.

"You know better than that."

"How do I know if you don't tell me? Tell me what happened that night."

"You know what happened." Henry continued to work over the horse's back.

"No, I want to hear it from you. I want to hear every detail. I deserve to hear every detail."

The whap of Henry's brush stopped. The horse whinnied and looked behind her, as if to see why no one was paying her any attention. Henry propped his elbows on her back, his face hard as rock.

"All right, I'll tell you. But there's not much to tell. Howard bet me he could put away more grain alcohol without getting drunk than I could. It was a stupid bet, but we were young, and I was too proud not to take it. So we set the date and bought two pints of moonshine with some grape juice to use as a chaser."

"Where'd y'all buy the moonshine?" Tom interjected. He laid his brush on the divider between the stalls and leaned back against a post.

"Same place we always did. The gas station across the river. Cecil Jenkins sold it under the counter there for years." Henry flicked the brush against the horse's coat again.

"So you'd bought from him before?"

"Sure. Everybody did. Howard and I drove the Buick out there that afternoon. Then, late that night, we came down here to the barn so Mother and Father wouldn't know what we were doing and started the contest." Henry's voice had lost its businessman's edge. He stopped brushing and patted the horse's flank. "It was a strange night. We sat on some hay bales and benches over there." He pointed at a dusty space between the rows of stalls. "I thought the way to win the contest was to drink as fast as I could and then show I was still sober, but Howard was drinking slowly. He wanted to talk a lot. At the time, I thought it was probably the effect of the liquor."

"What did he talk about?" Tom stared at the worn, gray boards behind the place where the brothers had sat. He had never heard this part of the story.

"I don't know. School. The army. Father. The mill. To be honest, I don't remember a whole lot because I was drinking pretty fast. But I do remember one thing he said. He said we were lucky to have the mill as our legacy, but a legacy could also be a curse."

Tom smiled slightly, wondering if Howard was talking about the same curse he felt. "What were you doing while he did all this talking?" he asked.

"Drinking. Answering him occasionally." Henry finished brushing the horse's rear. Suddenly, he looked up and threw the brush at Tom. "Are you going to help me with this horse or not?"

Tom caught the brush and started working on the horse's neck. After running his hand along the horse's hindquarters, Henry picked up a soft-bristled brush.

"The last thing I remember, Howard was sitting on a hay bale with his legs crossed Indian-style, holding the jar of liquor between them. He had a piece of wood that had broken off from one of the stalls, and he kept poking at the straw on the floor and pushing it around." Henry brushed the horse in long, smooth strokes.

"Then I must have passed out, or the alcohol just erased everything, because after that I have a vague memory of lying in the doorway at the house with Father shaking me, but it's very hazy. The next thing I remember with any clarity is Father waking me up the next morning to tell me Howard was dead." He raised his head; his eyes were heating up again. "And that is it—the whole story. That is everything that happened that night that I know anything about. It was a horrible accident—period."

His expression seemed to forbid any more questions, but Tom had to know more. "Did you buy the liquor or did Howard?" he asked.

"We both did. We stood at the counter and gave Cecil the money. He took the jars from under the counter and handed them to us. If he were still alive, he'd tell you that."

"And the jars looked exactly alike?" Tom picked up his brush and fingered the rough bristles.

"Yes, they looked alike," Henry said, "just like every other jar I ever bought from him."

"You said y'all bought two jars of liquor. Where did the third one come from?"

"How do you know about the third one?" Color began to rise in Henry's cheeks. His brushing strokes grew choppy.

"Lydia told me."

"That's it." Henry threw his brush against the floor with a resounding whack. The horse skittered away from him. "That woman is never setting foot in my house again."

"Don't get mad at her for knowing the truth." Tom tightened his grip on the brush he was holding. "Tell me about the third jar."

"I don't know where it came from," Henry said. "I never saw it until the next day. At least I don't remember seeing it. But it doesn't make any difference. It doesn't change one thing about what happened."

"What if that was the jar Howard bought, and somebody slipped the poison jar into the barn or gave it to Howard later? Was anybody else down there that night?"

"No. Just Howard and me."

"Did anybody hate you all enough to try to kill you?"

Henry stepped toward the horse, folding his arms across his waist. "That is preposterous. I told you. It was an accident." He walked around the horse and pointed his finger at Tom. "That is the truth. There is nothing else to know and no reason to ever talk about it again. Do you understand?" Tom held his grandfather's gaze and said nothing. "Well, you sure as hell better understand," Henry said. "This matter is over. There will be no more talk about my brother." He paused a moment. "And I meant what I said about that Colton woman. She better not ever come here again."

"How will you explain that to Nancy?"

"I don't have to explain it to Nancy. She's a child. She'll do what she's told. And I don't know what your involvement with that woman is, but you end it now."

Tom was burning to tell Henry he would do what he damn well pleased and Nancy would too, but he knew that wouldn't help. He needed time to decide if he believed Henry's version of what happened that night. Believing it was an accident meant giving up on his hope that the incident might give him a way out of Tanner, and he wasn't ready to do that yet. He turned a calm face to Henry and murmured, "I'll see what I can do."

"You'll see, all right," Henry said. "I'm going to take care of this, myself." Then he walked out of the barn and disappeared into the deepening dusk. Tom clutched the stiff-bristled brush and knew he had to warn Lydia that Henry was on to her.

14

A few weeks on high-powered antibiotics made Wilbur Meacham a new man, or so he told Jeff during morning rounds. Jeff was relieved the old fellow had more spark than when they met, but he knew Wilbur wasn't out of danger yet. "What's the matter, Mr. Meacham? Don't you like the nurses down here?" he asked.

He still had Wilbur on the medical floor. He'd considered putting him into the intensive care unit at first, but he decided the old man didn't need that level of care. He really didn't need the isolation. Wilbur needed to be around people, so Jeff kept him where he could have a roommate.

"The nurses are sweet as pie," Wilbur said, "but I miss Nurse Hazel. Bless her heart, she needs me. I'm the only one who can crack that old wet hen act of hers and make her smile."

"If you keep getting better, we'll have you back on the fourth floor before you know it."

"That's swell. Lester needs me too, you know. He'd stay buried behind that newspaper and never say a word if it weren't for me." Wilbur smiled a weak smile.

"I promise we'll get you back up there soon as we can," Jeff said, but he wondered how much longer they could keep him in the hospital. Wilbur's hip was healed. All he needed was some physical therapy, but he raised such a fuss about it that the therapist often let him skip it. Lying in bed had caused his pneumonia. Because he was who he was, the hospital staff had let him stay longer than necessary. He needed to go home.

Jeff hung Wilbur's chart on his bed and left the room. Staring at the clock in the nurses' station, he knew he couldn't prolong going to his office, although he dreaded it like hell. The office receptionist had left a message at the hospital that Henry Galloway made an appointment to see him at noon, but it wasn't for medical reasons.

Even though the parking lot at Jeff's building was nearly full, the Cadillac parked in the corner stood out. Henry had arrived early. Jeff went in through the back entrance, passed the examination rooms, and ducked into his office.

Dr. Evans had built the building that housed the medical practice, along with a law practice and an accounting firm. It was a solid brick building in the heart of Tanner, with big windows and spacious rooms. Jeff's office still had Dr. Evans' heavy oak desk, two of his book cases, and four upholstered chairs. Once Jeff had straightened the papers on the desk and removed yesterday's newspaper from one of the chairs, he called the receptionist to tell her he was in.

Henry Galloway was taller than Jeff remembered. When he stood to shake hands with his guest, he was surprised to have to look up at him. Or maybe it was just that he had never been this close to the man before. Henry's husky hand produced a firm grip. His dark-blue eyes shone out of a face solemn and resolute. Jeff offered him a chair, but he said he'd rather stand. Not wanting to appear anxious about the visit, Jeff sat leisurely in the chair behind his desk.

"This is not something I take pleasure in doing," Henry said, "but it has to be done. Do you know that your wife is running around town asking questions about my family? She's invading my family's privacy, and I won't stand for it."

Startled, Jeff took a deep breath while he searched for a response. "Excuse me, sir," he finally blurted out, "but I think whoever told you that about my wife has blown things way out of proportion. I'll admit, Lydia's an energetic woman with an active mind, and she's very interested in the people in Tanner, but I'm sure she didn't mean to do anything that would offend you or invade your privacy."

"Hmp. Then she has no idea what's offensive. She's asking about my brother, who died in a terrible accident years ago. If she doesn't think that's offensive to my family—not to mention none of her business—then she's out of her mind." Henry leaned against one of the chairs, grasping the back in clenched fingers.

Jeff's heart raced. "Look, sir, I'm sorry if Lydia hurt your family, but I promise you she didn't mean to. She just gets carried away. You know how women are when they get interested in something." He gave Henry what he hoped was a man-to-man look of understanding.

Henry's face didn't change. "I know when a woman has crossed the line of what's acceptable. And your wife is way over it. Now, I'm telling you to make her stop." Jeff wanted to say something, but he knew better than to refuse Henry Galloway. "And I'm also telling you to keep her away from my house. I better not ever see her at Foxrow again." Henry paused, as if waiting for Jeff to respond.

"I see," Jeff said, his face grown as hard as Henry's.

"This is a serious matter, Dr. Colton, and I hold you responsible for it."

"I realize that," Jeff said.

"I'm not sure you do. Tanner's a close-knit community. We all know each other and respect each other, and that means that what a family wants kept private is kept private. We like it that way, and we'll keep it that way. We don't have room for troublemakers in this town. We don't let them stay." Henry stepped closer to Jeff's desk. "Thank you for your time." Then he turned and left, without looking back.

Jeff didn't move. This was exactly what he had expected to happen. It was what he told Lydia would happen. Slowly, he massaged his forehead. So what was he supposed to do? After a few minutes, he picked up the telephone receiver and dialed.

"Hello, Lydia. Good, you're home. Stay there. I mean it. Don't you dare leave. I'm on my way home. I have to talk to you." He pushed and released the button, then dialed a single digit. "I have to go out for a little while. Apologize to my first appointment, and tell them I'll be back as soon as I can."

On the drive home, Jeff tried to calm down, but the more he thought about what Lydia had done, the more it enraged him.

Lydia had spent the morning cleaning out closets. Not that there was much to clean out, but she was filled with nervous energy. Malcolm was crawling now and screamed if she tried to keep him in the playpen, so she put up the baby gate at the door to her bedroom and let him crawl under the bed with some balls while she went through her closet. She didn't want to take her anxiety out on him. She had been tense ever since she ran into Henry at Foxrow.

She shouldn't have mentioned Howard, but it seemed like the thing to do at the time. Now she didn't know where to look next. The army discharge papers were interesting, but only confirmed what Wilbur had already told her. To have them mean something, she needed to find out what Howard's mental problems were. They probably didn't have anything to do with Henry, but they could. Maybe both twins had a mental illness. Maybe Howard's mental problems caused him to commit suicide. If he had a nervous breakdown, that could have been the case. Lydia's mother had a friend who had a nervous breakdown. That woman said that for a long time she wished she were dead. Or maybe Howard's problems were related to Nancy's condition, even though nobody ever said he was slow. "Mental infirmities" could mean a lot of things.

Lydia's mind whirled as she pulled clothes out of the closet and threw them onto the bed. She was starting on her shoes when Jeff called. After hanging up the receiver, she sat on the bed, her heart pounding. She didn't remember ever hearing him sound so disturbed. Fearing the worst, she picked up Malcolm and took him down to the kitchen, where she poured herself a cup of leftover coffee. It tasted strong and bitter, but the heat of it was soothing. She was sipping it when Jeff burst through the front door.

"Lydia, where are you?" His voice filled the small townhouse.

"In the kitchen." She set her cup down and waited.

Following her voice, he stormed into the room. His face was pale and strained as he looked down at her across the kitchen table. "Henry Galloway came to see me today," he said. Lydia's chest tightened. "He knows you've been asking questions about his brother, and he's furious." Jeff slammed his fist against the Formica counter top. "I told you this was going to happen. I told you to leave them alone. I told you they wouldn't take this lightly, and now you've done it. My career here's probably over. He said it was my responsibility to make sure you stopped asking questions." Jeff began to pace beside the table. Malcolm stared at his father, his eyes wide with bewilderment.

"Why does he feel so threatened?" Lydia asked.

"Didn't you hear me? He threatened *me*."

"But if he's that upset, he must have something to hide."

"It doesn't matter if he's hiding something or not. This is over for you." Jeff stopped pacing and glowered at her. "He also said that you have to stay away from Nancy, and you are not to ever set foot at Foxrow again." Lydia's feeling of defiance when he mentioned Nancy must have shown on her face because he immediately shouted, "Don't you get it? This is not me asking nicely for you to do something. This is Henry Galloway telling you what to do, and you will do it."

Lydia gathered a whimpering Malcolm onto her lap. "Why will I do it?"

"Because you want to live in this town. Because if you care at all about me and my career, you'll do it." Jeff took hold of her forearm. "Because you love me, you'll do it."

Somewhere in that angry face, Lydia saw the man she thought she loved. Their life together had been so hard for the last year or so—the stress of the baby and the fact that even the joy of the baby had not gotten rid of the longing she felt.

"I do love you," she said, but she couldn't go on. Besides Malcolm, the main reason she got out of bed in the morning was the possibility that she might learn something new about the Galloways.

"Then you're through with the Galloways."

Lydia studied her husband's face as she stroked the head of her son perched in her lap. She didn't want to give up the Galloways—she wasn't sure she could give up the Galloways—not when she was so close to understanding what they were about.

"And you won't see Nancy anymore." Jeff's voice was firm.

Nancy was going to be devastated over losing her friend, and Lydia didn't want to give up Nancy. Nancy needed a friend. She needed somebody to push her to do more than she was doing. And nobody seemed to care about that except Lydia.

"Say something." Jeff leaned across the table, bringing his face close to hers.

Lydia straightened her shoulders and met his gaze. "No," she said.

"No?" Jeff reared back as if he'd been slapped. "You are the most selfish, obstinate woman I have ever known. You don't give a damn about me or Malcolm. All you care about is yourself. You've always been like this. You jerked me around like a toy on a string until you got what you wanted. And now you're willing to throw it all away, and for what? To prove you're smarter than everybody else in town? Or more powerful? The only one able to drag up details about something that nobody gives a damn about anymore?"

"You think I'm the selfish one?" Lydia couldn't believe he would say that. "You're the one who made me come to this town. You're the one who told me what to do when we got here. You're the one who thinks you can run all our lives." Malcolm twisted in her lap, trying to climb down, but the muscles in her arms locked around him.

"Me?" Sweat dotted Jeff's forehead. "All I'm trying to do is earn a living. Why the hell can't you appreciate what all I do for you? I've given you a home and a good place to live. I'm not asking a lot from you. In fact, almost nothing in return for what I'm willing to give you, if you'll just quit being so goddamn stubborn. But that's not good enough for you. You know what? You're an ungrateful bitch. You don't deserve me or Malcolm."

Lydia's mind was reeling. "You pompous ass. You, with your hotshot country club golfing buddies and your know-it-all attitude about this town and its goddamn politics. You don't know squat about what makes people tick, and I tell you what, brother, you don't know me at all. You think being somebody big in this little town is important. Well, it's not. If you've got some hang-up about who your family was here twenty years ago, don't take it out on me. Grow up, Jeff. Get to know who your family really is and what we really need."

"Shut up!" Jeff thrust his arm across the table, knocking the sugar bowl, napkin holder, and salt and pepper shakers crashing to the floor. Malcolm screamed at the commotion and launched a series of piercing wails. "Don't tell me what to do," Jeff yelled above the noise. "I'm the one taking care of us. I'm the one earning a living and paying the bills, and I was doing a damn good job of it until you decided to sabotage me. You. You're the one causing trouble. You're the one who has the town in an uproar. You're the one who couldn't keep your nose out of other people's business. It's your fault, Lydia. It's all your fault."

Malcolm's screams grew shriller as he clutched at Lydia's blouse with tiny, sweaty fists. His face was turning red, and Lydia felt her own face flush as tears rose in her eyes. Maybe she was wrong. She really thought the risk she was taking was worth it, but now she wasn't so sure. Maybe the whole summer was a mistake. The whole summer—except for Nancy.

"All right," she said. "I give up. You win. I will never ask another question about Henry or Howard Galloway." Jeff's lips curled in triumph. "But," she continued, "I can't give up on Nancy. I just can't. She'd be heartbroken. She trusts me as her friend. And you don't know what they're doing to her. They keep her boxed up like some fragile doll. I can still be friends with her without ever setting foot at Foxrow again. Henry doesn't have to know." Hadn't they kept their library meetings hidden from Caroline for months? And now Lydia had this idea for getting Nancy a life of her own. She couldn't let that go. "You'll see. It'll be all right." Tears slid down her cheeks onto Malcolm's head. She clutched the baby close as her gut churned.

"No, it won't." Jeff's voice was raspy, strained. "I told you what Henry wants. There's no halfway here."

"Please, Jeff. For me, there has to be."

"No. You can't do this to us." Jeff pounded his palm with the fist of his other hand. "I won't let you. You're bound and determined to destroy me, aren't you?" He stopped pounding. "But I'll be damned if I'm going to stand around while you do it."

He swung around and stormed out of the kitchen. Lydia squeezed her crying baby closer to her. Jeff wasn't going to believe anything she said. He didn't care how she felt. She clung tightly to Malcolm as his father went out the front door and slammed it behind him.

15

If Jeff hadn't had patients waiting for him at the office, he would have driven the Mustang to South Carolina, where nobody knew him, and found some sleazy bar to drink away his frustration. How could Lydia be so blind? But he couldn't just run away, and by the time he finished five hours of patients, the urge had left him. He didn't have the energy to drive that far. He expected all afternoon that Lydia would call him or come to the office, but she didn't, and now he had to decide where to go. He would not go home, that was certain. He'd have to find a motel room because he wasn't about to tell any of his friends what was happening. And it would have to be a motel outside of Tanner, or word would get out.

But before he did anything, he had to eat. He had missed lunch, and the two Snickers bars he found in his desk weren't enough. He didn't want to go to a local restaurant by himself because that would cause talk. There was only one place he could go that wouldn't raise suspicion: the hospital cafeteria. He often ate lunch there and sometimes dinner during the week if he had to see a patient in the evening. The food wasn't spectacular, but it was cheap and plentiful.

He parked in the doctors' lot and went in through the back door. The small cafeteria, which served hospital staff only, was tucked into a corner of the basement. Pausing at the entrance, he surveyed the area, hoping to see no one he knew well. A group of orderlies in green scrubs were gathered at a round table, and a few nurses were scattered about at tables for two and four. A couple of doctors Jeff knew just in passing were waiting in line with their trays. He slunk in behind them and took a tray.

After choosing the baked spaghetti, he hurried through the cashier line and sat at a table hidden behind a post. He shoveled in the hot pasta, but it didn't make him feel any better. His life was a disaster. His wife had slipped out of touch with reality, and it looked like the only way to spare his medical practice from the damage she was doing was to separate himself from her. So that's what it came down to—a choice between his family and his career. He stirred the remaining strands of spaghetti around on his plate.

"Mind if I sit down?" Joanna stood in front of him, holding a tray of food.

"I guess not."

"So how's old Wilbur doing?" She set down her tray and took a seat across from him. "God love him, I hear he's taken a real liking to you."

Jeff twisted his mouth into a smirk. "I don't think it's me he likes so much. And he's not going to like me at all when I make him go home."

"Don't eat your heart out over that. Everybody knows he needs to get up out of that bed. Just nobody's had the gumption to make him do it. He's a pitiful old rich man."

Joanna dumped a liberal amount of salt on her chef's salad before she took a bite. Jeff shoved his plate aside, his eyes focused on the table while she chewed. Her perfectly manicured fingernails fluttered around her wooden salad bowl as she laid her knife across the bowl's edge and picked at the tomato wedges with her fork.

"What happened to happy Jeff?" she asked. "You're back down in the dumps, even lower than before."

"It's a long story, and it's something I can't talk about."

"Hey, we go back a long way. If you want an old friend to just listen, I'm here." When Jeff didn't respond, she went on eating her salad. Neither of them spoke. Jeff had nothing to say, but he liked the comfort of being with Joanna. She had a lightness about her, and at the moment, she was probably the only person in Tanner who gave a damn about him. So he sat in silence, soaking up her nearness, for as long as he could before he had to find a motel and deal with his life.

Joanna finished her salad and glanced at her watch. "My dinner break's about over. Is there anything I can do for you before I go back to work?" Compassion showed in her eyes.

"I guess not. I need to get going too."

They gathered their dining debris onto their trays, dropped them at the dishwasher's window, then walked out of the cafeteria toward the back door. Jeff expected Joanna to get on the elevator, but she didn't. She followed him out to the parking lot.

The sun had sunk behind the trees and hills, leaving the sky a milky blue, with a few clouds drifting lazily along. Soon evening would envelop the air in a purple haze. Jeff felt alone, more alone than he had ever felt before. The familiar surroundings seemed strange and haunting. Only the sense of Joanna next to him seemed right, like she belonged with him. She had said nothing since they left the cafeteria but stayed close to him.

When he reached the Mustang, he turned suddenly, pulled her to him, and kissed her. Her body was warm and tender, and at first, she returned the kiss. Then she backed away from him.

"Are you sure you want to do this?" she asked.

Jeff explored her face, surprised by his actions, as well as hers. She was beautiful in the fading light. He wanted nothing more than to pull her to him again. He was so alone. Betrayed by his wife. In the jumble of thoughts in his mind, the idea that Joanna had been seriously flirting with him for months became clear.

"Please," he said. "You asked me if I needed a friend tonight. I do, I really do." He reached for her, and she kissed him, setting his nerves on fire. "When's your shift over?" he asked when she released him.

"Not until eleven. But I'll tell them I'm sick and get out of here now. It's a quiet night. They won't miss me. Wait here."

Jeff nodded. She kissed him quickly, then turned toward the hospital. He watched her glide through the early twilight, a brawl of emotions beating against his chest.

When she returned a few minutes later, she pointed at her convertible and told him to follow her. She drove slowly, so he had no trouble keeping her in sight as she led him to a new apartment complex built on the land where Tanner's premier funeral home had once stood. Jeff was surprised when she passed the street he remembered as hers—a winding lane, dotted with one-story clapboard houses—but of course, she didn't still live with her parents. Daylight was fading quickly as they entered Joanna's first-floor apartment.

"It's small," she said. "But at least it's mine."

Jeff shrugged. "It's nice," he said. He could have been in a condemned warehouse, and he wouldn't have cared.

"Can I get you a drink?" Joanna tossed her purse onto a table.

"Sure." Jeff trailed her into the kitchen.

She took a new bottle of Jim Beam from the cabinet, poured some of the amber liquid over ice in two glasses, and pushed one into his hand. He took a long swallow and watched her sip from hers. She studied him, as if she were waiting for something to happen.

Finally, she said, "Okay, Jeff. What's eating you? Is it your job? Your family?"

He struggled to find a way to explain without revealing too much. He didn't want anyone, including Joanna, to know how his wife had offended Henry Galloway. But if he didn't say something, she might not let him stay, and at the moment, that was what he needed most. She was so beautiful.

"It's Lydia," he said. "She turned on me like some kind of vulture. She ripped apart everything I've worked for in Tanner. She doesn't care what happens to me. It's like I don't even exist anymore." His stomach tightened. "She just doesn't give a damn." He took another swallow of bourbon to wash away the memory of his wife's unflinching face. The way she sat there and refused to cooperate.

Joanna set her glass on the counter and slid her arms around his neck. She pressed against him, lacing small kisses along the edge of his jaw.

"I care what happens to you," she said. "I've always cared what happens to you." Jeff pulled her mouth to his with the fierceness of the animal clawing inside him. She tasted wild and satisfying. He forced his fingers into the tight French twist of her hair, sending hairpins flying. She was real, concrete, something he could get his hands on, and she led him to the cluttered intimacy of her bedroom. As they lay on her bed and hastily removed each other's clothes, he felt himself watching from the bedside, cheering them on, like a spectator at a wrestling match. Each bend of a knee or arch of a back brought more cheers until the final surrender, but they both won. Lydia was the one who lost.

At eight thirty the next morning, Jeff opened his eyes and stared in horror at the sunlight on the ceiling above Joanna's bed. He grabbed the clock radio and cursed himself for not setting the alarm. He was late for visiting patients at the hospital. There was no way he could see them now and still be on time for his first office appointment. *Shit!*

He dressed hurriedly while he debated whether to wake Joanna. Her blonde hair lingered across her face, like the wispy ends of dreams. Smiling, he quietly closed the bedroom door and slipped out the front. He would grab a cup of coffee at the drug store and go straight to his office. Give himself some time to catch up on yesterday's appointment notes, which he had completely ignored after Henry's visit. He could go by the hospital late that afternoon. If he waited until then, Joanna would be back on duty.

His fingers began to beat out a rhythm on the Mustang's steering wheel at the thought of another night with Joanna, when a jarring idea hit him. What if she told somebody at the hospital about them? The possibility was so disturbing that he forgot about the coffee and found himself sitting in the parking lot of his building.

"You fool," he said to himself. "If, by some miracle, Henry Galloway doesn't run you out of town, you're still ruined if word gets around that you're sleeping with one of the nurses at the hospital."

He rubbed his hand over his wrinkled shirt and wondered if anyone would notice he was wearing the same tie he had on the day before. He had to get back home to get some more clothes, but he didn't want to see Lydia. He never wanted to see her again. He slammed the car door and went into the building. He hoped Joanna's phone number was in the book.

When Jeff didn't come home that night or the next morning, Lydia called Suzanne. "For crying out loud, girl. You and Malcolm get yourselves over here right now," Suzanne said. "What has that man done to y'all now?"

So Lydia put Malcolm into the car and drove downtown. The stores were just beginning to open, with merchants sweeping the sidewalks in front of their doors or slipping off to the drug store for a cup of coffee and a Hostess Twinkie to start the day. Because the shoppers weren't out yet, Lydia found a parking place on the street in front of Suzanne's apartment. The hardware store owner, who was cleaning his display window, waved to her as she passed through the door at the foot of the stairs, and she waved back.

How can he be so fucking happy when my life's such a mess? she wondered. Do I look happy to him? Maybe his life's a mess too.

At the head of the stairs, Suzanne stood in the open doorway, with Frankie astride her hip. She was wearing a bib apron, and her hair had a bad case of frizz, like she'd just come in from a thunder storm. After hustling Lydia and Malcolm inside, she herded them into her tiny kitchen, where she put a cold Coke in Lydia's hand.

"Sit down, sugar, and tell me everything that happened," she said. "I wanna hear it all, but I have to time this steam. Give me a minute or two."

She turned to a heavy canner that covered two burners on her stove. Steam shot like a geyser out of the petcock as Suzanne watched the clock above the refrigerator. After two minutes, she closed the valve, checked the round pressure gauge, adjusted the heat, then looked back at Lydia. "So?" she said.

Lydia related every detail she could remember about Henry's visit with Jeff. Both babies began to squirm, so the women put them on the floor, allowing them to crawl into the living room. Lydia sighed. "Jeff thinks that if I don't do what Henry said, the old man'll turn our lives here into living hell and ruin Jeff's medical practice in the process."

"I've heard tales of shit like that happening." Suzanne reached for her Newports and lit one. "Not quite that bad, but along those lines."

Lydia rubbed her forehead. "Yeah, but you know, I decided that what I was doing was worth that risk. We can go someplace else if we have to. That's not what I'm worried about." She couldn't get Jeff's angry eyes out of her mind. "I'm afraid Jeff's not coming back. He may have left me for good." Saying the words out loud was worse than thinking them.

"Lord, Lydia, what did you say to him?" Suzanne laid her cigarette in the soap dish.

"I gave in. He yelled at me until I promised not to ask any more questions about Howard or Henry."

"Then why'd he leave?"

Lydia leaned over Suzanne's kitchen table and rested her chin in her hands. "Because I said I won't quit being friends with Nancy."

Suzanne wiped sweat from her forehead with a dishtowel. Steam from the pressure cooker had condensed on the kitchen walls and slid toward the floor in wavy trails. "Why in the name of heaven did you do that?"

"Because if I leave her now, she'll go right back to being like she was before, with no friends, cooped up like some kid with no say-so in her life. She's got not one iota of an idea about who she is or who she could be. She ought to get a job, but they're sure as hell not going to help her do it. It's like they don't see her. She's not real to them. She might as well be invisible."

Suzanne's expression suggested her mind had drifted somewhere else. "You know, you said that one time before."

"Said what?"

"That stuff about being invisible. You used those exact same words, but you weren't talking about Nancy. You were talking about you. All that stuff about not being real—you said that about you. Remember?"

Lydia sat up straighter, her mind grabbing at what her friend had said. "You're right. Goddamn it, you're right."

She jumped up from the table, knocking her chair over backward. Her awful spells of restlessness might have eased over the summer, but not the feelings of being unimportant, of not being taken seriously. Like those damn houses that Jeff wanted so badly. It didn't seem to matter what she thought. And why hadn't Jeff stood up for her with Henry Galloway? He caved in like she was some disobedient child. Good Lord, in a lot of ways, she was treated as much like a child as Nancy.

"You are so right, Suzanne," she said.

In her haste to hug her friend, she knocked over a couple of jars of green beans waiting on the counter for their bath in the canner. As beans and water poured onto the floor, Lydia walked back and forth in the tiny kitchen. "Nancy and me. We're so much alike. I don't know why I didn't see it before."

Suzanne squatted to wipe up the mess on the floor. "So what does that mean?"

"It means I need to fight for both of us. And I sure can't leave Nancy."

"What about Jeff? He's your husband, for Christ's sake. You love him, don't you?"

Lydia stopped walking. She had fallen in love with Jeff so gradually that it seemed like an organic thing that grew up between them and bound them to each other. It was part of who they were. At least it was back when she knew who she was. But now, like everything else familiar about her, it was slipping away.

"I know I used to love him," she said, "and I know I need him. And I sure as hell don't want him to leave me. But he's going to have to understand about Nancy and about me."

Suzanne shook her head. She had cleaned up the floor and thrown the dirty beans into the sink. "Well, I think you oughta give him some time to cool off," she said. "Men are like that. They blow up and need time to think about things, but they come to their senses later. If you don't hear from him by tomorrow, call him at his office. I bet he'll want to hear from you."

Lydia wasn't sure she would call him, but she would think about it.

Suddenly Suzanne looked over at the pressure cooker, which she had ignored through the whole conversation. "Oh, Lord. These beans are done." She cut off the burners beneath the cooker. "How about I fix you some eggs while this thing cools off? Did you eat any breakfast?"

Lydia shook her head, inspiring Suzanne to seize the skillet from the drawer beneath the oven.

After eating, Lydia hung around as long as she could, not wanting to be alone, but as the heat in the apartment rose with each batch of beans and Malcolm grew tired and fussy, she knew she had to go home.

"You're welcome to stay," Suzanne said. "I don't have to start making calls until two." But Lydia gathered up Malcolm and his things and left.

She drove home in the bright sunlight, wondering what Jeff's next move would be and if anyone had told Nancy they couldn't be friends. Through the long afternoon, she washed every scrap of laundry she could find, including the sheets and towels. Outside, the temperature climbed into the nineties, forcing the window air conditioners to work overtime. Lydia worried that it would be too hot in Malcolm's room for him to take a nap, but he managed to sleep for several hours. As she sat on the couch folding Jeff's T-shirts, she took comfort in the routine of it—her never-ending, rarely changing routine. And if he came back for his clothes, they might as well be clean.

Around five o'clock, she started rummaging through the kitchen cabinets, figuring out what to feed Malcolm for dinner—strained this or strained that—and looking for anything that might be appetizing to her. She hadn't eaten since Suzanne's eggs, but she still wasn't hungry.

Standing in the kitchen, she heard the front door open and close. The sound startled, then disturbed her. It had to be Jeff. No one else would walk in like that. Nervously, she waited for him to find her. When she heard nothing, she peeked into the living room. He was nowhere in sight, so he must have gone upstairs. Lydia's breathing quickened. She waited at the foot of the stairs, not knowing what to say to him. In the stillness, the thud of drawers opening and closing drifted down from above. She knew what he was doing. After minutes that seemed like hours, he came down the stairs, carrying a suitcase in each hand. His face was hard and tense.

"Where're you going?" she asked.

"I have a place to stay," he said.

"I have to know where you are, in case I need you for the baby."

"I'll call you."

And then he was gone.

Lydia sat on the steps, her knees suddenly weak. She was alone, with no idea where her husband was going or when he would return. Part of her was so angry with him, she wanted to scream. Since the beginning, he had never tried to see her side, never tried to work through it with her.

Yet part of her blamed herself. What was wrong with her that she couldn't be happy with things the way they were? Why did she have to get involved with the Galloways? But mostly, she was scared. What would she do if Jeff didn't come back? Thinking about the upheaval that would cause was so overwhelming she forced herself to focus only on the most immediate concern. She'd need money to take care of Malcolm. She pushed herself to her feet and went to the desk in the living room. The bank books showed money in both the checking account and the savings account. She was okay, for a while.

16

"It ain't right. It just ain't right. Keeping Lydia away from Nancy with the way Nancy dotes on her. What these folks thinking? And just when Miss Caroline was starting to like her a little." Stella clucked her tongue and rocked furiously in the chair beside the kitchen fireplace at Foxrow.

She had just about worn Pansy out, telling her what Caroline said about Lydia not being welcome at the farm ever again. In fact, she talked about it so much that Pansy went outside into the stifling afternoon air to string the beans for dinner rather than listen to her any more. It didn't matter. Pansy couldn't do anything about it.

Nancy had cried and cried when Caroline told her. Then she locked herself in her room and said she was not coming out until they changed their minds. Tom had been the one who finally coaxed her out for supper, but she had gone right back upstairs after she ate and stayed there most of the next day.

Stella hated to see her torture herself like that. She might seem happy and carefree most of the time, but Stella knew how fragile her feelings were. She loved everyone and expected everyone to love her back, and when someone hurt her, it cut her to the quick. Stella couldn't help but think that Tom's involvement with Lydia had caused at least part of the problem. Nancy and Lydia's friendship seemed so innocent and peaceful until he stepped into the picture. But maybe that was unfair. He said that the questions about Henry and his brother started with Lydia. Stella rocked and rocked and rocked. Whatever happened, Tom could take care of himself, but Nancy, now Nancy was another story. Nancy needed looking after, and Stella should know. She'd been doing it for twenty-three years.

Eventually, Pansy came back into the kitchen. "How long are you gonna sit there and rock?" she asked. "There ain't one thing you can do about this. She ain't your daughter. She belongs to Mr. Henry and Miss Caroline, and what they say goes. You just gonna have to live with it."

Stella's nose twitched. "I ain't so sure Miss Caroline wants this. I think it's all Mr. Henry's doing. I seen her face when she was telling Nancy about it, and she weren't happy."

"Don't make no never mind." Pansy rinsed the beans in a large metal colander, tossed them into a tall pot, covered them with water, and dropped in a chunk of fatback. Then she put the pot on the stove and turned on the heat. Water droplets that had splashed onto the outside of the pot slid down the sides and sizzled when they hit the hot burner.

"I'm telling you, Miss Stella, you might as well go on about your business and quit worrying yourself to death."

"Well, somebody's gotta worry about that child, and I may not have any say-so in this house, but when I takes her to town, she's mine." Stella stomped her foot on the floor. "And I do just as I please. If they think I won't, then they don't know me."

Pansy raised her eyebrows and took a bowl of washed blackberries out of the refrigerator. As she was mixing sugar in with them, Stella got up from the rocking chair and walked toward the stairs that led to her bedroom over the kitchen.

"There ain't no accounting for accidents, now is there?" she called over her shoulder.

Two days later Stella and Nancy left Foxrow for their usual morning visit to the library. Nancy hadn't wanted to go. She was still sulking in her bedroom, coming out only for meals, but Stella had lured her into the kitchen after dinner the night before and whispered to her that, if she went to the library, she might find a secret surprise.

Although she seemed excited about the surprise, Nancy was quiet on the ride into town. She had brought along two books that needed to be returned to the library. Sitting in the front seat of the car next to Stella, she silently flipped through one of them. Stella wondered what was going on in her mind—whether she suspected what the surprise might be and would she feel happy or guilty about it. Stella often wondered what was going on in Nancy's mind. She certainly didn't let on about everything.

Stella parked the Lincoln under a maple tree at the edge of the library lot next to the river. "A little shade just might keep the heat outa here while we gone," she said.

Down low in its banks because there hadn't been any rain for weeks, the river snaked along almost soundlessly. Even the waterfall was so thin it gurgled rather than roared. The air smelled dry and brown, like the grass at the edge of the road. Stella and Nancy, clutching her books, hurried into the coolness of the library's main room.

Only a few senior citizens were scattered about in the most comfortable chairs. Since there was no story hour that morning, the mothers were home with their children. Over by the windows, Stella and Nancy's favorite chairs were empty, as if waiting for them. Stella settled Nancy into one of the chairs and told her she was going to get a drink of water. Back by the door, she searched the room for the familiar black hair, but it was nowhere in sight.

As the librarian came through the door, the sound of baby stroller wheels creaking and scratching on the hardwood floor floated in from the front room. Stella pulled open the door, and there she was. Pushing Malcolm in his stroller, Lydia was on her way in.

"Lord, I'm so happy y'all came," Stella said. "Like I said on the phone, Nancy, she needs to see you."

"I need to see her too," Lydia said. Her face was pinched with worry lines Stella hadn't seen before, causing the old woman to wonder if Nancy was the only thing on her mind.

"Mr. Henry wrong to keep y'all apart. Nancy's been crying ever since Miss Caroline told her."

"I felt like crying too." Lydia patted Stella's thin shoulder. "I was glad when you called."

Stella held the door for Lydia to push the stroller through, while Malcolm chewed contentedly on a teething ring and stared at the rows of colored books on the shelves. When they rounded the last row of shelves leading to the windows, Nancy's face lit up like candles on a birthday cake.

"Lydia," she cried, causing the few old folks who were within hearing distance to look up from their magazines and newspapers.

Stella shushed her immediately, but Lydia leaned over and hugged her. "We're still friends, Nancy," she said. "We always will be."

"I was afraid I'd never see you again."

"We can't meet at your house anymore, but we can meet here."

"Long as you don't tell nobody, and we don't cause no scene," Stella said. "So keep your voice down. Don't talk like you some farmhand calling the cows."

Nancy stifled a giggle, while Stella tried to maintain a stern expression. If somebody took notice of their little gathering and mentioned it to one of the older Galloways, she could argue that they just happened to run into Lydia, but she didn't want to take that chance.

"No cows," Nancy said. Then she turned to Lydia with a puzzled face. "Why won't Granddaddy let you come see me anymore? Is it because of our treasure hunt? That's the last thing we did together."

"No. It has nothing to do with you or with anything you did," Lydia said quickly. "It's more to do with me." Her voice dropped into a pensive pool that surprised Stella.

"Is it because you wanted other people to see my sewing?"

"I don't think they knows about that, sugar," Stella said. "Do they?" She directed the question to Nancy, but she was really asking Lydia.

"No, it wasn't that, either, but I hope you've thought about what I said. I'm glad you told Stella." Lydia squeezed Nancy's hand.

"She told me about it, but I ain't so sure what I thinks of it."

"It's too soon for anybody to know what to think about it," Lydia said. "I need to get us more information. Do you want me to get more information, Nancy?"

Nancy smiled. "Darn tootin'," she said and giggled.

"Then, darn tootin', I will." Lydia leaned over to pick up the teething ring that Malcolm had thrown on the floor. "Did you finish that book?" she asked, pointing at the book in Nancy's hands.

"Yes. It was good." Nancy turned the book over to show Lydia the front cover, which had a picture of a large black horse with a white star on its forehead. "It's about horses, and it's told by a horse. He's a good storyteller." Nancy giggled again, and Lydia laughed too, as the worry lines in her face relaxed.

Yes, they does get along good, Stella thought. *It's like they understands each other.* Stella loved Nancy, but she didn't always understand her. She enjoyed being with her up to a point, but Stella was getting old, and some days she was just plain tired of the responsibility of Nancy. When Nancy was a little girl, Stella had more energy and could answer her frequent questions and take her where she wanted to go. But now, it was getting harder, and Stella had her own daydreams—dreams of settling down with her son, Sam, and his sweet wife and children. Just last week, Sam had brought the subject up again.

"Mama, why in the name of Jesus won't you quit that job and come live with me and Sharon and the kids?" he had asked. "You know those white folks don't appreciate you. You give 'em your heart and soul for years, and what have they ever given you in return? They're gonna make you run their errands and look after their girl till you drop. You don't have to do that no more. I can take care of you."

"I know that, Sammy," Stella said. "You done good, and I'm proud of you. But you ought not to talk that way about the Galloways."

"I'll say whatever I please about them bloodsuckers. A bunch of money don't give 'em the right to work you to death. Come on, Mama. We have a room just waiting for you. And you won't have to do nothing you don't wanna do. No more driving that big old car all over town. No more shopping for things you don't care nothing about. And no more picking up after a house full of folks who can't pick up after theirselves."

It sure sounded tempting. Stella had tried to imagine herself a lady of leisure.

"But if you wanna, and only if you wanna," he said, "you can tend to your grandchildren once in a while. Cook 'em some of those recipes of yours that they like so much, and tell 'em some of those stories they love to hear about the old days. They're crazy about you, and you know, Mama, they're growing up fast."

That's God's truth, Stella had thought. *One of 'em married with a baby, and the others in high school already.*

"Pretty soon, they're gonna all be up and gone, living somewhere off on their own. I tell you, Mama, you better come quick."

Stella had sighed and said what she always said. "You knows I can't leave Foxrow. Not now. I can't leave Nancy. If I leaves, who's that child gonna have to spend time with? And who's gonna take her into town? She'll spend ever waking moment out to Foxrow." The thought of that made Stella cringe. "No, Sammy. I just have to buck up my strength and keep going." Even more than all Stella's children and grandchildren, she knew that—right now—Nancy needed her the most.

The soft sound of Nancy's and Lydia's voices and laughter flowed like music. Stella smiled at the two women, deep into an animated conversation. Then she let her eyes rest on the shrunken river creeping over the fall.

Malcolm grew tired of chewing on the teething ring and of sitting still. He began to squirm to get out of the stroller, so Lydia set him on her lap, but he didn't want to sit there, either. He wanted to get down and crawl around, exploring the library, which Lydia knew would be a disaster.

"I'm going to take him for a ride in the stroller," she said. "I'll come back when he's settled down a bit."

Nancy wanted to go too, but Stella said they were better off waiting in their chairs by the window. Nancy's face puckered in a pout, but she did what Stella said.

Sally Whitney

Lydia rolled Malcolm quickly into the library's front room and parked him and the stroller in front of the librarian's desk. Despite everything that was going on, she couldn't put off her quest to get Nancy out into the world. If she was going to do it, she had to do it now. Otherwise, Nancy would lose interest, or she'd feel it as just another disappointment.

"Where would I find names and telephone numbers for the county social services department?" Lydia asked the woman behind the desk. After straightening the stack of sign-out cards she was reviewing, the woman pointed her toward a large, black directory on one of the reference shelves.

Lydia spread the book open on a table and flipped to the right county. A little searching and she had the names she wanted. She scribbled them quickly on the back of a blank check she found in her purse. By that time, Malcolm was fidgeting and fussing loudly, so she left the book on the table and pushed him hurriedly into the main room and over to Stella and Nancy.

"We have to leave," she said. "He's not going to settle down again this morning."

"Don't go," Nancy said.

"I have to, but we'll get together again, I promise."

"Let's us walk out with y'all," Stella said. "It's near about time for us to be leaving, anyhow." She looked at the heavy time piece on her wrist, causing Lydia to quiver, remembering where she got it. "Lord, yes. It's near about noon. We got to be going too." The old woman placed her hands firmly on the arms of her chair and pushed herself to her feet. "Come on, sugar," she said to Nancy. "Don't you forget to turn in that book."

Nancy rose slowly, frowning like a stubborn child. The three women and the baby left the main room, passed by the librarian's desk to drop off the book, and were soon outside in the hot summer day. Stella pulled the ever-present handkerchief from her pocket and wiped her forehead. "Lord, if this heat don't break soon, we all gonna melt," she said, dabbing at her cheeks and mouth with the piece of cloth.

"I'd just as soon melt, if I can't see Lydia," Nancy said, still frowning.

"We will see each other. I promise." Lydia tried to keep the exasperation out of her voice. Sometimes it took a long time to make Nancy understand something. "Let's set a date right now. How about Monday morning at ten, back here?"

Nancy smiled her agreement. Lydia looked at Stella. "Yes, ma'am, we can do that. Far as I know. Just don't tell nobody," the old woman said.

Lydia knew Stella was taking a big chance by bringing Nancy to see her, and she hoped the old woman wouldn't pay a price for it. Sometimes great courage was found in the smallest of acts. Impetuously, Lydia kissed Stella's cheek, causing her to cut her black eyes around in surprise.

"Then I'll see y'all on Monday," Lydia said as she pushed Malcolm toward the Camaro. She could hear Nancy chattering excitedly behind her as she and Stella walked in the other direction. Lydia hoped to have some good news for her friend by the time they met again.

While Malcolm took his afternoon nap, Lydia made telephone calls. Working her way through the county bureaucracy to find a person who could help her took some effort, but her persistence paid off, and it was good to keep her mind occupied. She finally got in touch with Abigail Price, a social worker who also did work for the North Carolina chapter of the National Association of Retarded Children.

Miss Price's voice was refined, with a softly southern accent, which suggested she had migrated south from the upper reaches of Virginia or maybe Maryland. She was interested in what Lydia had to say about Nancy, but she insisted she would have to talk with Nancy and her mother before she could offer any assistance. That was enough for Lydia at the moment. At least she knew help was out there. Now she had to convince the Galloways to take it.

17

Another night and no word from Jeff. Lydia lay alone in their double bed and listened to the crickets singing under the stars in the cloudless sky. The window air conditioner or even a fan would have given some relief from the sultry air, but Lydia craved the soft stillness of the night and flung open the windows to expose her body, draped only in a thin cotton nightgown.

Seven days and eight nights she had been on her own. She was still angry with Jeff. He hadn't even called to check on his son. And now that she was beginning to understand why she was so unhappy with her life, she wanted to shake him for not seeing what was happening to her. Over and over since he had been gone, she wanted to fly into his office and scream at him for letting all this happen and then walking out on her, but what always stopped her was the nagging voice that said part of it was her fault. Thinking about that kept her weighted down and motionless. If she had seen her life more clearly and found another way out besides the Galloways, maybe things could have been different. But then she wouldn't have gotten to know Nancy.

She twisted in the damp bed, clutching the pillow for comfort. She wanted to go back to when summer was new and start over. She wanted Jeff lying here beside her, like always. Gingerly, she ran her fingers down the side of the bed where his body was supposed to be.

Maybe she should at least call him, but she wanted him to call her. If she ran out of money, she would have to call him. So far, he hadn't taken any money out of their bank accounts, so she had that, although he had access and certainly could empty them. She could ask her parents for money, but she didn't want to tell them about Jeff. She could see the look of pity and disdain that would spread across their faces when they heard. To tell them was to admit failure as a wife and mother. She couldn't do that.

Maybe Jeff would call her today. Surely, he had had time to cool off and think things through. She would try again to explain why she felt so strongly about Nancy and assure him that she had kept her promise to drop the matter of Howard entirely. She was nearly bursting to find out what Howard's medical discharge papers meant, but she had done nothing about them. And she missed working with Tom, but she had stayed away. She would tell Jeff that. If he would meet her halfway, they could start over. Lying alone on the crumpled sheets, she shivered in spite of the heat. What if he refused to give in at all?

A streetlight cast a yellow haze on the wall opposite the bedroom window. Lydia stared at the haze, watching all her fears play out in its shadows until dawn. She got up before Malcolm began to stir and made a large pot of coffee. It was Monday, and she had promised Nancy she would meet her at the library. Remembering her conversation with Miss Price made Lydia smile faintly. At least she had something good to tell Nancy.

As she expected, Nancy was delighted with the news. But soon after Lydia explained about Miss Price, she drew Stella to another part of the library to talk with her alone.

"We have to set up a meeting," she said, "for you and me and Nancy and the social worker. And Caroline has to be there, and Tom should be there too."

"Tom? What we need him for?" The creases in Stella's forehead deepened.

"Because, believe it or not, he cares about Nancy. I think he'll be on our side, and he might help talk his mother into it."

"What you mean by 'our side'? And what's this Miss Price gonna do for Nancy?"

"She's going to help her find a life outside of Foxrow."

"Where? Doing what?"

"I don't know. That's why we have to talk to her. I still think Nancy is smart enough and has enough skills to get a job with a regular employer."

"I ain't so sure that's good for Nancy."

"Do you want her to spend the rest of her life at Foxrow?"

"No." Stella sucked in her thin lips and lowered her eyebrows.

"Then talk to Tom. Have him talk to Caroline. And don't tell her I'm going to be there, or she won't come."

The expression on Stella's wrinkled face turned thoughtful. "That might not make no difference. She was beginning to kinda see that you was good for Nancy before Mr. Henry said you wasn't allowed out to Foxrow no more."

Lydia couldn't help but smile at that. "Really?" she asked, and Stella nodded. "Well, I've got a feeling she won't like what we're going to talk about anyway, so you better make something up."

Stella's chest heaved. "Where we gonna meet?"

"At my friend Suzanne's. Tom knows where it is."

"I reckon I can give it a try," Stella said and went to check on Nancy.

———

They arranged the meeting for Wednesday afternoon before Labor Day. Suzanne left the apartment clean and tidy, although somewhat warm, with a hint of boiled turnip greens in the air. Lydia tried to crank up the window air conditioner, but it only sputtered and continued to spit out semi-cool air.

Miss Price was the first to arrive. A pleasantly stout woman with large round glasses, she was panting a little after climbing the stairs to Suzanne's front door. Inside the apartment, she dropped into Suzanne's beloved rocking chair and set her over-sized canvas carry-all on the floor beside her. Lydia offered her a Coke, but she declined and asked for water instead. As the two women talked about the current heat wave, Tom knocked on the door.

"I'm glad you came," Lydia said softly as she let him in. "We need your support."

After introductions, it took him fewer than five minutes to charm Miss Price and have her leaning toward him as he sat on the couch next to Lydia. He was in the middle of a story about his experiences at the county courthouse when Nancy's voice sounded from the stairs, high-pitched and excited in the new surroundings. Lydia drew a deep breath and inadvertently put her hand on Tom's knee, then jerked it back when she realized what she had done. When she opened the door, Stella stood before her, shielding Nancy and Caroline.

Stella started to speak, but Caroline blurted out, "Lydia! Why is she here? We can't stay." She turned and started down the steps, pulling Nancy with her, but Lydia called after her.

"Wait. Don't go, Mrs. Galloway. Tom's here. We need to talk to you."

Tom ran to the door. "Come back here, Mother," he said. His deep voice bounced off the walls, filling the narrow stairway. Caroline paused and turned to look at her son. Stella stepped out of the way, giving them a clear view of each other.

"Please, Mom," Tom said. "Just come inside for a few minutes and listen to what we have to say."

Nancy stood silently at Caroline's side, her high spirits dashed, her face twisted as if she were about to cry.

Caroline looked from her son to her daughter. "I thought I was coming here to talk about some new charity, not be hoodwinked by my own family. You know we're not supposed to have anything to do with her." She turned to stare at Lydia.

"Just give us a few minutes, okay?" Tom said.

Caroline's frown did not weaken as she slowly returned to the landing. Her broad shoulders squared defiantly as she swished into the apartment and directed her glare at Miss Price.

"How do you do?" Miss Price said, extending her hand. "I'm Abigail Price from the county social services department. I also represent the National Association for Retarded Children."

Caroline's gaze revealed a little interest.

"I've brought some information to show you about opportunities for your daughter," Miss Price continued, widening her eyes behind the large glasses and flashing a smile at Nancy. She seemed undaunted by Caroline. Her voice was soothing, and her chubby hands gestured calmly as she described social groups and classes and sheltered workshops.

"What are you telling me?" Caroline interrupted after about fifteen minutes of Miss Price's talking. "Y'all think Nancy needs to work in a sheltered workshop? For God's sake, why? She's well taken care of, I assure you. She doesn't need to work."

"A lot of our employees don't need the money," Miss Price said. "But they do need to get out in the world. They need to show they can do something that benefits other people. And they need to be around other people besides their families." She turned to Nancy. "Do you have a lot of friends?"

"Lydia's my friend," Nancy replied.

"Who else?"

Nancy shrugged. Miss Price nodded, as if she knew she had made her point.

"Which program do you think would be the best for Nancy?' Lydia asked.

"That depends on what Nancy wants to do. Let me show y'all some pictures of our classes and our biggest sheltered workshop."

Nancy slid out of her chair and crossed the room to look shyly at the pictures.

"Here's our brochure. Can you read this?"

Nancy responded by reading the words on the first page.

"Nancy is educated," Caroline said. "We've seen to it that she has everything she needs, including the best education for her. She has a good life."

Stella, who had scooted deep into Frank Jessop's La-Z-Boy, watched the conversation as if from a distance, arms folded and dark eyes following everything that was said. Occasionally, a hint of a smile played across her mouth, or her forehead wrinkled in concern, but she said nothing.

Tom asked a lot of questions about supervision, locations, times, and travel arrangements, while Nancy wanted to know about other people in the programs.

Caroline sat rigidly in Suzanne's red vinyl club chair until she finally asked, "So how many casualties do y'all have with these programs?"

"What do you mean by casualties?" Miss Price asked. "Our safety standards are really high, if that's what you mean."

"I mean, how many of the folks in your programs come for a while and then drop out because they can't do what y'all expect them to, or they're mistreated by the supervisors or instructors or somebody else in the program?"

Miss Price's smile faded, but her eyes remained steady. "Very few of our people leave the program, and if they do, it's usually because their families move out of the area."

"I'd have to see proof of that," Caroline muttered as she rose from the chair. "I'm sorry. I think we'd better leave now. Let's go, Nancy."

"I don't want to go," Nancy said. "I want to see more." Her face took on a recalcitrant expression that accentuated her resemblance to her mother.

"I've got more information, if you'll just give me a few more minutes." Miss Price reached into her carry-all and grabbed more handouts.

"No, we really have to go." Caroline walked toward the door. "Nancy, Stella, come on."

Nancy didn't move. Stella climbed out of the deep chair and straightened her skirt.

"Nancy." Caroline's voice was sterner; her eyes showed agitation. Still, Nancy didn't move.

"Well, we could get together some other time," Miss Price began.

"No, we don't have to do that," Tom spoke quickly. "I'll take Nancy home when she's ready to go. You go on, Mom."

"Yeah, let's us go on home, Miss Caroline." Stella put her hand on Caroline's back, her voice reassuring. The gesture reminded Lydia that Stella had told her she came to Foxrow originally to take care of Wallace when he was a child, and she was there when Caroline arrived at the farm as a young bride. The relationship between Stella and Caroline had always been ambiguous to Lydia, but she was seeing a small part of it now.

"That's right. You go on with Stella. I'll take care of Nancy. No problem," Tom said.

Caroline must have seen she couldn't insist any more without creating an unpleasant scene in front of a stranger, and her inbred gentility wouldn't let her do that, so she left quietly with Stella.

As Miss Price talked on about activities Nancy might be interested in, Lydia spoke up. "Nancy's really good with a needle and thread. I think she could work in some sort of job that involves sewing."

"If that's what she wants to do, it would have to be with a regular employer. Our workshop doesn't do that type of thing." Miss Price laced her fingers around her knee. "But we've been having a push for the last several years to teach companies about the benefits of employing mentally retarded people. And we've gotten some support from the Department of Labor for on-the-job training. I can sure check around with employers in the area that I think might be interested and willing to do it. Is that what you want, Nancy?"

"I guess so. I like to sew, and I'm good at it."

"We still need your mother to get on board with this." Miss Price's serene face darkened.

"I'll talk to her," Tom said. "We'll work it out. You just find a place for Nancy."

The foursome talked on until everybody ran out of questions and Nancy seemed tired. Miss Price gathered up her materials, gave a few to Nancy to keep, and tucked the rest into her carry-all. She thanked them for inviting her, shook hands all around, and said she'd be in touch soon.

In the apartment, the three who remained stood in a semi-circle, where they'd gathered to say their good-byes. Lydia's anxiety drained away, like she had holes in the bottoms of her feet. She had survived the meeting, and nobody had gotten hurt. Nobody had yelled or stormed out or offended anybody else—at least not too badly. It was a good start.

"Thanks for helping us," she said to Tom. "I wasn't sure you'd go along with this."

Tom put his arm around Nancy. "Me neither, until Stella convinced me to do it. Or at least she convinced me we ought to take a look at it. Nancy deserves a chance to do her own thing." He squeezed his sister, and she let out a giggle. "And I wanted a chance to talk to you." His clear-blue eyes were intense.

"About what?" Lydia knew what he wanted, but she wouldn't say it.

"About Howard. About those discharge papers we found. You can't fink out on me now. We still don't have any answers." He dropped his arm from Nancy's shoulders. She looked down to study the brochure in her hand.

"I can't help you," Lydia said. She didn't want to talk about what happened, but she figured Tom maybe already knew. "I don't know if you know this or not, but your grandfather came to my husband's office and threatened him. Told him to make me stop asking questions about your family. Now Jeff thinks Henry'll make him lose his medical practice here, so I promised I'd stop."

"And what the hell do you call this?" The blue eyes suddenly blazed. "If this isn't asking questions or at least messing with my family, I don't know what is. You pulled almost the whole damn family into a meeting with a social worker. What do you think my mother's going to say to my grandfather about that?"

Lydia's muscles tensed. She didn't want Tom turning on her. "I'll bet she won't say anything, thank you very much. Stella told me Caroline was starting to like me until your grandfather stepped in. This is between us and her, and I thought you were on my side, anyway."

"I am. But if I help you, you have to help me."

Nancy looked up from the brochure in her hand as Tom's voice grew more irate. "Don't get mad at Lydia," she said.

"I'm not mad at Lydia," Tom said, regaining his composure. "I just need her help."

If Tom only knew how much Lydia wanted to help him. She still thought Howard deserved that much. But she had promised, and she was afraid of what might happen to Malcolm and her if Jeff didn't come home.

"I told Jeff I wouldn't mess with anybody in your family except Nancy," she said. "I can't abandon Nancy. But I can't do anything else."

"Abandon me? What do you mean? What are you going to do?" Nancy asked.

"I'm not going to do anything. I'm just minding my own business."

"So what happens now?" Tom's voice had regained some of its edge. "I'm not ready to give up. I didn't promise anybody anything."

"Good. Then you can keep digging on your own. And I'll give you any suggestions I can, as long as nobody finds out they came from me." This was walking a thin line, Lydia knew, but technically Tom would be doing the probing.

"And I'll help," Nancy said with glee.

"So where should I start?" Tom asked. "I've already checked out the public library in Charlotte for information about mental health discharges during World War I. I tried to find out why they were usually given, but I came up empty. I've never heard anybody mention that Howard was sick when he came home or even had combat fatigue. He just went back to work at the mill, as far as I've ever heard. It doesn't make sense."

"Talk to Dr. Evans. Maybe Dr. Cathey told him something about Howard. Or maybe he knows about mental health discharges. He told me about the third jar in the barn. If he'll talk to me, he'll talk to you. It occurred to me that maybe Howard had a nervous breakdown. If that happened, he might have killed himself. Let me know what you find out. Meanwhile, I'll stay in touch with Miss Price." Lydia took hold of Nancy's hand. "We're going to find something fun for you to do," she said.

"Oh boy," Nancy said and grabbed Lydia in a bear hug that hardly let her breathe.

With a gentle motion, Tom pulled his sister away. "And what if Dr. Evans gives me the brush-off? What then?"

"Just ask him. If he won't talk to you, we'll come up with something else."

Tom looked skeptical, but he shrugged in resignation. "I've got to get Nancy home before Mom calls the FBI."

Nancy gave Lydia another hug, quickly this time, and Tom grunted, "Good-bye."

Alone in the silent apartment, Lydia collapsed into the La-Z-Boy. Leaning her head against the headrest, she closed her eyes. Nancy was on her way, and that felt good, but Lydia was tired. She needed to gather her strength. First, she'd have to give Suzanne a word for word description of everything that happened during the meeting. Then, she'd have to take Malcolm home, feed him his supper, and go through the evening routine all alone. Alone, that is, unless Jeff came home.

He'd been gone for more than two weeks now, with only one phone call to her, a call so short she hadn't said half of what she wanted to say. All he wanted to know was if Malcolm was okay and if they needed anything. At least he'd given her a phone number where she could reach him at night—a Holiday Inn about four miles out of town. She tried to tell him to come home, that she was keeping her promise about Howard, but he said not yet.

"Not until we make some changes," he said, but when she asked him what changes, he said they'd talk about them when he saw her in person. Probably he was still mad about Nancy.

He didn't mention Henry, so she assumed the man was keeping his distance, and he didn't say anything about losing any patients.

If she could deal with these changes, whatever they were, maybe their lives could go back to normal. She imagined him walking through the door with his suitcases, and her eyes flew open. She was kidding herself if she thought their lives would ever be the same again.

She had taken a chance and called Miss Price, knowing that Caroline wouldn't like it and Henry, if he ever found out, well, who knew what Henry might do? She had taken a chance and it had worked, at least so far. She liked the feeling she got from knowing she had maybe opened up the way for Nancy to have a new life. She liked the feeling, and she wasn't about to let go of it. Jeff would have to move over in their marriage and give it some room.

18

"Eat up, boy. Your clothes look like they've grown. You're not on that Atkins Diet my wife keeps yammering about, are you?" Avery Duncan slapped Jeff between the shoulder blades, almost causing him to choke on his iced tea.

"No, sir," Jeff sputtered. "I've just been so busy, I've hardly had time to eat." He turned in his chair to get a better look at Avery, who had walked up behind him as he was finishing his lunch at the drug store. Lately, he'd been grabbing most of his meals at the hospital cafeteria, but he was tired of the food there, and people were starting to give him funny looks. They probably wondered why he was spending so much time there.

Avery gazed down at him with paternal concern. A dapper man in his early fifties, Avery was president of Tanner's only bank, a position he thoroughly enjoyed. Being in charge of an institution as small as the Bank of Tanner allowed him to do whatever struck his fancy. He could be financial advisor one minute, loan officer the next, and chief executive the next. Right now, Jeff thought he was being annoying.

"Haven't heard any more from you about that house y'all were thinking about buying," Avery said. "Haven't changed your mind, have you? I can draw up the loan papers pretty quick."

Rotary fans hanging from the high ceiling of the old building whirred softly, blending with the murmur of voices and clatter of heels throughout the store. It was a steady din, but Jeff was sure the people sitting at the tables and booths around him could hear every word Avery said. He wished the man would shut up. The house was the last thing he wanted to talk about.

Jeff had spent a lot of lonely nights at the Holiday Inn out on the highway, and during most of that time, he tried to figure out how to pull his life together again. Henry's visit had shaken him badly. After that, he had been running on adrenalin and acting on impulse, but he had a better hold on himself now.

The nights with Joanna were a mistake. It had taken him a while to realize that, but he knew it now. He'd been so angry with Lydia, he would have done anything to hurt her, but that didn't change the fact that he loved her.

"We can't go on like this," he had told Joanna after a week at her apartment. "I need to go back to Lydia."

Joanna sat on the flowered sofa she rented for her living room. She was repairing the hem in one of her miniskirts, and she didn't look up. "She tried to ruin you," she said. Her voice was calm, composed, like she was at the hospital.

Jeff stood in front of the stereo. After starting the conversation seated next to her on the sofa, he realized her closeness made him uncomfortable. "Not deliberately," he said. "I may be able to fix the damage she caused. I have to try."

Joanna shoved her needle into the miniskirt, then raised her face so he could see it. He hated saying things to her that she didn't want to hear. He hated seeing anger rise in her delicate features. She meant a lot to him, but Lydia was so much more. In the end, Joanna maintained her dignity by telling him she never wanted to see him again, and she'd done a good job of avoiding him at the hospital.

Now he had to move forward. He missed Lydia, stubborn and willful as she was, and he wanted her back. He loved her. He loved her despite the problems she had caused. He just wanted her to help him clean up the mess.

"We've put the house on hold for a while," he said to Avery. "Decided there were other things we need to do right now."

"Sure," Avery said. "Let me know if you change your mind." He slapped Jeff on the shoulders again, a little less aggressively this time. "In the meantime, you oughta eat more." Patting his own protruding stomach, he strolled toward the door.

If Jeff had any appetite before, he'd lost it now. He pushed his grilled bologna sandwich and French fries away from him and stared at the swirled pattern on the Formica table top. The idea of a house sure as hell hadn't done what he wanted it to. He had to figure out what to do next. He dropped two quarters on the table and walked to the counter to pay his bill. Maybe he should just ask Lydia what it would take to make her leave the Galloways—all of them—alone.

He was so deep in thought as he left the counter that he almost didn't see Burt Evans waving at him from the magazine section of the drug store. He caught a glimpse of him as he was just about to walk out the door.

"Hey, Doc," he called as he tried to hurry on. He didn't want any long-drawn-out conversation at the moment, but the doctor was walking toward him, and it would be rude not to stop.

"How've you been? Haven't seen you in a while," Burt said. He was wearing his usual blue linen suit but without a necktie. The omission must have been his concession to the oven-like temperature outside. "How's that lovely wife of yours?"

"She's fine. Stays pretty busy with the baby. We both stay pretty busy." Jeff tried to keep from looking at the regulator clock on the wall above the soda fountain. He had patients waiting at the office.

"I don't want to take up too much of your time, but I'm glad I ran into you." The doctor motioned him over to the corner where the magazines were. "Come here for a second. I need to tell you something." Jeff moved away from the path of customers. "I've been thinking about Lydia because I got a strange phone call yesterday." He lowered his voice. His eyes behind the bifocals looked cautious.

"Tom Galloway called me, something I don't think he's ever done before. He wanted to ask me some questions about his grandfather's brother's army discharge papers. I didn't have any answers for him, but it seemed so peculiar. I'm telling you because it made me think about Lydia and all the questions she asked me about Howard Galloway and the night he died. Is she still prying into that?"

"No. No, she isn't." Jeff spoke more emphatically than he intended. "That was just a passing curiosity. She's over it now. I think her latest interest is the garden club."

Dr. Evans nodded in approval. "That's good. It's better if family matters stay in the family. I'll do what I can to help Tom, but I don't think there's anything new to be found there." He shook Jeff's hand warmly and patted him on the shoulder. "It's good to see you, Jeff. From what folks say, you're keeping my old patients happy and healthy." Then, with a hand on Jeff's back, he ushered the younger man out of the drug store and onto the scorching sidewalk.

As the doctor crossed the street, Jeff stood alone with sweat running down the sides of his face, whether from the heat or concern over what his friend had said, he wasn't sure.

He felt deflated, but he tried to reassure himself that this did not involve Lydia. This was Tom Galloway's doing, and it had nothing to do with him.

⁓

Tom wasn't satisfied with what Dr. Evans told him because the doctor didn't tell him anything. The last thing the doctor said was, "Why don't you ask your grandfather?" But that was impossible. Tom needed help, and Burt was the only person he could turn to. So he called the doctor back and arranged to meet him for lunch. He picked a tiny restaurant on the outskirts of town because the people he worked with didn't go there, and he didn't want to have to explain dining with Burt.

After changing management several times in the past few years, the restaurant was currently offering mostly Italian fare, with a few staples like hamburgers and French fries thrown in for broader appeal. While the tables had the obligatory red-and-white checkered coverings, selections from Italian operas played softly through speakers on the walls.

Tom and Dr. Evans both ordered pizza. By the time it was served, Tom was well into the speech he had prepared, a speech he hoped wouldn't raise any hackles yet would do the job. He told the doctor he couldn't talk about the discharge papers with his grandfather because, in his family, the subject of Howard was off-limits. Yet because Howard was such a close relative, he felt he needed to know what was wrong with him. Maybe what was wrong with Howard was associated with Nancy's mental problems.

Dr. Evans chewed his pizza thoughtfully, exasperating Tom almost beyond bearing. If he was going to say no, he should just go ahead and say it. Tom was beginning to think he had made a big mistake trying to push the doctor into helping him with his search, opening himself up to discovery like that. But finally, Dr. Evans spoke.

"I can't tell you anything specific about Howard or even about your family, but I know where you might could find some information that would help you. Mental problems of soldiers during wartimes is the kind of thing that lots of times gets written up in medical journals." He wiped his mouth with the checkered napkin and laid it next to his plate. The dim light in the restaurant made it hard to read his expression.

"Medical school libraries have the best collections of medical journals," he said. "The medical school library I know the best is Duke, so if you're game, I'll go down there with you next Saturday and see what we can find out."

The old man was a saint. This was what Tom was hoping for.

Saturday came on the heels of a week-long rain that took the punch out of most people's Labor Day plans but at least broke the back of the heat wave. The clouds moved out Friday night, taking a lot of humidity with them and leaving only clear skies and cooler temperatures.

Tom drove Dr. Evans to Durham in his Corvette, an experience the doctor said made him feel twenty-five again. As the farmland and towns rolled past, the two men talked easily about Tanner and briefly about the upcoming presidential election, although Tom was careful not to let the conversation slide into politics. Lately, he was finding more to like about Senator McGovern, particularly his support for draft evaders who had left the country, but he knew that would displease Dr. Evans. They were still chatting pleasantly when the gothic skyline of the Duke campus came into sight. The doctor directed Tom to a faculty parking lot—assuring him that classes were not in session, so it was all right—and then through the gray corridors and worn paths to the library.

Inside the reading room, arched ceilings rose above the towering windows, reaching up from the shelves and shelves of books. Tom couldn't help staring at the majesty of the room, breathing in the atmosphere of knowledge that pervaded it. After searching through several reader's guides and receiving a little help from a librarian, he and the doctor collected a respectable stack of psychiatry and psychology journals to peruse. They divided them evenly and started to read.

Tom slumped in one of the puffy, upholstered chairs, while Dr. Evans sat at a reading table, spread his first journal on the flat surface, and propped his chin on his palm while he read. Tom made his way through five of the articles without finding anything relevant to Howard. Burt didn't seem to be having any better luck. After nearly an hour, the doctor sat up and ran his hand across the back of his head.

"It says here that World War I was the first time the U.S. screened army recruits for things like schizophrenia or mental retardation. If they found any evidence of mental problems, they sent them home. So chances are, if Howard had anything wrong with him to begin with, he'd never have gotten into the army."

Tom looked up from the journal he was reading. "So probably something happened to him while he was in the service," he said, *or he faked something to get sent home early.*

"It's sounding more like combat fatigue," Dr. Evans said. "Do you know where he was stationed? Did he see any heavy combat?"

"Beats me. I know Grandpa was in France for a while, but I've never heard anybody mention what happened to Howard." Tom's family had hardly ever mentioned Howard at all.

They read on in silence until Dr. Evans spoke again. "Here's something about combat fatigue, or shell shock, as they called it then. Apparently, they set up treatment stations as close to the front lines as they could because they thought treatment needed to start as soon as possible after a soldier showed symptoms. Says they sent close to two-thirds of the men back to the front lines within a few days, so everybody knew shell shock didn't automatically get them sent home. Hardnosed bunch, weren't they? Says soldiers had to keep showing symptoms for at least six months before they got to go home."

Tom shrugged. Howard could have pretended symptoms for six months. That wasn't so hard to imagine. Slipping deeper into his chair, he picked up another journal. The article went through many of the same scenarios Dr. Evans had described, but a short paragraph toward the end caught his attention. It was nothing that was relevant to Howard, but it surprised Tom. He didn't think the army would have addressed that in World War I. He started to mention it to Dr. Evans, but then he thought, *why bother?* He finished the article and started another.

In all the articles he read, what struck him most was the lack of information about mental problems of soldiers in World War I. He and Dr. Evans had had a terrible time finding any articles that referenced the subject, which is why they asked a librarian for help, but even the few articles they found were mostly about World War II.

"I'm just not finding much," he said. "How about you?" Dr. Evans shook his head. "Where else could I look?"

"Your best bet may be to find a commander or a psychiatrist who served in World War I. There aren't many left, but you could probably find one. The army must have records you could tap into." The doctor closed his last journal and pushed his glasses, which had slid forward, back to the bridge of his nose.

"My guess is Howard had some form of combat fatigue. And maybe he got over it once he got away from the front, assuming he was ever at the front." He started gathering his stack of journals together, and Tom did the same. All that was left to do was drive home.

Since the next day was Sunday, Tom had plenty of time to think about what his next move should be. He lazed about in one of the wicker chairs on the front porch at Foxrow for so long that everybody at the house, including Stella, asked him what he was doing. Henry told him to go exercise the horses. Caroline tried to shoo him off to the tennis courts at the country club, but he didn't want to go anywhere. Mostly, he was sulking. The adventure he started with Lydia in July had been so full of promise: an early way out of the mill for him and maybe a fling with a pretty woman. But then Lydia gave up, and their most important discovery was going nowhere. *Fuck.* He spat on the painted oak floor in disgust.

Eventually, the afternoon sun crept under the porch roof, forcing him to go inside where it was cooler. He climbed the worn stairs to his room and took the discharge papers from his desk. No matter how much he stared at them, they didn't mean much. He might as well stick them with all the other documents in the boxes in his closet. He folded the old sheets of paper carefully—they were fragile and dry and felt like they could tear from the slightest stress—and slid them into the envelope they had been stored in. Then he opened a box on top of one of the stacks in his closet and shoved the envelope between some other envelopes, yellowed with age, and some miscellaneous papers.

As the pile separated, he saw a letter fragment he had glanced at the first time he went through the box's contents. It was less than a half sheet of stationery, obviously torn from a longer piece of writing. The penmanship was jagged, unlike

Sally Whitney

any other writing Tom saw in the boxes. There were only a few
sentences, signed by somebody named Benjamin, whom Tom
had assumed was a college buddy or business acquaintance
of one of the twins. He lifted the paper to read the sentences
again. Just as he was about to put it back, Nancy pushed open
the bedroom door and peeked in.

"What's that?" she asked.

"Nothing. Just an old scrap of paper." Tom dropped it into
the box.

"Let me see." Nancy hurried over to him.

"It's nothing. It's not even all there." He started to close the
box, but Nancy grabbed the paper and waved it in front of him.

"I got it, I got it," she said, waving it faster and retreating to
the other side of the room.

"Fine. You can have it. It's just a piece of trash." Tom closed
the box and shut the closet door.

Nancy held the torn letter in both hands and stared at it. "I
hope to see you again soon," she read slowly. "Last week was
good for both of us." Then she giggled. "Sounds like they like
each other," she said, blushing slightly.

Tom stared at his sister in astonishment. What made her
think that? It was just some business acquaintance, for God's
sake. "May I have it back, please?" he asked gently.

Nancy rolled her eyes, giggled again, and handed the paper
to her brother. "Let's look for the rest of it," she said.

"No, there's not any more. And I need to put all this away.
Did you have a reason for coming in here?"

"Granddaddy says he's fixing drinks before dinner."

"Tell him I'll be down in a minute."

Nancy slipped out the door and clip-clopped down the long
hallway. Tom read the two sentences Nancy had read and the
rest of the words on the letter fragment. Maybe Nancy was
right. He couldn't wait to talk to Lydia.

19

The wooden clock on the shelf in the townhouse said twelve fifteen. Lydia checked her watch to see if the clock was fast. It wasn't. Tom was fifteen minutes late. Maybe he wasn't coming. She went back to searching for snippets of ocean in the random pieces of the jigsaw puzzle spread out in front of her.

She didn't think of herself as a puzzle person, but in the weeks that Jeff had been gone, tackling at least a thousand pieces had filled the empty evening hours and sometimes given her solace during the day. The current challenge was a seascape with mountains in the background, which was especially hard since the sky and ocean were nearly the same color. Trying to match the particular shapes helped calm her jittery nerves. She had been even more anxious since Tom called.

The sound of his voice on the telephone was startling because he had never called her before. Since she had told no one except Suzanne that Jeff was gone, she was surprised Tom took the chance of calling her at home, although he had called in the morning when the odds were good that Jeff wouldn't be there.

Still, it was daring on his part, and she wondered what caused him to do it. She was taking a huge chance too, by letting him come there, but he said he didn't want to involve Suzanne, so her apartment was out, and there was hardly anyplace they could meet in public.

She kept the card table with the puzzle set up in front of a ladder-backed arm chair that usually occupied a corner of the living room. Today, she sat in the arm chair looking out the open front door. She was watching for Tom so he wouldn't ring the doorbell and wake up Malcolm. The baby had kept her up all night—he was undoubtedly teething—and she desperately needed a break from him. Through the screen door, the aroma of freshly cut grass was exhilarating. Her landlord had mowed that morning for the first time in nearly a month, after the Labor Day rain storms revived grass long dormant in the August heat.

At twelve thirty, Tom came strolling up the sidewalk. She had instructed him to park around the corner, or at least down the street, so her neighbors wouldn't see the Corvette. He moved casually, as if he walked up Singer Street every day of his life. The September sun reflected brilliantly from his red-gold hair, giving him an otherworldly appearance. Lydia rose to meet him and quickly shut the screen door, along with the main door, behind him. The darkened townhouse felt cozy and conspiratorial.

"What's going on?" she asked. "Is Nancy okay?"

"Nancy's fine," Tom said. He hesitated while a flicker of indecision crossed his face. "In fact, I guess I ought to tell you what happened last week before I tell you why I really came here."

Lydia settled in behind the puzzle again and gestured toward the couch. "Sit down," she said. Tom took a seat, his long legs stretched out in front of him.

"Mom threw a hissy fit about that meeting we tricked her into," he said, "but between Stella and me, we got her settled down. She's got a real attitude problem. She's so scared somebody will hurt Nancy. Anyway, we finally got her to agree that having a job might be good for Nancy, and she would at least think about it, since Nancy was so gung-ho about doing it."

"Thank heavens." The idea that they could make a believer out of Caroline made Lydia smile.

"It was a good start, but I still wasn't sure she'd come around." Tom raised an eyebrow. "Then, one night, she called me into the dining room and asked me what kind of work I thought Nancy would be doing at one of 'those places,' as she called them. I told her what you said about Nancy's sewing—only I didn't say you said it. Turns out I may as well have told her it was your idea. She's softened toward you. What she said next nearly blew me away.

"She said Nancy's been different since you've been coming around, and since Grandpa won't let you anyplace near Foxrow anymore, maybe it was time to let Nancy venture out some. If you could make Nancy happy, maybe somebody else could too. That was all she said to me, but I guess she made up her mind. A few days later I heard her talking to Grandpa about it. They were sitting on the front porch when I happened to come up from the garage. He didn't like the idea, but she told him it was necessary." Tom shook his head.

"Talk about a real shocker," he said. "That's the first time I've ever heard her stand up to him about us kids. She sure as hell didn't question anything he ever told me to do, but she didn't allow him any say-so about this."

"But he may still put a stop to it, don't you think?"

"I don't know. I'll bet, if that lady comes up with a job for Nancy, Mom'll let her take it."

Lydia wanted to hug Tom, but she didn't. Instead, she pummeled her fists against the card table, causing the puzzle to bounce up and down, before she remembered Malcolm and stopped. "Thanks, Tom," she said. "You came through on this one."

"It wasn't me. It was Mom. But that's not what I came to see you about." Tom looked at the mantel clock. Then he leaned forward with his elbows resting on his knees. "I think I know why Howard came home from the war. I think he was gay." Tom spoke calmly, but his eyes were dancing, like he was proud as punch about his discovery.

"Gay?" Lydia asked.

"You know—gay. Queer. Homosexual. Like the Gay Liberation Front."

"I know what it means. But what makes you think that?" Lydia spotted two pieces of sky that fit together and pressed them into place.

"It started with something I read in a psychology journal at the Duke medical library," Tom said. When Lydia looked up at him in surprise, he added, "I went there with Dr. Evans. I haven't had a chance to tell you about it. He was great—took me there, showed me around. But the point is, I found this article that said commanding officers sometimes let gay soldiers get out of the service with a psychiatric discharge instead of a dishonorable discharge. Otherwise, they actually could have been court-martialed and sent to jail because that kind of sex was a crime back then. That could explain Howard's discharge when nothing was wrong with him." Tom's voice sparkled with enthusiasm.

"It's possible," Lydia began, but Tom jumped in again.

"And then I saw this old letter in one of those boxes in my closet. It was just a piece of a letter, and I had seen it before, but Nancy showed up in my room, grabbed it out of my hand, and read it. What she said about it made me think it could be from a guy who was more than just a friend or business acquaintance." He smiled at Lydia triumphantly.

His excitement was contagious. Lydia had to push hard to keep her feelings buried in her stomach and not jump right in with him. She kept her eyes on the puzzle pieces, but the blues and greens and whites blurred together. Blinking, she pushed a few pieces around. She had to ask. "Has anybody in your family ever said anything about Howard being queer? You're really only guessing about this, based on a couple of pieces of information."

"Well, no. But they don't talk about him at all, so they wouldn't have said anything, would they?" Tom's tone was harsh as he frowned at Lydia's question.

Lydia gave up trying to focus on the puzzle. "Okay. Supposing he was queer or gay. What do you think that has to do with his death?"

"I don't know. Maybe Grandpa killed him, not for the mill but because he hated queers," Tom said. Lydia shook her head. "He could have," Tom protested. "I'm sure he would have been horrified and embarrassed to have somebody like that in the family back then. He probably would be now. Look how embarrassed he acts about Nancy."

Offended as she was that anyone could be embarrassed by Nancy, or Howard, for that matter, Lydia wasn't ready to use that to heap the blame on Henry.

"I think what you need to do first is find out whether or not Howard was gay," she suggested. "You may be right. It could be the key you're looking for, if you can just figure out where it fits. But first you have to know if it's true."

"I could quiz the people who knew him. Some of them are still around," Tom suggested.

Lydia frowned. "What are the chances he told anybody in Tanner he was gay? In 1919, it would have been scandalous. My guess is, there's only one person in this town who knows the truth. And that's your grandfather." She hated this fact, even as she said it.

"I can't ask him," Tom said. "He was furious that you even mentioned Howard's name to him. That's what got you kicked out of our house, remember? And why he went after your husband. I don't know what he'd do if I hit him with this."

"Where's your spine, Tom? It's a simple question about somebody in your family, and you have a right to know the answer. You're not accusing Henry of murder. Don't even mention Howard's death. You just have one question. Was he homosexual?"

"What makes you think he'd tell me? Assuming he didn't kill me first." Tom stood in a huff and walked over to face her across the card table.

Lydia turned her impressions of Henry over in her mind to try to give Tom a sound answer, but all she had was a gut feeling. The old man was ruthless, but he was honest.

"Given the right circumstances, I think he will," she finally said.

"What circumstances?" Tom picked up a few puzzle pieces without looking at them.

"Just you and him, to begin with. Don't let anybody else in the room. And tell him what you already know about the military discharge and the piece of the letter. You're the only grandson with the Galloway name. That means something to him, and I think, because of that, he'll tell you this family secret."

"And what if I'm wrong about Howard?" The puzzle pieces fell noiselessly out of Tom's hand.

Lydia took a deep breath. "Then I guess it's over, unless you know someplace else to look for clues about his death."

The mantel clock chimed the hour. "I need to get back to work," Tom said. He looked down and stirred some puzzle pieces with his finger. When he looked up, his eyes showed resolve. "I'll do it," he said slowly, "but only if you go with me."

Lydia shook her head. "That's crazy. If I'm there, the whole thing will blow up in your face. You know how much he despises me."

"He despises you because you make him feel threatened, and he's never felt threatened in his life. I might luck out, and he'd tell me the truth because of family ties, but our chances are better if he sees you aren't afraid of him, that you didn't stop just because he got in your husband's face. That'll push him over the edge because he'll realize we're going to find out anyway."

The old passion that Lydia thought she had pushed to the bottom of her soul came roaring to the surface. She wanted to talk with Henry so bad it hurt. This was the discussion she had been yearning to have all summer, the face-to-face, free-for-all that she had been building to every time she was anywhere near him. It was the discussion she feared she would never have, but Tom was offering her the opportunity—in fact, insisting on it.

If she went with him to talk to Henry, her promise to Jeff would be broken. She'd have no way to prove to Jeff that she loved him. He needed that, she knew, but this was a proof that he set up, not her. Did she really want to go on playing by his rules? *Oh, God*, she thought. *What do I do?*

If there was going to be room in their marriage for her to be happy about giving Nancy hope, then there had to be room for her to care about Howard too. Jeff said in his phone call that he wanted changes. Well, she wanted changes too. Mostly, she wanted him to see her as a person—an individual, distinct person—not just Mrs. Jeff Colton. As much as she wanted to continue being married to Jeff, she couldn't do it unless he saw the real her. This was the real her.

"All right," she said to Tom. "I'll go with you, but just us. I don't want Caroline or Nancy, or even Stella, the least bit involved. We have to be alone. Where should we do it?"

"At Foxrow. We want the strongest family vibe we can get, and that place reeks of it. Maybe Howard's even still there." Tom grinned mischievously, but Lydia had a tingling feeling that he might be right. She felt very close to Howard at the farm.

"Set it up, and let me know when," she said. "I'll need enough notice to get a babysitter."

Tom promised to stick to her rules about being alone in the house and to let her know in advance. Then he left, strolling down Singer Street with a little more kick in his step than before. Lydia closed the door gently, shutting out the last whiffs of newly cut grass. Summer was still alive, and so was her passion.

Filled with a tumultuous energy, she pushed the card table with the puzzle out of the way and danced around the living room, touching each wall and stick of furniture. She was thrilled with the news about Nancy and excited to near explosion with Tom's theory about Howard and the prospect of meeting with Henry. She was so energized, she had to do something. She danced into the dining room and picked up the telephone receiver. In seconds, she had Miss Price on the line.

"Guess what," she gasped, leaning against the old pine table, "Nancy Galloway's mother said yes! She said it's okay for Nancy to try working. All we have to do is find the right job."

From the depths of the drab cubicle where Lydia envisioned her sitting, Miss Price sighed. "I'm looking, Lydia, believe me, I am, but I'm not finding any employers in your area who're willing to hire her. I'm not sure if they're worried about hiring a mentally retarded person, or if it's more about who this particular person is. I've found a couple of places where I think she could use her sewing skills, but they're not interested." She sighed again, and there was a clink, as if the phone hit her glasses. "Maybe if her mother or her grandfather would call and say there won't be any problems."

"I promise you it's okay with her family."

"My instincts tell me this employer may be more worried about the reactions of people in town. Is there anybody in Tanner who could reassure him that it's all right to hire Nancy? If somebody could make this man believe that nobody in town will speak badly of him for hiring Nancy, I think that would help." Miss Price paused, but the soft sounds of her breathing still came across the line. "Is there somebody who could do that?"

Lydia paced next to the table as far as the telephone cord would allow. She thought Caroline would be their biggest obstacle. She never imagined that the good people of Tanner would throw up roadblocks, as well.

"I don't know that many people in town," she said. "I sure don't know who would have that kind of influence."

Mentally, she flew through her limited list of resources and lit on the only one who might be able to help them. Wilbur Meacham. A blessing from him might make a difference. She told Miss Price about Wilbur and promised to call him right away.

After hanging up the phone, she decided it would be better to visit Wilbur in person. He loved company and seemed to enjoy visiting with her. She would go the next morning if Suzanne could keep Malcolm for her.

Satisfied that she had a plan to deal with this unexpected glitch, Lydia started thinking about Howard again and the upcoming meeting with Henry. The conversation with Miss

Price had squelched her earlier euphoria, letting the cold reality of what she was about to do sink in. Her marriage might not survive this. But if it was to have any chance at all, she had to be honest with Jeff. No more keeping things from him, and no more trying to be somebody she wasn't. With trembling fingers, she picked up the phone and dialed his office.

20

A few wispy clouds marred an otherwise perfect sky on the day of the meeting with Henry. Summer was stretching deep into September and would continue until the pumpkins hung heavy on the vines.

Before leaving home, Lydia suggested the babysitter take Malcolm for a walk. He loved going outside, and it would make it easier to get him down for his nap. Tom had told her to arrive at Foxrow about one thirty. Henry was likely to hang around the house for a while after lunch on Saturdays, watching sports on TV, but unless he was particularly interested in a game or match, he was also likely to take off around two or three—headed back to the mill, Tom suspected. "So be sure you get here on time," he said.

Lydia left home earlier than she needed to for the trip to Foxrow. The last thing she wanted was to feel rushed when her nerves were already screaming. After getting out of town, she drove the two-lane highway slowly, thinking the best thing she could do was turn around and go home. She was gambling with her future, not to mention she still believed the meeting would work much better without her. But Tom had insisted that she come. She couldn't let him down, and she really wanted to be there.

"Damn it, Tom," she said as she turned off the pavement onto the dirt road that led to the farm.

More than six weeks had passed since Lydia's last visit to Foxrow. She was surprised at the changes those weeks brought. Tangles of new black-eyed Susans bulged along the road-side, almost hiding the tall grass in the fields. Corn stalks that stretched high behind the grass created their own forest and looked ready for harvesting. The life of the farm had gone on without her, like it didn't miss her at all. But the house hadn't changed. Its wide porch was welcoming as ever as she parked the Camaro in the gravel driveway. Most of the flowers in the garden were still blooming, reminding her of the afternoon she and Nancy sewed happily, hidden in their colors, until Tom invited them inside. That was the day she found the discharge papers, and the last time she talked to Henry.

Hesitantly, she climbed the wooden stairs. She could still leave. No one knew she was there. But as it had every time she saw it, the house drew her in. Soon, she was knocking on the heavy front door. Tom told her not to twist the buzzer because he didn't want Henry to know they had company. He must have been waiting for her in the hall because the door opened immediately, and he motioned for her to come inside. The hall, with its towering ceiling, was much cooler than the porch and yard. Lydia shivered.

"Scared?" Tom asked.

"No." She didn't want to tell him that her heart was pound-ing and her palms were soaked. "Where is everybody?" she asked. "Are we alone?"

Tom closed the front door without a sound. "The North Carolina ballet's performing in Charlotte today, so I gave Mom two tickets for Nancy and her. Stella took the day off to visit her son. Pansy's in the kitchen, but she won't come out." He pointed his thumb toward the living room. "Grandpa's in there. I guess there's no point in waiting." A muscle in Tom's cheek twitched, but his voice was steady. "Let's go."

He put his hand on Lydia's back in a gentlemanly gesture to let her go first, but she stepped aside. She wasn't about to go in first. Tom turned the knob, opening the door into the room. The voice of an announcer giving the play-by-play for a football game crackled out of the television in the corner. Henry sat on the couch, a magazine in one hand, his shirt collar open, his sleeves rolled up. He looked away from the TV when the door opened.

"Are the Tar Heels winning?" Tom asked.

Henry stared without answering, his eyes shifting to see who was coming into the room behind Tom. "What the hell?" he boomed when Lydia came into his line of sight. "What's going on, Tom? Get her out of here." He threw the magazine onto the coffee table and stood up, his face gnarled into a scowl.

"Not until you listen to what we have to say." Tom's voice had lost some of its firmness, and the twitch in his cheek had gotten worse, but he pressed on. "I have something to ask you. Something that's very important to me."

"Get her out of here," Henry repeated.

"No. She stays." Tom's voice was louder.

The old man grunted and continued to scowl. "I'm not talking to her. I don't want her in my house." He turned to Lydia. "Didn't you hear me? I said get out." Lydia closed the door to the hall and tried to look calm, although she could hardly breathe.

"No, Grandpa. Listen to me," Tom said. "I found some things in my closet. One of them I know belonged to your brother, and the other was in with some of his things, so I think it was his too."

Henry started toward the door. "I'm not listening to this," he said.

"Wait." Tom stepped in front of him. "Hear me out. I told you this is important. Howard was related to me too, and I want to know about him."

"There's nothing to know."

"Then why was he discharged from the army for psychiatric reasons?"

"How do you know that?" Henry's voice was gruff.

"I found his discharge papers." Tom stole a quick glance at Lydia. "They were in my closet. I want to know what they mean."

"They mean what they say. That's all."

"But nobody ever talked about Howard having any mental problems. What kind of problems did he have?" Tom sounded more confident. Lydia prayed that Henry would respond.

"That's none of your business."

Henry started to walk away again, but Tom grabbed his arm. "It is my business. It's my family. And I want to know." Henry jerked his arm away, but Tom kept talking. "Look, Grandpa. I did some reading, and I know that sometimes soldiers were given psychiatric discharges because they were homosexual. Is that what happened to Howard? Is that why you won't talk about it? Was he gay?"

"Gay?" Henry spat out the word, his face fixed in lines of anger. "I'm not going to dignify that with an answer."

"You have to answer me. I deserve to know." Tom's voice was louder, harsher. "I also know that Howard got letters from men, letters that sounded more than friendly. I found a piece of one of them." He reached into his pocket and pulled out the scrap of letter from Benjamin. "So tell me the truth." He shoved the paper in front of Henry.

Henry took the paper carefully in his hands. Without realizing it, Lydia had backed against the wall. As voices in the room grew silent, the football announcer chattered on, breaking up the bitter air that hung in the cavernous space. Tom and Henry were still, paused in a duel of wills, a duel of loyalties, a duel of family and individual pride. After staring at the words on the paper for long, agonizing minutes, Henry looked at Tom. His face was less angry, but still troubled.

"Why did you start digging around in Howard's things?" he asked. "What made you think you had the right to invade a dead man's privacy?"

"Lydia did," Tom said. "She made me see that Howard's death is like a pit in our family. It's a wretched pit that we cover up, but we drown in it every day. We never talk about him. We act like he never existed. And that's your fault. You did this to us. You taught us to hide him like we had something to be ashamed of, even though we didn't know why, and that's a contagious attitude. Look at what we've done to Nancy." His voice faltered when he said his sister's name.

"Lydia isn't caught in our hang-ups," he said, "and she saw what we're doing. But like me, she doesn't know why. Together, we're going to find out. We're going to find out for Howard because he can't defend himself." Drawing a deep breath, Tom collapsed into a chair, as if his words had sucked away his strength.

And for Nancy too, Lydia thought.

Tom said she saw what was going on, but she hadn't seen it clearly until he put his finger on it. For the first time, she understood the true connection between Howard and Nancy. It had nothing to do with mental disabilities and everything to do with the family's efforts to keep them where nobody could see them. It was what had gnawed at her about Howard. His mystery affected the whole family. That was why she couldn't let go.

Henry ran his fingers over the paper in his hand. "So you think this paper and the army discharge have something to do with Howard's death," he said softly.

"Yes, sir," Tom said.

"And you," Henry said, looking at Lydia, "you think you have a right to know this most private thing about my family."

"Yes, sir. You won't believe me, but I care about your family, especially Nancy."

"You don't know what it means to care. Neither one of you." Henry shot a menacing look back at Tom. "Caring isn't something you grab hold of one day when it's convenient. Caring is something you carry with you a lifetime. Caring makes you build a wall around yourself to protect a person. And you don't let somebody poke a hole in that wall for nothing, even if they're family." His face dissolved into drooping resignation, and he sat again on the couch.

"But if I don't tell you all, you'll find out somehow. You won't give up, will you? You're like dogs after a piece of meat. And you're going to make assumptions about Howard that you shouldn't make. Howard was an honorable man. He respected his family, and he was loyal to his country. He was smart and brave and trustworthy. He would have made an excellent soldier and an excellent businessman, but neither the army nor my father gave him a chance. They wouldn't give him a chance because of what he was."

Henry gazed at the floor. "Yes, Howard liked men. I didn't understand it then, I don't understand it now, and I will never understand it, but he was my brother, and I vowed to keep his secret. I kept it for fifty years." Henry was quiet, and then, reluctantly, he looked up at his eager listeners.

"So you're right about the medical discharge. A platoon leader found him with another soldier, and thank God, the commanding officer had some compassion for Howard. He could have had him court-martialed, but he gave him an out through the psychiatric discharge. Having mental problems on your service record was a disgrace, but God knows it was a better choice than Arthur Galloway gave him."

Henry paused and shifted his eyes away from the faces in front of him. Tom sat perfectly still, the twitch in his cheek frozen. Lydia felt ready to explode, and a sudden blast of music from the TV made her jump. She sidled quickly to the set and turned it off. The room was quiet. No one moved or spoke. Gently, the sound of Henry's labored breathing broke through the stillness. Lydia feared they had given the old man a heart attack, but he remained rigid and alert. Then Tom's strained voice rose above the breathing.

"Did Arthur kill Howard?" he asked.

"No," Henry said. "He didn't. He just tried to change him. He told him if he was going to take over Foxrow Mills with me, like he was supposed to, he'd have to put that part of his life behind him, marry some woman, and raise a respectable family. It was the only way Father could see things, and things had to be the way he saw them. He built the mill from the ground up, the same way he built his family, and no misguided son was going to disgrace either one of them. It was his responsibility to protect them, and now it's mine, which I have done with every bone in my body until today."

"Did you kill Howard?"

The words were hardly out of Tom's mouth when Henry jumped to his feet with a swiftness that belied his age and shook his fist at his grandson. "No, goddamn it," he yelled. "Don't you ever say I had anything to do with his death, or I promise you, I will take you apart with my bare hands."

The fist was trembling now, just like his shoulders. Both he and Tom seemed no longer aware that Lydia was in the room. She knew not to make a sound, but she was so transfixed she couldn't move if she had wanted to.

"Then it was an accident?" Tom asked.

Henry was trembling so badly, he appeared unable to speak. With a show of will, he grasped his upper arms and steadied himself.

"No," he said. "It wasn't an accident. It was suicide." He took several deep breaths and stared at Tom.

"Did you know he was going to do it?" Tom asked.

"For three years, I thought it was an accident," Henry said. "Then one day I went into his room and took his pocket watch from the drawer where he kept it. He must have figured that eventually I would do that because he knew how much I coveted it. The sad thing is, I didn't take it because I wanted it for myself. I took it because I missed him and wanted something of his to keep. When I opened it, I found the note. That's when I knew. And to be honest, I wasn't surprised. It tore me up like a bullet to my gut, but I wasn't surprised. I told y'all Howard was brave. He knew he couldn't be what Father or anybody else wanted him to be, so he took away the anguish, his and theirs." Henry covered his eyes with his hand, resting his forehead between his forefinger and thumb.

"Where's the note now?" For the first time since the conversation started, Tom's voice showed compassion.

"It's buried in my desk. I couldn't bear to look at it, but I couldn't bear to destroy it, either. The watch I kept close at hand so I could see it. I never polished it because Howard never polished it."

Henry's voice trailed off, as if his throat was closing up. With a jolt, Lydia realized that, if she had looked in the desk instead of the bureau on that early summer day, she might have found the note instead of the watch, and how different things might have been. But she still had one question she had to ask.

"Why didn't the police spend more time investigating what happened?" she said in a quiet voice. "If they had, they might have figured out it was a suicide."

Henry looked at her with years of pain in his eyes. "Because Father didn't want them to. He was afraid, if they probed too much, they would find out about Howard and his discharge from the army. Next to the mill, the family dignity was the most important thing in his life. And no amount of probing was going to bring Howard back."

"But they didn't even ask about that third jar of liquor." Lydia was still appalled.

"It didn't matter to Father. I wondered about it for years until I finally figured out that it was the jar Howard was drinking from until I passed out. Then he pulled out the jar he knew was poison. He didn't want to take any chances on me taking a swig from the wrong jar." Henry sighed.

Tom rubbed his eyes with his fingers. His shoulders slumped slightly under the weight of so much information. "Does anybody else know about this?" he asked.

"No," Henry said. "The suicide was just as horrendous as the men in Howard's life. I couldn't let anybody know about any of it. So just me. I've protected the family's dignity and Howard's reputation for most of my life. Until now." He looked from Tom to Lydia. "And even though neither one of y'all has offered an ounce of respect for Howard's privacy so far, I hope to God y'all will find some respect now. God knows, he deserves it."

Henry's face was drained. Tom was still again. Lydia felt a finality settle in her bones as sadness swept over the room. They had broken the old man, just not in the way she expected. *Wherever you are, Howard, I hope you found peace*, she said silently.

"I have to go now," Henry said, and no one tried to stop him. He left the living room door open, letting in the sound of his footsteps on the creaking stairs.

Tom looked at Lydia, but she couldn't tell what he was thinking. "Do you want me to leave?" she asked.

"I guess there's nothing else we can do," he said. "When it comes down to it, this doesn't change anything." He seemed bewildered.

Lydia reached for his hand and pulled him to his feet where she could embrace him the way she would a bereaved friend. He grasped her shoulders and pressed his cheek against her head. She could feel his chest rise and fall with each breath, his body slack as a blade of grass. Then he backed away and looked at her, and for a moment, she thought he was going to kiss her, but his eyes showed his thoughts were far beyond her.

Lydia searched for the right words and finally murmured, "At least we know what happened. That makes a difference to me. I hope it does to you." Tom shrugged, and she wondered, as she often had that summer, why he had been so eager to help her. "I'll be in touch with Nancy in the coming weeks," she said. "So maybe you and I can get together and talk about this, if you want to."

He shrugged again. "Maybe so," he mumbled and turned away.

Lydia left the room and let herself out through the grand old oak door that had so impressed her the first time she saw Foxrow.

21

On the fourth day after the visit with Henry, Lydia made
herself quit holing up at home. She had to reconnect
with the world. It was the middle of the afternoon, and Suzanne was on one of her Everclean calls when Lydia knocked,
but she yelled, "The door's open," so Lydia, carrying Malcolm
and his diaper bag, went in. Suzanne turned to wave at her,
then stopped, her smile twisting into a frown.

"Well, you just talk it over with your husband, honey," she
said into the phone, "and I'll call you back later." The receiver
dropped into its cradle with a clack as she wheeled around
to look at Lydia, who had collapsed onto the tie-dyed couch.
"What the hell is wrong with you? You look like you've been
run over by a Mack Truck. And why haven't you been answering your phone?"

"It's over," Lydia said, feeling the weight of the words, as
if they described a physical loss. "The mystery about Howard
Galloway that's been haunting me all summer is over. Henry
didn't have anything to do with his brother's death. The rumor's just a rumor."

"How do you know that?" Suzanne hunched forward, her eyes wide.

"Tom and I talked to Henry."

"Henry Galloway let you in his house?"

"Tom let me in and forced Henry to hear us out. It was one of the scariest and most God-awful things I've ever done."

Maybe coming to see Suzanne was a mistake. Lydia wanted to tell her so much more. To Lydia, the meeting had been an earth-shattering event, but it was a secret event. If she honored Henry's plea for Howard's privacy, she couldn't tell anyone. She owed Howard that.

"So what'd he say?"

"He didn't say anything different." The lie tasted foul. "But I believe him now, hearing it out of his own mouth. Like I said, it's over." She ran her fingers along the swirls of color on the couch. "From now on, I'm only concerning myself with Nancy. Other than her, I'm staying away from the Galloways completely."

"Seems to me like you said that before."

Lydia leaned back and stared at the ceiling. "Things are different now."

"Lord, I hope they are, for your sake and for your family. Have you heard anything from Jeff?"

"Yeah. He keeps calling me. He wants to come see me, but I said no. He wouldn't come home when I begged him to, so now I'm not ready to see him. I told him to stay away." Lydia sighed. "Do you know what he said to me? He thinks I'm sick, as in mentally disturbed. Like I'm nuts or something. He said I need help."

When she had called Jeff to tell him she was going to talk to Henry, he was with a patient and had to call her back. He had time to prepare what he was going to say, but his response still surprised her. The cool suggestion that she needed to see a psychiatrist was so out of left field.

"Can you believe that? I'm not crazy." She folded her arms across her chest and shook her head.

"No, you're certainly not crazy." Suzanne cleared her throat. Perched on a straight chair next to the telephone table, she considered what Lydia had said. "A little impulsive maybe, but not crazy. What you need to do—in your not-crazy state of mind—is take care of yourself and quit worrying about the Galloways or anybody else."

"I can take care of myself," Lydia said. "I just need some time."

"You've been saying that ever since Jeff walked out. I think it's time you did something. Talk to me about it."

"Not now. Maybe in a few days."

All the time Lydia was hiding at home, she had tried to come to grips with everything that had happened. She lined up the facts she knew for certain, and the one she kept coming back to was how much happier she was that summer. *I did something*, she realized. *Something nobody expected me to do. I found out the truth.*

Maybe now the Galloways had a chance at being more honest with each other. It had been a terrible journey, but it was worth it. Before that summer, she'd been living her life on the surface, hiding her true self in the shadows. Now she felt strong for the first time since . . . When? Since coming to Tanner? No, before then. Maybe she had never felt this strong. The question was whether she was strong enough to keep her marriage together, particularly since Jeff seemed to think she was either bonkers or on the verge of a nervous breakdown. She couldn't talk about that yet.

Suzanne stood up, put her arms around Lydia's shoulders, and kissed her forehead. "Okay. Have it your way. If I can't do anything else, I can at least feed you chocolate." She pulled Lydia toward the kitchen.

The fresh fudge lifted Lydia's spirits a little by the time she left an hour later. Suzanne almost always had that effect on her. She smiled gratefully up at the apartment door as she fastened Malcolm into the stroller at the foot of the stairs.

Walking along the sidewalk, she peered into the windows of the stores. Since it was closing time for most of them, a lot of the merchants stood at the front doors, telling shoppers good-bye as they left while preventing new customers from coming in. After a long day at the store, they were eager to get home to the children on their back porches and the dinner in pots on the stove. Lydia wanted to tell them what she had done, to share how hard she had worked for Howard and for Nancy. Even though she couldn't do that, she returned their weary smiles. She hoped all their secrets were good ones too.

To keep from worrying about Jeff during the drive home, she focused on Nancy. She realized she hadn't talked with Nancy in more than two weeks and not at all since her last conversation with Miss Price, which had given her the idea of asking Wilbur Meacham for help. When she'd gone to the hospital to visit Wilbur, she'd been surprised to learn he had gone home, but she found him easily at his house on Emory Street, not far from Dr. Evans' house. He seemed a little pale, but his spirits were good, and they had a lovely chat. When she asked him to reassure Nancy's potential employer that hiring Nancy would not cause trouble with the townspeople, he was more than happy to help.

"I know what that guy's afraid of," Wilbur said. "He's afraid if he hires Nancy, other people in town will complain that she's rich and doesn't need a job. They'll say she's taking a job away from one of them. Well, first of all, I don't think anything like that will happen, but if it does, I'll nip it right in the bud."

Yes, she had a lot of catching up to do with Nancy. She would have to go to the library on Friday, in case Nancy and Stella showed up.

Stella had a toe ache on Friday and wanted to do nothing more than stay home and soak her foot in hot water. Her arthritis was manageable most days, but every now and then it flared up. Friday was one of those days. Nancy, however, was bursting with excitement about the news from Miss Price, and although she had tried again and again to call Lydia to tell her, Lydia never answered the phone. Nancy thought maybe she would be at the library, so Stella just had to take her.

To tell the truth, Stella was pretty excited about her own plans and wanted to share them with Lydia, since she figured she owed the girl for putting all the wheels in motion, even if she'd created quite a stir at Foxrow all summer. Of course, it'd be just Stella's luck that she would drag her aching toe to the library and Lydia wouldn't be there.

"Come on, Stella," Nancy called from the hallway.

Stella gulped down three aspirins with a glass of water and followed her out the door. A dry breeze blew dust around the streets of Tanner. There'd been no rain in the weeks since Labor Day, and the town was shriveling up again.

"If it don't rain soon, the leaves ain't gonna have no color at all," Stella remarked as she pulled the car into the library parking lot. With their kids back in school, the mothers were busy with their own activities, leaving the library nearly empty. Stella found a parking space almost next to the front door.

"Don't look like there's nobody here," she muttered, but Nancy didn't answer. Nancy had said little on the drive from

Foxrow. She was too busy looking—*for the umpteenth time*, Stella thought—at the brochures Miss Price had given her.

"Lydia already seen those brochures," Stella said as she got out of the car. "And that ain't where you going, anyhow."

"I am for the first month," Nancy corrected her. "I'm going there to learn how to be a good employee." Stella grunted and limped along to the front door. The pain was definitely making her ornery, but she couldn't help it. Once inside the building, Nancy rushed to the chairs by the windows overlooking the waterfall, but no one was there.

"Maybe she's in the children's place," she said over her shoulder as she headed in that direction. Stella settled into one of the overstuffed chairs and propped her sore foot on her favorite wooden stool. Let Nancy run around looking. She was going to stay put. When Nancy came back, she would ask her to get some magazines from the rack.

In about fifteen minutes, Nancy returned, disappointment twisting her face. "I can't find her anyplace," she said. "Maybe she's not coming."

"Go get yourself a book and fetch me some magazines. Then sit yourself down and wait." Stella patted the chair next to her. "If she's coming, she's coming, and if she ain't, she ain't, and you can't do nothing about it."

That sounded cruel, but Stella didn't want to get Nancy's hopes up. Lydia had been acting a little strange lately, what with not answering the telephone and not coming to the library. But she had a good heart, so something was bound to happen. Nancy did as Stella told her and got them both something to read—*Reader's Digest* for Stella and a book about horses for herself.

Stella was deep into an article about sexual inadequacy when Nancy squealed, "There she is." Sure enough, Lydia was pushing Malcolm's stroller toward them, a smile as big as the sky across her face. Nancy jumped out of her chair and ran to hug her. Lydia hugged her back enthusiastically and then surprised Stella by stooping to hug her too.

"It's been a while since I've seen y'all," Lydia said. "Things have just kept me pretty busy, I guess."

"We've been busy too," Nancy said. "And guess what. I have a job." She clapped her hands and hugged Lydia again.

"My goodness. Tell me all about it." Lydia sat in the chair closest to the windows, dangling her car keys in front of Malcolm to keep him entertained. Nancy was too excited to sit down, so she pranced around in front of the windows. Stella loved seeing her so happy, and she loved seeing Lydia again too. There was something devilish about that girl, no doubt, but she could sure liven up a room.

"So where is this job?" Lydia asked.

"At the bloomer factory," Nancy exclaimed.

"At the what?" Lydia asked.

"Don't you call it that," Stella said. "A person ought to have some respect for the place they works at." Jobs could be hard to come by, Stella knew. An employer deserved loyalty.

"Tom calls it that," Nancy insisted.

"Well, Tom, he don't work there." Stella nodded her head for emphasis. "It's the ladies' lingerie factory down close to the railroad tracks," she said to Lydia. "I forget what it's called, but they makes underpants and nightgowns and I thinks maybe a few baby clothes. My sister worked down there for a spell, and seems like she give my grandbabies some little T-shirts. Maybe they was seconds."

"That's great," Lydia said. "So what're you going to do there, Nancy?"

"Sew," Nancy said. "Make things." Lydia turned a perplexed expression toward Stella.

"They thinks they can teach her to do some of the hand stitching on the ladies' gowns," Stella said. "And you gonna help with the packaging, ain't you, Nancy?"

"Yes," Nancy said as she did a half twirl on one foot. "Miss Price said I can learn to do lots of things. And they're going to pay me money." Her eyes lit up. "My own money. I was going to give it to Stella, but she's leaving." Her eyes dimmed.

"Leaving?" Lydia spun around to stare at Stella. "Where are you going?"

Now it was Stella's turn to beam. "I'm going home," she said. "Home to my son and my grandbabies and my great-grandbaby." She loved saying those words.

Nancy didn't understand it, but Stella was an old woman. She couldn't be sure how many years she had left. She had taken care of two generations of Galloway children, and now she needed to take care of herself. "Nancy don't need me no more," she said. "She a working woman now." It was hard to believe, but it was true.

"How's she going to get to work?" Lydia asked.

"There's a bus," Nancy said. "Miss Price sends it. It picks up me and some other folks and takes us where we're supposed to go."

"The county sends it," Stella said. "It takes most of the folks to the sheltered workshop, but some, like Nancy, goes other places."

"Well, Stella, that's marvelous," Lydia said, a note of hesitation in her voice.

Stella couldn't tell if she really thought it was a good idea or not. Nobody at Foxrow had seemed enthusiastic about Stella's retirement, except Stella herself. Caroline tried to talk her out of it, saying there was plenty for her to do, even if Nancy was going to be gone all day. Tom, in a move that surprised her, said he would miss her and that Foxrow wouldn't be the same without her. Pansy cried and said she just might have to quit too, if Stella left, but Stella knew she wouldn't. Henry hadn't said anything to Stella, but Nancy told her he mumbled, "That's too bad," when he heard the news. It was going to cause a big change in the Foxrow household, for sure, but there was already plenty of change afoot with Nancy's new job and something else Stella could sense but she couldn't quite put her finger on. Something was different between Henry and Tom.

"It's time for me to go," Stella said. "Ain't nobody at Foxrow needs me no more."

"I may not need you, but I sure want to see you," Lydia said.

"I want to see you too," Nancy said. "Can I come to your house?"

"Course you can come to my house. Both of y'all," Stella said. "Lydia ain't never met Sam or my grandbabies. We'll have us a grand time." The thought of Lydia and Nancy talking with her family made Stella smile. "Bring Malcolm too," she said. "He's near about the same age as my great-grandbaby."

The three women talked on as the morning slipped away. The pain in Stella's toe eased as she enjoyed watching the two younger women. Lydia really brought out the spunk in Nancy, and Nancy seemed to have a calming effect on Lydia. Lord knows, that girl could sometimes be in knots. Leaning her head back in the old chair, Stella looked at the library's high ceiling.

Thank you, Lord, she prayed, *for working in your mysterious ways.* Lydia's voice, rising and falling like a rollercoaster, broke into her reverie. *And please, Lord,* she added, *keep an eye on Lydia.*

22

As soon as Lydia got home from the library, she fed Malcolm and put him down for his nap. She couldn't wait to get to the telephone. She had two very important calls to make. The first was to Miss Price, to thank her for finding a job for Nancy; the second was to Wilbur Meacham, to thank him for convincing the manager of the lingerie company to hire her.

"My pleasure, Mrs. Colton," Wilbur said when she got him on the line. "Always glad to do a favor for a pretty lady. Glad to hear it all worked out." He paused. When he spoke again, his voice had lost some of its cheerfulness. "When you coming to see me again? This old house gets pretty empty."

"I'll be there soon as I can, Mr. Meacham," Lydia said. "And I know somebody else who I bet would love to come see you too." She was thinking about Nancy, who she knew would be grateful when she found out what Wilbur had done for her. "You won't be hurting for company."

A few minutes later, she hung up the phone and went to the kitchen to wash the lunch dishes. As the sink filled up with suds, the familiar longing came creeping back into her bones.

Something inside her was reaming out that hole again. She had felt so strong for the past few days. She couldn't bear to lose that.

In the corner of the kitchen, hung on the back of a chair, was one of Jeff's golf caps. Lydia picked it up and ran her fingers along the sweat-stained band. She could hear his voice, full of concern, telling her she was sick. That was bullshit. No sick person could have done what she did that summer. She got the Galloways to be honest with each other about Howard for the first time. She not only gave Nancy hope for a life outside Foxrow, she helped find her a job to make that hope come true. What if she had listened to Jeff and stayed away from Nancy like he told her to? None of this would have happened. What had he said when she told him she was worried about Nancy? Something like "that's just the way things are." Just like he said about the library card and the country club membership.

She tossed the cap back onto the chair. Jeff was wrong. Just because things are a certain way doesn't mean they can't be different. Maybe their marriage could be different. Lydia shut off the water in the sink and dropped into a chair. Resting her head on her arms folded across the table, she pictured Jeff. She missed him, for sure. But a scary thought poked at her for the first time. Did she miss him because she loved him or because she was afraid she couldn't get along without him? She raised her head as the realization came to her. She could get along fine without him. In fact, she had done what she did that summer in spite of him.

Slowly, she got up from the table and walked to the small desk in the living room. She took a few sheets of stationery out of a drawer, chewed her lower lip, and hoped she was doing the right thing. After a few minutes, she picked up a pen and began to write.

Sally Whitney

Dear Malcolm,

It may be that you'll never see this letter. I hope that's the case. I love you, and I want only the best for you, but right now you're not getting that.

They say every child deserves to grow up with both a mother and a father at home. I agree with that, but sometimes it's impossible. Your father isn't at home now because he can't live with me the way I am. So you're without a father. But if I let him come home to live with us again, then you won't have a mother, just as you really haven't had one since you were born. With him, I don't know who I am. I always thought this was the life I wanted, but now that I'm here, it's not what I thought it would be. The person I wanted to be doesn't exist anymore. She's changing, whether she wants to or not, and all you're getting now is a shell of a woman, who goes through the motions with you. I want to give you more than that. I want to give myself more than that. I want a life chosen not by your father, not by my parents, not by anyone else. I want a life that's chosen only by me. I know I can do that.

So, as of today, you and I are on our own. I don't know how long it will last. Maybe someday your father and I will understand each other better—maybe I'll understand myself better—and we can all be together again. If that happens, then I'll tear up this letter. But if it doesn't, and one day you ask me how it all started, I want to be able to show you how I feel today. I want you to understand how important it is to know yourself, and no matter how painful or inconvenient or scary it is, don't ever deny yourself. If you question that, I'll tell

you the story of people I met this summer, and then I'll
tell you my story, however it ends.

Lydia folded the letter carefully, knowing there was more to say. In days or weeks to come, she would add to it, but for now, she wanted to take the next inevitable step. She went to the telephone and called Jeff.

Lydia tried to call just as Jeff was about to show up at home, whether she wanted him to or not. He couldn't stay away any longer, torturing himself about what she might say to Henry Galloway and furious with her for not answering the phone. Something had to be done. She needed help. He needed help. Worried that she was disturbed beyond anything he could do for her, he had contacted Ted Jones, a psychiatrist he went to school with.

"I thought if I bought her a new house and gave her something to get excited about, she'd snap out of this spell she seems to be under. But she doesn't want a house. I don't know what she wants. She argues about everything. I swear, all she thinks about is what she can do to make me mad," he told Ted.

"If you bring her to Raleigh, I'll take a look at her," Ted said. "I can't tell you much without talking to her, but sometimes people with the symptoms you're describing need a total change of environment."

"I thought about that," Jeff said. "I'm afraid bringing her to this town was a mistake."

"Would you consider moving?"

"Maybe. I love my practice, but I could get used to a larger practice, I guess." Jeff hoped that was the case. It had never been what he thought he wanted.

"If you're serious, I could put you in touch with a couple of internist groups here," Ted said.

"Thanks. I'll get back to you."

Jeff dreaded telling Dr. Evans he might leave, but surely they could find another young doctor to come to Tanner. It would take time, but he could make it work.

He drove the Mustang to the townhouse as soon as he could get away from his patients that day. The late afternoon was still warm with remnants of summer, while children pedaled bicycles up and down the sidewalks, getting in one last ride before being called home to supper. At the front door, he hesitated. Should he ring the bell or just go in? Well, damn, it was still his home. He opened the door and walked in.

Lydia didn't seem startled by his intrusion. She was coming out of the kitchen, carrying a small vase of yellow daisies. "Just a minute. Let me put these down," she said with a wistful edge in her voice as she set the vase on the dining room table. "They're a little droopy, but they still have life in them."

She appeared calm, so possibly nothing terrible had happened with Henry Galloway, although Jeff wasn't sure when she planned to talk to him.

"I've been trying to get in touch with you for days, but you never answer your phone," he said.

Lydia smiled a sad smile and wiped her hands on her blue jeans. Water from the vase left dark streaks on the denim.

"Why haven't you answered the phone?" Jeff asked.

"I've had a lot to think about."

Lydia went into the living room and sat in one of the easy chairs. Then she got up and moved to the couch. Jeff followed her and sat at the other end of the couch. "Well, I've had a lot to think about too," he said. "And I have something important to tell you."

"I need to tell you something too," Lydia said, "but you go first."

Surprised by her comment, Jeff wasn't sure whether to go on or not. She might have something to tell him about the Galloways. Looking at his wife's face with its familiar curves and colors, the face he had kissed so many times, he didn't care about the Galloways. He just wanted her back.

"Okay," he said. "Here goes. We've made some mistakes in Tanner."

"You mean you think I've made mistakes." Lydia's face stiffened.

"No, *we've* made mistakes. But they don't have to destroy us. We need to be together. I want us to be together, but we need a fresh start. We can't stay here, so I'm looking for a new job in a larger city. We'll be happier someplace else." He waited for her reaction. For several seconds, she didn't say anything.

"That's not the answer," she said at last. "I'll be the same person in Charlotte or Atlanta or even New York City, for that matter. You can't run away from who I am, Jeff, and I can't, either." Her eyes softened, reminding him of the way she looked when she'd told him she wasn't pregnant after they'd been trying to conceive for months. It was the look that told him she was about to say something he didn't want to hear. She leaned toward him on the couch without moving any closer.

"I learned something about who I am this summer," she said, "and I'm afraid it's not the woman you married. I'm just not her anymore, if I ever truly was. I can't be the wife you want. I can't be an extension of you."

Jeff was confused. He thought she'd be thrilled to leave Tanner. In a new town, she could be anybody she wanted to be.

"I don't understand," he said. "You're not an extension of me."

"That's the problem. You don't understand. You can't see what's really going on between us, and, believe me, it's not all your fault. I didn't understand, either. And I still have a lot to learn about me and what I can be. About who I can be. About who I want to be."

"I can help you," Jeff said, thinking of Ted Jones. "We can figure this out together."

"No," Lydia said gently. "This is something I have to do on my own. With you here, we'll fall back into the same old patterns. I know we will. I need time to try out this new sense of who I am. To make my own decisions—totally. And if those decisions are mistakes, you won't take the blame." She drew a deep breath. "I want you to find another place to live, Jeff. I want a legal separation."

Jeff froze, not believing what he had heard. "What are you talking about?"

"I'm talking about us living separate lives, as much as we can. I think it's better if I stay here, since this is what Malcolm is used to. I want you to visit him as much as you want to, but you can't live here."

Jeff focused on the movement of her eyes, still trying to process what she said. He loved her, every wayward and stubborn bone in her body, and this was not what he expected. Certainly, not what he wanted.

"What happened?" he asked. "Why are you doing this?"

Lydia ran her hands across her thighs, then leaned against her knees. "The short answer is, I helped Nancy Galloway find a job. I got her out of Foxrow and out of her bottled-up life. But the more complicated answer is, I saw myself and my life for what it is. And I can't go back there."

"Please don't do this," Jeff said. "I swear, I can help you. Whatever you need, I can help you."

Lydia shook her head. "This is the way it has to be. For now, at least. I don't know what's down the road, but this is the way it has to be now."

"No. You can't do this. I won't let you do it." Jeff grabbed her arms, but she jerked away from him and jumped off the couch. He stood up and reached for her again, just as she backed away toward the dining room. Heat swirled through his body and hammered against his skull.

"Goddamn it, Lydia. Think about what this means."

"Believe me, Jeff, I have." The steadiness of her voice and the resolution on her face held him at bay. Breathing deeply, he didn't move.

"You may have thought about it, but you're not thinking straight," he said. "All this shit with the Galloways has really messed you up this summer. I know you've become somebody else. I was mad as hell at first, you know that, and I'm sorry for some of the things I said. I'm sorry I ran out on you, but I was worried about our family and what was going to happen to us here in Tanner." He took a step toward her. "But that doesn't matter anymore. We don't have to stay here. All that matters is you, and I'll take care of you, wherever we are. I want you to be happy."

Lydia folded her arms. "I will be happy. As soon as I figure out what that's going to take."

"What about Malcolm? Where is he in all of this?" Jeff grabbed for the argument he knew she couldn't resist.

"He'll be better for it. He really will." She nodded sadly.

"Let me take you to see a friend of mine. He said he might be able to help you. Let him figure out what you need."

"Jeff, listen to me. The last thing I need is somebody telling me what I need. My mind's made up."

No! He wanted to scream at her, but there was no use. She was hell-bent on going through with it.

"This isn't right," he finally said. "You know this isn't right, but if you're going to be so damn stubborn about it, I guess I don't have any choice. I hope to God you figure out what it is you want. And when you do, be sure to tell me, because I sure as hell don't understand. I don't know what I did wrong, but if you tell me what it is, I'll fix it. And I hope you realize what a mistake you're making."

He stared at her, unable to move. He couldn't leave.

"Jeff," she said quietly.

"I know," he said. "I'm still at the same motel, but I'll let you know when I find an apartment."

Lydia followed him to the door and closed it behind him.

Malcolm was fussy that night and didn't want to go to bed. He whimpered and grabbed at Lydia when she tried to put him down. She was afraid he sensed her tension. Also, for the past several weeks, nursing at night sometimes hadn't satisfied him, so Lydia had occasionally given him a bottle. It was probably time to wean him, although she didn't want to. Since rocking and singing did no good, she gave in and was feeding him formula when a soft knocking sounded on the door. The shelf clock said nine thirty. No one ever came to see her that late, especially without notice. Lydia carried baby and bottle to the door to ask who was there.

"Tom Galloway," said the voice on the other side.

Lydia opened the door, letting him slip in. He looked apologetic but pleased to see her.

"What are you doing here so late?" Lydia asked.

"I tried to call you, but you didn't answer, so I decided to take a chance and see if you were home." Tom stood just inside the open door, with the darkness and crickets' song mingling behind him. "I'm afraid I won't see you again," he said. "I doubt you'll be coming back to Foxrow."

"You're right about that," Lydia said as she settled into the rocking chair with Malcolm.

Tom leaned against the door jamb. "So what'll you do next? Go looking for somebody else's family skeletons?" He smiled his boyish smile, but there wasn't any joy in it.

"Maybe. If I find a family as full of stories as yours. But I doubt it. I've got a lot of catching up to do. I'm going to read some books and visit with Stella and her family at her house, and I'll have to find a job. Jeff and I are separated." She spoke the last sentence softly, trying it out for the first time.

"I'm sorry," Tom said.

"Don't be. It's what I want. But I doubt if I can count on him for anything except child support. Maybe I'll see if they need any chemists at the bloomer factory—you know, to develop their dyes or something. It'd be nice to work close to Nancy, and I bet I'd like the folks there. But mostly, I just want to spend time with myself." She lifted Malcolm, who was finally dozing off, to her shoulder and gently patted his back while she rocked him at a lulling, rhythmic pace. "I want to take some time to figure out what's important in this life. And where I fit into that. What about you? Did we completely screw up your future at the mill?"

Tom chuckled. "Not in the way you think. If we did, it'd be a blessing. I never told you, but I hate that mill. I don't want to spend the rest of my life there. It's just that Grandpa's bound and determined to keep me there to run the place when he dies. In some ways, I'm like Howard, a guy forced into being something I'm not."

He paused. The ticking of the clock alternated with the creaking of the rocking chair. Lydia studied his face in light of this confession.

Oh Lord, what we don't know about each other, she thought.

"The good news," Tom said, "is that now that I know about Howard, maybe I can use his story to make Grandpa see things differently with me. My God. He killed himself over what they were doing to him."

Lydia sighed. So much sadness.

"I hope you get what you want," she said. The limp weight of Malcolm's body told her he was well into dreamland. "I'm going to take him to bed, and I'll be right back."

She climbed the stairs to his room. When she returned, Tom was standing at the door, looking out into the night. There was just enough space next to him for her to be able to see through the screen door too. "Anything out there?" she asked.

"No ghosts or goblins," he said. "Not even the family ghosts we know." He turned to face her. "Thanks for helping me find the truth about Howard. Whatever happens to me, I'm better off for knowing this. And Grandpa's better off too, for telling me." His eyes were calm. "If you find any other adventures you want to take on and you need a partner in crime, call me. You know where I live."

He leaned over and pulled her tight against his chest, but before she could react, he let go and left. Out on the sidewalk, he stopped and waved at her. "Maybe I'll see you in town some time," he called, but since he almost never came to town, she knew that wasn't likely to happen.

In a few seconds, lights flickered on the Corvette, then the car roared away. Lydia walked outside, wondering if any of her neighbors were looking out their screen doors to see what was going on. The world was silent, except for the crickets and the rustle of a timid breeze in the maple trees. Moonlight covered the yard, illuminating the neatly typed nameplate on the mailbox by the door. Lydia removed the nameplate's glass cover and, with a pen she found in her pocket, crossed out "Dr. and Mrs. Jeffrey Colton." In clean block letters she wrote "Lydia Colton." Then she went inside and closed the door.

ACKNOWLEDGMENTS

Writing is a solitary task, but bringing a book into the world cannot be done alone. Ultimately, a novel has to communicate, and a writer can't know whether it does or not unless other people are involved in the creation from the beginning. These are my people, some of whom were there for me at critical stages of *Surface and Shadow's* development and some who walked with me nearly every step of the way. To each of them I offer my sincere thanks.

T. Greenwood and her novel revision class at The Writer's Center in Bethesda, Md., read the beginning of the novel before the end was written and showed me where the story really started.

My sister, Martha Newland, who worked with special needs children and adults for many years, helped me shape Nancy Galloway into an authentic character. She was also great at jogging my memory about details of the 1970s South.

After looking at the first drafts, early readers Rebecca Long Hayden and Mary Stojak told me where the story was too thin and where it was too fat.

Sonia Linebaugh spent so much time with *Surface and Shadow* I began to think she knew the characters better than I did. They resonated with her, and she gave me invaluable insights about them, as well as critical suggestions to improve my writing. Our regular critique sessions were eye-opening experiences, marked with a few epiphanies and lots of good advice.

I'm also grateful to Sonia for the novel's opening scene. She lived it.

Later readers Karen Bennett and Gary Garth McCann pointed out ways to refine the writing and smooth out rough spots in the plot.

Ally E. Machate and Harrison Demchick of the The Writer's Ally enabled me to take the novel to an entirely new level. Developmental editors extraordinaire, they gave me ideas for ways to reach the deeper layers without changing any of my vision for the story. Their detailed analyses helped me add dimension and richness to the novel.

Mark Willen gave me support for my writing, introduced me to Pen-L Publishing, and taught me about the publishing process.

Duke Pennell, Kimberly Pennell, and other editors and designers at Pen-L Publishing polished the manuscript and created the artwork with enduring patience and professionalism. Their knowledge and effort turned a story into a finished novel and helped me find ways to get it into the hands of readers.

I can't conclude a discussion of my appreciation for the people who shaped *Surface and Shadow* without mentioning my relatives and friends from North Carolina, many of whom once lived in small mill towns across the state and taught me about the loyalty and respectability that thrive in those locations.

And most important was my husband, Greg Whitney, who spent many evenings talking to me about the characters as if they were neighbors or unruly acquaintances. Greg believed in

Surface and Shadow, even when it was no more than a yarn flitting around my imagination. He kept me moving forward with encouragement and reality checks. He was sure the novel would one day meet the world. I wish he could have lived to see it.

READING GROUP GUIDE

How does Lydia treat Jeff when she meets him? How do her feelings for him and treatment of him change as the novel progresses? Are there any suggestions at the beginning that their relationship might not work out?

How much deception is there between Lydia and Jeff? Who causes most of it? How big a role does deception play in bringing about their separation? Can relationships survive deception?

Do you think Lydia ever really loved Jeff? Is it possible to think you love someone although you really don't?

What evidence is there that Lydia is treated like a child, not just by her husband, but by others in the town? Are there subtle ways in which women are still treated like that today?

Do you think Jeff's treatment of Lydia changes significantly after they are married, or is the change more in her perception of him?

Is Lydia fair to Nancy? Does she lead her on? Do her feelings for Nancy change? Is it all right to use someone if you make it up to him or her in the end?

Is Caroline a good mother to Nancy? What do you think Nancy needs most from her mother? How much choice does Caroline have about how she rears Nancy?

Why does Lydia think she wants Jeff to come home after he leaves? What changes her mind? What are some common ties that bind couples together? Are all of them valid?

How did Howard's death affect Henry? Is this a common reaction to the death of a beloved family member?

If you were Henry, would you have hidden the truth about Howard for so many years? Why do you think Henry kept the secret? What secrets do families feel obligated to keep today?

In Chapter 6, Lydia says to Suzanne, "I've got everything I ever wanted, but sometimes I just feel like I'm nobody. Like there's not one person, except maybe you, who really sees me—like I'm invisible." What or who do you think is making her feel invisible? Is it Jeff or the people in Tanner or is she doing it to herself? Or is the problem something else entirely? Have you ever felt invisible? Why?

Lydia decides in Chapter 19 that if her marriage to Jeff has room for her to be happy about giving Nancy hope, then it must have room for her to care about Howard too. Does a marriage have to have room for everything each partner wants?

To what extent are Lydia, Jeff, Tom, Caroline, Henry, and Stella products of their environments and the expectations put on them? What questions does this raise about free will? Is Lydia's choice to be a wife and mother really her choice? And are Jeff's expectations for marriage really his own?

In Chapter 4, Jeff thinks his success in Tanner will be Lydia's success too. Is this a valid assumption? Can one person achieve success through another? Is this attitude important to a successful marriage? In what ways can your partner's success be your success? In what ways can it not?

In Chapter 13, Lydia says, "Earning money is the way we measure what a person contributes or how good they are at something. It's our only yardstick for value." Do you agree?

What do you think is the real cause of Lydia's unhappiness with her life?

If Lydia is the protagonist of the novel, who's the antagonist? Is there really a villain?

How does Lydia's motivation for learning the truth about Howard's death change over the course of the novel? How do these changes affect the way she feels about herself?

Is asking for a separation from Jeff the answer to Lydia's problem?

Is Tom doing the right thing by staying at the mill although he hates it? What's more important—family obligations or personal freedom?

Did Lydia make the right choice in the end? Should she have worked harder to keep her marriage together? What would you have done?

How important is the issue of control in the characters' lives? How important is control in most people's lives? How important is control in your life?

If you would like Sally Whitney to discuss *Surface and Shadow* with your reading group, please contact her through her website, sallywhitney.com. She is happy to meet your group in person within geographic limitations, or she can join you via Facetime or Skype.

ABOUT THE AUTHOR

PHOTO BY KAREN LEIGH STUDIOS

Although Sally Whitney has spent most of her adult life in Pennsylvania, Ohio, Kansas, and New Jersey, her imagination lives in the South, the homeland of her childhood. "Whenever I dream of a story," she says, "I feel the magic of red clay hills, magnolia trees, soft voices, sudden thunder storms, and rich emotions. The South is a wonderland of mysteries, legends, and jokes handed down through generations of family storytellers, people like me."

Sally is a fan of stories in almost any medium, including literature, theater, and film. She'd rather spend an afternoon in the audience across from the footlights than anywhere else, and she thinks DVDs and streaming movies are the greatest inventions since the automobile. She loves libraries and gets antsy if she has to drive very far without an audio book to listen to.

The stories Sally writes have been published in literary magazines and anthologies, including *Grow Old Along With Me—The Best Is Yet To Be*, the audio version of which was a

Grammy Award finalist in the Spoken Word or Nonmusical Album category. Her stories have also been recognized by the Syndicated Fiction Project and the Salem College National Literary Awards competition.

In nonfiction, she's worked as a public relations writer, freelance journalist, and editor of *Best's Review* magazine. Her articles have appeared in magazines and newspapers, including *St. Anthony Messenger*, *The Kansas City Star*, *AntiqueWeek*, and *Our State: Down Home in North Carolina*.

Sally currently lives in Maryland with her cat, Ivy Rowe, and is delighted to be once again residing below the Mason-Dixon line. When she isn't writing, reading, watching movies, or attending plays, she likes to poke around in antique shops looking for treasures. "The best things in life are the ones that have been loved, whether by you or somebody else," she says.

Surface and Shadow is her first novel.

YOU CAN FIND SALLY AT:

BLOG: SallyWhitney.com
FACEBOOK: SallyMWhitney
TWITTER: @1SallyWhitney

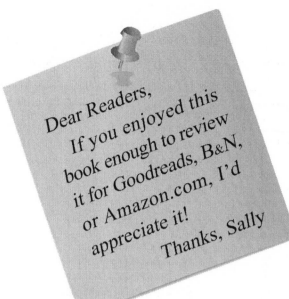

Dear Readers,
If you enjoyed this book enough to review it for Goodreads, B&N, or Amazon.com, I'd appreciate it!
Thanks, Sally

Find more great reads at
Pen-L.com

Made in the USA
Middletown, DE
17 September 2017